I0722532

UNTIED

A MASTERMIND NOVEL

LYDIA MICHAELS

Untied
A Mastermind Novel
Lydia Michaels

Romance

Second Edition Copyright © 2023 by Lydia Michaels

All rights reserved.

No part of this book may be reproduced in any form or by any electronic or mechanical means, including information storage and retrieval systems, without written permission from the author, except for the use of brief quotations in a book review.

PRAISE FOR THE MASTERMIND NOVELS

"This author is a romantic MasterMind and I look forward to reading more!"
—*The TBR Pile*

"I'm absolutely in love with the nerds of the Mastermind Series."
—April, *Goodreads Reviewer*

"Through these characters, Lydia Michaels shows that vulnerability is neither weak nor old fashioned. This series proves nerd love is the best love."
—*Love at 1st Read*

"The art of intellectual stimulation was done to perfection. From mildly titillating to pure carnal desire, this book [Blind] holds you in it's grip on every single page."
—*Author Cassidy London*

"Nerdy and adorably different!"
—*Goodreads Review*

"This first book of the Mastermind series is sheer brilliance in my opinion. The real Mastermind here is Lydia Michaels, and this book is truly her Masterpiece."
—Loren, *Goodreads Review*

For Daniela.
You're a true romantic with a spicy soul.
When I started writing this you were chasing love.
In the end, true love found you.
See ... fairytales do come true.
xo,
Lydia

Listen to the Blind Playlist!
Click Here to Listen!

Listen to the Untied playlist here!

1

———————

"Here you go, Mr. Garnet." The waitress placed the billfold holding Elliot's credit card to the right of his napkin as he continued to read an article from the *New York Times* website.

"Thank you, Tracy." She was his regular server, one who understood he dined at the restaurant out of necessity, not because of a need for company or idle chitchat.

"I've made a fresh pot of coffee for you. I'll be right back with it."

It was also convenient that she knew he followed

every supper with a cup of dark roast Brazilian coffee, and a generous helping of half and half—not
those little individual vessels that sat out warming
and cooling for God knew how long. And he preferred sugar in the raw.

"Thank you." He appreciated her attention to
detail, her lack of tediousness, and his appreciation
was reflected in his tip.

As subtle as a breeze, she returned with his
coffee and a small dish of cream, the packet of sugar
resting beside his cup on the saucer. Elliot slid the
billfold back to her, having removed his card and left
a cash tip. "That's for you."

She nodded her appreciation and slipped it into
her apron. "Will there be anything else, Mr. Garnet?"

"That's all, thank you."

She stepped away and he set to mixing his coffee.
As he swallowed the first sip, he applied his focus to
relaxing, a practice that eluded him of late.

Nine o'clock on a Tuesday there weren't many
patrons dining, which dictated his reservation time.
However, there were always a few case studies of so-
ciology and human nature that would make Henry
David Thoreau spin in his grave.

The world had become an endless race of lab rats
in a quest to mimic human nature when, in all reality, there seemed a lack of humanity sweeping the
species, a drought of tolerance for diversity, and a
cruel chill that froze him out of social circles since
childhood.

What did he care anyway? He had no interest in
pop-culture or keeping up with the Joneses. He was

far past the time of caring what others thought of him, and his isolated existence was by choice, not assignment.

Tedious, pretentious illusionists more concerned with performing on social media than accomplishing anything worthwhile. Where would they be if that carefully fabricated veil, threaded with fragile heartstrings, came down? At least he knew who he was and didn't pretend to be anyone else.

But tonight his observations were more envious than complaining, a rare occurrence that bristled. It had always been him and them. Backsliding into a place of feeling left out only wasted time and energy better spent elsewhere.

Having created the leading social media network, he reaped the benefits of every shallow performer out there. Perhaps it was a bit of profit on the old adage *those who can't ... teach.*

He'd failed, time and time again, to be more than a social misfit, but he studied others enough to see the tools in demand and make a penny off the fodder of egos, a.k.a. social media. He and his friends had created the world's greatest virtual playground, yet still remained sentenced to the shadows of social belonging. Some things never changed.

His eyes scanned the other diners, not really lingering on anyone in particular, but noting the various couplings. Always couples.

Why did people take such issue with enjoying a meal unaccompanied? There was no deficiency in his life, though extroverts seemed to assume his introverted preferences implied there were plenty. He simply savored solitude and detested the chore of cooking—and small talk for that matter. Eating alone exploited opportunities for reflection. There was nothing wrong with—

The broken record of justifications halted as every muscle in his body tightened. The air filling his lungs thickened, turning his breath heavy and jagged as his gaze snagged on a familiar form.

Nadia.

She was sitting only a few tables away. How had he missed her?

Her sleek black hair was twisted away from her striking face, gathered in a heavy knot atop her head that unveiled the soft wisps at her temples, finer than baby's breath. Her caramel skin gleamed from every angle, drawing his attention to the sharp slant of her exotic eyes as her dark irises flashed like polished onyx.

There had never been a woman so perfectly put together, so flawlessly female. He swallowed thickly, his natural reflexes requiring mental commands that shouldn't be necessary. Spellbound, he forced himself to breathe and blink as her arresting presence gripped him like an all-encompassing paralysis.

His gaze drifted to her throat, exposed by the deep V of her crimson dress. Her breasts lifted and his body tightened. Her ruby lips parted, a look of distress stealing over her face.

Elliot's brow pinched as he tried to recall a time she looked anything other than happy—not that he was an expert, after only meeting her twice. Barely sparing her dinner partner a glance, he registered she was with a man. Of course, she was. Women like Nadia were hardly short on company.

Her companion dominated the conversation, gesturing with his hands as his body language implied he was closed off to whatever they were discussing. When he reached for Nadia's fingers resting on the table, she tucked them into her lap, drawing her narrow back into the seat, away from the table.

The urge to interfere was unwise and unprecedented, a reflex he immediately stuffed away. Self-preservation radiated from her poise and graceful posture, enhancing her beauty with a silent show of pride. She tipped the scale of intimidation so off balance Elliot sank back in his own seat, but his shoulders weren't nearly as stiff or assured as the woman he watched. She was simply unreachable by every standard, yet she captivated him in ways no one else ever had.

The stiff set of her spine contradicted the plume-like grace she usually held. The sharp divot between her high-arched brows and the brisk flutter of her thick lashes were unspoken signals of her upset.

The irrational instinct to protect her pounded harder, but too many unpleasant experiences from his past kept him still. There were heroes and then there were men like him. It was best not to confuse the two.

Her long fingers twisted the linen napkin, tossing it down as she abruptly stood. His throat dried as his heart hammered in his chest. Her lithe body, pure flawlessness, was hugged by that deep red dress, accentuating every curve and denoting what seemed a billboard for the devil's truest temptation. He wanted to be that dress, wrapped tightly around her every curve.

Swallowing against the dryness of his throat, he casually adjusted the napkin over his lap. She was the only woman to ever cause such an intense reaction in him without fail, and it was happening again. Damn it.

The man—her boyfriend most likely—stood and Elliot sank deeper into his chair. He was *exactly* the sort of man he'd expect a woman like Nadia to date, rife with testosterone, the clichéd societal ideal of masculinity. Every chiseled muscle was defined to the public eye, despite his clothing. The man was palpably attractive, everything Elliot was not, and he likely shared an intimate knowledge of Nadia.

Elliot's glance dropped to his coffee as envy burned through him like a glowing poker. All of his life he'd diverted his desires with things he could legitimately earn. He didn't enjoy craving things outside of his reach, yet here he was coveting *her*.

Nadia was his darkest desire, someone he shouldn't know—*didn't* really know—but there was no diversion from the suffocating hunger he suffered in her presence. The agony of looking into her beautiful eyes was indescribable—a torture he'd experienced twice and had no interest in repeating. She was too breathtaking and every time he'd been in her presence he felt like something inside of him was dying.

He lifted his gaze as she brushed past her date. The man grabbed her arm and Elliot's shoulders locked. Sliding his coffee away with unsteady fingers, his lips faintly trembled as he watched the heated couple, the tension between them unmistakable to anyone watching their argument unfold.

She jerked her arm out of her date's hold. Elliot's breath sucked past his teeth. What right did that man have to touch her so aggressively? He was three times her size—twice *Elliot's* size.

"Nadia, wait," the man snapped, going after her.

"Get away from me, Ian."

"God damn it, Nadia..."

Checking his pockets, Elliot quickly gathered his belongings, stashing his iPad in his shoulder bag, and followed them to the exit, keeping a safe distance. Lingering in the shadowed vestibule by the ATM, he watched the two argue just outside the entrance of the restaurant. Their muffled voices rose as they likely assumed they were without an audience.

Elliot edged closer to the glass to better make out their words. Nadia's long legs and pointed heels paced over the pavement.

"This means what?" she snapped, an indignant set to her brow. "You sublet our home because you suddenly needed a change? *Lófasz.*"

The Hungarian lilt of her voice heated his blood, sinking deep into parts of his body usually left cold. Why did she have such an effect on him?

"Nadia, it's nothing personal—"

"Nothing personal?" She laughed coldly, her exotic eyes narrowing. "You ... you think I'm an idiot, Ian. A man does not just decide to sublet his home and two days later he is moving. I know these things take time. No. A man does not do anything like that. A scared little boy does this!"

"I gave you a place to live."

She scoffed. "And I gave you plenty in return. Where am I to go? Hmm?" She poked her finger into her date's chest, her courage mesmerizing as she crowded the giant. "My mother's? No. You know she is flying to Budapest in a few days."

"What was I supposed to do, put my life on hold until your family got their shit together?" the man argued, shoving her sharp-nailed finger away from his chest. "Nadia, we had fun, but this was never meant to be permanent."

She went completely still. Elliot craned his neck to better see her expression and his blood chilled. That look... It was not kind.

A threatening glint filled her eyes. "Oh, I did not realize my being your lover was holding you up from other endeavors. And what might you be planning, Ian? Is it blonde or red-headed?"

Ian shuffled back a step but she continued to crowd him. A lioness closing in on her prey.

"I. Am. Not. A. Fool." The sharp knife of her fingernail jabbed into his chest again, punctuating her words. "You go. You run away, *coward*. I do not want to be with a man who trembles at the thought of a future. You are a weak little boy, running away. And I am too much woman for you, little man. Go."

Ian snatched her hand on the last jab, his grip noticeably firm around her dainty fingers. "Poke me again," he growled, eyes threatening.

She yanked her hand out of his grasp and

stabbed her finger in his chest. "Or what? You'll throw me out? Ha! Too late."

His somewhat tolerant expression transformed with hostility as his hands flew out, jerking her narrow shoulders hard. "This is why I'm done! No sensible man would put up with this shit. You were never supposed to be more than a fuck! You're an uneducated, glorified stripper, mistaking trashy clothes for sophistication and class. Champagne taste on a beer budget. Be grateful it lasted as long as it did." He released her with a push. "You're not worth it."

"Get away from me." She took a staggering step back and Elliot noted her hurt, the shimmer of unshed tears in her eyes.

"Gladly! You have until Friday morning to get your shit out of my place."

Her lips remained tight as he stormed away, leaving her on the dark, vacant sidewalk, all alone. Elliot's heart pounded against his ribs. She didn't burst into tears or even turn to watch him go, she just stood there.

He backed into the shadows and considered his options. Long ago, he'd learned not to interfere in other people's business. It never ended well. But the threat of the other man was gone, leaving only Nadia, and he couldn't leave her there alone like that, could he?

His attention returned to her. Her posture wilted as she lowered her head. Where did that man expect her to go? This was why people were better off living unattached lives. Or at least taking the time for formalities like renter's insurance and cohabitating lease agreements. Regardless, codependent relationships were always dangerous.

He should see if she needed anything. Chances were she wouldn't even remember him, being that the second time they'd met, at his friend's wedding, he lacked the balls to even say hello. She wouldn't remember him.

Still ... she might be stranded. Offering help would be the chivalrous thing to do...

Drawing in a deep breath, he wiped his clammy palms down the side of his slacks, adjusting his glasses and straightening his tie. He could do this.

Stepping out of the shadows, strangely aware of how loud and jagged each breath left his lungs, he pushed the door only to collide with the handle when it didn't budge. Nadia's attention jerked to the glass. Damn one-way entrances.

He pulled it open and cleared his throat. Their gazes held for an infinitesimal second that had enough longevity to somehow lift every hair on his body.

His skin chilled as his chest warmed. Mouth dry, his lips moved over the silent shape of her name and he cleared his throat again.

"Na ... dia," his nerves butchered her beautiful name.

She frowned at him, no sense of recognition in her expression.

He wanted to disappear, but he couldn't move, so he tried again, voice shrinking to a whisper. "Hello, Nadia."

Her head tilted as if trying to place him. The breeze caught her mysterious scent and his body reflexively stiffened.

"Do I know you?"

Stuffing his hands in his pockets, he tried to disguise the inappropriate reaction her nearness was having on him. "I'm ... Asher Roan's friend, Elliot."

She snapped her fingers and clicked her tongue, startling him. "Yes, Elliot Garnet. You were in my dance class when Asher started taking lessons."

He nodded, shoving away the obstinate memory of the torture he'd endured for his best friend's sex life. As far as first impressions went, that had been the worst.

Change the subject.

"Are ... are you okay?"

Her entire demeanor softened as she offered a comprehending sigh, obviously understanding he'd witnessed the argument. "I..." Her throaty laugh sent chills dancing over his spine. "No. No, I'm not okay."

This is your chance. "Do you need a ride somewhere?"

It was late and he couldn't just leave her stranded. Despite her impressive boldness, she was clearly shaken. Even the strongest creatures had their own personal kryptonite.

She smiled, her full lips unveiling pearl white teeth. *That mouth.* He swallowed thickly and tried to draw his body away from the constricting material of his pants.

"Aren't you sweet." Glancing away, she seemed to consider her options. When her gaze flicked back to him, her dark eyes stole his breath. "Would you like to grab a drink with me, Elliot?"

Surmising home was the last place she'd want to go, he quickly measured the probability of humiliation versus fantasy. If he let her do most of the talking he could probably keep his presence neutral, at least get to sit close to her for a minute or two. The slithering sense of social suicide snaking through him was slightly overshadowed by the gains. He might even learn a thing or two about her.

"Sure. I could do that."

The moment he agreed his heart murmured and he sucked in a strained breath, a prerequisite to what usually ended with him breathing into a paper bag. He forced himself to remain calm. He was getting a chance to talk to Nadia. *Nadia.*

Her brown eyes lit as her smile showed genuine relief. "There's a little place around the corner. Walk with me?"

Unable to find his voice, he nodded, falling into step beside her. She was tall, matching his height within a centimeter, but she also wore heels.

He kept his focus on the pavement ahead despite her distracting presence. He was walking with Nadia. They were going to *grab a drink.*

Hardly a fan of alcohol, he rarely patronized bars. His mind was suddenly preoccupied with feasible drink orders. What would be palatable yet manly? The thought of bitter beer turned his stomach and wine usually gave him a headache. Perhaps the effect would be minimized if he ordered something with seltzer or club soda? What did people generally mix with—

"You do not talk much, do you?"

His gaze jerked to her and back to the pavement as they rounded the corner. The lit awning of what he assumed was their destination hung at the end of the block.

"Not unless I have something to say." He mentally grappled with topics of conversation, knowing people generally took his reserve as rudeness, which it wasn't.

She nodded, the soft click of her heels tapping a delicate pattern on the footpath. "I didn't realize anyone was watching me. I'm not sure how much you overheard."

Though he didn't want to intrude, he needed to talk, so he went with what he witnessed. "Was that your boyfriend?"

"No."

He frowned. "I thought..." He let the comment drift away, accepting her relationship with her dinner companion was none of his business. Maybe they could find something else in common to discuss. *Not likely.*

"He was my lover."

Blurred eroticism flashed through his mind saturated in Nadia's essence but too far out of reach to depict clearly. Breath weighed heavily in his lungs taking so much space he had to concentrate on exhaling. He hadn't realized there was a distinction between the two terms but suddenly hated his logical mind for immediately noting the difference. "I see."

She shook her head, laughing quietly. "I was foolish to assume he was anything more than cold company. It's probably best we ended things."

Slowing her steps, she approached the entrance of the pub and he shifted in front of her to grab the door before she had a chance to touch it. She smiled as he stepped aside to let her enter first.

"Thank you."

The tavern was dim, lit by accent lights and votive candles distributed on each table. A few men sat at the bar, focused on a sports game playing on all three flat screens while a couple dined in the far corner. Following her lead, they settled in at a tall bistro table by the front window.

"Do you mind the window? I like looking at the street lights and people going by."

"That's fine." He liked looking at her and was still processing the anomaly he'd be able to do so for however long people typically *grabbed drinks*.

She scooted onto the tall stool, her long legs crossing gracefully at the knee. Throat parched, he swallowed and took the chair across from her.

She tucked her purse beside the standing menu and rested her elbows on the table, folding one arm elegantly over the other. Realizing he still wore his shoulder bag, he lifted it and hung it from the back of his chair. When he faced her she smiled and he stilled. Was he supposed to do something?

Say something. Talk about the weather. "Summer seems to be dying down." Could there be a more hollow topic?

"I like your glasses."

He blinked trying to recall which pair he wore and alarmed she was looking close enough to notice he wore glasses at all. "Thank you."

"I used to have a pair like that, but they broke."

"You wear glasses?" He couldn't imagine her in them, but the idea turned him on. Flashes of her standing in a library, glasses sliding down her thin nose while looking over the teachings of Pythagoras filled his head. He was instantly hard. *Fuck.*

"I've needed glasses since I was a kid." She pointed at her eyes. "Contacts. I wish I could wear the colored ones. A blue would be nice, don't you think? But I have a ... stigma and the colored ones are hard to find for that condition."

His brow creased. "You mean astigmatism?"

"Yes. Sorry." She shrugged. "English words. Sometimes I fumble them."

He found her attempt unguardedly charming. "I think your eyes are pretty the color they are." They were brown, but the most shimmering shade, a deep agate with flecks as vibrant as tourmaline and quartz.

Her head tipped to the right, the candlelight reflecting in the dark highlights of her ebony hair. "You do? They are too dark, no?"

"Not at all. They're so dark they're almost crystalline. They're ... exotic." The moment the words left his mouth mortification choked him. What was he doing? He didn't flirt.

Clearing his throat—a nervous tick he wasn't used to—he reached for the drink menu. God, he didn't know what half these things were. "What do you like to drink?"

Steepling her fingers she laughed, the melodic chortle drawing his body to full attention, every decibel an erotic stroke up his spine. "I think tonight is a night for tequila."

Shit. If she was going with hard liquor he'd have to keep pace. "Sounds good." He placed the drink menu back where it had been.

His neck heated as he searched for a waitress. Maybe the bar was out of tequila. When he spotted a server he raised a finger catching her attention. As the waitress approached, his drink order played like an untried script in his head and he prayed not to botch his words.

"What can I get for you?" the waitress asked, dropping two cocktail napkins on their table.

"Two tequilas, please."

The waitress raised a brow as if waiting for more information—information he didn't have. Damn it. He was definitely sweating.

Nadia leaned in, all charm and grace as if she and the waitress were old friends. "Make it two Patrons on the rocks with a splash of water and a twist of lime, please."

The waitress nodded in complete understanding. When they were again alone, Nadia smirked. "Not a tequila drinker?"

His face heated. "Not usually."

"You could have ordered something else."

But he didn't have a clue what something else might be. Better to trust her taste. "I'm not opposed to trying new things." That was a lie. But for some reason, when it came to her, he'd try almost anything.

The waitress returned with two stout cocktails, clear liquor frosting the glass.

Nadia lifted hers. "*Egészségére.* Or ... to health, as you say."

Lifting his glass he tapped it to hers. "Cheers."

She took a long sip, giving the misleading impression of smoothness. Tipping his glass back he balked as the sharp, putrid burn hit his tongue. Disguising his dislike, he closed his lips and lowered the drink. Hers was a quarter empty while his looked untouched.

"Do you like it?"

No. "Sure."

She laughed. "You don't have to lie, Elliot. We can get you something else."

As she turned to find the waitress he snatched up his glass. "No, it's fine."

His esophagus scorched as the fiery liquid burned its way to his belly. Oh, God... Everything inside of him wanted to send it back up.

"You have a reckless side to you, I think," she teased and smiled, her full lips pursing. He'd drink poison to keep her looking at him like that.

She sipped her drink again and he did the same, forcing the swallow of what might as well be battery acid down his throat. Silence hung heavily with every passing second. Within a minute the conversation had gone from cordial to complicated. That quickly, they'd run out of things to say.

He had to keep it going before she finished her drink. "So that man," he hedged, refusing to use the term lover. "How long have you known him?"

Her thumb dragged over the frost of her glass leaving a dewy trail. "A few months. We were never supposed to live together, but..." She shrugged. "I suppose it's pointless to live somewhere else when you wake up in that person's bed every morning."

His knuckle brushed his Adam's apple as he loosened his tie. His mind fumbled over images of Nadia in a bed. Did she wear pajamas? What color were her panties? He wasn't sure if he was even blinking.

"Did you love him?" he rasped.

She laughed dryly. "No."

"But you were ... lovers."

Now she was really laughing. "Didn't you ever have a lover just because they were good in bed? Satisfied an itch?"

His face burned. There had been that horrid episode on his twenty-fifth birthday when Jet sent a woman to his hotel room.

Flashes of how fast he'd humiliated himself made him shove the memory back to the farthest recesses of his mind. The only purpose that night served was to get the guys off his back about still being a virgin. Little did they know the only thing that woman left with was a stain on her skirt and pity in her eyes. He refused to address the subject when they asked about it in the days that followed.

Glancing at Nadia, her flawless skin, and those full lips, he couldn't imagine ever embarrassing himself like that in front of her. The other woman meant nothing—a stranger. But Nadia... She was the only woman who ever made him lose sight of his limits long enough to consider the possibility of something more. Foolish. Part of him hated that she tempted hope where there was none.

A dark sense of inadequacy blanketed him, snuffing out all ambition where she was concerned. His gaze dropped to his barely touched drink. This was a mistake. "It's getting late. I should go. Do you need a ride?"

"We just got here."

He shook his head, unable to catch his breath or meet her gaze. His tie was choking him and he had no business speaking to her about such personal matters.

Itching to leave, his hand brushed the strap of his bag hanging from his stool. "Will you be okay?"

"Did I offend you?" Her voice turned low as she eased closer, not helping matters.

"No, but you're probably tired and—"

"Please don't go." Her fingers brushed his and he stopped breathing, blinked at her perfect nails. "You haven't even finished your drink."

His neck prickled. Why did she make him so self-conscious? He was Elliot Garnet, co-founder, and CEO of GeekPeek. His net worth left men like Warren Buffet jealous. Yet, he was absolutely power-less when it came to her.

Easing his weight back into the chair, he nodded and brushed away the trace of perspiration gathering beneath the rims of his glasses. She slid his cocktail forward, suggesting he take a sip without speaking a word.

Ice rattled as he lifted his drink to his lips, draining it with a swallow so large it hurt his throat. He sputtered, welcoming the burn and praying it might fortify his courage—or knock him out.

As surreal as her presence was, it was equally painful. The bizarre circumstances that led him here were unprecedented and too improbable to ever happen again. Leave it to him to spoil a once in a lifetime opportunity.

Her eyes studied him as he set the glass of ice on the table. Her chin dipped, commending his effort, just before raising her own glass and emptying it as well. Suddenly, the whole situation seemed comical, so he chuckled roughly.

She laughed as well, soft and delicate. Her posture relaxed as her long arms draped over the edge of the table.

"I like your laugh. It's deep the way a man's laugh should be. Tell me about yourself, Elliot. I think I want to know you better."

His humor vanished, as did his hard-on. He had a Googleplex of questions for her, but not one interesting thing to share about himself. Shit. "How about another drink?"

He needed time and alcohol to ease the sting of what was likely going to be one of the most humiliating evenings of his life. He flagged down the waitress and pointed to their empty glasses then turned his attention back to Nadia. "What do you want to know?"

2

Nadia studied Elliot, finding his peculiar mannerisms refreshing and honest. Her anger toward Ian quelled as the alcohol slowly relaxed her temper.

She had no idea what she'd do about her living situation. Two days—what could anyone do in two days?

Right now she didn't want to think about that. She wanted to escape her problems—how nice that Elliot had offered to help her.

"You work with Asher, right?" she asked, hoping

to keep him invested in their conversation, as she didn't plan to leave until the tequila soaked up the last of her troubles. Not to mention she had absolutely no idea where she would go.

He nodded, his neatly parted brown hair catching the light. Every strand was combed into submission and her fingers itched to rumple such calculated perfection.

"Our company turned thirteen years old this June, but I've known Asher since kindergarten."

Asher's success loaned itself to Elliot, making him a safe distraction but far out of her league. Perhaps that's what put her so at ease. Men like Elliot Garnet didn't date women like her, so there was no threat she might ruin the last salvageable shred of her self-esteem.

"And you do computer stuff?"

He smiled, but the motion seemed tense. "I design monolithic applications based on binary coding that operates via BitTorrents and HBase data storage. I also do some of the in-house accounting."

Her eyes widened. "That sounds very intellectual."

"It's rather simple. Data's read from log files, separated and clustered every one-point-three seconds. The more popular a piece of data becomes the less real time it is. If a bit becomes raw it's removed."

She sipped her drink, not sure what he was saying and certain if she made any comment she'd sound foolish. Maybe she should change the subject. "What do you like to do when you're not working? I assume you don't like to dance since you never returned to my class."

A tinge of color darted over his cheeks as his gaze dropped to the table. "I'm always working."

"You must have a hobby."

Rubbing his hand over the back of his neck, he mumbled, "A few, but they're not worth mentioning."

"But I want to know."

Dropping his hands into his lap, he glanced away and hesitated. "Okay." He looked around and stood. Moving to the bar he grabbed something and returned to his seat. He held out a *fogpiszkáló*.

"Your hobby is toothpicks?"

"No," he said, snapping off the sharp ends and breaking the wood in half so he had two small sticks. "You take this one."

She cupped the small shard of wood as he pinched the other half between his index finger and thumb. "Hold it like this, tight so it doesn't slip."

She pinched her half just as he held his, the wood tips forming divots in the pads of her fingers. "Why am I doing this?"

"Do you have it tight?"

"I think so."

He took her hand holding the half toothpick and pulled it close to him. "See how there is no way for anything to get past your grip?"

"I could let go."

"Don't let go." He held up his fingers pinching the other half. "Watch." Turning his fingers so the two sticks crossed like a T, he tapped his piece against hers. "One," he whispered, liquor scented breath teasing her cheek. He tapped again, slowly. "Two." Her eyes strained, anticipating something great to come. "Three." Another tap.

She gasped, as his fingers, still pinching the wood, were now linked with hers on the other side of her toothpick.

"How did you do that?" She pulled and the pieces wouldn't give, their fingers latched together as the wood held.

"Magic."

Her lips parted, as she laughed a bit breathless. "Amazing!"

"Now, you count."

As he tapped her piece from the inside of her fingers she said, "One. Two. Three." She gasped again, as their fingers were unlocked, his toothpick back on the outer side. *Impossible.*

He smiled and flushed, tossing the wooden piece onto his cocktail napkin. "It's just a parlor trick."

She picked up his half of the toothpick and compared it with hers. There were no splits, no soft spots, yet he somehow made it slide through hers. She pinched them in both her hands and tried to repeat the trick, but couldn't figure out how he did it.

Frustrated, she tossed the pieces on the table and smiled at him. "Can you do more?"

"Sure." He glanced at the bar. "Hold on."

She waited as he left the table to speak to the bartender. He returned a moment later with an unopened beer bottle and a straw. He ripped the top of the wrapper off the straw. "Do you like magic?"

"Yes." Not that she'd ever met a real magician

until now, or given such talents much thought, but she couldn't stop smiling, both anxious and enthralled to see what trick he would do next.

"Are you familiar with Star Wars?"

She cupped her hands over her ears, mimicking the shape of side buns. "Princess Leia? The girl with the buns?"

"Yes, well, she's one character. The Jedis—the good guys—believe in a power called *The Force*. It's a sort of telekinesis."

"What is *telekinesis*?"

"The power to move objects with your mind." He withdrew the straw from the wrapper and centered it on the cap of the unopened beer. "Watch carefully."

Holding his palm out, he slowly moved his hand toward the straw but didn't touch it or the bottle. She sucked in a breath as the straw suddenly pivoted and rotated in a clockwise motion without falling.

"*Te egy varázsló!*"

He stilled his hands and the straw stopped moving. "What?"

"*Varázsló...*" she repeated, then translated, "You're a wizard!"

He grinned, a playful glint in his eyes as he winked. "Jedi."

That subtle wink accompanied by the dimple in his shadowed jaw unraveled something inside of her. It was so genuine, so sincere. The usual tension she felt around men wasn't there. This was something new and different. Perhaps a platonic association she didn't usually experience.

"Do you want to try?"

She drew back, as she'd been hovering over the edge of the table in awe. "I can't do magic."

"Sure, you can." He slid off his stool and rounded the table. "Stand up."

She stood and he stepped behind, taking her hand in his.

"You have to concentrate." His voice was low, his breath lifting the stray hairs that escaped from her bun. "Focus on the straw and send all your concentration to the tips of your fingers. Ready?"

Swallowing, she nodded, very aware of her fingers as he lightly angled her palms. Her gaze was fully committed to the straw still balanced on the beer cap. He slowly moved her hands forward.

"Keep your palm open." His breath teased another strand of fallen hair and she shivered.

She gasped, as the straw shifted, her hand no less than four inches away from it.

"Steady," he whispered, guiding her palm in a slow circle over the bottle. "Don't break your concentration. Picture it moving and your mind will move it."

All of her focus concentrated on the teetering straw. She giggled, in awe. As he directed her hand the straw rotated, picking up speed and twirling like a propeller. It didn't make sense.

"How am I doing this?"

He chuckled, releasing her hands. The straw teetered and rolled to the table.

She turned and faced him, eyes wide with shock. There had to be some explanation. Her mind wasn't magic.

"Tell me how it works."

Gray eyes squinted behind the lenses of his glasses. A tight smirk twisted his lips. "A magician doesn't divulge his secrets."

Disappointed, she pouted. "Oh."

He slid into his chair and she did the same. He continued to watch her. "I'll tell you."

Surprised and enchanted, her smile returned.

"It's an imbalance of electric charges. The straw's made up of atoms that are equally positive and negative. Before I placed it on the bottle, I used the wrapper to separate the protons and neutrons, causing an imbalance. The neutral charge of my hand repels and attracts the opposite polarity."

She snorted. "Now, I'm more confused than before."

"It's science. Do you ever hold a balloon and your hair stands up?"

"Yes, it tingles and floats."

"That's all it is. Static electricity."

She frowned, still not understanding the method, and teased, "So you're not a Jedi after all."

He smirked. "Just a boring scientist."

She tsked, disliking that he'd think himself boring. She was thoroughly entertained. "You are not boring, Elliot. I think you're fascinating."

His grin trembled and he looked away. Unsure why her words would upset him, her own smile faded.

Perhaps he was anxious to leave. Now that she thought about it, he probably had somewhere he needed to be. Maybe someone was waiting for him at home. Reaching for her second drink, she finished it so he wouldn't feel obligated to stay.

"Thank you for telling me your secret." She nudged her glass, showing him it was empty.

His attention returned to her, uncertainty playing in his eyes. "Will you go to his place?"

She grimaced. No amount of tequila would change her reality. It was all waiting on the other side of the pub walls, unchanged and unflattering as usual.

"Until I find a better option." She thought of all the complications she now needed to address. "Lord knows where I'll be in two days."

"I'm sorry he did that to you."

Her smile was sad. "Me too. But I did it to myself. You're very nice to blame him, though." Her situation wouldn't be so hard to swallow if Ian were truly to blame, but, like always, the cause of her problems could be traced back to her.

She could almost pinpoint the exact week their sex life shifted from pleasure to obligation. There was a specific moment in time when her attraction became less about Ian and more about the security he offered, which proved to be no security at all.

From then onward, her sexual appeal seemed a tarnished coin and each time she put it to use her dignity paid the price. But her looks had always been her most valuable asset—her only asset when it came to persuading others. It wasn't the first time she needed to lean on her appearance and it likely wouldn't be the last if she didn't start making more money at the studio.

Suddenly tired, she slouched and groaned. "This is a nightmare."

His head cocked as the dim overhead lamp cast a glow on his rosy complexion. He seemed more at ease since he'd started his second drink. "Why?"

Humiliation pinched as she faced the truth. She didn't want him to see her as pathetic, so she kept to basic facts. "Because I'll never find an apartment in two days. My mother is moving back to Budapest and I have no other relatives here. I'll probably end up sleeping in my studio until I find a place, but if my landlord catches me it will be bad. I'm not allowed to sleep there."

"You can stay with me."

She stilled, certain her ears were playing tricks on her.

By his wide eyes, his words clearly caught him off guard as well.

"No," she declined, loathing a possible repeat of her last few male relationships.

Elliot was different. He wouldn't stand for messy. Though she didn't know him well, his tidy appearance and guarded mannerisms gave the impression he wasn't like the men she usually associated with. And by his tight expression, his invitation had been an accidental one.

"Thank you, though."

If he was relieved she rejected his offer, he hid it well. "Where will you go?"

"My studio." It was her only option.

"Does it have a kitchen? A shower?"

"No, but I'll figure something out."

His forehead creased as he glanced away. He appeared rather put out by her situation. "I can't let you go there."

Her brows lowered. "Pardon?"

His focus returned to her, his eyes determined. "You can stay with me. My house is large enough. I have plenty of bathrooms. You can stay until you figure things out. You shouldn't have to sleep in your studio."

His generosity overwhelmed her, but she couldn't accept. "Elliot—"

"What other option do you have?"

"I told you."

"It's not a problem. I'm gone during the day and my nights are usually quiet. I won't be in your way."

She scoffed. "It's *your house.* I'd be the one in the way. I couldn't possibly impose on you like that."

And what would happen if he wanted her to go before she found something? She didn't have the money for a new apartment and saving that much would take time. Her stomach soured at possibly having to offer some sort of *compensation* to a man as classy as Elliot.

No. She couldn't accept his offer. It seemed too … intimate for reasons she didn't understand. "We hardly know each other."

"So?"

She frowned at his persistence. Typically, men only made offers like this after sleeping with her. What sort of man invited a woman he just met into his home? She thought he was different, but maybe he wasn't. Maybe he saw this as a way to get her into bed. True, they met before, but tonight was the first time he ever spoke to her. She couldn't allow herself to impose on him, not after Ian took the last of her pride and threw it in her face. She didn't want Elliot to become the next Ian. She didn't want him to look at her like that.

"I can't."

"Why?"

"Because you don't know me, and I don't know you." But she liked the impression he'd made in such a short time. Perhaps it was all magic, or one distraction hiding the abrasive reality. Regardless, she didn't want to shatter the illusion that Elliot Garnet was somehow different. Her bleeding heart needed to believe good men existed, or she would have to admit her life was just a played-out love song full of unfulfilled hopes and dreams.

Disappointment flashed in his eyes as he lowered his gaze. "Do you have money for a new place? I can give you money."

She drew back, forcing her hands into her lap. "I'm not taking your money, Elliot. I'll be fine. Trust me. I've survived much worse."

A V formed above the bridge of his glasses. "Why won't you accept my help? I wouldn't charge you rent. It's a free place to stay until you get back on your feet."

"Elliot." He was rather persistent and the temptation put pressure on her morals. "I think you've had too much tequila."

But he was determined. "Nadia, take the offer. Let me loan you money or at least give you a place to stay. I promise, there are no strings attached. I'm trying to be a gentleman. I can't let you sleep in an empty dance studio. Don't be stubborn."

"*I'm* stubborn? Do you hear yourself? You're inviting me to live with you and we only met an hour ago."

"We met more than a year ago."

But the shy man who participated in her class over a year ago didn't resemble the determined, sweet man keeping her company tonight. "I'm messy."

"I have a maid."

"Of course you do." She was again reminded of how affluent he and his friends were. "I don't know how long it will take me to save up for my own place. Most of my income goes toward rent at the studio."

"There's no timeline."

Her lips pursed. It wasn't right and she didn't want to take advantage of such a nice person. She didn't want to be indebted to him, either. Or discover he could take advantage of her the way other men had. "Why are you doing this?"

He paused, the question seeming to catch him off guard. "I ... just want to help you. Do I need a reason?"

"There's always a reason, Elliot."

"Then ... blame chivalry. It's the right thing to do."

She frowned at him, waiting for him to laugh and tell her this was some sort of joke. Nobility? When had a man in this lifetime *ever* spoken of such outdated ideals? "You're a strange man."

"Is that a yes?"

She sighed. He seemed safe *and* dangerous. Somehow vulnerable and all too cocky. She hated the possibility that she might take advantage of his kindness, so she swore this wouldn't be like all the other times. Elliot was different and that meant the situation had to be as well. "Perhaps just tonight."

3

———————

~Sheldon Cooper
The Big Bang Theory

Elliot anxiously tapped his fingers on the steering wheel as he waited for Nadia to return with her belongings. It was almost midnight and he still was processing how he'd gotten himself into this mess.

True, he didn't like the image of her sleeping on some cot in an empty dance studio lacking all the habitable necessities a woman might need, but that didn't make it his duty to fix her problems. Since when did he involve himself in other people's drama?

Never. The answer was never. So why was he suddenly taking some homeless dance instructor back to his house? This bordered on every possible creepy stalker scenario out there and he was the pitiful culprit, justifying his motives as noble. Pathetic.

The door to the apartment complex opened and he sucked in a breath, doing his best to appear relaxed as she carried a large bag to the car. Wrenching open the door, she wedged her belongings behind the passenger seat, slid in beside him, and growled.

Her words, mumbled Hungarian, tickled his brain, but he couldn't decipher a single phrase. He made a mental note to pick up a book on the language.

When she finished her foreign tirade, he glanced behind her seat. "Is that everything?"

"Yes," she grumbled, crossing her arms over her chest.

Not one for translating female body language, he shifted gears and edged onto the road. He'd always heard women were heavy packers. Maybe that was a myth because she apparently lived with very few clothes. The apartment wasn't in the nicest area, so hopefully, they wouldn't have to return.

The ride to his house was made in silence. Her sour mood seemed to escalate as if her temper was actually heating the interior of his car. The closer they came to his home the higher his anxiety spiked. He should have offered to put her up in a hotel.

The idea of actually exposing his personal quarters to someone as complex as Nadia left him nauseous. What if seeing his private home disappointed her in some way or she found his house strange? Some people's homes had a smell. Did his? He was starting to sweat.

The ingrained practice of hiding his vulnerabilities from the rest of world was something he mastered long ago. The sense of exposure, even or especially to Nadia, formed a knot of dread inside his stomach so tight he suddenly recalled humiliating moments from childhood with painful clarity, embarrassing events he'd assumed were buried and forgotten. It wasn't a welcome sense of nostalgia.

He turned the car toward the entrance of his property, pausing to key in a code at the gate. As they eased up the long, winding drive, his gaze bounced between her shadowed presence and the dark road.

Her scowl lifted as the house came into view. "*Ez nem egy ház.*"

"I don't speak Hungarian." He was definitely picking up a book tomorrow.

"This is not a house. This is a fortress."

He cherished his privacy, which made his decision to let her into his home all the more startling. But it was definitely a house. Just a big one.

"The gate code's three one four, but I ask that you keep that to yourself." Once she left, he'd have to change it. Such a slight inconvenience, but it felt mammoth in his well-ordered world.

Still, an unfamiliar part of him wanted her there. He disliked this indecisive side of himself very much and wasn't used to wavering, emotionally or otherwise. This was why women confused things.

Parking by the front steps he shut off the engine

and they sat in utter silence. Her hands fidgeted in her lap, her soft fragrance overpowering the delicate leather scent of the upholstery.

"Are you sure about this, Elliot?"

Every time she enunciated the "T" in his name his body shivered. Despite his reluctance to let anyone in, some definitively masochistic side of his psyche demanded he do this. Perhaps it was some skewed sense of decency that insisted he help her, but more realistically it seemed a perverted chance to be near her—even if *near* was as close as they'd ever come. This was going to be torture.

"Yes, I'm sure." He opened his door and she followed suit.

She gathered her bag and met him at the foot of the steps. He took the duffle from her, surprised by its light weight, and led the way to the door.

"The front entrance code is one five nine."

His entire security database was programmed to the digits of pi, but she'd only need to know the gate, front door, and alarm. No need to go into the many other codes protecting his belongings. As he typed in the code, the door chirped and opened, flaying his composure and tempting him to rescind his invitation and escort her to a hotel.

The light blinked on the security panel and he quickly typed in the disarm code. "The alarm code is two six five."

"Will you write the numbers down for me?"

"Yes." Switching on a few lights, he drew in a stabilizing breath that barely steadied him at all. "I should let you know the house is under surveillance, not the bedrooms or bathrooms, of course, but all the common areas have cameras on them twenty-four-seven."

She probably thought he was a pervert. *You are.*

"It's just for security."

"Why?"

He shrugged, not wanting to revisit the memories of having his home robbed while he hid in the pantry, terrified. That was a different house, but still. "I have a lot of valuables in the house. I'd rather be vigilant than sorry."

She nodded and turned, taking in the expansive foyer. "Where do you sleep?"

"Upstairs. I'll show you the guest rooms." Hefting her bag in his arm, he led her up the staircase and paused at the first closed door. "This room's private."

No need to risk her judgment. Most grown men didn't have an entire chamber dedicated to Legos. Building things with his hands helped him relax and some of his best ideas had been born in that room.

"This is my room." He continued to walk, pointing out the purpose of each door. "Closet. Game room. Home theater. Arcade. Library. And this is a powder room."

Her expression was unreadable, so he went on. "This is one of the guest rooms. You can take a look to see if it suits. There are four more."

She stepped forward and eased open the door. He wasn't much for frills, finding methodic practicality necessary in many cases. Whenever his work required attractive design schemes, he passed the ball to Ash or Hunter. If it was out of their league, they hired a specialist.

She didn't appear enchanted or disheartened by the room's dark color scheme. Though there was no label, he often referred to the room as The Penguin Suite—the villain, not the aquatic bird.

"This is very nice."

"I'll show you the others." Leading her down the hall, he opened the door to The Riddler Suite. Deep green walls made the violet comforter pop.

"They're all so nice. It's like a hotel. Do you have guests often?"

Never. "Not really." He opened the door across the hall and showed her The Joker suite. Bright teal drapes contrasted the damask mauve wallpaper. The bedding and shams were done in green and orange to match the Joker's vest and ascot.

"How do you pick your colors? They're so vibrant."

His neck heated. She probably thought his taste was abysmal. "I, uh, base them on characters from comics."

"Like Garfield?"

"Not quite." He shut the door, wanting this painful experience over. "The last guest room's at the end of the hall."

Opening the door to the Poison Ivy suite, he hoped she chose this one. It was more feminine than the rest, and he found it easy to imagine her lying on the emerald duvet embroidered with tiny silk vines. The walls were deep ruby, providing an almost sensual atmosphere.

"Oh, Elliot... It's lovely." She pivoted, a slow smile forming at her lush mouth. "I may pick?"

He swallowed tightly, under her spell once more. "Of course."

"I choose this one." She stepped to the bed and collapsed to her back.

His gaze fastened to the flash of soft flesh showing at her thigh where her skirt had risen. His stare zeroed in, lingered, and slowly traveled over her crimson dress, and up her hips, pausing again where her breasts jutted upward. He needed to get out of there.

Dropping her bag to the settee at the foot of the bed, he back stepped to the door. "So you have everything you need? The bathroom's through that door. There are linens in the closet—"

"Elliot?"

Glancing over his shoulder, he found her resting on one elbow, her body curving with feline grace. His brain short-circuited as his breath seized.

Her smile was all too trusting. "Thank you for letting me come here. I promise I'll be gone soon."

"Take as long as you need," he rasped, betraying every insecurity raging inside of him. "You're my guest."

Crossing the threshold before she noticed the mountain of rock hard cock jutting below his belt, he shut the door behind him and blew out a rigid breath. This was definitely not how he expected his evening to end.

He went to his room, and as soon as the door shut he adjusted himself. "Unacceptable," he muttered, trying to disguise the unrelenting bulge in his pants.

Growing frustrated, he removed his glasses and crimped his brow in a hard grip. "Get a hold of yourself."

But there was no hope. Every time his eyes shut, glimpses of Nadia stretched across his guestroom bed flashed in his mind. He marched into the master bath. Five minutes later he was only slightly relieved —and hard again.

"Damn it!"

His flesh and blood fantasy was down the hall, and if he didn't get a grip, he'd be walking around with a hard on until she left. He grit his teeth and marched back to the bathroom for a second demeaning attempt.

This was exactly why women and the feelings they produced were tedious.

After jerking off twice, he was still too wired to go to sleep and too much of a pussy to venture outside of his room. Watching his phone like a teenage boy watches the hot neighbor's windows, he settled into bed. After hours of stalking the cameras for any movement outside of Nadia's room—there was none —he managed to fall asleep sometime around three.

The following morning, as he dressed and knotted his tie in a perfect half Windsor, his gaze continuously drifted to his cell, which still had the security app open. He was leaving in a few minutes and feared he wouldn't see her before he left for work.

Once his shoes were on, he paused at his bedroom door and returned to the desk. Pulling out a sheet of paper, he hesitated...

Nadia,

I hope you slept well. There is cereal in the pantry and eggs in the refrigerator. You may help yourself to whatever you need. Martha is my maid and she will be here between 10:00am and 3:00pm. She knows where everything is kept. My cell number is

"Shit." He crumpled the note. Letters were so impersonal.

Brushing a frustrated hand over his hair, he moved to the dresser, and smoothed out his part, hesitating as he faced the door once more.

With a huff, he marched down the hall, pausing outside of the Ivy Suite. Their proximity produced a sort of diaphoresis, and he couldn't remember ever sweating to such a degree outside of gym class.

Raising his hand he tapped lightly and waited.

Muffled shuffling met his ears and light filtered beneath the wood of the door. Stepping back, he braced himself, directing his gaze at the carpet. The door opened and two small feet stepped into view. Her second toe was a smidge longer than the first, but her nails were painted in the sexiest shade of red, the skin on the top of her feet as dusky and striking as all the rest.

"Good morning, Elliot."

His regard traveled upward over tapered calves,

feminine knees, and lush thighs. He'd never seen so much flawless skin and his heart rate accelerated the higher his eyes traveled. He'd yet to run into a stitch of clothing. His breath gusted out of him when he reached the apex of her thighs, covered in tight little black shorts that looked more like men's underwear than actual attire.

Blinking, he stared a moment too long at the expanse of satin flesh shown at her flat belly. This was what she slept in? Men's briefs and a tank top?

His face went numb as his attention rose to the peaks of her unconstrained breasts. And there were her nipples. "Um…"

"Are you okay? You look irritated." She stepped forward and he sucked in a sharp breath as the back of her cool knuckles pressed to his clammy brow. "Your skin's warm. Are you sick?"

"Yes." *What?*

He seemed to have no control over his words at the moment. But she was wearing glasses, wearing the fuck out of them, and he couldn't fathom how a woman as sexy as Nadia had gotten more attractive overnight.

"You should rest. Let me use the bathroom and I'll take care of you."

Her hand pulled away, leaving him dizzy as she turned. His attention fastened on her toned ass stretching the material thin and his dick throbbed. Did she say she was going to *take care* of him?

"You might have a fever, but I have just the thing." She gazed over her slender shoulder and smiled, knocking the breath out of him again. Beautiful torture.

"Go on back to bed. I'll be there in a few minutes."

She was coming to his bed? "Okay." Another word he had no control over.

He didn't move.

"Go on. Bed."

When she disappeared into the guest bath, he looked down the hall, his vision narrowing to pinholes. *What are you waiting for?*

His brisk steps carried him back to his room where he turned in a confused circle in the same place over and over again like a dog seeking its resting spot. Lowering himself to the edge of the mattress, he pulled out his phone and dialed.

"Think Tank."

"Jet, it's Elliot."

His friend waited as Elliot tried to focus, capable only of the simplest facts. "I won't be in today."

"Everything all right?"

He hadn't taken a day off in … eleven years. "Yes. I'll call you later." He ended the call as he heard her soft steps brushing over the carpet.

The door opened and she tsked. "I said, back to bed. You need rest. Under the covers you go, mister."

Without paying him much attention, she straightened his bed covers and fluffed his pillows. As she folded back the sheet, she looked at him and clucked her tongue. "Do you plan on wearing your suit and shoes to bed?"

She nudged him back and gracefully kneeled at

his feet, her big brown eyes flashing as her gaze seemed to physically stroke over him before lowering to his feet. Her small fingers untied the laces as she slipped the shoes off his feet.

His mind jumped to a forgotten place in time, the shoe store his mother used to take him back when shoe salesmen actually measured customers' feet. There was a fish tank he liked in that store. But he liked this better.

As she rose, her elegant motions put him in a trance. Her body moved so gracefully as if gravity didn't have a hold on her the way it held everyone else. Every motion its own dance. His gaze tripped over her breasts and his chest tightened with desire as his fingers twitched to feel her supple flesh.

The leather soled shoes clopped to the floor, jarring him out of his head. She leaned close and he held his breath as she clutched his tie, loosening the knot and sliding the material free with a practiced pull.

"No need in wrinkling your dress clothes. Where do you keep your lounge pants and t-shirts? I'll grab some for you."

He blinked at her, afraid if he moved he might spontaneously combust. "I don't have lounge pants." Or t-shirts for that matter. His undershirts were as close to casual as he got, and he never wore them without something on top.

"What about sweatpants?"

He shook his head as she stripped him of his jacket.

"Pajamas?"

He couldn't tell her he slept nude. Making a mental note to pick up loungewear—whatever that was—he rasped, "These pants are fine."

"Don't be silly. They're dress slacks. They'll get creases."

Her hand went to his belt and he sucked in a breath, catching her brazen fingers, and stilling her progress. *"What are you doing?"*

An inch south and she'd realize what a depraved pig he really was. Her dark eyes widened. Fuck. Did she already know?

Her hair was down, tumbling all the way to her hips and over her shoulders. She still wore those ridiculous boy shorts. Her full lips formed a shy smile. "I'm just helping you."

He pressed her hands away, panic driving his heart into a frantic hum. "I can undress myself."

Her arm drew back and she frowned. Did she honestly expect him to disrobe in front of her? This was totally inappropriate. He wedged a pillow over his lap.

"Perhaps you could find some tea?" Anything to get her out of there and away from his constricting pants.

Seeming to understand she'd crossed a line, she nodded and backed to the door. "Okay." Her dainty fingers rested on the frame, drawing his attention to the slope of her hip. "But you stay in bed. I'll be back in a few minutes with something. We don't want you getting the flu."

The door closed and he stared dumbly at the empty room, as helpless as a child under the decree of a stern mother. This was not at all what he wanted. He didn't need her to think him some feeble man who couldn't handle a slight cold.

You're not even sick!

Disturbed by his pathetic appeal to her good nature, he stood and marched to his dresser, opening a drawer and snapping it shut when he found nothing but well-ordered socks and briefs.

"Why don't you have normal clothes?" He unlatched his leather belt, coiling it with the others in the top drawer. "Ridiculous. And now she thinks you're sick. Pathetic."

He continued to berate himself as he stripped out of his dress shirt and tossed it in the hamper. As he climbed into bed still wearing his slacks and undershirt, he fussed with the pillows, refusing to lie there like an invalid. *Now what?*

Being that he couldn't alleviate the pressure in his pants, he did the next best thing and reached for his phone.

4

"THE ART of medicine consists in amusing the patient while nature cures the disease."

~Voltaire

Nadia rummaged through the well-stocked fridge for produce, glad to see Elliot had everything she needed. She found a chicken in the freezer and sat the carcass in the sink to thaw. Placing the kettle on the stove, she went about organizing her supplies. The enormous counter was covered with hearty vegetables and an array of leafy greens.

A door opened and she frowned. *I told him to stay in bed.* Men were so stubborn.

She set a heavy cutting board on the counter. "You should be in bed, mister."

A stout, older woman stepped into the kitchen wearing a startled expression on her crepe thin, wrinkled face. Not Elliot.

"Hello." Nadia waved nervously.

The woman's wide eyes scaled Nadia from her shoulders to where the counter cut off her view, just beneath her ribs. Maybe she should have dressed. She wasn't expecting company.

The woman took a step back, her hands clutching a large pocketbook. "Who are you? Where is Mr. Garnet?"

"I'm Nadia. Mr. Garnet's... guest. He has a cold."

"You're Mr. Garnet's guest?" The woman frowned. "Are you a relative?"

She asked the question as if Elliot were some sort of recluse and this was the first time he had a woman in his house. A man like Elliot surely had lots of guests, but perhaps he chased his companions out before—whoever this was—arrived.

"I'm Nadia. Just a friend. I didn't catch your name."

"Oh." Silence blanketed the kitchen. "I'm Martha, his housekeeper." The teakettle let out a sharp whistle.

Nadia turned and moved it off the burner. When she faced her again the woman's gaze reverted to the counter. Uncomfortable, she mumbled, "I wasn't expecting anyone so I didn't dress. Elliot's sick, so I wanted to make him tea before anything else." She gestured to the mess on the counter. "And soup."

The woman's frown remained as she nodded slowly. "I'll go check on Mr. Garnet." She disappeared, her silent steps leaving Nadia with no clue to her whereabouts in the large house.

"Strange woman."

Dropping a teabag in a mug, she poured the hot water and stilled as a thought crossed her mind. Placing the kettle back on the burner, she scanned the room, pausing when her gaze landed on a tiny black globe in the corner by the crown molding.

Awareness crept over her, tingling every square inch of exposed skin as she looked into the hidden camera. Was he watching her?

She didn't know if the cameras were linked to a computer monitor or the televisions, or, in this day and age, she wouldn't be surprised if he could watch from his phone. She waited for a sense of violation to sink in, but there wasn't one.

Oddly, the thought of Elliot watching awakened something dark in her, like performing on a private stage for him and him alone. Her hand slowly lifted, her fingers fluttering in a wave as if he might somehow answer the gesture.

She quickly turned back to the counter and caught her breath. No. She shouldn't think about him like that. He was simply doing her a favor by letting her stay here. Only a fool would mistake his kindness for more. And damn her for falling into the same trap she always did when a man was nice to her. She needed to stop living in a fantasy world and start seeing things the way they actually were.

Look at his home, the way he lived, he probably thought she was class A trash borrowing his guestroom and traipsing around in discount underclothes. No wonder the maid was shocked. She probably looked nothing like the other women he brought home. And he was probably mortified his employee just saw her like this. Nadia would make it clear to the maid they weren't involved. At least then Elliot would be saved the chore of making excuses for her presence.

What was she thinking accepting his invitation last night? She'd gone from one man's inconvenience to another's. The difference was, she liked Elliot and didn't want him to resent her the way Ian did. She'd see to his soup and then start looking for somewhere else to stay.

5

"THE RIGHT MAN *in the wrong place can make all the difference in the world.*"

~Half-Life 2

$\mathcal{E}$lliot's lips parted, as Nadia looked right at him through the security camera. He'd told her the house was under twenty-four-hour surveillance, but maybe she didn't believe him. Her head quirked and her hand slowly lifted in a shy wave. A breath of laughter caught in his throat. She was so damn cute and she was in *his* house. He preferred watching her from a distance when she couldn't see how much she rattled him.

A sharp knock landed on the door and he stashed his phone under the covers, like a kid sneaking a glance at a dirty magazine. His throat cleared. "Come in."

"Mr. Garnet," Martha called, peeking inside. "That woman said you weren't feeling well, but I didn't believe it. Is there anything I can get for you?"

Embarrassed he now had the maid worried about him, he considered coming clean but that would only add to his humiliation. "I'm fine, Martha. Thank you. As a matter of fact, why don't you take the day off? I'll probably just get some rest and be back to my usual routine tomorrow."

The older woman hesitated, her creased eyes rife with confusion. "There's a woman in your kitchen—"

"Nadia. She's a friend. She's staying in the suite at the end of the hall. If you could—before you go—just see if her room needs any attention."

"You're sure you don't want me to stay? I don't mind."

"I'm sure."

No need to have more witnesses to the spectacle he was making of himself. For God's sake, he was a decade overdue for a day off. There was no need for sirens or a parade.

"I'll just take your dry cleaning down." She disappeared in his closet. "Your friend seems to think you have the appetite of ten men by the amount of food she set out to prepare."

He'd noticed. It touched him she would go to such lengths, but he assumed it was more about repaying his hospitality than any real concern. "I'll make sure the mess is cleaned up."

Martha emerged with an armful of suits, her smile uncertain. "I'll leave you to resting. Call if you need anything. Once I check her room, I'll be on my way."

"Thank you, Martha."

When she shut the door he let out a breath. Reaching under the covers, he felt for his phone. Sliding his finger over the screen he frowned when he didn't see Nadia. The door opened without a knock and he threw the phone back under the covers, wincing as he used too much force and it slid clean off the mattress onto the floor.

Nadia stilled, brow arched as she held a tray laden with steaming items. "I brought you breakfast."

He cleared his throat, trying not to look at his phone displaying the view of the kitchen from where it rested on the carpet. Perhaps if he ignored it, she wouldn't notice. "Thank you."

He scooted back as she carried the tray to the bed, resting the legs of the tray on either side of his knees. She handed him a linen napkin and he was distracted by the scent of autumn spices rising from the bowl of what looked like porridge. "Is this oatmeal?"

"Gruel. My *dédanya's* recipe." She squeezed his bicep, sending blood rushing to his lower extremities. "It will make you strong."

Thank God there was a tray over his lap. "*Dédanya?*"

"Great-grandmamma. She made the best gruel." Turning, she bent to scoop up his phone, glancing at the screen before handing it back to him. "I'm also making you soup for later, but I guess you figured that out with all your sneaky cameras." She smirked. "Are you a spy, Elliot?"

His face heated as he tried to match her playful smile and failed. "Sorry. I ... wanted to see if you needed anything."

"I met your maid. She's very nice, though I don't think she was expecting to find someone like me in your kitchen." Making herself at home, she lowered herself to the edge of the mattress, her curvaceous body brushing his knee through the covers. "Why is that? You must have women stay over from time to time."

Distracting himself by searching for a spoon, he cleared his throat. "I don't entertain much."

"Yet you have all the cameras. I assumed a lot of people come to your home."

People, not beautiful women. "Mostly employees." And even that was rare.

"Do you not trust the people that work for you?"

She asked a lot of questions. "I don't trust anyone."

Her head tipped to the side, a dark curtain of chestnut waves falling down her arm. "Not even Asher?"

"I trust my partners, but that's about it."

"Yet you opened your home to me."

Something he still didn't understand the logic behind.

It's because you're pathetic and you're using this as

an excuse to get close to a woman who wouldn't notice your existence otherwise.

"You needed a place to stay." He took a bite of the gruel, surprised by the sweet flavor that filled his mouth. "What is this exactly?" He went in for another bite.

"Family recipe. I make it from spices and nuts. You have a great kitchen. It makes it fun to cook."

Holding the bowl in his palm, he practically inhaled the stuff. "Thank you. Feel free to use it whenever you like. This is delicious."

She laughed, the sound overriding his appetite with other urges. "I'm glad you like it."

Placing the bowl and spoon back on the tray he sighed. "Gruel. Interesting. I'm definitely a fan."

"Wait until you taste the rest."

He stilled, his body throbbing. Her lips pulled tight as she held his stare. She was talking about soup, right? Definitely soup. Had to be soup.

"Drink your tea before it gets cold." He reached for the mug just as her knuckles pressed to his brow, testing his temperature. "You still feel warm and your skin's flushed."

"I'm sure I'm fine." He couldn't keep lying to her, although illness seemed a great excuse for the symptoms of arousal he couldn't hide. But the last thing he needed was her thinking him fragile—although he wasn't as sturdy as the men she was probably used to.

"Still, you'll rest." She stood, removing the bowl and surveying his room. "Do you want anything else?"

His gaze clung to the curve of her hips, the soft, nearly invisible hairs dusting the flesh beneath her belly button. "I'm sorry, what?"

"It's not nice to stare, Elliot."

Mortified, his stare jumped to her eyes. "I'm sorry. I'm not … used to this."

His heart thundered, and he diverted his attention to the mug in his hands, scalding his tongue. He grimaced as the robustly potent flavor filled his mouth and forced himself to swallow when he wanted nothing more than to spit the tea back in the mug. Maybe gruel was the only good thing she made. If not for the trace of cinnamon, he wouldn't be able to swallow whatever was burning the shit out of his tingling esophagus.

"You don't like my tea?"

He forced it down and made a face, ensuring it stayed down. "It's … different."

"Well, you need it. Drink up. It will make you sweat out whatever bug you have."

The mug suddenly seemed dauntingly large. And he didn't want to sweat any more than he already was.

"I'm going to check the soup." She carried the empty bowl to the door.

He frowned. Despite the luxury of her attention, it wasn't right for her to do so much under false pretenses. "Nadia?"

She turned, too much trust in her gaze.

"Don't you have to go to work?" She ran her own dance studio. He'd feel terrible if his playing hooky interrupted her schedule.

"Not today. My next class is tomorrow night. My days are usually free."

Tell her you're fine. "Well ... thank you ... for this."

She smiled and left the room. Picking up his phone, he waited until she was back in the kitchen to dump the tea down the bathroom sink. Whatever that was, it was intense and more likely to make him sick than actually make him well—which he already was.

He sighed, not looking forward to a day wasted in bed. He should've just told her he wasn't sick. Instead, here he was, shuffling around in his undershirt letting her wait on him hand and foot.

"You're so screwed up."

At precisely nine o'clock, his phone rang as it did every morning. Figuring a day off wasn't so bad, he told himself it was a mental health situation so the workaholic in him would ease up. His thumb slid over the phone.

"Hi, Mom."

"Good morning, sweetie. How's your day going?"

"Good. I, uh, took the day off."

"Oh, no. Are you sick?"

He shut his eyes. He couldn't lie to his mother. "No. Just ... relaxing."

She laughed. "Because you needed a challenge? You already sound flustered."

No one, not even the guys, knew him as well as his mother. She'd put up with his tireless attention to detail since before his toddler days and she was probably already wagering he'd be back in the office by noon. He never handled idleness well.

"I have a house guest visiting for a few days. A woman."

The line silenced. "O—okay. Is this a girlfriend of yours?"

He laughed without humor. "No."

"Who is she?"

"Just a friend who was in a bind." The term friend might be a stretch, too. He didn't want his mom getting her hopes up. "She's a bit out of my league."

She tsked, always his greatest champion even though she was also completely biased. "What makes you say that?"

While his mother, an ever-persistent optimist, only saw the triumphant moments of his existence, there were eons of painful interludes he'd managed to hide. Suffice it to say, his earlier years were enough to scar him for life.

"She's just different."

"Different is good, Elliot. You're different."

"I mean different in a good way."

She tsked again. "Every difference is a good thing. We don't need a world full of clones."

He smirked, appreciating her justification. "She just got out of a relationship."

"You like this woman."

He sighed quietly, sparing his mom the hollow details. "That doesn't matter."

"Elliot, you have to take risks to get what you want in life. You, of all people, should know that. Look at your success."

"I know, but some risks aren't worth the consequences."

"But are they worth the reward?"

His mind came up short every time he tried to imagine the reward of connecting on an intimate level with Nadia. There were just too many obstacles to navigate and he was exhausted by the idea before making a single move.

Of course, his mother assumed he was an average bachelor with thirty years of life experiences under his belt, but in truth, dating was and would always be an unsolvable conundrum to him. It was the epitome of tedious socializing and therefore best avoided.

Realizing his mother was still talking, as she would continue to do until satisfied she'd pulled him out of whatever slump he was in, Elliot slipped in some false reassurance.

"You're right, Mom." He wasn't sure what he was supporting but offered his agreement all the same.

"Good. And when it works out you bring this friend over so I can meet her. I'll admit, I'm intrigued. She must be pretty special for you to tell me about her. You're so private about your lady friends."

He didn't have lady friends. She was getting ahead of herself. Way. Ahead.

"Well, I don't think she's interested, so I wouldn't assume too much. We're better as friends." It was more realistic to call himself Nadia's temporary landlord than her friend.

"Well, I have faith in you. What else are mothers for?"

The door pressed open and he winced as Nadia stepped in. Shit. Had she been listening to his conversation—with his *mother*? "I have to go. I'll call you later."

"Okay, sweetie. Love you."

"You too." He ended the call.

"I didn't mean to interrupt."

He should lie and say it was work. "The tea's gone. I feel better already."

She stepped closer and brushed her fingers over his brow. "Your skin's still warm to the touch, but that's okay. It's likely working. Was that your girlfriend on the phone? Your voice was different with her."

Dear God—his girlfriend? He inwardly cringed. "Who said it was a female?"

She tapped her ear. "I heard her call you sweetie."

Shit. He gave up and grimaced. "It was my mother."

Her mouth curved into an approving smile. "You're close with your mother?"

Awkward. This was so damn awkward. "She's an important person in my life." He needed to make it clear he wasn't a momma's boy. He adored his mother, of course, but his need for closeness stemmed from a deeper concern. "My dad passed away last year. I try to touch base with her for a few minutes each day to make sure she's okay."

"I'm sorry about your father. Were you close?"

His mouth opened but he hesitated. "He was one

of my closest friends and my hero." He glanced away. "I ... don't like talking about it."

She patted his leg through the covers. "You're a good son. Not many men talk to their mothers every day."

She bent to lift the tray, distracting him with her body as she leaned in front of him. The sight of her full breasts only slightly retained by her top had his mouth watering and he swallowed, unable to blink. "Are you close to your parents?"

"My mother is not a citizen and she's going back to Hungary. I should probably call her."

That wasn't necessarily a yes. "Is your father in Hungary?"

"No. He's gone." There was little emotion to her answer.

"Are *you* ... a citizen?"

Her smile beamed with pride. "Yes. I have been for some time. My aunts raised me when they lived here in the States. My mother only comes to visit every few years. She stays for a few months. This time was the longest so far."

"Are your aunts still in America?" Why hadn't she stayed with them—not that he was complaining.

"My Aunt Petra passed when I was twenty and my Aunt Mira went home a few years ago to be with family. She's not doing well, which is why my mother is leaving."

"I'm sorry to hear that. Will you go back?"

The thought of her returning to her homeland actually disturbed him, though he had no claim to her time here.

"It's expensive." She rubbed her fingertips to-gether. "I can barely afford a taxi ride at the moment. The studio doesn't do well during the warmer months, but I have new classes opening this week."

He frowned, wondering what dance instructors made as far as income and irritated he didn't know.

"I'll leave you to rest."

As she lifted the tray, he blurted, "You don't have to go."

She smiled and glanced at the tray. "I'll come back. I want to wash these dishes and check on the soup."

He didn't know if he should be excited or scared about lunch. The slight scent of something unfa-miliar was drifting up the stairs, but it wasn't strong enough to sway him either way.

"Maybe we can watch a movie—since I'm appar-ently bedridden today."

She laughed. "Rest will do you well. Sure. I'll be back in a little bit."

When she left he used the remote to trigger the television behind the wall. Searching through his col-lection, he tried to find something she might enjoy but didn't have a clue about her taste in cinema. By the time she returned he still hadn't selected anything.

"You have a television in here too? I've never seen a house with so much... What is the word for electric stuff? It's like a space house."

"Technology?"

"Yes. You have lots of technology. I like it."

She'd changed, replacing her distracting boy

shorts with a tight pair of black pants that did nothing to disguise her figure. The straps of a teal bra showed underneath her black tank top, making it a thousand times harder to breathe.

"What kind of movies do you like?" he asked, voice strained as she invited herself to sit on the other side of the bed.

"I like drama, but I mostly watch foreign films. What do you like?"

He hesitated, pretty sure his preference would seem juvenile in comparison to foreign films. "I like science fiction and fantasy."

"Make believe?"

He grimaced. "Yes."

"Then we'll watch that. Pick a good one, Elliot, or else I might fall asleep on you. Someone woke me up extremely early this morning."

His chest tightened as she scooted close to his side, her bare arm brushing his. Though his thumb directed the remote, his eyes made no sense of what was on the screen. Her hair tickled his arm and he had to remind himself to breathe.

"Have you ever watched Star Wars?"

"No."

"Well..." He swallowed again, his voice seeming to dry up under the scent of her body so close to his. "There're two ways to watch them. We can go in order of production or in order of the series. The first one didn't come out until 1999, but the fourth one aired in 1977."

She frowned. "Why did they do it that way?"

Finally, something he could discuss without feeling like an utter moron. This was his arena.

"George Lucas started by writing what he called a Space Opera, but it was so long he chopped it into nine parts, breaking it into three trilogies. Not knowing if the movies would succeed, he started with the only part that could be viewed as having a beginning and an end. It was a huge success, of course."

"Then I say we start at the very beginning. If there are nine, we have a long journey ahead."

"Well, the third part of the trilogies is being produced by Disney. You can see the difference. I saw the last one eight times in the theater." *Too much information!* He stopped talking as his enthusiasm made him sound like a zit-faced, no-life teen.

Her eyes creased as she smirked. Was she laughing at him?

"We don't have to watch it," he said quickly, directing his attention back to the television.

"Oh, no! Not after you talked it up so much." She scooted lower, her hair now touching his pillows. "I want to see why you love it."

He studied her, trying to weigh her sincerity, but distracted by her presence in his *bed*. Holy hell. She was in his bed. *Don't get hard!*

She seemed genuinely curious. *Star Wars* wasn't just a saga about outer space. It was political symbolism, epic battles, breathtaking scores, and timeless trials of good versus evil. He didn't know if he could handle how much hotter it would be if she actually enjoyed the series as much as he did. That was just unrealistic.

We'll see if she falls asleep...

He cued up *The Phantom Menace* and placed the remote between them. As the Twentieth Century Fox lights showed and trumpets played, she stretched her body over his chest, and he froze as she shut off the lamp.

Glancing over her extended arm, she whispered, "I like movies in the dark."

In perfect timing, the symphony instruments burst into a climactic eruption as her breast brushed his arm. And he died for a split second as she slid off of him. Shutting his eyes, he willed his body to behave.

"Who is that?"

He hardly had to look at the screen, knowing the movie by heart. "That's Obi-Wan and Qui-Gon-Jinn. They're important."

Her eyes followed the characters across the screen. Along her temple were baby fine hairs, dark, but delicate. He'd give half his mint collection of priceless collectibles to trace his fingers there.

She turned, catching him staring again. "You're not watching the movie, Elliot." Her dark lashes fanned low while his eyes could barely blink.

Everything seemed heavy, even the breath filling his lungs doubled in mass. What was this woman doing to him?

"Sorry." He looked at the television, promising himself he'd be more careful.

She shifted, sitting up a bit, her attention back on the movie. "Why do you look at me like that, Elliot?"

"I'm sorry?" He turned back to her because it was easier than looking away.

She gave him a pointed stare and he understood how unnerving it could be. "Why do you do it?"

"I..." What the hell was he supposed to say? *You're the prettiest woman I've ever met and it makes no sense that you're sitting in my bed watching Star Wars with me?* Come to think of it, this had to be a dream. He pinched his arm. *Shit! That hurt.*

Her body twisted so she sat on her knees and fully faced him. "Is it because I bother you or because you think I'm nice-looking? Or is it something else?"

Mouth dry, he moistened his lips. Pressing back his glasses, he glanced away. "You're very pretty, Nadia." His breath literally shook as it left him.

When she said nothing, he spared her a quick glance and stilled when he found her smiling. What on earth was this woman doing here?

She eased forward and he drew back as far as the headboard would allow. "What are you doing?"

She stilled. "I was going to kiss you."

Oh God. "Why?"

Her eyes darted to the side and her cheeks tinged with pink. "I don't know. I just decided to do it. I didn't really think about it."

"Why?" he repeated, questioning her sanity.

She shrugged and sat back on her heels. "I just thought... you think I'm pretty, so..." She shrugged again. "I won't if you don't want me to."

Idiot! You open your mouth and ruin everything!

"It's not that..." What the hell was he doing? They should just watch the damn movie. "You don't have to kiss a man to say thank you, Nadia." That came out totally wrong! "I mean—"

She laughed, but now there was insincerity tucked within the sound. "Is that what you think, Elliot, that I was paying you thanks with kisses? I should be offended, no?"

He pushed his glasses up again. "No. No, that's not what I meant. I just... You shouldn't feel obligated to do that just because I state the obvious."

"Obligated?" Her brow creased, her gaze sinking lower with each botched explanation. "I'm not obligated. Maybe I just wanted to see what it would feel like to kiss you."

Again... "Why?"

She tsked. "Forget it." Turning, she dropped her back to the pillows and frowned at the screen. "Now, I missed something. Who are these people?"

Without taking his eyes off her, he answered, knowing the scene well enough. "That's the queen and Palpatine."

She didn't look at him so he continued to study her, noting everything from the slight rise and fall of her breasts to the subtle parting of her lips. This woman—*this woman*—wanted to kiss *him*?

Without taking her focus off the screen, she whispered, "Elliot, you're staring again."

This time he didn't apologize. "Maybe..." He swallowed, unable to take his gaze off of her. "I want to see what it feels like, too."

Dear God, did he really just say that out loud? His heart was going to explode if it beat any faster.

Her lashes lowered, her dark eyes turning to find his. She looked almost ... skeptical. "Is that so?"

Her accent seemed thicker, more sensual than usual, which he thought was impossible, but what the hell did he know? His IQ was dropping by the second. Unable to move, he breathed without blinking, anxious to see what would come next.

She reached between them, picked up the remote, and paused the movie. Sliding back to her knees, she turned and faced him. "So kiss me."

She wanted *him* to do it? No. That wasn't the plan. Blinking quickly, as if making up for lost time, he let out a staggered breath, all his curiosity corroding with trepidation. There was no way he could make the first move.

Lame. He was so lame. Chickening out, he reached for her small hand and lifted her fingers to his lips, brushing a kiss over her knuckles. *I hate myself.*

She raised both brows and the last of his manhood disintegrated into dust. "*That* is how you kiss a woman?"

"I hardly know you." It wasn't what he expected to say, but he was beyond thinking. He didn't even know her last name.

"What do you want to know?"

What your skin tastes like. He shrugged. "I don't like to intrude on people's personal business."

"You're not intruding. Ask me anything. I have no secrets."

Bullshit. Everyone had secrets. The trouble was he wanted to know all of hers. "How old are you?"

"Twenty-six. How old are you?"

"Thirty-one." The number stabbed into his self-esteem. He had the track record of a twelve-year-old when it came to women. This was a terrible idea. "We don't have to do this."

She caught his hand. "When's the last time you kissed a woman, Elliot?"

His face burned as he shifted uncomfortably. "I don't want to play this game."

"What game? We're just talking."

"I don't discuss my personal life." His words came out curter than he'd wanted, but he was not discussing it with *her* of all people.

"Last week?"

He picked up the remote, aiming it at the television and she took it from him.

"Last month?"

"Nadia—"

"Last year?"

"I don't kiss women!" he snapped and she drew back.

Her lips slowly parted. "Men?"

"What? No! I..." His skin burned as if under an interrogation lamp. "I don't date."

"What does that mean, you don't date? *Ever*?"

He gritted his teeth. "Let's just watch the movie."

"Elliot, are you a virgin?"

"Of course not." He took the remote back, hit play, and she caught his jaw in her hands, forcing him to meet her penetrating stare.

"You're thirty-one."

"I'm perfectly aware of my age, Nadia. Now, if you aren't going to watch the movie I'm going to go to work. I feel fine." Or at least he would once he got away from her.

A small kink formed on her brow, but she backed off, sliding onto the pillows and turning her focus to the screen.

This whole episode might have permanently ruined *Star Wars*. Then what would he have left? He flinched as she touched his hand. The breath in his lungs stilled as her fingers entwined with his. *What's happening?*

"What are you doing?"

She didn't look at him. "Holding your hand."

He couldn't take his eyes off their intertwined fingers. An abnormal amount of warmth bloomed between their palms, radiating up his arm and heating his chest. His blood turned heavy and he shifted his legs, other things reacting. Staring at the covers draped over his lap, he shut his eyes and willed himself to calm the hell down.

Her head nestled into his shoulder and his eyes shot open. The scent of her hair permeated his senses and his body caught fire. He had roughly one hour and forty minutes left of this torture before the movie ended. And God only knew how long she'd remain his houseguest.

"I don't think I've ever met a virgin that was a man," she whispered, her attention still on the television.

His gaze jerked to her and he scowled. *"I'm not a virgin."*

He hated that term. He was a man, goddamn it. A fucking man. Pulling his hand away, he shoved himself into a seated position.

"Elliot—"

"There's no definitive explanation for that term by today's standards. What might be virginal to one culture isn't to another. It's all relative."

She shrugged. "I think it's nice. The men I'm used to just want sex, sex, sex. I think you're the first man to ever kiss my hand."

The tension in his shoulders eased as her response baffled him. "Really?"

She smiled at him, not venturing to verbalize her answer. When her attention returned to the screen, he casually slouched and rested his palm between them. Waiting.

Unbelievably, she took it.

A thousand volts of electricity shot through his body as his common sense drifted out of reach. He slightly tightened his hold and she snuggled into his side again. What was this?

For several minutes, he mentally debated the truth of the issue, knowing full well he'd never slept with a woman. How pathetic that this moment was likely—no, *definitely*—the most erotic moment of his life? If she thought it was nice, why lie? But his ears couldn't bear the truth.

He didn't have the patience or fortitude for all the social tedium sex required. But he thought about it enough, despite his avoidance. Tedious. It was all so tedious. The expectations, the silly social rituals, the castigating that came when you weren't what someone expected. The sheer amount of focus romance stole from other, more important issues after it obliterated an otherwise logical person's common sense. Who in their right mind would chase something so life altering with so many drawbacks?

When Asher got involved with Scarlet, his friend became obsessed. Jet, who was overly satisfied, hardly said goodbye to one conquest before making plans for the next. And Hunter... Well, Hunter was a little more paced, but still, if any one of his friends had a choice between ComiCon and sex, sex would always win. Elliot was the only one to find the whole topic repellant, due to its addictiveness.

Sex was like a drug and he didn't need such distractions in his life. The others didn't seem to mind. They were already gone.

Sex made men short-sighted and he didn't want his brain clouded by overzealous hormones like it had been in his teens. It was a personal choice, not a deficiency. He liked order and control. Sex was capricious and contingent on others.

He wanted Nadia to know it was a matter of choice and that there had been opportunities, especially once his career took off, random opportunities for him to choose otherwise. But again, none of those women seemed genuinely interested in him.

"There was a woman," he said, distracting her from the movie. "A few years ago. My friends arranged for her to come to my room."

Her gaze drifted to his. "What happened in your room?"

His chest constricted as his lips tightened. "Nothing. Well, some things, but then I sent her away. I didn't know her well enough and I had no interest in..." He had no reason to feel ashamed. "Sex is personal. I don't understand how people make it casual."

"Was there anyone else?"

Swallowing, he lost the courage to hold her stare. "No."

"Are you ashamed of this?"

"No. Not really. But there's a stigma."

Her brow furrowed. "Like my eye."

He smirked. He loved the charming way she fumbled with the English language. It made her ... human. Less intimidating.

"That's astigmatism. A stigma is a sense of disgrace in relation to a certain circumstance. Men are defined by their virility. I'd prefer to define myself by intellectual feats."

"Just because you don't have sex doesn't mean you're not virile, Elliot. Perhaps it means you're more patient and disciplined than others."

"That's not the reason."

"No? You've waited thirty-one years. That's patience. Some men can't wait three minutes."

And he'd likely be waiting thirty more years. "I'm very particular. People get on my nerves. Half the world's fake, the other half's cruel. I have no interest in tying myself to artificial people who..." Why was he telling her all this? "I'm just a private person."

"Yet you let me stay with you, in your home."

Because she was different. "We've been through this. You had nowhere to go."

She shook her head. "I don't believe that. I think you're a good man and you saw another man being mean to me and did the honorable thing. There is a word for that. You said it last night. What is it?"

"Chivalrous?"

"Yes. You are very much that, Elliot. *Gallant*. I think I like these things about you."

Breathing deeply, he turned away. "Did you remember me? If I hadn't mentioned Asher, would you have had any idea who I was?"

"No. But I have a lot of people come into my classes and never return. I did recognize you, once you jogged my memory." She smirked. "You were very tense in my class that day. You wouldn't loosen up when I danced with you." A slow smile took form. "But I remember you gave me evil eyes when I left you to dance with your other friend, the one with the darker hair."

"Jet."

"Yes. He's quite handsome from what I recall."

His molars locked. Every woman noticed Jet. There weren't many that escaped Jet's attention either. "He's popular."

She laughed. "You say that as if we're kids."

"Well, he was popular then, too." He shook his head never quite understanding how some people possessed such magnetic charm while others seemed repellent. "He's charismatic."

"That may be true, but that's not where his sex appeal comes from. It's his confidence. You feel it coming off him in waves and it draws women in. It's not easy to resist, but a wise woman would."

"Why?" There was plenty to envy about his friend but never enough to think badly of him.

"No woman wants to be second prettiest in a relationship. It's too much work."

He wasn't sure if he should be relieved or offended. Wait. She was like Jet. She was too pretty, too exotic to go unnoticed by other men. "You and Jet have a lot in common."

She giggled. "Perhaps, but I want to know what you mean by that."

"People notice you. You're confident—"

She held up a finger. "I'm not as confident as people assume. I'm always nervous I'll speak wrong or say something foolish and others will laugh at me. People notice me because I'm foreign and look different. Do you know what that tells me? That I'm not like everyone else when that's all I've ever wanted to be. I love being here, but as soon as I speak people look up and their opinions change right before my eyes, judging me on the spot."

"But you're so ... fearless. If they pay attention it's only because you're so striking."

"Not always a good thing." She shrugged. "Maybe there's a stigma to being different. See that? I learned a new word."

He chuckled. "Yes, you did." He never considered she might have insecurities similar to his own. He thought about his mother's words from earlier. "There's nothing negative about diversity."

"That is how America should be, no? We're all mixed up here. Everyone is different." She smiled. "There is so much flavor. When my aunts offered to bring me here, my father fought with them. But I wanted to come here too much. I finally got my way." She nudged his shoulder with hers. "You Americans are a tricky bunch. You tell a woman how special she is, but it's not very special at all if you tell *every woman* those things." Her lashes lowered as her gaze softened, freezing him in place. "I wonder if you tell all the ladies they're special."

He hardly spoke to women and never met anyone as unique as her. "I don't."

A playful purse twisted her lips. "What do you like in women, Elliot?"

Stumped, he blinked at her. "I never gave it much thought."

"Oh, you are full of it." She pushed on his chest, teasingly. "Every man wants something."

"I just want to be happy." He'd settle for good old contentment. So far, his greatest happiness came in isolated moments of satisfaction. Outsiders usually made him self-conscious.

"Do you believe in love?"

Love came with risks. "I don't know if I believe in an unconditional love, aside from familial love. The rest seems illogical and mind-numbing."

She giggled. "That's the fun of it. I'm what they call a hopeless romantic."

It didn't sound fun to him. "I like feeling in control. I don't want to balance my happiness on someone else's."

"You are a cynic, then?"

"I guess I am."

She lifted their entwined hands and pressed her lips to his knuckles. His breath held as he watched her pouty mouth slowly pull away.

"When you get brave, you come find me and we'll see if I can change your cynical mind ... maybe even leave it a little numb."

It was already happening. Surely that concoction she'd tried to poison him with had knocked him out and he was hallucinating. His voice seemed far away as he rasped, "What do you mean?"

She laughed. "You heard me. Don't play dumb. I know you're smart, with all your technologies and magic tricks. If you want to be brave and see if you're wrong about love, I'll be your experiment."

What the hell was she offering? "Are you talking about sex?"

She shrugged. "That depends on you. You have to kiss the girl before *ágytorna*."

"What is that?" Screw it. He was downloading a Hungarian eBook tonight. These language barriers were becoming a nuisance.

Leaning close, she smiled and whispered, "It means a good, solid fuck."

His eyes widened and his blood solidified in his veins, burning his body from inside out. "Nadia..."

"Elliot..." she echoed with a bit of challenge, holding his stare. "Do you want to kiss me now?"

"Yes," he rasped, but couldn't find the strength to move a single muscle. At any moment he'd wake up.

Shutting his eyes, he willed himself awake. *Wake up. Wake up! Wake—*

The blankets shifted as the heat of her body touched him before anything else. Sweet breath teased his lips as his glasses slid off his face. He couldn't breathe, couldn't open his eyes, and couldn't do anything other than sit there in unadulterated panic.

Her soft lips pressed his. "Let me help you..."

Pulling in a long breath through his nose, he trembled as her mouth pushed against his. He tensed as her fingers gently brushed his jaw and combed through his hair, traveling behind his ear. When her tongue skated over his lips he jerked back, knocking his head against the headboard, he blinked at her.

"Good?"

"Why are you doing this?" Was it because she felt indebted? Pity?

"Because I think you're very handsome and you rescued me last night when I really needed someone to save me from doing something stupid. Also because my aunt always told me a man who treats his mother nice will be kind to all women. Am I wrong?"

There was other stuff, but he'd lost focus after her first reason. "You think I'm handsome?"

She smiled. "Yes. You know you're attractive."

Her fingers pulled at his ear, the strangest little tug that seemed to reach down to his toes, stroking everything in between. He studied her, but every-thing was blurred.

Reaching for his glasses, he slipped them back on his face. His fingers hesitated, then detoured and traced the soft hair at her temple and his body tightened to the point of excruciating pain. She was so damn beautiful.

His thumb feathered over the outline of her lips and they twitched. Easing closer, he brushed his mouth against hers and she released the softest moan. That little hum seemed to vibrate his soul. With choppy breaths, he pulled back, waiting for her to tell him to stop, but she didn't.

Her eyes softened, as did her shoulders. The strap of her bra showed, tempted, and he wanted to touch it, but wouldn't.

She thought he was handsome. *Him.* There was no logical explanation, which only increased his skepticism. She was right. He was cynical. But he wasn't an idiot and only an idiot would walk away from this situation without taking the opportunity of a lifetime.

This was Nadia, not some random woman. He'd fantasized about her since the day he walked into her studio.

"Elliot?"

"Hmm?"

"Are you done kissing me?"

Shit. He got distracted, his damn analytical mind weighing every aspect. "No. I was thinking."

"About what?"

"You."

"Oh?" Her brow lifted. "What were you thinking?"

"I can't figure you out."

She glanced away. "I'm not that complicated."

"But you are. You... I thought about you, Nadia. It wasn't like I had to stop and place you last night. I recognized you right away. As a matter of fact, you're the only woman I've ever thought about at any length."

"Me?" This seemed to genuinely please her as her cheeks darkened and her lips parted in a smile. "Why?"

"I don't know. That's what I'm trying to figure out. For all my thoughts, not once did it cross my mind that you might someday be sitting in my bed asking me to kiss you. That ... that kind of thing doesn't happen."

"Maybe it doesn't happen because you're not an opportunist with women."

Yet he was with business. He rubbed his hands over his brow and let out a breath. This was intense. "I wasn't expecting this."

"And?"

"And I'm not sure I know what to do." Frowning, he amended, "I mean, I know what happens, but I... Jesus." His palms were burning up. "I've never done anything like this before. I feel like an idiot and I *hate* feeling like that."

"Don't feel that way. I know you don't have many experiences with women."

Try one. He inwardly scoffed. He should have taken the guys up on their offer. Never did he expect to regret sending that woman away, but he did now. Thirty-fucking-one years old and this was what it had come to? Pathetic. Utterly pathetic.

If he weren't such a perfectionist, he'd slide her onto her back and do his worst, but he didn't want to disappoint her. Damn it. How long would she sit through his endless deliberation? *You. Are. Ruining. It.*

"Fuck it." Throwing caution to the wind, he surged forward and sealed his mouth to hers. She toppled back to the mattress and giggled.

His body electrified, as her fingers slid over his scalp to the back of his head. His shirt tightened as she fisted the material and pulled him more on top of her, twisting her lips as she tilted her head.

The soft brush of her tongue sent blood tunneling through his veins as he caught his weight on his hands. Pulling back, he drew in an unsteady breath.

She stared at him through those thick lashes. "Don't stop." But her words froze him in an inescapable moment in time.

He couldn't believe this was happening. "You're so pretty, Nadia." He'd meant to compliment her, but she seemed unfazed. She likely heard words like that a million times a day.

She tugged his shirt, pulling him closer with a hand tangled in his hair. The tension in his body made it almost impossible to move. Lowering his lips by the slightest degree, he traced his mouth over hers again.

Lush lips opened beneath his as wet heat closed over his lower lip and sharp teeth nipped him. *Ouch!*

He drew back, touching his lip. "You bit me."

"You're teasing me."

Not intentionally. If he let himself go full throttle he'd come at her like a ballistic missile. But maybe he could let go a little more.

"Sorry. I didn't know." Leaning over her again, he pressed his mouth to hers, this time shutting his eyes and letting the sensations lead.

Her grip on his hair loosened to a slow stroke down his neck as he gently moved his tongue over hers. That little touch sent his muscles on an avalanche of pleasure, threatening his hold on his composure.

Her body lifted, arching into him as he teased his tongue with hers. A fire lit beneath his skin, burning from the inside out as she tightened her grip on his shoulders. He was abundantly hard and there was no hiding it in their position, especially as her knee hooked over his hip, pulling him against her body.

He sank into her and immediately pulled back. "Am I hurting you?"

"No. I want more."

A slow throb pumped through his brain as her words sank in. Panting, he nuzzled her jaw. "I … I can do more." He hoped.

Finding her lush mouth again, his entire body trembled. Meeting her halfway, he tasted her mouth. Sweet mother of God, he could die like this.

As her body arched again, he pressed into her, shivering at the relief that came with the slight friction. Her kisses turned hungry, almost greedy as she took as good as she gave. Losing sight of their surroundings, he gave in to the unparalleled thrill of pressing his body to hers. Need built to an unmanageable degree as he dragged his fingers through her hair and rocked his body against the heat of hers.

Throaty moans vibrated from her the longer they kissed. Every press of her nails through the fabric of his shirt delivered a carnal sting. Though they were hardly moving, he was winded, panting with the desire for more.

Ripping his mouth away, he caught his breath. He was going to explode.

"Everything okay?"

"Yes," he panted, blinking at the familiar surroundings from an angle he'd never occupied. They were twisted in his covers, her hair a curtain of black waves across his pillows, rippling like an ocean under the night sky. And he was about to come. "Maybe we should slow down."

"We're only kissing."

Glancing away, he confessed, "It feels like more."

Despite her agreeability, he didn't want to spoil their connection. Sitting back, he covered his lap with a pillow, painfully aware of how flushed his face must be. She slowly sat up and folded her hands on her thighs.

Shy? That was new for her—at least to him. Unsure if he'd offended her, he asked, "Are you all right?"

"Yes." Her lashes lifted, showing him the softest view of temptation he'd ever witnessed first-hand.

They needed a distraction. "We should finish the movie. You have six more to get through."

Nodding, she scooted back to the pillows as he searched for the remote. Once he found it, he hit play.

She laced her fingers with his. Warmth settled over him as an unfamiliar sense of contentment—no, *happiness*—blanketed him.

6

---

*"THERE'S **no terror in the bang, only the anticipation of it."***

~Alfred Hitchcock

*W*hy did she do these things? Elliot was a perfectly nice man and she'd gone and spoiled it by being her invasive self. As she picked the chicken off the bone, adding the fresh cuts of meat to the boiling soup, she silently berated herself.

She couldn't go on using men like this, and she *hated* that her insecure, weak will let her do exactly what she swore she wouldn't and put Elliot in a category with the others. Her misery was her own doing. But her actions...

What had she been thinking, coming onto him like that? Upstairs, something had come over her.

But now that she was downstairs and away from those charming eyes she realized what she'd done. The same stupid thing she always did. She turned him into a safety net when she hadn't meant to. Damn her.

But what if Elliot was her only hope of getting back on her feet? She couldn't go back to Hungary, back to the life she left, because even there, her problems hadn't been much different. At least here, she had a choice in the men she selected.

She shivered. She couldn't go back to Roland. Finances and the thought of *him* made the idea of home the most unwelcoming thought she could conjure.

Every day her heart broke a little more knowing her aunt was closer and closer to the end, but if she flew home it would drain the last of her finances, if not overdraw her accounts completely. She'd be forced to stay with her mother and it would only be a matter of time before Roland discovered she was nearby. She had no doubt he'd take full advantage of her financial limitations, and that was something she simply couldn't stomach. *Never again. Not with him.*

She glanced at the little camera in the corner and her face heated with shame. Was he watching her? Her heart fluttered at the thought and didn't that just make her a fool? Whoever Elliot saw, it wasn't real.

He didn't see the filthy secrets she kept or the dirty past she hid. She liked that he saw her differently, but the characteristics he assumed also filled her with a terrible guilt.

Elliot was a special man, different. It didn't make

sense that he didn't have a lover. He was very attractive, but beyond that, he was a true gentleman.

He's not for you.

The air filled with the delicious aroma of cooked vegetables and fresh stock. She took extra care dressing his tray, folding the linen napkin like they did at restaurants and polishing the spoon for good measure before placing it beside the bowl. Once she ladled out a hearty helping, she carefully carried his lunch upstairs.

Her heart fluttered again as she backed into his room. It was almost impossible to keep her expression casual as their gazes connected. "Lunch."

He scooted, sitting with his back against the headboard of the enormous bed. "I don't think I've had this many meals in bed since I was six and sent home with the chicken pox."

"Sick boys need tender love and care. Careful, it's very hot." She set the tray over his lap as he took a deep breath of the soup, laughing as his glasses steamed. She carefully sat on the edge of the bed and waited for him to taste, anxious to see if he approved.

"Aren't you eating?"

"I will."

"You could have brought yours up here."

She'd thought of that, but worried he might want some privacy. They'd spent the entire morning together. "I have to clean up some things downstairs."

He frowned and she remembered the cameras. If he'd been watching her, he'd know the kitchen was already spotless. Carefully blowing on a spoonful, he leaned forward and took a bite.

"Oh, my God," he practically moaned. "This is incredible. You made this from the stuff in my kitchen?"

Smiling at his praise, she nodded. "Give me a chicken and a few vegetables and you'd be amazed what I can do."

"Consider me thoroughly amazed." He took another bite. "Delicious."

"How are you feeling?"

"Great. I think you've healed me."

"It was probably the tea."

He didn't answer, more focused on gobbling down his soup. He sure had an appetite, yet he wasn't a thick man. His body was lean, not overly rugged, but not frail either. He had the trim, muscular build of a swimmer, or a man who never indulged to the point of excess. He was very proper, with his neat and tidy hair always combed to the left and his freshly shaved face. Clean.

His exotic American eyes, bright gray like a hazy dawn, creased as he smiled at her. She liked the square angles of his jaw and the way she often caught him watching her with those piercing eyes. "I should go clean up."

He stilled. "Stay. Or go get your lunch and come back."

She laughed nervously. "Aren't you getting tired of me?"

"No."

She wanted to kiss him again but held back. He was sick after all and she couldn't afford to catch a cold, something she should have thought of earlier, but the temptation was too strong.

She'd get her lunch and eat with him, but then she'd let him rest. And there would be no more kissing. He'd stopped her for a reason. "Did you want a second helping?"

"Please. This is the best soup I've ever had."

"It's just chicken and rice."

He shook his head, swallowing down the last drop. "I love it."

Taking the tray, she returned to the kitchen and prepared two more bowls. She couldn't shake her despondent mood, still trying to rationalize what on God's green earth would make her think she could get away with coming onto a man like Elliot. He probably thought she was a whore. Maybe she was.

She was being hard on herself, but after last night with Ian, she had every reason to. Her mind stressed over the unknown, finding no security in the spiral her life had taken. But she would not use Elliot or take advantage of his kindness. He was different from the other men she knew. She didn't know why, but there was something special about him.

It wasn't bad enough being publicly dumped and left on the curb like day old trash. She didn't want him to see her the way Ian did. But maybe that was how all men saw her.

That was her fault. "Stupid," she mumbled.

How had she been so stupid? Of course, Ian didn't love her. Men didn't love women that took no effort. She'd made it so easy for him, and the man before that and the one before that. She should know by now that wasn't how love worked, being that not a single one ever claimed to love her or stuck around longer than a few months—except Roland.

Her mind cringed. Over the years, with every rejection she delivered, his determination only grew. Men, it seemed, only wanted what they couldn't have, building the unknown to unattainable heights. But Roland had his chance and never forgot. He held their past over her head, dangling it like a lewd chandelier of regrets to cast shadows over the rest of her life. He claimed to love her, but he only wanted to control her.

When she entered Elliot's room again he smiled. She focused on the tray, afraid if she looked into those eyes too long nothing but *yes* would come from her lips. His hospitality was an immeasurable gift, one she not only appreciated but also needed. There was no room for awkwardness. No room for games.

"Do you want to watch Episode Two?"

Two more hours of sitting by his side? "You should probably rest."

"I feel great."

She bit her lip. "Maybe a little bit, but then you need rest."

"I am resting. I haven't been out of bed all day."

As she slid onto the mattress, keeping a safe distance, he moved the tray between them with a smile. He needed to stop looking at her like that.

She sat cross-legged and ate the soup while he worked on his second helping. It was like a date—a date on a bed over a picnic, with all of that first date edginess. Leave it to her to make out with the man before they even had lunch.

"You're being quiet."

Taking her time to swallow a bit of chicken, she stared at him. "I'm just thinking."

"About?"

Her shoulder lifted and she took another bite, buying more time. He was more talkative than he'd been this morning. "How long I'll be here. I'll know my fall roster by the end of the week. Then I'll have an idea of what sort of money I'll be making. I'm saving up a down payment for a new apartment."

Her stomach turned as she considered how long it would take to save first month's rent, a security deposit, and continue to pay her studio rent. Lowering her spoon, she let it drift deeper into the broth, no longer hungry.

"Hey."

Bracing herself, she returned her gaze to him. A small divot creased his brow just above the bridge of his glasses. "What's wrong? You don't have to stress about being here. I told you, you're welcome here. You can stay as long as you need."

But this wasn't how she wanted to live. She couldn't be some drifter incapable of supporting herself. She never imagined things would go this far.

"I hope you don't think I'm helpless."

"Why would I think that?"

She shrugged. "My circumstances ... they're an accident. When my aunt returned home, the apartment was transferred into my name. I had a home—a nice one. Nothing like this, of course, but it was mine. When my mother came to visit it seemed to shrink so I ended up ... sleeping out a lot. Then it sort of became hers. When she asked what to do with the lease, I said forget it, knowing I couldn't afford it and thinking I'd continue to live with Ian. I was a fool to think that."

He laid his spoon on the tray and frowned. "You don't have to apologize or explain how you got here, Nadia. I know your situation wasn't part of your plan. I get it."

She let out a deep breath. "You're very understanding."

One side of his mouth lifted into a half smile. "What was your favorite part of your apartment?"

"My favorite part?" It had been a while since she lived there, her mother making it hard to breathe in the cramped space. "There was a little window in the kitchen leading to the fire escape. I had a planter packed with fresh herbs. In the winter I'd move it to the sill, but in the summer I'd hang it outside. It was my own little farm. I could reach right through the curtains and pluck fresh basil right off the vine."

"You like cooking, don't you?"

"It depends. You have so many boxed meals here. It's easy, but cooking from scratch is a labor of love. That's all we do at home."

"Do you miss home?"

The hollow longing she lived with for nearly a decade seemed to hiccup inside of her. "Yes, but I'm happier here. This is my home now. I think I'd miss America more if I left."

"Do you ever visit?"

"I've been gone so long I feel like if I returned the ache might get sharper when I had to leave again. But my aunt..." Her eyes blinked as the sharp awareness of time fleeting by pinched her heart. "My aunt was *home* to me and soon she'll be gone. It's very sad."

The gentle weight of his fingers pressed to her knee. "I'm sorry. She must be very special to you."

Nodding, she let out a breath, shoving away the heavy emotions. "She is. I was closer to my aunts than either of my parents and soon I'll have lost them both."

"You should visit her before it's too late."

Her chest tightened. She wished there was some possible way that could happen. But under her current circumstances, there wasn't. "It's very expensive."

"Let me buy the ticket."

Her head jerked up and she frowned. "What?"

"I'll buy you a round trip ticket and you can have the closure you deserve."

"Elliot, no." Was he insane?

"Why not?" He shrugged. "It couldn't be more than a thousand dollars round trip. You should be able to say goodbye to the woman who raised you, Nadia."

"I can't let you do that. Besides, I have obligations here. I have classes and—"

"This is your aunt. You could be back in a matter of days. How much would it really interfere with your work?"

"It's a twenty-four-hour flight."

"Not if you don't stop for layovers," he argued. "You could get there in under sixteen hours, stay for a few days, and be back by the weekend."

It scared her how simple he made it seem. So tempting. "Thank you, but no."

Going home would complicate things. She wasn't ready to see all those memories in living color, face everything she left behind to transport her entire life to the States with nothing to show for her time away.

"I appreciate the offer—*so much*—but Elliot, I can't accept."

He frowned, appearing genuinely disappointed she couldn't accept. Maybe he was looking for a way to ship her out of his house.

"Is it because of the cost? If that bothers you we can call it an IOU. You can pay me back down the line when you're back on your feet."

Damn him. He had a way of breaking down everything into manageable little pieces. "I would absolutely pay you back regardless, but the answer's still no. You've already offered me too much."

His expression blanked as he stared at the tray for a moment. When his head lifted there was a calculating glint in his eyes. "What if I told you I was going to Budapest on business and my colleagues backed out, leaving me with a non-refundable ticket?"

"I'd say you are a liar and a terrible one at that. What business do you have in Budapest?" She tossed her napkin at him. "You have too much of an honest face to fib, mister."

"It's true," he insisted, not convincing her. "We have shareholders there."

Pursing her lips, she arched a brow. "What shareholders?"

"Time Warner, Noki, and the developers from other platforms we collaborate with."

Maybe he was telling a half-truth, but she knew there was no trip. He was trying to manipulate her into accepting his offer. "And you weren't planning on going because...?"

He shrugged, his gaze flicking about the room as if the lie made his eyeballs skittish. "I, uh, was planning on postponing until one of the guys could join me. But this actually works out. You'd be much more helpful, sort of like a translator."

He didn't speak Hungarian, so she could see why he'd need a translator. He'd done so much to help her. If he needed something in return she couldn't let him down. If he would be making the trip eventually anyway...

She was wavering. "It would help you?"

"Definitely. I wouldn't have to postpone any meetings and we'd be able to close the deal we've been negotiating. I'd have meetings most days so you'd have plenty of time with your aunt and relatives."

It sounded too perfect, too simple, and smelled a bit too much like bullshit. "When is your trip?"

His eyes skittered to the right and she detected more fibs. "It was actually supposed to be this week. I think we were scheduled to leave on Saturday, but I have to check. It was booked months ago. I almost forgot, because once the guys said they couldn't make it, I assumed we'd postpone."

He was either getting better at lying or he was really telling the truth. "Okay, no more, Elliot." She didn't want him to lie because he was too good for that. "Look me in the eye and swear this is the truth."

His face blanked as he met her stare head-on. "I swear I want you to come to Budapest with me so I can meet with our foreign associates."

She pursed her lips. He had to be telling the truth. No one learned to lie that quickly. "Fine, I'll go. But I'm paying you back for my ticket."

His face lit with a satisfied grin. "Great. Perfect. You're really helping me out."

She narrowed her eyes, still not fully trusting this story but finding it impossible to disappoint him. "Then we shall go."

7

"I'm going to Budapest. My flight leaves on Saturday at four a.m. and I'll need a car to the airport and some meetings scheduled for Sunday night. Can you arrange that, Hunter?"

The meeting squealed to a halt as Jet, Asher, and Hunter all frowned at him. "Budapest?" Asher asked, brow knit in confusion.

"You're going to Hungary?" Hunter wore a look of equal misunderstanding. "Why?"

"We haven't touched base with some of our shareholders in a while and I think we're overdue."

"So shoot them an email," Jet suggested. "That's a long ass flight. If we go anywhere it should be to Hong Kong. I thought we were scheduling China this quarter."

Elliot shook his head. "No. We can do Hong Kong, too, but Budapest is happening. I've already booked the flights."

"When?" Asher continued to scowl. "I thought you were sick yesterday."

"I just took the day off. I booked the flight this morning."

Easing back in his chair, Asher adjusted his glasses. "How long are you staying? Scarlet only has one week left before school starts, so I can't go. And we won't be able to schedule much on such short notice. Sunday's out of the question. We could probably swing Tuesday at the earliest."

"My return flight isn't until Wednesday night. Tuesday works." He'd just have to occupy himself other ways until then.

"A little notice would have been nice," Hunter grumbled. "If you're planning on sitting down with Zen, maybe I'll go."

"You can't go."

"Why not?"

"Because no one else can go. You're all busy."

Asher leaned forward, looking him square in the eye. "What the hell's going on, Elliot?"

"Nothing. I'm taking a trip and it has to be a business trip—a solo one."

"We don't do solo," Jet pointed out, now frowning

like the rest of them. "Are you negotiating a deal we don't know about?"

"No, I…" Shit. This was why he hated lies. "I'm traveling with someone."

"*Who?*" The three of them asked at once.

Say Mom. He buttoned up.

Hunter tossed the file he was holding on the conference table. "I'm not booking shit until you tell us what's going on."

The three of them glared at him. He adjusted his tie. "Forget it. I'll arrange everything myself. Just be informed I won't be here next week."

Standing, he collected his laptop and the files he was working on and escaped to his office. Within an hour he had a car arranged and Martha busy packing his suits. They were leaving in two days.

The guys continued to send him shady looks every time they crossed paths. When it came time for lunch he was anxious to heat up the leftover soup Nadia had packed. He wasn't sure what her secret ingredient was, but he was absolutely addicted to her cooking—sans the tea.

As he waited by the microwave, the guys unloaded orders from the restaurant downstairs onto the table. "Why'd you brown bag it today?" Jet asked.

"I had some soup left over from yesterday." Elliot carefully carried the bowl to the table and dug in his bag for a napkin and spoon.

"That smells good. Where's it from?" Hunter asked, hovering over his lunch.

"Back off," Elliot snapped, not willing to share even the scent of the magical mix.

Hunter rolled his eyes and plopped into his seat, unwrapping a long sub. The first bite of soup was hot and savory, reaching his belly on the tails of a sigh. The guys were quiet, likely still pissed about his *private* business trip, but they'd get over it.

Reaching for his napkin, he jerked back as Jet suddenly snatched it out of his fingers. "What the hell is this?"

Elliot's eyes widened as Jet flashed the backside of the napkin, displaying a scribbled heart and the words *Have a good day!* His face heated as he snatched the napkin back and stuffed it on his lap. All eyes on him.

"Did Martha pack your lunch?" Asher asked, a concerned, almost aghast, twist to his brows.

"I'd like to eat without an inquisition," he mumbled, taking another bite.

Hunter's nose wrinkled. "Martha? She's in her seventies, man. What's going on in that house of yours?"

Jet shrugged, taking a bite of a sandwich that barely fit in his mouth. "Martha's okay," he mumbled. "Nice round ass."

Elliot curled his lip, not wanting to think of his elderly housekeeper's ass while eating. "Do you mind?"

"Not at all," Jet answered and laughed. "How long you been diddling the maid?"

He dropped his spoon. "I'm not doing anything with my maid. Knock it off. You're ruining my appetite."

Asher's knowing stare weighed heavily on Elliot

as he retrieved his spoon. He'd be the hardest of the three to deceive. First, because he'd recently fallen in love and likely knew the symptoms, and two, because he knew Elliot the longest.

Wait. What?

His brain backtracked. First of all, he was *not* in love. That was a slip. Pure, unconscious laziness on his part. What he felt for Nadia was affection, lust. His baser instincts longing for something he'd never experienced before.

There was no love in the equation. He liked her, yes, but that wasn't love. Love was serious, and their situation was more circumstantial than anything else. Whatever happened yesterday morning didn't happen again, so clearly they were not involved in any sort of romantic arrangement. It was a fluke. A hot, erotic, freak accident that would probably never happen again.

"What's wrong, Elliot? You're all flushed."

Jet snickered. "He's probably picturing Martha naked."

Narrowing his eyes at Jet, he grit his teeth. "Shut up." Taking the last bite of his lunch, he bagged up his Tupperware and pushed away from the table. "I'll be in my office if anyone's looking for me."

"If Martha calls we'll put her right through," Hunter called and they all laughed.

Assholes.

Once he was at his desk he texted Nadia. She was helping her mother pack today and had a class tonight. When he'd left for work she was still sleeping and he didn't want to disturb her.

. . .

How's your day going? I checked the schedule and we're leaving Saturday—early in the a.m. A car will deliver us to the airport.

Hitting *send* he waited to see if she'd respond right away, grinning like an idiot when he saw the bubbles indicating she was typing. His phone buzzed.

My day is good. How was your soup? Don't push yourself too hard after being sick.

Again came the guilt of making her believe he was ill when he was perfectly fine. He should confess but after letting her tend to him all day he felt like a total jerk for taking advantage of her kindness. He'd just have to suffer the guilt.

Soup was delicious and I feel great.

His phone vibrated.

. . .

I'd hate to do this but I have a favor to ask...

Typing back he asked what she needed, liking the idea of coming to her aid when she needed rescuing. His phone buzzed as her reply came through.

I hate having to ask this, but would you be able to drive my mother to the airport tonight? I have to teach a class and I'm worried I won't get her there in time to get through all the security checks. So sorry to put that on you.

He sat back in his chair. She wanted him to take her mother to the airport? Alone?

He supposed he could manage that, but from what Nadia told him, her mother didn't speak a lick of English.

There was a knock at his door and he looked up as Asher stepped in. "Hey. You got a minute?"

"Sure." He casually flipped over his phone so the screen didn't show. "What's up?"

Asher lowered himself into a chair and leveled him with a stare. "What's going on, Elliot? If you're arranging something with our shareholders I need to know."

He sighed. "I'm not doing anything like that.

Come on, Asher. I just told you I *need* meetings scheduled. I have nothing prepared for this trip."

"Then why go? What's in Budapest?"

His phone buzzed. "Hold on. I need to check this text."

I'm sorry. That was a lot to ask after you've already done so much. Don't worry about it. I'll call a cab company. Enjoy the rest of your day.

"Shit."

"What is it?" Asher asked, frowning.

"Nothing."

He quickly responded, telling her it wasn't a problem at all and that he was in a meeting and would get back to her in a few minutes. When he placed his phone back on the desk it buzzed again, but he resisted the urge to look at it with Asher there.

His friend appeared very distracted as the buzzing continued every few seconds. Elliot ignored it.

"I'm sorry. You were saying?"

"Aren't you going to get that?"

"It's fine. I'll deal with it later." The phone buzzed again.

Asher's eyes narrowed behind the lenses of his glasses. "What exactly is happening here, Elliot? You have hearts on your napkin, you're planning a sudden trip out of the country, and you're texting. You never text."

"I text."

"With who? Your mom? She calls you." Asher shook his head, glancing away for a brief moment. "Are you seeing someone?"

He tugged at his tie. "No."

"Who drew on your napkin?"

"Look, Asher, I know you have certain things figured out now that you're married and a father, but I'd appreciate it if you didn't make my life another case study of yours. My private life is private."

His friend drew back, appearing genuinely affronted. "Why won't you tell me what's going on?"

"There's nothing to tell."

"Who's going to Budapest with you?"

The phone buzzed again. Girls had so much to say and he wasn't used to that. "If I tell you you'll make a big deal out of it and it's not a big deal."

"Then why keep it a secret?"

God, this was tedious. "Fine. It's Nadia—"

"Nadia? The dancer?"

"Yes. Her aunt's dying. This is her last chance to say goodbye."

"Wait." He shook his head, a baffled expression on his face. "Nadia, Nadia? My dance instructor, Nadia? How do you know all this? You met her once."

"Twice. I also saw her at your wedding."

Asher rolled his eyes. "Have you ever actually talked to her?"

Elliot pursed his lips. "As a matter of fact, yes, I have. I ran into her at a restaurant Tuesday night. We stopped to grab a drink afterward."

"You *grabbed a drink*—with *Nadia*? Who are you

and what have you done with my antisocial best friend? You never drink." He laughed. "And you never get involved with women."

"She needed someone to talk to. Don't overthink it."

"Wait, wait, wait. You're serious? You've actually been spending time with *Nadia?*"

"Yes, *Nadia!* It's nothing personal." Total bullshit. It was the most personal connection he ever shared with a woman.

Asher held up his hands. "Look, I'm the last person qualified to give relationship advice. The fact that I wake up beside the woman of my dreams every day still boggles my mind. But you are talking about Nadia, the exotic, Hungarian dancer you could barely breathe around when I dragged—literally *dragged*—you to her class. You're involved with her?"

"It isn't a relationship. I'm helping her out. That's it."

His friend looked truly confused. "Come on, Elliot. I was in love with my wife since high school. Do you think I'm going to judge you for caring about Nadia? You wouldn't grab a drink with her if it was just a philanthropic gesture."

He shifted uncomfortably. "This is what I didn't want. My feelings are irrelevant. She's in a tight spot and could use some help. What's a trip to Hungary for me? Nothing. But it's everything to her. She wouldn't go unless I convinced her I was already going on business and had an extra, non-refundable ticket."

Asher's eyes widened. "You lied to her?"

Not just about that either. He was likely developing an ulcer from the weight of his guilt. First playing hooky and now the trip. But he swore that was the last of the lies. From here on he'd be nothing but honest with her.

And Asher was the last person who should throw stones at glass houses. "Like you can talk."

"Yeah, but you saw where my lies got me. Elliot, you're the most honest person I know—*painfully* so."

"It's only a lie if I'm not there on business. If Hunter would set up a damn meeting this wouldn't be an issue."

Sitting back, Asher crossed his arms. "You could take the Noki guys out to lunch. That's easy." Seeming to consider their options he tilted his head. "It's noble, what you're doing for her, taking her to see her sick relative."

He didn't want the gesture to go to his head. He wasn't doing it for any sort of recognition. He was simply doing it because she took care of him like he was on his deathbed yesterday and he wanted to do something nice for her in return.

Plus, he knew what it was like to lose a parent. She obviously loved this aunt very much. It was only right she got to say a proper goodbye.

"She's nice. I wanted to help her. I don't expect anything in return."

Asher held up his hands. "Hey, I've known Nadia a while now. She's a very sweet person. From what Steve says she's really tight with her family. It has to be difficult for her with half of them on the other side of the world."

He frowned. "Steve, your trainer? How do they know each other?"

"I think they used to date. Sometimes she teaches Zumba at his gym."

"Nadia dated Steve?" His mind filled with images of the other man, a total contrast to himself. The guy was cut from granite, towering, and—from what Elliot could recall—a decent person. "Why did they break up?"

"I'm not even sure I have the facts straight. Maybe they were just friends—"

"Well, you should really know the difference before you go spouting off accusations," he snapped.

The thought of Steve touching Nadia was a lot more threatening than a guy like Ian. Steve was ... smart enough to own his own business, good looking, and successful.

Jesus, his tie was choking him.

"Are you okay?"

"I'm fine," he barked. "Scarlet likes Steve, doesn't she?"

"I think you're missing the point here, Elliot."

"Does she like him or not, Asher?"

"Yeah, but why does that matter? She met Steve during the whole Mr. Stone debacle and he was good to her when I ... wasn't."

"Can you find out why he and Nadia broke up?"

"Elliot, I think you're focusing too much on the irrelevant. Who cares if they have a past? Nadia's beautiful. I'm sure there are lots of men—"

"Get out."

"What?"

"Get out. I'm not discussing this. Forget what I told you and don't mention it to Jet or Hunter. I'll schedule my own meetings and handle everything myself."

"Why are you suddenly pissed off?"

He didn't have a clue, but at the moment he wanted to throw something. "I just have a lot of work to do and I'm going to miss next week dealing with this."

Easing out of the chair, Asher held up his hands. "I didn't mean to upset you."

"You didn't." *More lies. Fuck!* "I just have a lot on my mind." Like Nadia with other men. "I'm sorry I snapped at you."

"Okay. Well, why don't you come to the house tomorrow night and grab dinner? Anakin would love to see his uncle."

He should. He hadn't been there for a while, but what about Nadia? He didn't want to miss her at home and he wasn't ready to let Asher know she was staying with him. "Maybe after our trip."

"Promise?"

"Yeah. I'll bring Anakin back a souvenir."

"He'd love that. And whatever happens, Elliot, I'm glad you're finally putting yourself out there."

Elliot exhaled when the door closed. Sweeping up his phone he found five texts, each one gushing with gratitude for his assistance with her mother. She used those stupid emojis he hated. Only now they didn't seem so stupid. He especially liked the one with the yellow face blowing a kiss.

Texting back a quick *you're welcome*, he got to

work, scheduling a meeting with their contacts across seas. Once that was handled, he downloaded a book on common Hungarian phrases and studied it as if he had the final of a lifetime in a few hours. The airport was a solid forty-five-minute drive and he couldn't fill it in silence.

8

———————

Ocimum Bacilicum: A common herb comprised of endothelial and other healing properties. Also, that which makes Nadia smile.

~*Musings of Elliot P. Garnet*

Knocking on the door, Elliot drew in a bracing breath and smiled as a petite woman peeked through the crack under a chain lock. She looked like Nadia, but with a wider nose and lighter hair. She was also shorter by a foot.

Keeping his voice friendly, he said, "*Helló. Én vagyok Elliot. Nadia barátja.*"

The woman's brows twitched, but she opened the door for him. Turning, she pointed to her luggage on the floor and rattled off words faster than he could translate. She waved her hands at the three suitcases.

"*Ez minden?*" he asked, wondering if that was everything.

The apartment was vacant of personal items, aside from tattered old furniture. Nadia had said much of what her family owned was already shipped back to Hungary.

The woman spoke again, her rapid words flinging across the room as her little finger poked in the direction of other rooms. Aside from a few verbs and the random mention of Nadia, he was at a loss. Perhaps after their twenty-four-hour flight, which he intended to use for studying he'd be better equipped to decipher the language.

"I'll carry your bags," he said slowly, raising his voice like dimwitted people often did when faced with a language barrier. *She's not deaf.* "I'll be right back."

Lugging the baggage down to the parking lot, he popped the trunk and stowed the suitcases in his car. When he returned, the woman continued to watch him.

"Do you have anything else? *Van még?*"

"*Ez az,*" she said and shrugged.

Giving each room a quick inspection, in case she left anything personal behind, he checked to make sure all the windows were locked and—he paused as he stepped into the kitchen. There, on the sill, was an old wooden box with various herbs growing out the top. Examining the box, he noted the hooks that allowed it to hang from both sides of the window.

Opening drawers, finding them all empty, he searched for a screwdriver. Nadia's mother came into the kitchen and frowned, rambling accusing words he didn't understand.

"Screwdriver?" He gestured, twisting his hand in a poor charade. "I was going to take this to Nadia." And he was shouting again. Like that helped.

"Nadia?"

"Yes, Nadia. She wanted these herbs. The plants." He pointed.

The woman frowned and shoved him aside. Using both hands, she lifted the window box off the hooks and held it out to him. "*Adj Nadia.*"

He took the box, which was rather heavy, and placed it on the counter. Pointing at the hardware that let the hooks hang from the wall, he said, "Tools?"

"Ah!" She left the room and returned a moment later with an old Swiss Army knife and smiled.

"Perfect. Thank you."

He had the hardware removed and in his pocket within two minutes and Nadia's mother held the door as he carried the herbs out of the apartment. Dirt sifted from the bottom and soiled his shirt, but he was more worried about the seat of his car.

Flipping over a floor mat, he covered as much of the leather seat as he could and placed the herb box on top, holding it in place with the seat belt for good measure. Nadia's mother watched him from the passenger seat.

As he slid behind the steering wheel, he checked his watch. They had plenty of time. "Ready?"

She frowned and shrugged.

"Okay," he said to himself, backing out of the parking lot.

As he backed out she pressed her open palm to the glass as if waving goodbye to the apartment. Though it wasn't much, they all seemed rather attached to the place.

It was a shame Nadia said it was already leased to new tenants. He would have helped her keep it. What he should do was offer her a loan to put a deposit on a new place—a better place. However, he was coming to appreciate their current living situation, so he didn't dwell on the thought too much.

There was very little talking on the ride to the airport. Though he'd studied many words that afternoon, only a few common phrases stuck with him. When he tried to use English, it was clear she understood very little. Perhaps if he met Nadia's aunt it would be different, depending if she had the strength to speak. Elliot didn't know how terminal the woman's health was.

When they reached the airport, he unloaded her luggage and put it on a cart. After directing her to the right door, he pointed out which terminal she should use, showing her both the directory signs and the matching words on her ticket.

She smiled. "Köszönöm, feleségül veszi Nadia házat?" She pointed to his car. "Te gazdag vagy, nem?"

He laughed nervously and shrugged. "Sure." Not a clue what she just said, but she seemed happy. "Have a safe trip."

She patted his cheek and wheeled the cart toward the terminal, taking some of his tension with her. A forty-five-minute drive home turned out to be a two-hour experience in rush hour traffic.

When he walked through his front door, leaving a trail of soil behind him, Nadia still wasn't home. He carried the herbs to the kitchen and considered his windows. They were much larger than her little window and lower to the ground. Figuring which one would get the most sun he set the box on the floor and went to the garage to find a drill.

Do I even own a drill?

Luckily, he found his old tool set in the garden shed. When the hardware was secure and the box was hung, he stepped back. Well, it didn't seem to have the same charm it had in her little kitchen, but it worked. The window sort of dominated the little flower box, but he was certain she'd get it. There wasn't much she didn't appreciate.

9

———————

*"A KISS CAN BE EVEN DEADLIER **if you mean it.**"*

~Catwoman

The cab dropped Nadia off well after dark. It was getting chillier at night and she needed to remember a sweater, unsure what happened to her warm clothes from last season. As she reached the door, she bit her lip. Another code.

Opening her phone, she checked the texts that Elliot sent her with all the numbers she needed to know, smiling at his last one stating that her mother made it to the airport safe and sound. He even attached a smiley face.

As she punched in the code the door beeped and unlocked. The house was quiet.

"Elliot?"

"In the kitchen," he called.

Placing her bag by the door, she toed off her sneakers and followed his voice. She found him sitting at the table looking at his iPad. Her heart skipped a beat. His hair was in perfect order as usual, but his tie was loose, hanging a few inches below the collar. Spotting the smudge of dirt on his crisp white shirt she frowned.

"You're dirty."

"I brought you something." Smiling, he stood. "Go look at the window."

Rounding the counter, she sucked in a breath of surprise. "My herbs!" The sight of her basil and cilantro momentarily pushed all of her worries away. Turning, she beamed at him. "You brought my flowerbox!"

His smile was tight, his cheeks slightly tinged. "I figured you wouldn't want to leave it behind."

Touched by his thoughtfulness, she moved without thinking. Rising on her toes, she cupped his sweet face and pressed her lips to his. He stiffened briefly before his hands rested tentatively on her hips.

Pulling back, she whispered, "You are very, *very* sweet."

He stared at her, his face blank and his eyes holding a bit of shock. He gradually leaned down and brushed his lips against hers again. She leaned into the kiss, pulling him close as her blood started to heat.

She tried so hard not to think of him in a romantic sense, but he was always doing nice things for her like letting her stay there or explaining words she mixed up or letting her join him on his trip to Hungary. And now, bringing the one thing she missed from her apartment to his house. It was impossible to ignore how genuinely sweet he was.

His palms burned through her thin dance clothing and she moaned softly. He shifted forward, deepening the kiss, surprising her with a glimpse of aggressiveness as he backed her against the counter.

The spike of intensity charged her desire, driving it higher. She wasn't sure feeling any higher around Elliot was a good idea. It would make the plummet back to earth that much more lethal.

Breathless, she braced a hand on his chest and turned her cheek. She hadn't meant to stir things up again, but somehow, not five minutes after walking through the front door, she landed herself right in his arms. She had to be careful, with him and with herself.

"I need a shower," she murmured, grasping at any excuse to escape and find her bearings. He had a way of undoing her before she realized she was coming undone.

He stepped back, not meeting her gaze, and nodded. "Sorry. You probably didn't want to be mauled the minute you walked through the door."

She stilled and frowned. She kissed him first. "You don't have to apologize for kissing me." If she gave in to her wants she'd have him naked by now, but she was really trying to keep her composure. Her gaze drifted back to the herb box he'd hung. It wasn't easy. He was so damn sweet.

Elliot took a step back. "I lost my head. I shouldn't have... I'm sorry."

Why did he sound so disappointed in himself? It was *her* fault. She started the kiss. And she pulled away, because the minute he flashed that aggressive side he ramped her need into dangerous territory. *She* was the one who feared coming off too strong. "It's fine, Elliot. Really."

"Did you eat dinner?"

He obviously wasn't comfortable discussing it. "Yes. Did you? I could make something."

"That won't be necessary. Martha usually leaves something in the fridge."

Had he been waiting for her to eat? "I could heat it up for you."

He shook his head. "Go do what you have to do."

Feeling like an irritant, she drew back. He shouldn't have waited for her. "I don't mind—"

"Go shower, Nadia." The command in his voice took her off guard. He was clearly flustered by her presence.

"Thank you again for helping with my mother." She should have taken her herself.

"No problem." He still wouldn't look at her.

Nodding, she silently left the kitchen.

She was so confused by him. Maybe she shouldn't have cut off the kiss. Maybe he needed that and now he felt rejected. She was only trying to protect them both from muddying their relationship. She should have never touched him. All day she told herself she wouldn't confuse their situation by sexualizing their interactions, but she'd done exactly what she wanted to avoid two minutes after walking through the door.

Or maybe he wasn't irritated about the kiss at all. Perhaps he had a bad day and asking him to take her mother to the airport was too much. She shouldn't have imposed on him like that. From now on she'd only look to him as a last resort.

Her shower was wonderful. Of course, Elliot had state of the art bathrooms complete with heating vents and radiant flooring. Brushing out her hair, she considered how strange her week had been and how much stranger it was bound to get. It still hadn't registered that in two days she'd be home, a place she hadn't been in years.

Braiding her hair into pigtails, she reached for her glasses. She wanted to ask Elliot about his schedule over the next few days, but she didn't want to be a pest. Still, she needed to double check if he would be staying in a hotel or with her family, so she could let them know.

Slipping her cable knit cardigan over her arms, the one that belonged to her grandfather, she went in search of her housemate. He wasn't in his bedroom or the kitchen or the den. Venturing back up the stairs, she surveyed the many doors, knocking quietly at each one. The house was silent and big enough to lose a person.

Pursing her lips, she stared out the window and stilled when she spotted movement. In the distance, just beside the blue reflection of the pool, she saw him sitting in a lounge chair.

Sliding the glass door open, it beeped, and then

she took the patio steps toward the pool area. His yard looked like a private resort, accented with well-placed landscape lights that made it colorful even at night.

"I couldn't find you," she said as she approached so as not to startle him. He turned but didn't smile or speak. "May I sit with you?"

He nodded so she took the chair beside his, stretching out and looking up at the starry sky. "Wow. There are a lot more stars here than over the city."

Without looking at her, he said, "It's the same sky, same amount of stars. Overpopulation causes light pollution, making it difficult to see nebulae or distant galaxies. Same sky. Different perspectives."

She smirked. "You're a bit of a know-it-all, I think."

He faced her and arched a brow. "Did you really want to go on believing the stars favored one part of the sky over the other?"

"Maybe they do, smarty pants."

"They don't."

"Then why are they moving?"

"It's implied motion—the Earth's rotating on its axis. And there's turbulence in the atmosphere, which refracts the light, making them twinkle."

She rolled her eyes. "What about shooting stars, mister? They move."

"They're not stars. They're meteors—rocks. They only light up because they're traveling so fast their heat glows as they pass through the atmosphere."

"You are ruining the sky for me, Elliot. Stargazing is supposed to be romantic."

He stopped talking and she split her attention between the sky and him. Maybe he didn't have a romantic side. But how would he explain the window box? Perhaps he'd only meant to be kind or sweet and she was, once again, misinterpreting another man's intentions.

After a long bout of silence, he asked, "Do you see that strip of light sky there?"

Her gaze followed his finger. "There?"

"Yes. That's the Milky Way. It's actually quite tragic how it came to be, if you believe in fairytales."

"Oh, I do." She shifted so she could look at him. "Will you tell me the story?"

His gaze remained on the sky. "There was a daughter who wove beautiful fabric and her father loved how talented she was, but she was also lonely and would often cry. She couldn't weave with tears in her eyes, so when she was sad her toiling stopped. He loved his daughter very much, so he introduced her to a cow herder and they fell madly in love."

Nadia grinned, knowing he didn't believe a word of what he was saying, but thinking something had to make him recall the fable. "Did they marry and have children?" Perhaps their family was the haze over that part of the sky.

"No. Once she was in love, she was too distracted to weave for her father anymore. He got angry and separated the lovers by a heavenly river of stars, but his daughter was so heartbroken she cried more than she had before—no longer weaving at all."

"Shame on him for interfering with love. Did her lover beg for the father's approval?"

"No, a flock of magpies sympathized with her pain and made a bridge of wings for her to cross."

Nadia smiled. "I think this isn't a tragic story at all, but a story of how love knows no distance."

"The magpies only came on the seventh night of the seventh month. It's said that if it rains, they won't come and she can't cross. She has to wait the entire year again."

The warmth in her chest dissipated and she scoffed. "Well then, I will hope it doesn't rain so she can cross to her lover's side and never return to her selfish father again."

He chuckled. "I don't think it works that way."

Snapping her tongue against the back of her teeth, she rolled her eyes. "What do *you* know? You think shooting stars are rocks. I happen to know on good authority they're wishes."

"Good God."

"Don't laugh at me, Mr. Cynic. I make a wish every time I see one."

"And how many have come true?"

"Oh, shut up, Elliot."

They stared at the sky in silence, which was probably what they should have done from the start. As her eyes grew heavy, she thought about all the questions she had about their upcoming trip but didn't want to disturb the tranquil moment.

The sky dulled with each sweep of her lashes and soon she was drifting off, dreaming of magpies and lovers reuniting under a blanket of stars. The brush of fingers down her cheek woke her and she shivered.

Elliot looked down at her, expression blank. "It's getting late. We should go in."

The air had chilled and she could no longer see the Milky Way. "What time is it?"

"Almost midnight."

He'd sat out there all that time? How did someone tolerate so much silence?

She shifted and put her feet on the ground. He held out a hand and helped her stand, keeping their fingers clasped while they silently made their way back to the house. As they walked upstairs, he shut off lights. When they reached his door he let go of her hand and a physical emptiness took hold.

She couldn't read him. He was either staring at her with too many secrets in his eyes or pushing her away. There had been two kisses, but both times he'd acted as if he regretted touching her. Maybe he did.

She also had regrets. Mainly, not meeting him sooner, before she threw so many pieces of herself away on men who turned out to be shallow and unkind. His quiet life and kind heart had a way of casting a blinding light on all of her mistakes and poor choices. She was attracted to him, yes, but more than anything she wanted him to be her friend.

"Do you not like me, Elliot?"

Sometimes they kissed, sometimes they held hands, but there was little clarity in between. She shouldn't be so affectionate with him if he wasn't interested in her as more than a friend.

He glanced at his bedroom door. "I like you."

Then why did it seem to pain him to say so? "Is that as a friend or...?" Perhaps they were mere acquaintances, him helping another person out because he was simply kind and generous.

His brow tightened and he shifted closer to the door. "It's whatever you want."

"What does that mean, whatever *I* want? What do *you* want?"

He opened the door and she caught his arm.

"Elliot, wait. Tell me what you want."

He grimaced and she braced for some unknown level of insult. "I don't want to get hurt. You're beautiful, Nadia, but beyond that, you're thoughtful and caring and a very nice person."

That hadn't been what she was expecting. "You're all those things, too, Elliot."

"No," he argued. "You aren't seeing the real me. Whatever you see when you look at me, I assure you, no one else sees the same. I don't think you really know who I am, and I'm worried that the more you get to know me, the less appealing I'll be. So maybe it's safer to just be friends."

He was scared she'd be disappointed? In him? She worried about the same issue, that he might hate what he found if he got close to her. She couldn't imagine what he had to hide, but she desperately wanted to understand him. "There are things you don't know about me, too."

He shook his head. "I'm not nice, Nadia. I'm intolerant and exacting. I get extremely impatient with social niceties and artificial bullshit. I don't want to lead you to believe I'm someone else because I know for a fact I don't have the tolerance to pretend to be anything other than the man I am."

"Do you know what I think, Elliot? I think you're everything I see, but other people see you from a different view. You're like a starry night. Consistent. Quiet. Misunderstood at first glance. Like you said, same sky, different perspective. I see you. And I think you're quite beautiful just the way you are. Maybe that will change, but I don't know that it will. There's nothing wrong with being who you are from where I'm standing."

She brushed a kiss on his cheek. "Goodnight, Elliot."

When she reached her door, she turned and found him standing where she left him, his hand touching his cheek where she'd pressed her kiss.

10

____

"NO CAPES!"

~Edna
The Incredibles

BY THE END of Nadia's last class on Friday night, the week had caught up with her. Once the last student was gone, she changed the music to her favorite playlist and went to use the bathroom. As she was washing her hands the bell rang and she shut off the faucet. Had someone forgotten something?

Creeping into the main studio she drew in a slow breath as Elliot appeared. "Elliot. What are you doing here?"

"It occurred to me you'd take a cab home and I figured why not do a favor to the environment."

She loved that he passed his thoughtfulness off

as practicality, loved that he'd thought about her even when she wasn't with him. "You're a terrible fibber."

His mouth twitched. "Is everyone gone? I wasn't sure what time you finished."

He looked so handsome in his work clothes, which she was coming to discover were a part of his day-to-day wardrobe. Elliot's attire was nostalgic of a time when men weren't as wrinkled and blends were more than cotton.

His hands wedged deep in his pockets and his sleeves were rolled at the elbows. Today his tie was red, deep like rubies. This was as casual as he got, such a flagrant contrast to her in stretch pants and a tank top.

"My last class just left. Let me get my things."

"Take your time."

How nice to not have someone rushing her for a change. She gathered her bag and switched her jazz shoes for sneakers. When she returned to the main room he was lingering by the back window.

"I'm ready."

"This is where we first met. I was standing right here, plotting my friend's death."

She laughed, recalling how uptight he'd been. It was no secret he hadn't wanted to be there but was doing a favor for his friend that day. "Asher's a very good dancer now. He and Lettie still take lessons on occasion."

"How... How did Asher learn about you? There are a lot of dance studios in the area."

That was a long time ago, so she had to think. "I think Steve hooked us up."

"And you knew Steve before Asher?"

"Yes." She shifted her bag on her shoulder. "Are you ready?"

He hesitated, his stare direct and holding her in place. "How did you know Steve, Nadia? Was he an old friend or something?"

Her smile fell, a strange sense of self-preservation waking inside of her. "Why are you interested in that?"

He shrugged. "Just curious."

No, that wasn't a spontaneous question. He had a reason for asking and she wasn't sure what he was hoping to find out. "Does it matter one way or the other?"

He glanced away, something people often did before distorting the truth. "No."

The warmth that filled her when he arrived chilled. He was making some sort of judgment about her and she didn't like it. "Steve and I met at the gym—the one he worked at before he bought his own. I used to teach Zumba classes there and he was a trainer."

"Did you ever date each other?"

And there it was. This was exactly why her guard had gone up. "Do you have a problem with Steve?"

"I hardly know the man."

"But you dislike him?"

"I didn't say that."

She frowned. Elliot was usually direct and didn't do well at beating around the bush.

"Then why don't you say what it is you mean to say, instead of asking all these roundabout questions? You want to know if Steve and I slept together, is that it?"

He broke eye contact but didn't object to hearing the truth. Her throat tightened as a sharp bite of unexpected shame inched into her chest.

Blinking, she stared at him and confessed, "We went on a few dates, but he never made it to my bed. Are you satisfied?" Why was she suddenly on the brink of tears?

Sensing her upset, he returned his gaze to her face. "Nadia, I'm sorry—"

"What do you want, Elliot?" she snapped, flustered by her doubts about things from so long ago—things that meant nothing and hadn't even been the worst of her past. "Do you want me to tell you I've never been with another man? I can't."

"I know that. I don't care."

"Then why this sudden obsession with a man who asked me out when I was eighteen?"

"You were eighteen?"

"Yes! What does it matter?"

He shook his head. "It doesn't. I'm sorry. I don't know why it was bothering me. Asher said you two used to date and—"

"Asher?" She threw up her hands. "What does Asher know? He was only a student of mine."

"I know that. That's why I figured I'd ask you directly, but I didn't do it to upset you."

It was none of his business, but she also didn't want to lie to him. She wanted him to know who she really was but still feared the truth might scare him away. This was going too fast. They hadn't even clarified what they were to each other. At the moment, they were friends who shared a few awkward kisses and an address.

Pressing her lips tight, she glared at the ceiling, refusing to cry over nothing. "Why do you care who I dated? The *truth*, Elliot."

His jaw twitched and he glanced away. "It ... pissed me off. I don't know the other men, but I know Steve. When Asher said you might have dated, I couldn't stop picturing it. I couldn't get it out of my head. I wanted to hit the guy, but I can't because he's three times my size."

Her anger subsided as she blinked at him, his words slowly sinking in. "You're jealous."

"No." He shook his head. "I don't get jealous."

"Oh?" She lifted her brow. Everything he just described sounded like jealousy.

Stepping closer to him, she tugged his tie. "It seems a strong reaction, is all."

He caught her hand and held it in his large fingers. "I have a vivid imagination—"

"I bet you do."

"—and sometimes it gets away from me."

"What is it you imagine—about me—Elliot?"

His Adam's apple made a slow dip as he swallowed. "Your door was unlocked. You should have something more than a bell to let you know someone's in the studio."

She laughed, the abrupt change of topic jockeying her away from what was important. "What is that, a trick you do? You don't want to answer the question so you just start talking about something else?"

"I don't have an answer to your question."

"Hmm." Sliding her hand out of his grip she stepped back. "Well, I'm still curious, so when you figure it out, let me know." Walking to the wall, she flipped off the switch, leaving him standing in the dark.

She jingled her keys. "I'm going to lock the door now. Don't want any dangerous burglars sneaking in."

He followed. "I'm serious about the lock. It's late and this isn't the best area."

"This is a fine area. Don't be a snob, Elliot. Besides, dance studios don't have anything to steal." They took the steps and she locked up. "There. Safe and sound."

"I wasn't worried about your belongings. I was worried about you."

Her smile faltered, surprised to hear him admit such a personal concern for her safety. "Oh."

This was just another example of the nice man he was and her reading too deeply into his character. It wasn't necessarily about her. To put him at ease, she said, "I know self-defense and keep pepper spray with me."

This didn't seem to appease him. "You should have cameras and a buzzer to let people in and out."

"It's not my building. I take what the landlord gives me. Come on, it's chilly."

She wasn't going to debate the security of her studio. She had the best she could afford. Not everyone lived in a space house with fancy alarm systems like he did. Besides, she hadn't had any problems since renting there.

"Did you eat?" he asked as he backed out of the parking lot.

"No."

"Do you want to stop somewhere?"

"Like Burger King?"

"I was thinking something a little nicer."

"I'm wearing sweaty clothes and sneakers."

Briefly taking his eyes off the road, he glanced at her. "I think you look nice."

"Says the man in a dress shirt and tie."

"Trust me, you could wear a sack and I'd still be the inappropriate factor in the equation. Let's stop and have dinner. We'll go someplace small and quiet."

She sighed. "Fine. But you have to take off your tie and un-tuck your shirt."

"What?"

"Either that or I'm not going. I look like a slob."

His fingers noticeably tightened on the wheel. "Fine."

When they arrived at the restaurant, a little corner place with outdoor seating and Italian cuisine, Elliot stood at the car door and loosened his tie. After unclasping the top button of his shirt, he frowned at his hips.

"My shirttails will be wrinkled. Can't this be enough?"

She laughed at how uncomfortable the idea of wrinkles made him. "Fine."

Untwisting the clip in her hair, she flipped her head over and shook out her waves, hoping to hide the fact that she was in an old tank top with a bleach stain on the side.

Flipping back, she paused as she caught him staring. "What?"

His eyes were wide behind his glasses. "Nothing." He shook his head and looked away.

He took her hand and escorted her into the restaurant. The smell of delicious pasta cranked up her hunger. The hostess greeted them, and before Nadia could manage a word, Elliot asked for a private table in the back. They were escorted to the rear of the restaurant, far away from all other patrons.

"Do they know you here?" He seemed to have some pull.

"No, but if you make a direct request people don't often tell you no."

She raised a brow. "I'll have to remember that trick."

For as gentle as he was, he had a knack for being equally commanding. His clout was subtle but undeniable. She wondered if he even realized the influence he held over others. He wore authority very well.

As they perused the menu, she struggled to decide what she should eat. "What will you order?"

"Probably just penne. You?"

"I can't make up my mind. My mouth's watering over the thought of steak, but I don't know if I feel like being a meat eater tonight." She gave him a flirty smirk and batted her lashes. "Should I pretend we're on a date and act like I have a dainty little appetite to impress you?" Really, she was just fishing to see if this counted as a date.

"Why would you base your dinner on our circumstances? If you're hungry, eat."

She shrugged. "Women do all kinds of silly things to get a man's attention. For instance, they might play footsie under the table."

She brushed her foot against his and scrunched her nose when the rubber sole of her shoe snagged against the soft fabric of his pants. "Sorry. I don't usually wear sneakers on a date. Is this a date, Elliot?"

His gaze lowered as he straightened his silverware. "I suppose that depends on how you define the term."

"No, no." She waved a finger at him. "No fancy smart talk. Is. This. A. Date? I'm being direct, so you have to give me an answer."

Meeting her gaze, his nostrils flared as he drew in a slow breath. "Yes. It's a date."

Playing off her relief, she opened her menu again. A slow heat bloomed in her belly as she inwardly celebrated. "Good. I'll have a Cobb salad."

The waitress arrived and took their drink orders. "Do you need a few more minutes to decide?"

Elliot, again, spoke before she needed to. "No, we're ready. I'll have the penne in the vodka sauce and my date will have a Cobb salad with the filet mignon."

Her eyes went wide, that was *not* what she planned to order.

"How would you like that cooked?" the waitress asked and he looked at her.

"Um ... rare, please." Once they were alone she gave Elliot a pointed look. "I said salad."

"I don't expect my *date* to starve herself for my benefit. You said you were in the mood for steak, so I ordered you exactly what you wanted. End of story."

She sat back and folded her arms loosely in her lap. "You can be quite bossy when you want to be, mister."

"Direct," he corrected.

Whatever. She liked it.

The meal was delicious. She only managed to eat a quarter of her filet, but it was worth every bite. "We should bring this home and have it for lunch tomorrow."

"We won't be here. Our flight leaves before dawn."

The entire week passed in a blur and she was hardly prepared for the trip. "I still have to pack and now you've put me in a food coma."

"How much could you possibly pack? You came to my house with *a* bag."

"I picked up more of my things this morning. I was missing some sweaters."

His hand stilled as he held his glass to his lips. "You went back to Ian's?"

"I was only in and out."

"I didn't realize. Did you see him?"

She laughed. "No, Ian was not there. Thank God."

He visibly relaxed. "Customs will only allow a seventy-pound bag."

"That should be enough. I hope."

"Well, if you still have to pack we should get moving." He looked for the waitress.

"Don't you have to pack too?"

"No. Martha took care of that."

"You had your maid pack for you? Aren't you worried she might have forgotten something?"

He shook his head. "I wear the same thing every day. It's a little difficult to screw up."

"Why do you dress like that? Do you wear ties on the weekends when you're sitting around at home?"

He again looked for the waitress. "Everyone has a preference."

"Yes, but I wear heels because I think they're sexy, not because they're comfortable. Why do you prefer to wear a tie around your neck?"

He shrugged, notably avoiding her question and gaze. "Where did the waitress go?"

"Relax. We have plenty of time. Tell me why you're always so buttoned up."

He adjusted the position of his butter knife. "I like it. It's proper."

Her lips twisted. "That's not the reason. Tell me why you like it."

Giving up on his search for the waitress, he huffed. "Why does it matter? When I was a boy it was how I always imagined I'd dress. Men wear suits."

"Not all men."

"The sort of men I admire do."

Perching her chin on her palm she studied him. "And what sort of men do you admire?"

He rolled his eyes. "This is stupid."

"No, it's not. Tell me. I won't laugh. When I was a little girl I wanted to be a unicorn. You can imagine my disappointment when I realized that was impossible."

He chuckled, an unguarded dimple forming under the slight flush of his cheeks.

"Please," she cajoled, desperate to know how his mind worked.

Drawing in a deep breath, he flashed her a bashful glance, so teasing and boyish her heart skipped a beat. "I wanted to be like the best of them, Bruce Wayne, Clark Kent, Tony Stark, James Howlett, and Matt Murdock."

Tone teasing, she laughed. "I can't believe I told you I wanted to be a unicorn for that. I don't know who any of those people are."

"*What?*"

She shrugged, not believing they were presidents or anyone she should recognize. "Who are they?"

"You don't know who Bruce Wayne is?"

"Should I?"

"Yes! He's Batman!"

"Oh, I know who that is. Christian Bale."

"No, no, no, no, no, no, *no!*" he grumbled, dropping his face into his hands. "Christian Bale was just one actor who played him. Batman originated long before Bale was even alive, in DC Comics back in 1939."

It was amusing how scandalized he was that she didn't know this. "Sorry, I'm a girl. I don't read comic books."

"Plenty of girls are into comics."

"What girls?"

"When we go to conventions there are lots of women there."

"Really? Are they mothers, taking their sons to buy comic books?"

He narrowed his eyes, his smile fading. "No. Forget it."

Okay, so he really liked these comic characters. She regretted taking her mocking too far. "I'm sorry. I was only teasing."

He shrugged, no longer in a playful mood. "I'm used to it."

She frowned. She hadn't meant to offend him or make him feel foolish. She told him she wanted to be a *unicorn. That* was foolish.

Not only did she regret pushing his buttons, she wondered if she was somehow lacking because she didn't have this comic book connection with him that other women might.

Folding her napkin on her lap, she murmured, "Do you only like girls who are into these characters?"

"They're heroes, and I think it would be awesome if a girl understood them like I do."

She bristled, trying not to take his remark personally. "Will you teach me to understand them?"

His mouth opened, but no words came out. He

blinked and frowned. "You don't have to pretend to be interested—"

"But I am. Please tell me about them."

He hesitated. "I'm not really sure where to start."

She truly wanted to know what made him feel so fervently about them. She wanted to know that passionate side of him, more than she was willing to admit.

"Tell me about your favorite ones. What do they do?"

"The characters are cool, but it's not just about what they can do. Comics were a source of escape for me. Even the bad guys ... Lex Luther, who had nothing, taught me not to sulk about the things I couldn't have. Peter Parker showed me I could pursue a career while still acting as a student. There are hidden morals. They taught me people aren't always what they seem. That was something I really needed to learn at one point."

"Why did you need to learn that?"

His gaze skated away, his voice dropping. "Because for a very long time I hated everyone."

She drew back in her seat, unable to imagine a cruel side to him. "Why? Hate is such a strong word, Elliot."

Keeping his focus on the table, he whispered, "There are a lot of mean people in the world. I think I met half of them before I was fifteen. Comics made me strong enough to walk back into hell ... day after day after day."

"Hell?"

"High school—and middle school—and a good

part of grade school. I hated most of school—*hated it.* I love learning, but the entire process of social integration has always eluded me. Comics gave me hope that one person could suddenly show up and change everything. It's what got me out of bed each morning, the hope I might find that person."

He shook his head, his eyes staring off just beyond her shoulder. "But no one ever showed. When I realized the real world was short on heroes, I decided to try to be one. I run a club for kids like me, and I try to show them intellect's more of a superpower than anything else. They don't have to be ashamed because they love math or chess or whatever makes them tick. It gives them a reason to enjoy school when so many social factors make it unbearable."

Nadia tilted her head and studied him, assuming she should see some physical shift from the impact this man's words had on her. It was quite an evolution from who she assumed he was that morning and it was difficult to imagine him being picked on or hurting in any way—even if his pain was over a decade old.

"You make children brave? Build their confidence?"

"I try."

"I think that's amazing." Most people didn't go to such lengths to make strangers feel better about themselves. She thought he was just a computer guy.

"If I believed what others saw in me as a kid ... I probably wouldn't be here. So, yeah, figuring out that underdogs can sometimes be the most powerful men of all is a lesson that stuck, a lesson I got from reading comics."

She had no idea how to respond. There was nothing lacking in Elliot's appearance that made him seem ... less than anyone else. The truth was, once she cracked his shell, he was hiding so much more than most men. This man had depth, and she'd only grazed the surface.

Here she thought comics were just picture books and movies about people with supernatural powers. To think something so simple could have such a complicated impact, it gave her a new appreciation for the genre. "I'm envious."

He blinked at her. "Why?"

"Nothing's ever made such an impression on me. I'm sorry I teased you about it, Elliot. I see now that they're much more than children's books."

He smiled and drew in a breath to say more, but the waitress suddenly returned, interrupting the moment. Though he never said whatever he was going to say, he seemed to forgive her for making light of something that carried substantial weight in his life.

The ride home was quiet and though she should have been planning what to pack, all she could think about was this sweet man overcoming some sort of childhood adversity. He'd managed to bury the pain and evolve into one of the gentlest souls she'd ever met.

Elliot parked by the front steps of the house. "Wait, I'll get your door."

As he jumped out of the car she laughed. He truly was a gentleman in every sense of the word.

As they walked up the steps he reached for the keypad and she caught his hand, her heart rattling in her chest as she went against all of her good advice to simply be his friend. But after their dinner, and the week she had, there was no disguising how much she wanted him.

"I believe it's customary to kiss your date at the door," she whispered.

She didn't want to kiss him out of gratitude or any sense of indebtedness. She wanted to kiss him out of sheer attraction.

His head lowered, not turning toward her in any way, but she knew he heard her. Maybe he didn't want to kiss her. Embarrassment made a slow crawl up her spine and her heart quivered.

It hurt, realizing he might not find her as attractive as she found him, but she accepted that might be the case. The more she learned about him, the more she realized he had a right to hold a high standard. He was, after all, a great guy.

"Elliot?"

His brow creased, an internal debate playing over his shadowed features. She shouldn't have said anything.

"It's okay. You don't have to."

The soft scuff of his shoes over the pavement had her sucking in a breath. Without saying a word, he tucked a strand of hair behind her ear and tipped up her chin. His gray eyes glistened under the porch light. "But I want to."

Looking up at him, her body trembled. "Okay."

Soft lips brushed hers and an uproarious wave of

pleasure swelled in her belly. She rose on her toes and slowly wreathed her arms around his shoulders, her chest tightening with the thrill of having his lips on her once more. As he deepened the kiss, his palm dragged low, stopping just above her hips and he pulled her closer. She loved the way he kissed, so focused on the actual act rather than what might come next.

Sliding a hand down his arm, she followed to his wrist and nudged his fingers lower. His body tensed for a moment and then his grip tightened on her ass as the kiss doubled in intensity. His other hand sifted through her hair, tightening and holding her to him as he squeezed her close.

When he broke away he was panting. She licked her lips and pressed her cheek to his chest. "You're very good at that," she whispered, wishing they could do more, but enjoying the anticipation he was so skilled at dragging out.

"So are you."

His grip on her body loosened as he stepped back, clearing his throat. Her front chilled the moment he pulled completely away. The lock buttons beeped and the door opened.

"Do you need anything? Luggage or...?"

She'd never met a man who could slam on the brakes so abruptly and show no signs of distress. His ability to hide any signs of arousal or discomfort left her off balance and unsure. "No, I should have everything I need. What time do we have to leave?"

"A car will be here at two-fifteen."

That was in a few hours. "Will you go to sleep?"

"For a little bit. I don't sleep well on planes. I try to get what I can while I'm home."

She nodded, figuring she'd likely wrap up packing around two-fourteen. "Well then, I guess I'll see you here in a few hours."

They took the stairs in silence. The entire journey she wordlessly begged for him to take her hand, but he kept his distance. When he stopped at his bedroom door a pinching ache formed in her chest. She deeply wished he'd kiss her one last time. But he didn't.

"Goodnight, Nadia."

She stuffed away her disappointment and tried to smile. "Thank you for dinner."

When she reached her room at the end of the hall, he was gone. This time he didn't watch her go and she didn't know what that meant. His restraint made her desire seem imbalanced. She shouldn't be so forward with him in the future.

She didn't want to be some wanton woman, too eager for a good man to appreciate, too easy for any man to turn down.

She wanted it to be real with him. Elliot definitely had control over their situation and she wasn't even sure he'd call it a "situation"—romantically speaking. To him, it could be a dilemma.

11

---

*"Once we accept our limits, **we go beyond them.**"*

~Albert Einstein

Elliot watched the belt at baggage claim go around, waiting for their luggage to appear while Nadia hung at his side, falling asleep on his shoulder. He'd never seen a woman sleep for practically twenty hours straight, but somehow she managed it, only waking up for a few minutes here and there during the flight. And she was still tired?

While she had slept on the plane, he learned as much as he possibly could about her language. Her grogginess kept her close to his side, however, so he wasn't complaining.

"There's my bag." She lifted her head and reached for her suitcase.

Watching the rubber curtain, he waited for his to appear. A new load came through and several people surged forward to claim their belongings, but he still didn't see his. The longer they waited the more his concern grew.

"Do you think we should file your name with baggage claim? They'll contact us when they find it."

"Let's just wait a little longer. Here come some more." His stomach knotted at the horrifying possibility he might have to make do without his things.

"None of these people were on our flight. I think our lot's done."

His jaw ticked as he tried not to lose his temper. He didn't want Nadia to see how much a little setback could rattle him, so he worked hard to keep it together. Of course, his bag was the only one missing on the entire flight. That was just his luck. Forcing out a deep breath, he grit his teeth. "Fine."

After filling out the superfluous forms and leaving Nadia's aunt's phone number, along with his cell, they found their way to the exit. It was just after six a.m. and the sun had yet to rise.

Loading their carry-on and her suitcase in the trunk of a cab, he focused on keeping his breathing even and held her door. Nadia gave the driver the address and they were on their way.

"It's so strange being back. Everything looks exactly the same, yet so different."

Budapest was lovely. The European architecture always impressed him, but Nadia didn't live directly in the city. Her family resided just outside the city limits in the town of Érd.

Congested streets gave way to thoroughfares in ill repair, so narrow at parts two cars wouldn't fit. Scrubby land left wide-open patches of earth, adjacent to terracotta-roofed homes packed tighter than sardines. It made his skin itch, seeing the two-hundred unit apartments and imagining close to eight hundred residents crammed into one building.

The number of older citizens out and about, on foot, had his brow lifting. Hungarians were not an idle people. It was clear the country was not at its economic best, but an evident work ethic was implied after only a brief glance.

Nadia sighed, stealing his attention from the road.

"Are you okay?"

"Yes." She smiled softly, her hands wringing in her lap. "Anxious."

He should do something to ease her tension. His mind shuffled through the traits of the men he admired, wondering what they might do in such a situation with a beautiful woman. He could say something clever to distract her or... Sliding his hand across the tattered cab seat, he slipped his fingers around hers and squeezed. Her eyes turned to him and there was a moment of sharp doubt in his chest that faded when he caught her smile. Her fidgeting stilled and he slowly pulled away his touch, satisfied that he'd helped her in some small way.

The cab slowed outside of a pale, stucco home and her fingers started fidgeting again. The lawn showed dry patches where the soil seemed made mostly of dust and two of three shrubs were dead, long without leaves and showing nothing but gnarled branches that looked dry enough to snap with his fingers.

Reaching into his pocket, he removed the money he'd transferred. "How much do I give him?" he asked Nadia in a low voice.

Nadia took the bills, sorted out a few and handed them to the driver. "*Köszönöm.*"

She appeared a bit shaky as they retrieved their belongings, pausing at the iron gate to draw in a steadying breath. "*Otthon,*" she whispered and he was pleased to identify the word. *Home.*

Before they reached the door it opened and he recognized her mother. Rapid Hungarian words flew between them, caught with smiles and tethered in welcoming hugs, yet Nadia still appeared tense.

Was he the only one picking up on her nerves? Her family should notice such things.

"*Mama, emlékszel Elliot,*" Nadia introduced, pulling him to her side.

"*Jó újra látni, Kisné Rozsa,*" he greeted with halting efficiency.

Both Nadia and her mother smiled, but then lost him as they rattled off words too fast for him to track.

They bustled inside and his nose took a moment to adjust to the unfamiliar fragrance. A bantam old woman with hair wrapped in a silk scarf crept into what appeared to be the parlor and clasped her work-weathered hands tight as she smiled.

"Nadia," the older woman spoke affectionately, tears shimmering in her eyes.

Nadia's face reflected equal affection. "*Nagymama.*"

The fondness the two shared was evident in their embrace. They whispered a few soft-spoken words and the woman touched Nadia's face with evident affection, her eyes again glazing with unshed tears.

Nadia held the woman's arm and walked her over to where he stood. "Elliot, this is my grandmother." She turned to the little woman. "*Nagymama, ez az én barátom Elliot.*"

He nodded and greeted. "*Örvendek.*"

The women chatted as he was shuffled into a small kitchen that smelled ... curious. He was handed a glass of water and shoved into a seat. The grandmother continued to ask him questions, but none of the words she used were in his vocabulary aside from a spare few.

Nadia was so animated, laughing and smiling. When her grandmother spoke, she listened, her brow tightening in concentration and her eyes illuminating. She burst into melodic laughter. He had never seen her so animated or unguarded. The sight of her evident happiness filled him with deep satisfaction and he was certain bringing her here had been the best thing he'd done in a long time.

The mood quieted as Mrs. Rosza, Nadia's mother, said the word *néni*—aunt. Nadia's chest rose as she took a deep breath and all humor vanished from her expression. "Elliot, will you come with me?"

He nodded and stood, surprised and flattered she'd look to him for support in such an emotional situation. Taking her hand, they left the kitchen and

Nadia led him through the house to a back room. The scent of illness was faint, but there.

He recalled that same scent from just before his father passed away. No matter how many times his mother washed the windows and polished the furniture, there was only so much one could hide when a person was reaching the end. His stomach tightened against the unwelcome return of sorrowful memories, reminding him just how hard it was to say goodbye to loved ones.

The door creaked as Nadia stepped into the room. A small woman rested on her back, hair thin enough to see her scalp, her face serene. Nadia's hand tightened in his and her faint sniffle met his ear. Instinctively, his hand rose to rest at the base of her spine, offering her his physical support as she moved into the room.

They approached the bed slowly so not to disturb the woman. Nadia's finger traced the frail bones of the woman's hands folded over her chest and the weary eyes gently opened. "Nadia?"

"Néni Mira," she responded, dropping to her knees and resting her brow at the woman's side.

The woman's frail hands brushed weakly at Nadia's dark hair. "I did not expect to see you again in this life."

Elliot stepped back, wanting to offer them privacy, but not wanting to abandon Nadia. The aunt's English took him by surprise, but he supposed it made sense, being that this woman had raised Nadia in America for most of her life.

"I'm sorry I couldn't come sooner," Nadia rasped, her fingers gently crawling over the quilt.

"You're here now, baby. No apologizing. *Ki ez az ember?*" *Who is this man?*

Nadia gave a throaty laugh and sat up, wiping her eyes. "This is Elliot. He helped me get here. Elliot, this is my Aunt Mira."

"*Jóképű,*" she said, openly appraising him. His neck heated as his mind recalled *jóképű* was the word for handsome.

Nadia took advantage of his limited linguistics as she spoke in fluent Hungarian. Her words threaded together like fine silk and he lost track. They gestured and laughed. It was clear they were talking about him.

"Elliot."

He turned as his name was called from the door. Nadia's grandmother held a bowl of bright pink liquid, looking like a cross between Pepto-Bismol and yogurt. She asked him a question, but, again, he was at a loss.

"She made soup for you," Nadia translated. "Fruit soup. Try some. It's delicious."

Delicious like chicken soup or delicious like the dreadful tea Nadia had fed him?

"Will you be all right?"

She nodded. "Yes. I'm going to visit with Mira for a bit. You go eat."

He followed the little old woman back to the kitchen and was again urged to sit. The bowl slid in front of him as she wrapped his fingers around a spoon. Giving him an expectant look, she said, *"Eszik." Eat.*

He slowly dipped his spoon into the pink broth. It was cold.

The grandmother smiled expectantly, nodding, as he brought it to his lips. He prayed this was going to be a Hungarian dish he liked. The unexpected blend of berries met his tongue and his taste buds danced.

Smiling with relief, he nodded appreciatively. "It's good."

The woman patted his shoulder and came back with a crock and ladle, filling the rest of his bowl. It was spectacular, a cross between rich spices and tart fruit. He hoped Nadia knew the recipe because this was definitely something he'd like to have again—of course, he could always get the recipe from her. There was no promise she'd ever prepare food for him again and it wasn't wise to entertain such hopes.

When he finished his second helping, he carried his bowl to the sink and the old woman swatted him away, directing him back to the chair. She placed a plate in front of him with links of meat and waved a hand for him to try.

He patted his belly. "Thank you, but I'm full."

She nudged the plate closer and smiled.

Giving in, he took a small slice of meat, popped it in his mouth, and paused. The salty morsel had a venison flavor, similar to sausage but lacking the give of pork. He held it in his mouth, not quite sure how to process it.

Nadia came into the kitchen, looked at him, the

plate, and then her grandmother. She said something in Hungarian and laughed. Turning back to him, she said, "Do you like that?"

Still not through the first bite he shrugged, not wanting to offend anyone.

"It's horse sausage," she said, passing him a napkin.

He took the napkin and turned, spitting it out before he gagged. Reaching for his water, he took a gulp and swished until the taste was gone.

Nadia giggled and whispered, "If she offers you *hurka* say no thank you." He didn't know what *hurka* was, but he trusted her judgment. No horse and no *hurka*.

The door opened and Nadia noticeably stiffened. A man, about Elliot's age with a rugged build, stepped inside and stilled the moment he spotted them. Was this another relative?

A slow grin exposed tobacco stained teeth as the man practically purred her name. "Nadia."

"Hello, Roland." Her welcome was as curt as his was lascivious.

The man—Roland—strode to her in two steps and took her into his arms. Elliot stiffened, his body going as taut as Nadia's appeared as the newcomer leaned in to *kiss* her. She arched away and Elliot stood, clearing his throat.

Roland turned as Nadia peeled herself out of his grip. His gaze scrutinized Elliot as if just noticing his presence. "Who is this?" he said, his Hungarian gruff and basic enough for Elliot to translate.

Nadia, not using her native tongue, stepped to Elliot's side. "This is Elliot. My boyfriend."

Elliot stilled at the label, his mind jetlagged and his thoughts racing to keep up with the cultural differences while making a decent first impression, but he was certain he'd have noticed if his greatest fantasy had come true and he and Nadia formed a relationship. There would be no missing that detail and she was clearly lying for reasons having to do with this man, whom Elliot disliked on principle. So he didn't object to the label. He also disliked seeing random men touch her.

Placing his arm around her shoulders, he met the man's assessing stare. His insides coiled as the larger man seemed to stare through him and see his deepest insecurities. Elliot envisioned Bruce Wayne's armor covering his skin, impenetrable and protecting him from that stare. It didn't protect him, but it made it easier to hide his timidity.

Nadia's body relaxed once she realized he'd play along. "Elliot, this is Roland, our neighbor."

The larger man folded his hands across his broad chest, drawing Elliot's attention to the extra pounds packed on his trunk, and openly sized him up.

"Boyfriend? For how much time?"

His English surprised Elliot, but Roland wasn't nearly as fluent as her aunt. His words were slow and clumsy, but he suspected he'd learned the language as a way to connect with Nadia—much like Elliot learning some Hungarian.

"We met over a year ago," Nadia informed, lacing her arm in his. "We live together."

She didn't necessarily lie. She was staying with him temporarily. They'd been kissing and had an official date last night. Did that mean she actually saw him as her boyfriend? Of course not. This was just a ploy to keep this Roland's hands off of her. He knew why she lied, but his chest swelled with satisfaction as part of him wanted to believe the lie.

The man grunted, his beady eyes narrowing on Elliot as his ruddy complexion darkened. "Nadia is my fiancée."

His inflated chest deflated as the man's statement punctured the fantasy. Elliot frowned and Nadia snapped in Hungarian, her words cutting through the air like the lash of a whip.

Fiancée? She was engaged? How true was their engagement? Nadia didn't seem to care for this man, and she'd never mentioned having a fiancée. Although, why would she mention that to him?

The man barked back, craning his neck and exploiting his strength. But she didn't cower, nor did she soften her tone. Her dark eyes flashed with sharp dislike as her words cut through the air, pointing accusingly at the man who claimed to be her fiancé.

Elliot didn't need a translator to understand the situation. Apparently, this Roland fellow missed the memo that the wedding was off. Elliot grinned as relief settled over him.

His eyes widened as the man crowded in, towering over her and growling some sort of demand while pointing at him. While she might not be intimidated by this brute, Elliot knew he was outmatched.

The man was an oak, his meaty fists the sort that could swiftly snuff out a life.

Elliot kept his voice level. "Nadia, maybe we should—"

The man's cold stare landed on him, threatening, and Nadia shoved his barrel chest, drawing his attention back to her. He grunted and let his stare wander down and up her body, before mumbling something that sounded like a promise.

Her eyes narrowed and her nostrils flared as she met his glare. "I hope when we return, you're gone," she growled at the man, pulling Elliot into the parlor.

"I'll be here, Nadia. You can't get rid of me."

She handed Elliot his carry-on. "I'll drive you to your hotel. My aunt's resting."

"I can take a cab if you'd like to stay." He didn't want her to stay. He wanted her as far away from that giant as possible, but she was here to visit with family.

She hesitated, glancing back to the kitchen where Roland watched her through narrowed eyes. "No. I think I'd like to go with you."

The car they borrowed was a dated, compact blue model, a cross between a sedan and a station wagon. Nadia managed the roads well but laughed when she forgot her way.

"It's been a while. Sorry. I swear I'll get you there."

He was hardly paying attention to the roads, his mind still trying to make sense of the man claiming to be her fiancé back at the house. "Why does that man think you're engaged to him?"

She huffed, her tapered fingers gripping the wheel. "Because he's a fool. My father wanted us to marry and told him so. I was only a girl then, but I knew I'd never marry him, whether my father gave him permission or not."

"Have you told him that?"

"Yes." Her lips pursed. "Roland has money and he helped my grandmother when the banks wouldn't. He thinks we're indebted to him."

"Has your grandmother paid him back?"

She scoffed. "No. She has no income. My aunts used to send her money, but those days are over. I send what I can. My mother will find work and help out, but, with Mira sick, it's a struggle. He always collects his debts one way or another though. I know they aren't being honest with me."

He shifted in his seat to face her. "What do you mean?"

"I think he's been giving them more money lately. I told them not to take anything from him." She shook her head, clearly annoyed with the situation. "My mother shouldn't have come to the States. She should have stayed here and kept an eye on things, but the money is better in America. She sent what she could, but who knows what happens here when we're not around."

"That man thinks you're going to marry him over a family debt?"

What year was this? He couldn't stop replaying

the entitled way he went at Nadia and how ... undisturbed her family appeared by his actions.

"I don't care what he thinks. My answer's been the same since I was thirteen. People cannot buy wives."

"How much money has he given your family?"

"I don't know. They don't tell me those things. They just tell me they need more and I send it."

"You send them money too?"

"Money, clothes, whatever I can, but I haven't been able to for some time. The yard looks like hell and my mother's worried, I can tell."

They entered the city limits and he let the topic rest. However, the closer they came to the metropolitan area, the more he worried about lodging so far away.

"Will this man be at the house a lot?"

"Probably. He's like a fly you can't get out the door, always touching shit and buzzing too close to your face."

"But you told him I was your boyfriend."

"Yes, sorry about that. I just wanted to make it clear he shouldn't touch me."

Disappointment nipped. He'd figured it was a ploy, but a small part of him wished her statement was genuine. Actually, he wondered why it wasn't.

He'd never entertain such an absurd idea, but he also never expected to be talking to Nadia like this. Not only were they speaking, they were living together, traveling to her family home, and... He laughed. It all seemed ludicrous.

"What's so funny?"

"This—our situation. I just never..." She wouldn't understand his perspective. "It's just unexpected."

Gripping the wheel, she glanced at him. "I'm very appreciative for your kindness, Elliot. I might not say it enough or clearly, but you bringing me here is the kindest thing anyone has ever done for me. You're a very special man. You're very special to me."

And then she went and said things like that. What was happening between them? How was this possible? Everything seemed to be moving in his favor and if things were as incredible as they seemed, he might as well go for broke.

"Maybe I *am* your boyfriend."

Her attention pulled from the road and she glanced at him then back at the oncoming traffic. "Is that what you want?"

"I don't know." *Yes, you do.* But he also didn't want to humiliate himself or put her in an awkward position. But dear Lord did he want her—so much it bordered on pain. "What do *you* want?"

She chuckled. "Well, to start, I want a boyfriend who knows what he wants."

His mind filled with juvenile words he couldn't outmaneuver. He tried to phrase his statement in a manly manner, but it was impossible. Even in the most direct manner, his query sounded infantile. But he had to ask, had to see if his luck had run out. "Will you be my girlfriend?"

She smiled, her cheeks flushing deep pink. "Yes. I think I will."

He stared as if this were all a dream. A warm, satisfying heat spread through his chest as he sat back and stared out the windshield. *Well, this is a first.*

It should have seemed more monumental, being that he'd never had a girlfriend, but it came so natural—easier than he expected. Holy shit. Nadia was his girlfriend. Maybe he was still processing.

Thinking of all the various relationships he'd watched over the years, he figured he should make a few things clear. "This means we're monogamous."

"What is that word?"

"No other men or women. Just us."

She nodded. "Yes. No one else."

She took this news without argument as if they were merely discussing the weather. Didn't she have concerns about dating a man like him? Why was this so simple? Something seemed off.

His body prickled and he stretched his limbs as much as the little car would allow. Beautiful women weren't interested in men like him. It wasn't a hunch. It was fact. So what the hell was going on?

Despite his misgivings, his ego swelled. He suddenly felt bigger and that was a dangerous assumption because he was still himself. Maybe he should test this new label.

Glancing to his side, he reached his hand to her knee and cupped her thigh. She smiled. Just smiled. She didn't slap his hand away or reach in her bag for pepper spray. Interesting. Now what?

His hand was on her thigh—Nadia's lush, warm thigh. Blood surged to his cock and he swallowed, throat tight. Jesus. He was dating Nadia.

12

———————————

"I CHOSE THIS LIFE. *I know what I'm doing. And on any given day, I could stop doing it. Today, however, isn't that day. And tomorrow won't be either."*

~**Batman**

"What do you mean it hasn't arrived?"

"Let me help, Elliot." Nadia placed a calming hand on his arm and spoke softly to the concierge in Hungarian.

Great. This was just great. He had five days here and no one had a fucking clue where his belongings were.

The airport told him they'd deliver everything once it was located. Other than the items in his carry-on and the clothes on his back that reeked of a day's worth of travel, he was screwed.

After speaking to the concierge she edged him away from the counter. "Elliot, there are shops. We can get you something to wear."

He wanted *his* clothes. "I know that, but this is ridiculous. Five hundred dollars' worth of luggage and God knows how much in clothing." He wasn't being cheap. It was the principle. "How do they just lose a person's personal belongings?"

"It happens. Come on. Let's put your carry-on in your room and we'll visit some stores."

He sighed, exhausted. It was still early, but he hadn't slept the entire flight. "I think I need to rest."

"Okay." She led him to the elevator. "I've never been in this hotel before. It's very luxurious."

He'd booked the Four Seasons, unsure how much time he'd be passing in the hotel while she visited with family. Now, limited by his lack of wardrobe, he was grateful for the amenities.

The elevator dropped them off on the top floor. The tower suite was at the end of the hall, the most private room they offered. As he slid his key into the door, they were greeted by the scent of freshly pressed linens and soap. Nadia gasped as he flipped on the light.

The large king bed was dressed in ivory and draped in gauzy fabric that hung romantically from the ceiling. Overstuffed club chairs and ottomans faced the foot of the bed. Cozied between the two chairs was a small accent table with a bottle of champagne on ice.

"This is magnificent," she said, awe coloring her expression.

She fell to the bed and the lush blankets rippled in her wake as she stretched and sighed. Shutting the double doors, he placed his lone bag on the chair and stared at her.

Catching him watching her, she smiled slowly. "You're staring again, mister."

He blinked but didn't look away. "I can't help it. You're beautiful."

Her eyes turned shy as her lashes fanned low. Rolling to her hip, she held out a hand. "Come here."

Everything inside of him wanted to rush to her while his muscles locked up and held him in place. With halting steps, he approached the bed and placed his hand in hers. She tugged and he sat on the edge of the mattress.

No matter how much he tried to appear relaxed around her, he wasn't. Crawling beside him, she crept to her knees and he drew in a breath as she slid her leg over his lap and straddled his thighs.

"Wh—what are you doing?"

"Are you always so tense?" Her warm breath fanned over his cheek and his body hardened. "Relax." Her body lowered and he grunted, mortification choking him. There was no way she'd miss his raging hard-on sitting like that.

His hands hovered at her hips a moment and then touched down, catching her weight. "You should get back—"

"Hush. We have plenty of time."

For what? Several seconds passed, rife with excruciating intimacy as she looked directly into his eyes. His heart hammered like a metal mallet in an empty room, echoing throughout his body.

"Nadia..."

"Elliot?"

"I don't know what your intentions are, but—"

"My intention is to help you relax."

She was doing the exact opposite.

Delicate fingers loosened his tie and she whispered, "This is a lot of hotel for one man. You might get lonely here all by yourself."

You can keep me company. Fuck, he was hard. Did she not realize the effect she had on him? "I'll manage."

His conscience seemed trapped in a polarized battle with his libido. Everything inside of him itched to toss her to the bed and climb on top of her, kiss her, touch her... But that was insane. His pulse seemed to move south, throbbing hard along the length of his dick. This was not good.

Her dark gaze held his as she slid his tie out from under his collar and tossed it onto the floor.

His throat went dry as he swallowed. "Careful with that. It's my only one."

"Oh, no." She pouted, mocking him. "What will you do without a pressed tie?"

His insides jerked, his defenses coming out of the lust induced coma and rising to like a shield. "You're making fun of me."

"Of course not." Her hips shifted, pressing into him as her fingers tunneled through his hair, destroying his part. She grinned and nuzzled her nose against his. "Did you know this is how Eskimos kiss?"

Conversing soothed the irritating panic building inside of him, but the more she touched him the more challenging it became to maintain an outward calm. His luggage had drifted to a secondhand thought, his sole focus now the beautiful woman on his lap. If he didn't focus on their dialogue he might do something too forward and she might never sit on him like this again. He wanted her to sit on him like this every day for the rest of his life.

"It's actually a greeting used by Inuit. Traditionally, it isn't nose to nose, but nose and lips to cheek or brow."

She cocked her head, her long hair tumbling down her arm. "Show me."

"How the Inuit kiss?"

She nodded, her expression blank and her full lips tempting. Even nuzzling her was dangerous. She was too beautiful, too perfect.

"Do you not want to kiss me, Elliot?"

He wanted to kiss her and so much more. Drawing in a breath, he slowly leaned forward, his eyes watching hers as he pressed his nose to her cheek, lightly teasing his lips along her soft skin and breathing her in.

"They breathe their loved ones in," he rasped, loving her intimate scent as he softly nuzzled her throat and shut his eyes.

She shifted her arms loosely around his neck, pressing her nose to his cheek and breathed deep. "I like the way you smell."

Her mouth dragged over his jaw where his beard had grown in and she licked him, humming as her tongue slowly, sensuously scraped over the stubble. His body hardened, encroaching on a point of pain, and his fingers tightened on her hips. The effort it took to hold his control was agony.

"This is how Americans kiss," she murmured, pressing her lush lips to his.

His eyes closed as his heart thundered, his jaw trembling as she gently teased his mouth.

"And this is how the French do it." Tipping her head, she slid her tongue between his lips.

Breathing deep, he tightened his grip as her fingers massaged their way back to his hair. Her body slowly rocked over his, awakening every part of him as she deepened the kiss. Pleasure turned to pain as his desire rapidly grew.

Pulling back, he drew in an unsteady breath.

She smiled nervously. "You always pull away from me. Why?"

His heart was racing, his body hot and hard. "It's too much. When I kiss you ... I feel like everything..." *Tightens. Throbs. Yearns. Hungers.* "It hurts, in a way I can't describe. I feel weak yet strong."

Her hands brushed over his shoulders and down his chest, toying with the line of buttons on his shirt. "It doesn't have to hurt, Elliot. It can feel very, very good."

He shivered under her touch, waiting for her to stop, at the same time praying she wouldn't. Swallowing tightly, his mind flashed with erotic images he'd seen in movies and on television, coming up short when he tried to picture himself doing some of those things to Nadia.

He wanted to. He just didn't know how. "I don't want to disappoint you."

"You won't."

He'd never ogled magazines plastered with air-brushed women or chanced his computer's safety by scoping out pornography on the Internet, but now he wished he had. He had absolutely no finesse with women beyond knowing point A connected with point B. His fascination with her breasts could occupy him for days, but what fascinated her? He couldn't screw this up.

His hand lifted, hovering between them then dropped to the bed. Damn, this was frustrating. Glancing away, he muttered, "Tell me what to do."

She eased back and studied him for a silent moment, pulling his attention back to her with a gentle touch to his jaw. "You want to do more?"

Nodding tightly, his finger teased under the hem of her shirt, barely touching the inside of the material. She said she liked a man who knew what he wanted. He definitely wanted her.

"Yes."

Her hand covered his, her hold light. Easing back, she lifted his palm and set it over the swell of her breast. "You can touch me here."

His heart beat erratically as he cupped her through the layers of clothing. His body swelled under her weight as blood pumped heavily through his veins. She was so warm.

She hummed softly as his thumb dragged slowly

over her curves and her nipple beaded beneath his gentle touch. Swallowing, he rasped, "Can I see you?"

She reached for the hem of her shirt and lifted, exposing her trim, tan belly where a tiny jade stone flashed. She tossed it toward the pillows.

He sucked in a breath as her bra—black lace—filled his view. She was the sexiest woman he'd ever seen, and she was here with him, sitting on top of him, as his girlfriend. A shiver of excitement snaked through him, triggering things inside of him, and he quickly looked away, blanking his mind and silently begging for self-control.

Please no...

"Elliot? Is everything all right?"

He swallowed as he tried to focus on her question as well as not coming in his pants. "You're very beautiful."

She turned his jaw, drawing his gaze back to hers. "Then why don't you look at me?"

It never hurt so much to look at anything. Breathing heavily, he blinked, mesmerized by the delicate swell of flesh and smooth expanse of olive skin. Reaching forward, he brushed the back of his fingers over the pebbled tip of her nipple. Her spine elongated as she moaned, and he paused. He glanced at her in question, wondering if this was what she intended or if he'd gone too far.

Her gaze turned heavy as her full lips curved into a smile. "You can do what you like, Elliot."

Finding nothing but trust in her stare, he returned his attention to her breasts. There was a small clasp in the center of her bra. Carefully, he pressed the catch together, plumping her breasts, and then drew the material apart. The lace gathered and dragged over her flesh, exposing heaven. His hands shook as he stared in awe.

Full, lush, and mouthwatering, her dark nipples tightened before his eyes. Keeping his touch tentative and gentle, he feathered his fingertips over her areola and it puckered tighter. Her breathing rasped as he trailed his touch to her other nipple and tiny goosebumps rose on her shoulders.

Her chest lifted with each breath as she watched him. She was a work of art, every single inch of her a flawless masterpiece. She was exquisite feminine perfection, each little mark, freckle, and blemish proving she was real.

"You're ... gorgeous," he whispered in a hoarse voice.

Nudging his head lower, she threaded her fingers through his hair and brought his face to her chest. "Taste."

Glancing over the frames of his glasses, he studied the way her eyes had dilated and her cheeks flushed. She was aroused—aroused by *him*. He nuzzled his nose to the side of her breast, pressing his lips to the soft flesh as he breathed her in— nuzzling.

She giggled. "You're quite good at Eskimo kisses."

His body was rigidly hard, his arousal insurmountably constricting in too many ways. Feeling with his lips, he glided his mouth over every slope and contour, until they finally brushed the firm tip of her nipple. He placed a kiss on the side of her areola and slowly licked over the delicate crest.

Her breathy sigh met his ears as her fingers threaded through his hair and her thighs tightened over his hips. She lifted, dragging the tip of her nipple over his parted lips and he kissed her flesh with slow, succulent pulls, drawing her deeper.

She keened and took up a gradual rhythm, canting against his hips with each soft pull of his mouth. He drew back, fascinated by the damp skin, now darker from the flow of blood beneath the surface. Turning his attention to her other breast, he did the same, pulling, sucking, tasting her. A thousand volts of electricity seemed to dance up his spine as his need expanded and greed unraveled inside of him. His hands coasted down her back, holding her to him as he took his time pleasuring her.

Her moans, breathless and needy, came closer together the harder he pulled. Her hands tugged at his hair, his clothing, and her hips contracted over his, rolling and creating a delicious friction between them. If it felt this incredible to have her rubbing against him, he couldn't imagine how mind-blowing it would feel to actually be inside of her.

Her hand drifted down his chest. The weight of her fingers brushed the bulge of his erection. He jerked back and gasped as her palm closed around his solid length and stroked through his pants. Her finger traced the buckle of his belt, almost question-ingly, as she lifted her lashes and looked into his eyes.

Was this how it happened? Shouldn't it be more orchestrated? Romantic? Formal?

Physical need overruled romantic ideals and he pressed his hand over hers, holding her to him. The weight of her touch satisfied something dark inside and he shivered, almost coming then and there.

Sliding off his lap, she dropped to her knees, fitting perfectly between his thighs. He held his breath. He didn't want it to end, but if she actually touched him, flesh to flesh, it would be over in a matter of seconds.

"Nadia..."

"Shh. I want to."

Her dainty fingers unlatched his belt and unclasped the top button of his pants. He sucked in a breath as she gazed up at him and slowly dragged the zipper down, parting the constricting material.

His heartbeat resounded in his ears and his breathing grew unusually loud. He lifted his hips as she nudged his pants lower on his legs. She reached into his briefs and his eyes rolled shut.

He beat back his nerves, distracted by the worry he might disappoint her in some way. Her fingers brushed the flesh of his cock and he hissed in a breath. Nothing had ever felt so exquisite, so carnal, so agonizingly right. Licking his lips, he peeked through his lashes and watched as she withdrew him.

Struggling to calm his breathing, he focused on her fingers folding around his throbbing flesh and let out a jagged exhalation. "Christ."

"Has a woman ever done this for you before?" she asked, her hold tightening as she stroked slowly.

Unable to form words, he shook his head. It felt *nothing* like when he touched himself. Her hold was so warm and firm, but delicate.

"I'm glad I'm the first. I get jealous, too." She smirked.

As she tipped her head, her hair stole his view. Every muscle in his body locked as wet heat closed over him. Bowing against the bed, he hissed as she lowered her mouth, sucking him to the back of her throat even as she stroked him.

"Fuck. Fuck. Fuck," he cursed, unable to rein in his control.

Wanting to see what she was doing, he gathered the wild mass of onyx waves and pulled her hair away from her face. His toes curled as pleasure knifed through him, more potent now that he could see her mouth gliding over him. Her cheeks hollowed with every pull. Her lashes threw tiny shadows on her tantalizing skin.

Frantic not to come, he tried to catch his breath. She literally stole his breath, stole it right from his soul.

His head tipped back reflexively. His eyes rolled in delirious pleasure, and he let out an agonizing moan as his control spun away. An explosion of fantasies fabricated into reality, and his mind shattered. This was actually happening and it was a million times better than his darkest dreams. There was no drawing back his orgasm now.

As his release tunneled through him, his body

quaked under her erotic touch. Her moans sent little vibrations through his cock. The pleasure was too intense.

Waves of ecstasy ripped through him as a guttural moan ripped from his chest. He fisted the blankets and gritted his teeth. "Nadia. Nadia, I'm ..."

Her tight mouth released him and she smiled, her hand still stroking, dragging his urgent release through his veins too fast for him to stop it from happening. He cupped his hand over his cock.

Didn't she know what she was doing to him? "I'm going to..."

She brushed his hand away and stroked harder. "On me."

He grunted as the first spurt shot across her breast. *Jesus Christ.* He couldn't hold back. Gasping, he shut his eyes and let go. Relief morphed into utter mortification as he lost control in those finishing seconds and came across her breasts.

He shivered and flinched, her lingering touch too much to tolerate. He fell back on the bed, panting.

When he finally opened his eyes, he was painfully aware of how exposed he was. His cock had softened but still throbbed, remaining thicker than usual. He covered himself with his hand and sat up, stilling when he saw her.

Her breasts were slick with his come. Her hair was as wild as her eyes. Lips parted, she smiled and gazed up at him.

Unsure what to do, he tucked himself away and stood, taking her hand. As she rose from the carpet, he gave her a moment to find her bearings—and a moment for him to find his fucking brain. He wasn't sure he'd ever be the same again.

It was too quiet. Unsure how to proceed, he led her to the bathroom and lifted her onto the vanity. Turning the faucet to warm, he grabbed a fresh washcloth from the rack. Once the cloth was warm and wet, he carefully washed away the evidence.

She watched him carefully but didn't say a word. When he had her cleaned up and dry, he met her gaze, his full of mortification and apology.

It was only then they truly looked each other directly in the eye, fully aware that this changed everything. Something inside of him shifted, internally growling as he stared at her and smiled. Territorial pride washed through him, wiping away any traces of regret as she seemed happy about what just happened.

She wasn't angry with him or shocked by his behavior. Relief swept through him as his mortification flipped to pride. She was pleased and he could sense her pleasure, see it in the way her eyes sparkled and her mouth smirked. An unfamiliar voice in his head growled, catching him off guard, but his body seemed to rattle with the inward claim.

Mine. He would never willingly give her up.

Leaning forward, he brushed his lips against hers and kissed her deeply. Once again shocked that she let him.

Her gaze turned shy, as they broke apart. "Should we cuddle now?"

His chest warmed at the thought of holding her in his arms. Nodding, he led her to the bed and drew back the covers. She slid under the sheets and smiled up at him, but he hesitated.

Part of him feared if he shut his eyes he'd wake up and she'd be gone. "I feel like I'm in a dream. Promise you won't disappear."

Her throaty laugh broke the silence. "You're a strange man, Elliot. Come hold me. I'm cold."

His fingers unbuttoned his shirt and he hung it carefully over the back of the chair, then awkwardly slid under the covers. She snuggled close to his side and he kept his eyes open as long as possible, but eventually, exhaustion defeated his strength of will.

Sometime later he awoke to a soft chirp of the door and opened his eyes, squinting at the unfamiliar surroundings. Budapest. Disoriented and unsure of the time, he blinked and searched for a clock.

"Where did you go?" He must have slept soundly. He hadn't felt or heard her leave the bed.

"Did you sleep?"

"Like the dead." He stretched under the covers, taking her in with his eyes, and scooted over, inviting her to sit. "Where were you?"

"I went shopping and stopped home to pick up some things." Placing the last of the bags she carried on the chair, she came to the bed and sat beside him. She wore a skirt, which was quite different from her usual dance attire.

"You look nice."

She grinned. "I found some of my old clothes. I haven't worn this dress in years."

"Any word on my luggage?"

"No. Sorry."

He sighed.

"I bought you some things. I hope you don't mind."

He frowned. "You didn't have to buy me anything."

"I wanted to surprise you."

She shouldn't be wasting her money on him. "I can pay you back—"

"Consider it my gift to you for being so kind and bringing me here. You were so upset about your luggage. I wanted to do something nice for you after all the nice things you've done for me."

"You went clothes shopping for me?" Embarrassed she'd seen the side of him that could so easily get bent out of shape over lost luggage, he tried not to focus on his earlier behavior.

"Yes. I might have gone a little overboard, but I think I did well. I think Bruce Wayne would approve."

He laughed, touched she would take time away from visiting family to do something so thoughtful. "Thank you." He'd figure out a way to repay her for the money she spent, but the gesture... It was so incredibly thoughtful. His attention drifted to the drawn curtains. "What time is it?"

"Almost midnight. You slept most of the day."

The time change disoriented him. "How's your aunt?"

Her smile turned sad. "Not well. She doesn't have much strength left."

"I'm so sorry, Nadia." He took her hand in his and

squeezed. She shifted, filling the space at his side as she lay down on the bed, facing him.

Her fingers pulled at the sheet, lowering it to his ribs and his nipples tightened. Her fingers teased his chest, her breath feathering over his skin. "It's good I'm here. It makes her happy. The house seems so sad I can only bear it a little at a time. I like being able to come back to you for an escape."

"Then I'm glad I came with you."

Her fingers explored, treading softly from his chest to his jaw. "I'm not used to seeing you with facial hair."

"I need to shave. I should shower and see about finding food."

"My *nagymama* sent something for you."

He grimaced. "Not more horse, I hope."

She laughed. "No. A sandwich. She makes the bread herself. You'll like it."

"I like that you know what I like." For the most part.

"I'm learning." She settled and sighed, appearing tired.

He, of course, was wide-awake. "We seem to be on opposite sleep schedules."

"Mmm," she answered, and he tipped his chin, seeing her eyes had closed as her cheek rested on his chest.

He lightly touched her hair and rolled onto his back to stare at the ceiling. He could probably sleep some more if he had something to eat. "Where did you say the sandwich was?"

She didn't respond.

Sliding out from under the blankets, he replaced his chest with a pillow. She didn't flinch. The woman could sleep.

Eyeing the bags, he didn't see anything that looked like food. He'd find it later. Right now he needed something quick.

After using the bathroom he dialed room service and ordered a plate of what he hoped was eggs. While he waited, he shot his mother an email.

She worried whenever he traveled and emailed him twice already, asking if everything was okay. Email was the most dependable form of communication when overseas and typically he'd have checked in when he landed, but he usually traveled alone. Nadia had distracted him. He apologized for the delay but avoided any mention of his travel companion—certain more talk of Nadia would only get his mother's hopes up.

He'd begun to explain his frustration with the airlines and the hassle of losing luggage, but then deleted his comments, no longer as irritated by the situation. Despite the absolute inconvenience of it, he was surprisingly ... over it.

He paused from writing his email and blinked. His mind worked to fathom this unfamiliar, inner calm he felt. His gaze drifted to Nadia. Was she responsible for this strange sense of tranquility? Usually, he was wound tighter than a top, but at the moment his body was relaxed, at total ease regardless of the unexpected hiccups of the trip. How strange.

He concluded his email with a peculiar *every-*

thing's going great. It wasn't his typical tone, as he often complained to his mother—the one person who never seemed to tire of him. But today, he had no complaints. With a strange grin, he closed his laptop.

He showered but decided to shave in the morning. Room service delivered two eggs, one hardboiled, the other poached. There was also toast, beans, and several slices of questionable meat.

He picked at the toast then went searching for the sandwich again. She was right. He liked it. The bread was fresh and the meat was mild. There was some sort of sauce he suspected was made from avocados, but all in all, it was filling and delicious.

Nadia slept soundly. He'd removed her sandals and covered her with the blanket, supposing she'd stay there the night. It was too late for her to drive back alone.

Passing time, he checked the rest of his email and stocks and then caught up on some of the shows he'd missed that week. By three o'clock he was dozing off, so he placed his iPad on the nightstand, folding his hands over his chest as he stared into the darkness.

Nadia sighed and nestled deeper into his body. Her natural affection showed a softer side he adored. She never hesitated to touch him or kiss him. So why was he restraining himself?

He studied her under the shadows for several minutes. Lifting his arm he carefully draped it over her narrow shoulder. She sighed and her slight weight nestled closer. This was not at all what he expected a week after running into her, but his expectations were shifting, his standards climbing. He was considering things he was afraid to even admit, even to himself, fearful those expectations would somehow turn to disappointments and this would somehow blow up in his face.

His hand tightened on her shoulder as he leaned down and kissed her temple, breathing her in. His mind drifted to images of her family ... her ... fiancé. The man didn't pose much consequence, being that he was here and they were leaving in a few days, but Elliot didn't like the way he groped Nadia. Hopefully, now that his position had been clarified, there would be no more issues there.

It was one thing to pretend to be her boyfriend, but now that he actually was... There would be no other men touching her—especially not a Hungarian beast twice his size.

13

"YOUR BODY IS NOT *who you are. The mind and spirit transcend the body.*"

~Christopher Reeve

"This shirt is plaid."

Nadia peeked out from the bathroom, a towel twisted on top of her head like a turban. Her body an absolute distraction. "Yes."

"I don't own plaid."

"Now, you do."

He frowned and rummaged through the bags. "Why are all these pants so narrow?"

"That's the style in Europe."

"Wonderful," he mumbled. "Did you get any ties?"

"I bought you some *sálak*—scarves."

"Scarves?" While James Bond could pull off an ascot, he could not.

Pulling out one of the many scarves, he frowned. There were a lot of patterns happening here. "How am I supposed to know what goes with what?" Everything clashed.

She stepped out of the bathroom, ripping his attention from the clothes in his hands to the damp towel swathed tightly around her body. "You are being fussy, Elliot. It will not kill you to try something new. Here."

She took the plaid shirt out of his hand and bent to dig in the bag of pants. Her tapered thighs peeked out beneath the terrycloth as she rummaged and he swallowed.

Rising, she turned and held out a handful of denim "Wear these."

"Jeans?"

"Yes. Jeans."

His nose crinkled at the sight of all that denim. "I'll look like a cowboy."

She snorted. "Trust me, you won't. Get dressed. I promised my *nagymama* I'd be home for lunch." She returned to the bathroom and he sighed.

I should sue the airport for losing my luggage.

Sliding into the stiff pants that left little breathing room, he grimaced. The shirt didn't help matters and the pattern made him dizzy. "I look like a reject from a Gap commercial."

Nadia tsked and approached. She'd dressed and he considered how unfair it was that she would look good in anything. "You are supposed to cuff the sleeves. Stop frowning. This is very in style right now."

She fussed with his clothing and then ran her fingers through his hair, sifted the strands out of order and destroying his part.

"I just combed—"

Her lips pressed to his, silencing him. His lashes lowered and he caught her waist, his body responding instantly to her nearness. She slowly pulled away.

"You were saying?"

What had he been saying? "I forget."

"You look very handsome, mister. Let's go."

When they returned to Érd the house was full of unexpected guests. Apparently, in Nadia's culture when a person was on their deathbed, the family hosts a sort of living wake before the relative passed. Food was spread out on every open surface and numerous people mingled around the small home.

His ears had adjusted to the sound of Hungarian, but his brain was still frustratingly slow at picking up the language. Though he could decipher short sentences, whenever anyone spoke more than a few words at a time he was lost. So many strange names and unfamiliar faces, he found it best to sit in the parlor and simply watch.

Nadia stayed by her aunt's bedside, only coming out to refill the pitcher of water or check on him. He'd assure her he was fine and she'd smile, the other guests learning to ignore the strange American in the corner.

As he observed, he noted many qualities of Hungarian people. They were, overall, a serene bunch, relaxed and laid back. One woman even tried to help him with some common phrases, which he appreciated. He could see where much of Nadia's generosity stemmed from and thought it a shame that so many years had passed between now and her last visit.

As the sun set, the crowd thinned. He'd lost track of what day it was, realizing he'd probably recover from feeling jetlagged just in time to get home and back on American time. But it was worth it.

Thinking the last of the visitors had left, he gathered some dishes from the parlor and carried them to the kitchen where Nadia's grandmother and mother tidied up.

"Elliot, akkor nem kell tisztítani," her grandmother said, taking the dishes out of his hand and tsking. He sensed he was being yelled at so he went to find Nadia.

She wasn't in her aunt's room or any of the other rooms he passed. Returning to the kitchen, he asked, *"Hol van Nadia?"*

"Garázs," her mother said, pointing out the window to the shed in the back. That was where they kept the spare freezer and much of the folding tables he'd helped bring inside that morning.

Traveling through the house, he let himself out the front door and followed the broken path to the backyard. His nose twitched at the familiar and irritating scent of aftershave. Frowning, he stepped softly onto the crabgrass and stilled at Roland's deep voice.

The man spoke quickly, his tone level, but not

necessarily kind. When Nadia spoke, her voice sounded harried and almost waspish, causing Elliot to take a quick pace forward.

She stacked folding chairs against the wall. Elliot scowled at the way Roland towered over her, not offering a single hand to help her move the items. Roland's face was set in disapproval as he rattled off too many Hungarian words for Elliot to decipher.

He grit his teeth, recognizing a phrase about America and definitely something about family and marriage. This guy needed to back off.

Nadia turned, not noticing his presence at the door. Her glare hardened on the other man and her shoulders stiffened. "*Elég*! When will you get it? This is not my home and I am not yours."

The man scoffed. "Because of your American boyfriend? You come here, with your fancy English. I speak English, too. I hear him asking you all his silly questions. The man does not have a clue about our culture." He crept closer. "You need a real man, Nadia."

As his hand closed around her upper arm, an indignant rage took hold of Elliot and he growled, "Don't touch her."

The moment the words left his mouth, bearing more threat than he could uphold, he regretted speaking. Fear snaked through him, snapping with knee jerk regret and worry for his safety. It was a response he hadn't suffered since high school, but so ingrained in him, so familiar and beaten into his memory that his insides recoiled and he had to swallow back the bile rising in his throat.

He tried to soften his tone without sounding like a total pussy. "She..." His words withered and Nadia yanked her arm out of the other man's grip.

Roland glared at him. "You're not invited here."

Certain this man could knock him out with one flick of his fat fingers, Elliot panicked but didn't back down. Gritting his teeth, he stepped into the shed. "I... Nadia asked me to be here." If his heart beat any faster he'd pass out.

Roland laughed. "This is not America, little man. You are in my home."

Nadia scoffed and slammed a metal chair against the others. "This isn't *your* home."

Roland squinted at the ceiling, his gaze traveling through the shed door as he craned his neck. "It is if I pay for it."

Elliot didn't know the extent to which this man helped her family and didn't want to damage any agreement that benefited them, but he would not stand by and let him harass his girlfriend. He knew a bully when he saw one.

Elliot held a hand out to Nadia and she took it. Pulling her out of the shed and a safe distance from Roland, he met the man's stare and swallowed back his fear. "Touch her again and you and I are going to have a problem."

Roland's harsh laugh mocked him. "I'd like to see you try to give me a problem."

Burying his anxiety, he edged her toward the yard. "Come on, Nadia. We can deal with this later."

Without sparing the man a second glance, they returned to the house and he fought the urge to puke. Once they were inside, he turned to her. "I'll be right back."

"Are you okay? I'm sorry you had to see that."

"I'm fine," he lied. "Excuse me."

By the time he made it to the hall, he was trembling with adrenaline. Locking himself in the bathroom, he turned on the faucet and gripped the lip of the narrow sink, catching his breath. His pulse was wild and his neck was sweating. Glancing over the frames of his glasses, he looked at his reflection. He was white as a sheet.

"Fuck," he breathed, shutting his eyes, trying to steady his breathing.

Dragging a hand down his face, he pulled off his glasses and collected himself. He wouldn't survive another run-in with a man like that. He could be many things, but he was not a fighter. Bullies terrified him for good reason.

Closing his eyes he suffered through countless recollections of run-ins with people similar to Roland. He could smell a bully's stink from a hundred miles away. And though the bruises always healed, the scars under the surface never seemed to fade.

"You're safe," he whispered, the words hardly carrying a sound as he forced out a breath. "You're a grown man. You're successful. You're in charge of your life." His heart rate gradually slowed.

Shutting off the faucet, he dried his hands, took a galvanizing breath, and opened the door, taken aback by the sight of Nadia waiting for him in the hall.

Her brow pinched as her eyes showed regret. "Are you okay?"

His gaze darted away from hers. "I'm fine."

"You don't have to involve yourself with him. I can handle Roland."

Was she insinuating he couldn't handle the asshole? She was right, but he didn't want her making such assumptions. "He shouldn't put his hands on you."

The other man's entitlement made him livid, but aside from empty threats, there was little he could do to stop him.

"He means nothing, Elliot. I just ignore him." Despite her blasé attitude, he could tell the other man had upset her.

"He shouldn't bother you anymore," he offered lamely, almost laughing at himself for sounding so arrogant and equally ignorant. They both knew Elliot's threat hadn't intimidated Roland one bit, but he wanted to pretend it had. God, he was such a pussy.

Her head tipped as she studied him for a moment, a peculiar curve to her lips. "Do you want to get out of here for a while?"

Yes, he wanted to get as far away from there as possible. "Sure."

After saying goodnight to her relatives, she met him at the car and stashed a little bag in the back. His mind immediately made assumptions about what was inside said bag, but he didn't ask.

They returned to Budapest and stopped at a small café. All he'd done was eat all day, but Nadia was hungry, so he had coffee while she devoured a baklava strudel.

"I miss this food," she said as she pleasantly hummed over the last bite. "I make it at home, but it's never as good."

He knew of a small Hungarian restaurant in the city and made a mental note to take her there. He liked watching her eat—which might be a strange thing for a boyfriend to enjoy, but he didn't care. "Do you eat horse?"

She laughed. "I've tried it, but I don't like it. Horses are too pretty to eat."

"You don't think cows and pigs are pretty?"

"I do, but I like meat too much to give them up. What is the word for that? *Húsevő.*"

He chuckled. "Hypocrite."

She lightly smacked his arm. "No. I'm trying to say meat eater."

He arched a brow. "Carnivore?"

She smiled. "Yes, I am a big carnivore hypocrite."

They walked the streets until dark and he enjoyed having such a well-informed tour guide. When they stood outside of the Four Seasons, she hesitated.

"I should probably get back."

He thought about her bag in the car. Thought about how they'd slept in each other's arms last night and how much he wanted to have her in his arms again. "Or you could stay."

Her gaze searched his, the energy between them tightening. "Is that what you want?"

God, yes. "Only if you want to."

She looked down, her eyes appearing troubled. "Promise me something, Elliot."

"What?"

As she lifted her face, a deep V formed between her brows. "If I stay with you, will you still look at me the same in the morning?"

His chest tightened, the slight ache indefinable. Why would she think he would look at her any differently? "Nadia, there's nothing you could do to make me look at you differently."

"Promise me."

Stepping closer, he whispered, "I promise. But we don't have to do anything. You could just stay."

The worry lines surrounding her eyes remained. "I like you, Elliot. So much it scares me. I don't want to go too fast and spoil what we have."

His breath caught as his own fears of inadequacy battled with excitement. As much as he wanted to see what it was like, he was terrified he'd ruin it as well. "We'll take it slow. Let's not decide until we get there."

Appearing slightly relieved, she nodded. "I brought a bag."

As she pulled her luggage out of the back, he took it from her and carried it into the hotel. Awareness settled over him, tense and prickly. Adrenaline heated his blood and his stomach swooped with every step closer to the room.

The waiting became agonizing as they took the elevator to the top floor. He needed more time to collect himself. He wasn't sure what to expect once they were on the other side of the door.

"I think I need a shower," he announced, figuring that would buy him ten minutes.

"Okay," Her voice was just below a whisper. Maybe she was nervous, too.

Sliding his card through the key slot, he held the door for her. She stepped in and walked right to the window, giving him her back.

"I'll be out in a few minutes," he said, emptying his pockets on the dresser. She nodded, so he left her to her thoughts.

Although it seemed like he was taking an almost rude amount of time to shower, he felt unprepared to return to the room. Cursing under his breath, he stood in only a towel in the steamy bathroom, realizing the rest of his clothes were still on the chair.

His heart wouldn't settle and his head seemed to be pulsing. Drips fell from the faucet every few seconds, a ticking clock waiting for him to make a damn move.

Taking an unsteady breath, he turned the knob and stepped onto the carpet. On the ottoman was a pile of neatly folded clothes and he recognized Nadia's skirt—the one she'd been wearing.

Slowly rounding the corner, his steps staggered as she turned, wearing the hotel robe. His gaze drifted to the nightstand where she'd placed something and he swallowed thickly. That was definitely a condom.

He hesitated, unsure if he should make the first move or let her come to him. "Sorry I took so long."

"Do you know what I like about you, Elliot?"

He hadn't a clue. "No."

"You're genuine. You don't say much and I know you are always thinking, but when you look at me I find you trying to see beneath the surface." Something sad flashed in her eyes and in that moment she was so strikingly stunning he could have fallen to his knees. "Most men only care about the surface. Very few think I have depth."

He swallowed. Of course, she had depth. He wanted to know everything about her. "I like getting to know you." He looked down then returned his gaze to hers. "But I also think you're the most beautiful woman in the entire world."

Her mouth curved into a smile as a pink tinge crested her cheeks. Her hands went to the belt of the robe as her fingers untethered the fabric. His eyes widened as she parted the material, unveiling a smooth expanse of skin. The flash of her bellybutton ring registered just before the material fell to the ground.

Dear God, she was totally naked. His mind blanked, as she stood before him utterly bare. Blinking, catching his breath, his gaze wandered down her smooth belly landing on the V of her sex. A chill swept over his shoulders as his body hardened. His towel wasn't much of a disguise for the response she caused in him.

Lifting his gaze to her face, he searched her eyes. There were no signs of laughter or teasing in her gaze. This was real. This woman—Nadia—was offering herself to him. Dear God, he was going to have a heart attack. Without thinking, his weight dropped to the ottoman and he sat.

"Elliot?"

"I just … need a minute."

Silence. "Do you want me to leave?"

He shook his head. No, he wanted her to stay. He wanted to touch her and pleasure her better than any man ever had, but he didn't have the first fucking clue how to do that.

Stupid! He'd been reading Hungarian on the plane when he should have been studying other topics. But the possibility of actually sleeping with her never crossed his mind. This moment was so far from the realm of realistic possibilities he could barely process it. And now she was right in front of him—naked.

She shifted, hiding her sex with a turn of her lithe body as her hip jutted forward and her arms closed over her chest. "I'm sorry. I'll—"

"Wait."

She blinked at him, midway to picking up her robe.

Forcing himself to his feet, he pressed his lips tight. He couldn't let her think she'd done anything wrong. This was *his* problem. And it was hardly a problem. Having the woman of his dreams naked in his hotel room was a complaint no man ever made.

Drawing in a steadying breath, he confessed, "I want to do this right, Nadia, but I don't know how."

Her relief was palpable as her posture eased and she exhaled. "Let it come to you. Natural." Her feet whispered over the carpet as she approached slowly. Her fingers laced with his. "You do what feels right."

Nothing had ever come to him without immense

focus and well-calculated determination. "Tell me what to do. I want to know what you like."

She held his hand and stepped closer to the bed. "I like when you touch me."

His other hand lifted, first cupping her hip, and then gliding slowly to her breast. Her skin was like silk, her fragility never more clear than in that moment of matched vulnerability when he heard her breath catch. He drew in a sharp breath as her nipples pebbled under the faintest caress.

Directing his other arm, she placed his fingers over the soft patch of hair at her apex. "And here."

His blood thickened. She was so warm, so delicate, slightly wet. His fingers slid lower as dewy heat greeted. She was soft, like a flower, and he feared bruising her.

Turning his palm, he gently cupped her breast as his thumb treaded lightly over her nipple. Sliding the finger of his other hand forward, her folds parted before his touch and she drew in a long breath.

He stilled, measuring her expression. "Is this okay?"

"Inside," she whispered.

His brow tensed as he curved his finger, tucking it into her tight, hot slit and she moaned, catching her hands on his shoulders. With very careful movements, he fed the finger deeper. Heat engulfed his knuckle as her body tightened on his digit. The deeper he moved his touch inside of her, the more her slick heat gripped him.

Her scent intensified, and his body reacted, tightening with dark yearning.

Lowering herself to the bed, she pulled him closer. "Don't stop."

Everything inside of him wanted to ... ravage her, but he feared if he let his instincts take the lead he'd screw everything up and terrify her, never getting a moment like this back again.

Her fingers cupped his jaw, turning his face to her as she pressed her mouth to his. "It's okay, Elliot. I like your fingers inside of me." Her hand traced over his. "Deeper."

His cock throbbed with desire. Breathing her in, his gaze caressed her breasts. He nudged his touch deeper and a soft gasp caught between them.

Her knees fell open as he traced her folds, sliding his finger back and inside again. "Kiss me," she whispered.

His mouth closed over hers, greedy and savoring every taste of her. His fingers continued to slip through her arousal, fondling her delicate folds and getting lost in her heat. She moaned into his mouth, her hands tightening on his shoulders.

"More," she pleaded.

He kissed a trail down her neck, not stopping until he reached her breasts. Her body writhed and arched beneath him as her hand tightened over the one between her legs, directing his touch deeper.

Her fingers tunneled through his hair while her other hand guided his. His lips closed over her nipple, pulling and sucking. Cool air teased his back as the towel snagged on the covers and fell away. She directed his wet fingers, sliding them over the tiny nub at the top of her sex. Following her lead, he rubbed in gentle circles and her breath caught, little sighs sewn together in a symphony of need.

His mouth continued to suckle her breasts as he swapped his fingers for his thumb, rubbing as well as penetrating. Tiny hiccups met his ears as her body trembled and tightened.

"Igen, igen, igen..." she cried, and her channel tightened around his intruding fingers as her body tensed, quaking with feminine shivers.

Her hands slackened and fell to the bedding. He glanced between their bodies in awe as her belly rose with each quick breath. His fingers glistened. He studied her face, noting the gentle way her smile curved and her half-lidded eyes watched him.

Should he let her rest? "Are you finished?"

She laughed, her head lolling to the side in charming invitation. "I hope not. Women don't need time, like men."

"Should I keep going?"

She shifted her arms over her head, stretching out beneath him. "Please."

He could do more. Sliding his fingers between her legs, she gasped and sighed, opening her thighs wider. He pressed deep, slowly pumping in and out. This time she got there faster. Her body arched, rocking into his touch as she moaned his name, which drove his desire to a point of no return.

Her feet burrowed into the mattress as she rocked her hips, urging him to penetrate faster. *"Istenem,"* she cried, her entire being trembling as a rush of heat met his hand.

Mesmerized that he could do that to her—*twice*

—he scooted lower. Her folds were glossy, darker than her skin elsewhere, and that little bud seemed to swell and throb. Keeping his touch light, he teased and she sucked in a breath, her knees falling open.

His eyes widened as he saw the deep pink of her inner channel. His cock twitched, unbearably hard. Leaning forward, he placed a kiss on the little bud and she moaned, her legs curling around his shoulders and pulling him closer.

"Please. Don't tease me, Elliot."

He hadn't realized he was teasing, so he licked and she let out a litany of Hungarian words. Sliding a finger inside of her, he closed his lips over what seemed the central source of her pleasure and sucked. She arched, her fingers fisting his hair, holding him to her as he pulled and pumped his wrist.

"Igen! Harder..."

He thrust another digit inside of her, pumping quickly as he pleasured her with his mouth. She was wild, writhing, and greedier than he'd ever imagined.

Her cries doubled as her sex contracted, squeezing his fingers. A guttural moan left her lips, sounding like his name, garbled with other syllables as she peaked and found her third release, this one the most dramatic of them all as every drop of her ecstasy seemed to flavor his tongue and her body arched beautifully off the bed.

In awe, he stared at her trembling muscles, skin glistening with a sheen of perspiration. He'd never been so aroused in his entire life.

His gaze darted to the nightstand. Condom.

Catching his breath, he swallowed and searched her face. Her eyes were closed as sharp breaths passed her parted lips. Should he ask or just do it? *Fuck.*

Dragging a hand over his mouth, he stilled as her scent perfumed his skin, her pheromones clinging to his fingers and lips, mixing with his own scent and driving his arousal up another degree. He crawled over her and kissed her lips. Startled, she opened her eyes and smiled, pulling him in for a deep kiss.

"Are you ready?" she whispered against his lips.

God, he hoped so. "Are you sure this is what you want?"

She smiled up at him, looking like a goddess beneath him. "I've wanted you since the night you rescued me, Elliot. I don't think I'll make it another day without having you."

Fuck, he had to be dreaming. Reaching for the condom, he examined the foil, searched for a tear line, his fingers slightly trembling with anticipation.

Her hand closed over his. "Let me."

She placed the condom on the tip of his cock, the slightest touch making him flinch and suck in a fierce breath. Looking into his eyes, she grinned and rolled it down his length.

Once it was in place, she eased back to the mattress, pulling him over her. Should he say something? Maybe he should thank her or remind her he'd never done this before?

She moved her legs outside of his knees and waited.

He broke eye contact, fumbling to find the right positioning as he shifted lower. The heat of her sex brushed his hand as he held his cock close to her opening, but he couldn't bring himself to enter her, not without looking at her.

His heart was beating so fast he feared he'd die before he ever got the chance to truly be with her. Something told him it would be different with anyone else. Easier. Less significant. But this was Nadia. Nadia, who he...

Swallowing tightly, he lifted his gaze and stared into the prettiest brown eyes he'd ever looked upon, and froze. So many unfamiliar feelings raced through him, each one equally as pleasant as they were frightening. In that moment nothing was certain aside from his desire, and he understood so much about the weakness of man in the throes of passion.

Perhaps he loved her. It made sense since no one else had ever captivated him to this degree. But how could he be sure of his feelings? Relationships weren't a science. They were buoyant and flimsy and often irrational. It made no sense why a woman like Nadia would want a man like him.

"Where have you gone, Elliot? I've lost you," her soft voice murmured.

He blinked down at her, a crushing fear that the consequences of their actions might swallow him whole and leave his well-organized world in a pile of rubble. While he might love her, she would never love him—at least not to the same degree.

In order to move forward, he had to accept that

he would always care about her more. "I'm here. I was just thinking."

She laughed and pulled him a little closer. "Think later. I want you."

The perfect example of irrational logic. "I want you too."

"Then take me. Stop torturing me and making me wait."

Pulling his head low, her lips sealed to his and his body sank forward, her body welcoming him. Sharp ecstasy electrified his spine as her heat engulfed him. He didn't pause until he was fully seated, and then he simply breathed. *Amazing.*

Her hands coasted over his shoulders, down his back, and she lifted her hips. Jesus, she felt incredible. He drew back and thrust deep, knowing he only had a few seconds of ecstasy before he was spent—if that.

Each stroke of her body against his stole more of his breath. Every thrust sent intense sensations through him until the effort to hold back any longer became excruciating.

The over sensitized nerves in his body screamed for him to finish. He never wanted to come so hard in his life. The effort to last left him trembling and he hated that he couldn't offer her something better.

"I'm sorry, I need to... finish." Even talking was torture.

"Go ahead," she whispered and he thrust hard, groaning as his release tunneled forcefully through his body. His soul felt turned inside out, wrung of every last drop of desire, but his wanting bloomed again with his next breath.

He shut his eyes and lowered his head to her shoulder, catching his breath as his body quaked with relief. She combed her fingers through his hair as she held him, giving him time to recover as he trembled. It was heaven.

"You're not a virgin anymore, Elliot."

He chuckled. "No, thank God."

"Are you sorry?"

He laughed harder. "No."

She nudged his chin until he looked at her. She whispered, "I have a part of you now, something no other woman can claim. I think I like that I was your first. You'll never forget me."

Forgetting her had never been an option. "You're incredible. I want to do it again, but..."

She giggled. "We have time. You wore me out."

He rolled to his side, shivering as his body withdrew from hers. "I need to clean up."

She pulled the covers to her chest and smiled as he left the bed. In the bathroom he removed the condom and winced, his entire body sensitive to the lightest touch.

Catching his gaze in the mirror he paused. He looked the same, but something in his eyes was different. Quietly laughing to himself, he shook his head and whispered, "Nadia."

She'd never know how much this meant to him and he might never know what it was to be a part of her intimate world for more than a day, but he knew this moment and the few that would follow. He knew he'd never forget this feeling or the way she smelled on his skin. And whether she'd ever know how he felt, he knew no other woman would ever have this strong of an effect on him.

Smiling, he washed up, anxious to return to her. When he exited the bathroom, her eyes were closed. The sense that he was trespassing wasn't as strong as before. He climbed under the covers and she curled into his side, welcoming him close to her body.

Nadia.

This was definitely heaven.

14

"Don't Panic."
The Hitchhiker's
Guide to the Galaxy

ELLIOT AWOKE to the distinct sense that someone was watching him. As he opened his eyes he was greeted by a vision. Nadia, her dark waves appearing almost black in the shadows, her face wearing a serene look of pleasure.

"Good morning, Mister Sleepy Head."

"Good morning." His hand lifted to her hair, hefting the thick weight between his fingers. Softer than silk.

"You have your meetings today, no?"

He shut his eyes, regretting his need for an unnecessary schedule. However, she'd be with family most of the day and this trip was really about her having time with loved ones. "I'm afraid so."

"Will I see you tonight?"

"Of course. My meeting's at noon and then I have another at four. I should be back to the hotel by six. Did you want me to come to the house?"

"No, I think I'll come here and surprise you."

He laughed. "It's not a surprise if I'm expecting it."

She tsked. "I have lots of tricks up my sleeve. You are not the only magician in this bed."

"Is that so?"

"Mm-hm." Her hand slithered under the blankets and he sucked in a breath as her cool fingers closed around him.

The novelty of her nearness still took his breath away. He doubted he'd ever adjust to her touching him like this. Every graze of her fingers, even a spare direct glance... She completely disarmed him. "Nadia..."

"Yes?"

He shook his head, nothing to say, only needing to hear her answer to prove this was real. "I love when you touch me," he groaned, stretching onto his back. As her hand slowly stroked, the muscles in his legs flexed, waking and stretching in a deliciously tantric seduction. He was completely under her spell.

"Me too. I like touching you and I like how you touch me. I'm not sure I believe I was your first."

He nearly snorted. "Trust me, you were."

She brushed the covers away from his hips and continued to stroke him slowly. It was strange letting someone see him so exposed, but what she was doing with her hand subdued any sense of self-consciousness.

"I think I should also be your second." Sliding her hand under the pillows she produced a condom. "Look... Magic."

He laughed. "I think your tricks are more impressive than mine."

"Oh, I don't know about that. You're a Jedi. Maybe I'll wear my hair in braids like the Queen for you."

Jesus. It was the holy grail of fantasies—Princess Leia in the gold bikini. "I love when you talk *Star Wars* to me."

She tore open the condom and slid it over his length. "You'll have to point it out."

"You'll know when you see it."

She straddled his legs and rose above him, slowly dragging his cock against her hot sex. There was nothing as gratifying as his body touching hers.

He'd assumed now that Pandora's Box had been opened the haze of shock would dissipate. He'd been wrong. Though he was no longer a virgin, he was still a novice and the sheer pleasure of her delicate flesh stroking along his rigid cock sent his mind into meltdown mode. It was almost too intensely satisfying to take. Almost.

His chest lifted as she seated herself, sliding him into her tight channel and engulfing him in heat. His hands cupped her hips as she slowly rocked. He was still acclimating to the intense sensations linked to being inside of her.

Her dark hair covered her breasts as she rode him at a gentle pace. She gathered it off her shoulders, piling it high on her head as she stretched and elongated her body, utterly breathtaking.

His fingers tightened on her hips. It was still surreal he could touch her like this. Stretching forward, he pulled her closer, capturing her nipple in his mouth and she lost her balance.

"Sorry." He needed to work on his finesse.

She cocked her head. "Did I hurt you?"

"No. Not at all. But I wanted..."

Onyx tendrils tumbling over one narrow shoulder, she tipped her head and smirked, her hands lifting to cup her breasts, lifting them like a sacred offering. "You wanted to taste?"

"Fuck..." His rasp was a plea for stamina because such eroticism should only exist in fiction but she was warm flesh and hot blood and she was riding his cock. "Come here."

She giggled and lowered. The moment her dark nipples were within reach he captured one turgid tip in his mouth. She let out a sharp gasp that had his dick twitching inside of her and thickening—ready to burst.

Her fingers dug into his shoulders as he lifted his hips and the sharp tips of her nails scraped along his skin. What would drive a woman to scratch a man like that? Was it a reflex or something she did because she saw it done in the movies? His mind went to all the various things he'd seen over the years, his greedy libido wanting to try every single one—yesterday.

"Nadia?"

"Hmm?"

"Can we try something?" He needed to switch things up before he finished.

Her hips slowed as her body lifted, and her gaze met his. Her dark hair formed a curtain around them. "What do you want to try?"

Everything. God, she was so damn beautiful. "I want..." His throat was suddenly dry, and he feared foolish words of inexperience would spill out and scare her away. He was falling in love with her and she... She didn't love him.

The hair surrounding them seemed to trap them in a secret world where their breath mingled and their eyes locked. It was a place secrets couldn't exist between them, intensely intimate and somewhat overwhelming.

"On your knees," he rasped, hoping she didn't detect how much she beguiled him. Men probably shouldn't feel this much emotion with sex.

She hesitated and then nodded. As his body pulled from her heat he let out a silent moan, his eyes rolling back. The suction of her tight, wet heat made it deliciously painful to leave. Shifting behind her, he pressed her hands into the mattress so she was on all fours. He hoped he wasn't being too demanding.

She arched a brow as she peeked over her shoulder, a playful glint in her eyes. "What are you planning to do back there?"

He wasn't really sure. Right now his eyes were focused on the plump curve of her ass. Kneeling behind her, he dragged a finger slowly down her spine and she arched like a cat.

His palm brushed over her bottom and she moaned, shifting closer until the hair of his legs rasped against her smooth thighs. Taking himself in hand, he guided his body back to hers, aligning his swollen flesh with her glistening folds. His mind short-circuited and plunged forward, sinking deep.

She gasped and he stilled. "Did I hurt you?"

"No. A little aggression is good."

"It is?"

"Yes. I'll tell you if it's too much."

His hands glided to her hips, holding her in place this time, as he thrust again. She gasped and pushed into him. Every way she moved sent a different sensation spiking through his nervous system.

His grip tightened, as his thrusts grew surer, harder, and with each deep stroke of his body, she appeared more excited. Finding his rhythm, he pumped faster, firmer, and his lungs burned with exertion.

Though he'd outlasted his first experience, he was still on the verge of finishing too soon. It seemed impolite to come without bringing her release, so he slid his hand beneath her belly and touched where their bodies connected.

The color leached from her knuckles as she fisted the blankets and he groaned as her body gripped his so tightly it became difficult to move. She gasped and rocked into him with quick little pumps of her hips, and her shoulders collapsed.

The pulse of her contracting sex broke his control and he called out her name, trembling as his body blanketed hers, his hips jerking as come spurted hard into the condom. Catching his breath, he lifted his weight off of her and withdrew, collapsing to his back.

She curled into his side and pulled the covers over them as they panted. He couldn't recall another moment when he was so damn content.

This couldn't have been what normal sex felt like. It seemed too incredible, too much the result of his feelings for her. But maybe it was like this for everyone. Maybe this was why the rest of the world seemed fixated on all things sex.

Jesus, he was just like the rest of them. The thought amused him more than he expected. "I like sex," he announced and laughed, never having the courage to entertain such possibilities before.

Two weeks ago, he'd have denied the appeal at all costs. He was an ignorant fool. If he'd known what he was missing he wouldn't have been the world's oldest virgin.

She giggled. "Not many people dislike it."

If only she knew how much effort he'd wasted trying to avoid the subject in thought and action, somehow convincing himself he wasn't missing anything. Despite his IQ, he was a fucking idiot.

Deep down he knew he'd like it. Too many people desired it for there to be no appeal. But how deep were his trust issues that with knowing sex would likely be incredible he still avoided it? He'd never wanted to give anyone that sort of hold over him. And now he'd given it to Nadia—the one woman who already affected him more than anyone else ever could.

15

---

*"A HERO CAN BE ANYONE. **Even a man doing something as simple and reassuring as putting a coat around a young boy's shoulders to let him know that the world hasn't ended.***"*

~Batman

*E*lliot took the elevator, hoping to find Nadia waiting for him in his hotel room. His meeting had been unremarkable, but Asher was happy to hear they'd received a proposition from their shareholders, so all was not wasted.

As he slid his key through the door and twisted the knob, disappointment washed over him. His room was dark and empty.

He checked his watch. It was only six-fifteen. Maybe she was still finishing things up with her family. Unsure if she'd eat with them or wait to have dinner with him, he ordered a light snack from room service and passed the time responding to emails.

When his food arrived with a knock at the door, he stowed his laptop. Opening the door—

"Nadia."

Her face pinched as she looked up at him with red eyes, tears streaking her face. Seeing her so upset and not understanding why it hit him like a punch to the gut. His first and only instinct was to fix whatever was wrong.

"What happened?"

"Mira passed," she rasped, her shoulders shaking as she fought back a sob and lost the battle.

His heart fractured as she struggled to hold the pain inside. He pulled her into his arms and hugged her tight, pressing his lips to the top of her head. He couldn't fix it. Losing a loved one was a pain that only time could ease, but even time wasn't powerful enough to totally erase the grief. He wished he could do more for her, but all he could do was hold her.

"I'm so sorry, Nadia."

She sniffled and wrapped her arms around his waist, squeezing tight. "I was there, holding her hand, and she just looked at me and said, *Én kész vagyok most.*"

Damn this language barrier. "What does that mean, sweetheart?"

"I'm ready to go now." Her tears seeped through the fabric of his shirt as she crumbled in his arms.

He ushered her into the room and sat her on the chair. Opening a bottle of water and gathering the box of tissues, he sat on the ottoman, pulling it close so their knees touched as they sat across from each other. "Take a sip of water."

She drank and he pulled out a tissue, blotting the shed tears before they dried. "Just think, she left this world holding hands with her favorite niece. That had to mean a lot to her."

She wiped her nose and nodded. "It meant something to me, too. Thank you so much for bringing me here, Elliot. I can never repay you for such a gift."

"You don't have to thank me. I wanted to do it."

Wiping a hand over her eyes, she held her hair away from her face and sighed. "My eyes are killing me. I need to get these contacts out." She scrunched her nose. "I must look like a disaster."

Honestly, she looked gorgeous, though sad. If not for her heartache he'd be all over her. "Do you have your glasses?"

She nodded. "In my purse." The knock on the door noticeably startled her. "Are you expecting someone?"

"It's just room service. I ordered an appetizer because I didn't know if you had dinner or not."

"Oh. I haven't eaten since this morning."

"I'll get dinner then. You go find your glasses."

He patted her knee and stood to get the door. Stepping into the hall, so she had privacy, he asked the attendant to bring up dinner for two using a lot of hand gestures and butchered Hungarian. The attendant seemed to understand and left to go relay whatever the hell he'd just ordered to the chef.

Nadia stepped out of the bathroom and he

stilled. She looked like the sexiest nerd in the world when she wore glasses.

"I ordered dinner." He couldn't blink. "It should be here soon."

She sniffled and nodded. "Thank you."

Trying to be tactful, yet practical, he sat her back down and took both her hands in his. "We can stay longer. I can arrange a different flight. I just need to know what day the service will take place?"

"There's no service. We don't do things that way in our family. Mira will be taken tonight and there is no embalming. She'll be cremated and her ashes will sit beside my Aunt Petra's in the sacred corner."

Recalling all the formality of his father's burial, this seemed incomplete, but it wasn't his place to judge one tradition against another. Now it made sense why they held the open house.

"It's nice she was able to see so many loved ones in her last days."

His analytical mind wasn't satisfied with leaving so soon after she suffered such a loss, so he silently continued to evaluate any options that might make this easier on her. Their flight was scheduled to leave tomorrow night, but he didn't want to rush her when she was mourning.

He tucked a strand of hair behind her ear and wished there was a way to take some of her pain. "Do you want to stay longer, Nadia? Even if there isn't a service, we can stay so you have time to be with family."

"I can't afford to stay any longer. I have classes I need to teach."

"I'm sure your students would understand."

She laughed without humor. "They would, but my landlord wouldn't. I need to get home so I can pay my studio rent. No classes, no money."

He hesitated, knowing she'd likely say no, but wanting to help her any way he could. "I could handle your rent. Why don't you let me talk to your landlord? You and I can work out the details later." He'd never take a cent from her, but if she knew that, she'd definitely decline his offer.

She smiled, cupping her hands at the side of his jaw in a way that made him feel awkward, yet told him she was giving him complete sincerity. "You're a very sweet man, Elliot, but no. I'm not going to let you do that. I came to say goodbye to my aunt and I have. There's no need for me to stay here. I can mourn at home."

He missed his house, his language, and American food, but he'd stay another year if it made this easier for her. "Are you sure?"

She nodded. "Tomorrow I'll say my goodbyes to my mother and *Nagymama* and then I'll be ready. Will you come with me?"

"Whatever you need."

She shut her eyes and sighed. "I'm tired."

He stood and pulled back the covers of the bed. "Rest. Do you want me to wake you when the food arrives?"

She climbed onto the bed, her motions lethargic and weak. "If I'm awake, I'll eat. If not, I'll eat later."

He tucked the blankets around her shoulders and pressed his lips to her brow. Pulling off her glasses, he folded them on the nightstand. Her hand caught his arm and he looked at her in question.

"No one's ever been so nice to me, Elliot. I don't always know how to accept such kindness, but with you... I want to. I want nothing but truth between us. No games. No lies."

"I wouldn't lie to you." He'd done some truth bending to get her here, but in the end, the trip had served a business purpose. "I don't want games either."

Her eyes were tired, but as he held her stare he noticed a weighted concern in the depths. "I care about you, Elliot. And I never make the right choices with men, it seems, but I want this to be right. I don't want to be wrong about you."

Her words knocked him back, but he stayed outwardly still. The pressure not to disappoint her doubled as he understood how much she wanted to believe everything she assumed about him, but she was so far out of his league he wasn't sure he'd ever measure up to being good enough.

All he could offer was the truth. "I don't want to disappoint you."

"I don't think you could, if this is really who you are."

"Nadia..." He swallowed, overwhelming pressure mounting. All of his life he dreamed of being a hero only to be brutally reminded that he was simply ordinary. "Just ... be patient with me. No games. But ... at one point I'll need a learning curve, okay?"

She smiled. "I don't know what a learning curve is, but okay."

"It means you remember this is new to me and I have no experience."

"For a man with no experience, you seem to be a natural at finding your way into my heart, mister. When I'm scared, my mind goes to you and I feel safe again. You're there when I need help. Dependable. Your endless kindness is such a refreshing surprise to me. I've never met anyone who made me feel that way before."

His expression blanked. Maybe she was too exhausted or too emotionally wrung. "Nadia, my kindness has limits and I'm not such a nice guy."

She laughed, her eyes closing in a long blink. When her lashes lifted she looked up at him through dark slits. "You promised not to lie."

"I'm not lying." He was dead serious. "I'm impatient, short-tempered, and intolerant of other people's bullshit. It's why it's easy for me to be alone."

Her eyes closed and she shook her head, a smile pressed loosely to her full lips. "Hmm... Maybe you don't know everything after all. I see a different man."

Her voice tapered into nothingness but not before her words burrowed deep in his soul, tending to some repressed, broken part of him he hardly thought about. In a way, she made him feel safe as well. And hopeful and surprised. But she also made him long for things that came with no guarantee.

He nuzzled his nose to her cheek and breathed her in, pressing a soft kiss to her skin. "Get some sleep, sweetheart."

He caught room service before they could knock

and ate quietly in the dark, watching her sleep. His mind bounced between worries. She might see the real him and everything they shared would suddenly vanish. Or he could exhaust himself trying to be the good man she believed he was. Just the thought of meeting her expectations seemed daunting. His main shortcoming had always been social ease, but she didn't see that. She saw him as a man—the sort of man he'd always wanted to be. Did she see him as a hero?

Could he be that for her? Damn. He wanted to. He wanted to be the man she looked to, the one that solved all her problems and always made her feel safe. Most of all he never wanted to let her down.

He was falling in love with her—maybe he was already there. He wanted her to love him back, but he wanted to earn her love.

After moving the tray outside and slipping Nadia's dinner into the mini-fridge, he crawled into bed beside her. Lying on his back, he stared at the ceiling. He was going to win her over. He was going to be everything she expected and more. He was going to rise to the man she deserved—he just had to figure out how.

When Elliot awoke, the sky was still black. Nadia slept soundly beside him. He frowned into the shadows, a troubling thought on his mind.

Slipping out of bed, he grabbed his laptop and moved to the chair.

Once he found the site he was looking for, he typed in the address to Nadia's house and plugged in his credit card information, purchasing access to a fully inclusive report. The property was listed under Ada Szoke, her grandmother. He jotted down the name to get the spelling accurate.

Within thirty minutes he had everything he needed, the land and tax evaluations, all previous sale information, and the most recent appraisal of the property. While on the site, he also did a search on the neighboring property, that of a Mr. Roland Hegedus. The man had remortgaged three times and was looking at thirty more years of payments with practically zero equity.

While that man barged into her family's lives parading about like the gaudiest form of wealth, he had nothing to show for it. His funds were liquid and his property belonged to the bank more than her grandmother's, yet he had them convinced he could somehow bail them out of financial crisis.

Sitting back, Elliot laughed quietly to himself. "You son of a bitch."

Closing his laptop, he checked his watch. They had roughly nine hours until they were on a plane back to the States.

Calculating the time difference, he grimaced. He shot a text to all three of the guys, hoping at least one of them would get it before morning.

Tossing the phone aside, he gently nudged Nadia. She opened her eyes and smiled. "Hey, you."

"Hey."

She rolled onto her back and frowned, noting the sun had yet to rise. "What time is it?"

"It's early still. I need to talk to you."

She rubbed her face. "Is something wrong?"

Taking her hands, he chafed them gently. There was a good chance his nosing around could upset her.

"Nothing's wrong. Nadia, is your grandmother's name Ada?"

She frowned, her eyes suddenly guarded. "Yes. Why?"

Relieved, he relaxed a bit. "She owns the house. Did you know that?"

"How do *you* know that?"

"The information's accessible online." No need to mention he paid for that access. "My point is, if she sold the property to you at a much lower cost, the taxes would be taken out of escrow and the payments could be stretched over time."

She frowned. "I don't know what you're talking about, Elliot. I don't want to buy that house, nor do I have that sort of money."

"I'm talking about a loan. Let's say the house is valued at a hundred thousand dollars, but she sells it to you for only twenty. You stretch that out over thirty years with a very low interest rate and you're only paying a little over a hundred dollars a month with taxes figured in. Your mother could definitely afford that and still live a decent life."

"Elliot, I don't have twenty-thousand dollars. And I don't want that house."

"Why? You don't need to have the money up front. You just need to get approved for a loan. Your mother would be maintaining it."

"That will never work. I once tried to buy a car

and they laughed at my credit score. I'm not worth anything."

He scowled. "First of all, yes, you are. Second, if you've never had a loan and don't have any substantial debt, you don't have bad credit, you just don't have *any* period. You have to build it. I can help you do that."

"How?"

"I'll cosign for the loan."

She shook her head and slid out of bed. "No."

"Why?"

Pacing, she flung out her hands. *"Ne keverjük a szerelem és a pénz. Nem akarom, hogy tartozom neked semmivel, és—"*

"English, Nadia."

She paused and shook her head. "I do not want to owe you anything. What if I mess up and it hurts you?"

Over twenty-thousand dollars? She honestly had no concept of his wealth, which was endearing.

"You won't. As cosigner, I'd keep abreast of all transactions, penalties, and fees. If there was an issue with making a payment, I'd intercept before the banks could."

"Then you'd be paying for my family's home. No."

"I wouldn't be paying. I'd be a safety net." A legitimate one that wouldn't lord it over her or her family.

"And what happens when we can't make ends meet? My mother isn't reliable. She has to work, but if she thought she could get away with no job, believe me, she would. She doesn't have the same work ethic as the rest of my family. You don't want to do business with her and neither do I. Don't get involved."

He frowned. "But you'd let Roland bail your family out?"

"That's them, not me. My father trusted him, so they automatically think he's a good person. My grandmother's old, Elliot. She doesn't know him the way I do. And my mother ... she is lazy. She will always take the easiest shortcut."

"Don't they care how he treats you? You can't negotiate with bullies. They're never satisfied."

"He doesn't bully them. Just me, and we're going home tonight. He can't get to me in America."

"But he keeps you from visiting."

"Money keeps me from visiting."

And yet she continued to send them money. "They shouldn't bargain with him, especially when you're sending them money on occasion. This is your home, too, Nadia. If your family knew how he actually treated you, they'd probably feel differently."

"You're wrong. It doesn't matter why he helps, only that he does. When my grandmother couldn't pay the taxes he saved them from being put on the street. I couldn't help them, Elliot. I can send things here and there, but not to the degree Roland can help. He gains nothing in return and never will, but they keep a roof over their heads. He can threaten me all he wants—"

"Threaten you?" He was on his feet, uneasiness taking hold of him. "He threatened you? When?"

She waved a hand. "He does it all the time."

"*How* did he threaten you?"

Rolling her eyes, she explained, "He says if I don't move home and be his wife, he'll buy the house out from under my family the next time the banks come calling. Then they'd have to pay rent to live there or get evicted—unless *we* are family."

"Family as in in-laws?"

"Yes, but he's crazy, Elliot. So long as I let him believe what he wants to believe, he won't do anything to hurt us."

Something shifted in her eyes, betraying her bravado. That man scared her to some degree and he didn't like it.

"Nadia, when I was a kid I excelled in school. I didn't have a lot of friends, but it didn't take friends to notice I was a hell of a lot smarter than the rest of my classmates. Some people asked for help and I helped them, but those who demanded it, threatened me, they never cared about what happened to me. The minute I didn't do exactly what they wanted they made my life hell. Bullies are bullies. There are no nice ones. There are just bad ones. You have to stand up to them or they never go away."

"I do stand up to him." She waved her fingers. "You'll notice there's no ring on my finger. I'm not his wife and he's not the boss of me. I'd never give into someone like that."

But she still had to put up with him. He still made her uncomfortable in her own home. "I don't like the way he treats you."

She pinched the bridge of her nose. "He can't

hurt me when I'm in another country. You're all wound up and talking nonsense."

"It isn't nonsense," he snapped, frustrated she trusted that man to guard her family's interests when he was offering a better solution. "Why won't you let me help you? This will get that asshole off your back. He won't barge in or feel entitled anymore. You'd never have to go to him again."

"I don't want you to be that to me. Why can't you just be my boyfriend?"

"I don't want to be your boyfriend when another man thinks he's entitled to call you his future wife!"

She blinked at him. "Don't shout at me."

Surprised by his outburst, he took a step back. "I'm sorry. I..." He'd assumed after everything she'd said last night it would be simple to save her from this situation now that he had a solution. He never expected her opposition. "I don't understand why you would choose to remain in an unhealthy situation with this other man when I'm offering you an out."

"It's not an out, Elliot. There is no out. I'm broke and when I'm not broke, I'm poor. All you're doing is transferring the sense of indebtedness from one man to another. I don't want that sort of relationship with you."

He dropped into the chair and thought for a minute. "What if I promised not to interfere? If you lose the house because you can't make the payments, it'll be your choice. I'm just setting the mortgage up to give you more control over the situation."

Her dark eyes held skepticism. "That's all?"

He'd do his best to keep his word and make sure her family kept the house no matter how many financial burdens fell on them, but he'd have to respect her wishes. The woman had a lot of pride and that only added to her appeal. "That's all. Take the deal, Nadia. It's a good business decision."

Shutting her eyes, she blew out a breath. "I can't do anything without talking to my *nagymama*. And she won't like a stranger poking around in her finances. She's very private."

"So am I. I know this is a lot, but if you trust anything about me, trust that I'm good with money and not out to harm you or your family."

"Fine. But for the record, I'd much rather wake up to sex than this sort of stress."

"Who says we can't have both?"

She stilled and glanced over her shoulder. "You'll have to catch me."

She squealed as he sprung from the chair and tackled her to the bed. His lips found hers, and when he broke the kiss, she laughed.

"Caught you," he whispered.

"Maybe I let you catch me." She nipped at his mouth and lifted her hips.

"Well, I'm not letting you go."

"Is that a promise?" She kissed him. "Once my *nagymama* lays into you, you might change your mind. You're going to see where I get my stubbornness from."

He pulled her arms from his shoulders and pressed them into the pillows above her head. "Then I better make this count."

She stretched beneath him, her hard nipples poking against the material of her clothes. "Oh, I think you better."

He growled and pinned her to the bed, kissing her with promise and not stopping until he followed through on his word.

16

~Yoda

$\mathcal{N}$adia pinched the bridge of her nose as her mother continued to shout. Luckily, Elliot's Hungarian was terrible so he likely wasn't taking too much offense to her mother's cutting words.

"You bring this stranger into our home and disclose our personal business!" her mother accused. "This is none of his concern! He is not family! At least Roland has a stake in saving our home."

"What stake? Momma, all he wants is to blackmail me into his bed."

"He wants marriage, Nadia. Stability! Which is all your father asked of you years ago. You are too bullheaded, running off on American adventures when your family needs you here!"

"I'm making a living—"

"What living? You are jumping from one man's bed to another and always crying you have no money. At least as Roland's wife, you'd have your dignity."

Elliot cleared his throat, his English disrupting their argument. "If I might say something..."

Her mother rolled her eyes, continuing to speak over him in Hungarian. "This man! What more does he have to say?"

Nadia turned to Elliot, having heard enough from her mother. "Go ahead."

He opened his mouth and paused, glancing at her. "Will you translate?"

She nodded.

"If you transferred the house to Nadia, you wouldn't be in debt to a man who wants to do something that would make your daughter very unhappy. The ownership would be divided between the three of you. That would ensure you never missed a payment and your taxes would be figured into your monthly payments, instead of required once a year in a large lump sum. It would be more manageable for all of you and it would be *yours*. No need to ask for help from Roland anymore."

Her mother gave her a pointed look and she quickly translated. Before she even finished, she was shaking her head.

"No. We are fine the way we are."

Dropping her face into her hands, Nadia groaned. "I told you this wouldn't work."

Her *nagymama,* who had been sitting silently for the past hour, placed a hand on Nadia's arm and whispered in Hungarian, "Do you trust this man, Nadia?"

"*Igen,*" she answered immediately. At the moment, she trusted him more than anyone.

"Then I trust him, too," her grandmother said in Hungarian.

When her mother tried to interrupt her grandmother silenced her with a halting finger.

"You had your time to talk. This is my home and I haven't been able to afford it for a long time. If Nadia wants to buy it from me, and she can figure out how, then I will sell it to her."

"But Roland—"

"Look at your daughter. She does not want to marry Roland. She is young and beautiful and he is not what she wants. I think it's time you let go of your husband's dying wishes and accept what is."

Her mother stood, mouth tight and eyes full of anger. "He was a good man and deserves a good daughter who would honor his dying requests." Her glare cut to Nadia. "What a disappointment you've become. This is a mistake. What happens when this man leaves you like all the rest and wants his money back?"

Nadia winced, her mother's words stabbing deep into her insecurities. "It's not *his* money. He's only cosigning the paperwork. You would be paying the mortgage."

"No man does something for nothing, Nadia. When will you learn that? Besides, this is your plan, but the burden will be on *my* shoulders."

Gritting her teeth, she swallowed her response. This was exactly why she moved to the States.

Her grandmother's fist came down on the table, rattling the silverware. "And you have lived here your entire life. You raised your family in this house, and since Nadia's father passed, I've paid for everything. Do you think Roland will always be there to pay what we can't afford? Nadia does not want to be his bride. If she did, we would have had a wedding by now. Enough."

Her mother glared at her for a moment and then stormed out of the kitchen.

"What's happening?" Elliot whispered.

Nadia took her grandmother's hands in hers. "Are you sure this is what you want?"

She shrugged. "I'm old, Nadia. The house will eventually be yours anyway—if we manage to keep it that long. I can't take any of these things with me when I go. None of it is worth fighting over."

"I'd understand if you wanted to keep things as they are."

Her grandmother smiled sadly. "Your mother needs to pull her weight. I've lost two daughters who worked their entire lives. She's all I have left and I think it's time for her to do her part, let you live your life where you want."

Nadia smiled, relieved to have her grandmother's blessing, and faced Elliot. "She says yes, she'll do it."

He sighed with relief and she wondered once

again why he'd take such joy in carrying her family's burden. He faced her grandmother. "It's a good plan."

She shrugged, not understanding his English.

Nadia translated and the moment they shook hands, Elliot was off making phone calls and contacting banks. They only had a few hours left and Nadia didn't like leaving her mother while they were at odds.

"I'm going to find, Momma," she whispered to her grandmother so as not to disturb Elliot.

Her mother wasn't in her bedroom or any other room. When she searched the yard she found it empty. She stilled as Roland's back door opened. Her brow creased as her mother slipped out of his house and bustled to the gate.

"Where were you?" Nadia asked, clearly startling her.

"I went for a walk to calm down."

She frowned at the blatant lie. "We're leaving soon."

Her mother's gaze drifted to the front door. "Of course."

"Momma, you have to understand this is for the best. Roland—"

"I'm not discussing this with you anymore," her mother snapped.

Nadia scoffed. "Why?"

Her mother shook her head, her eyes narrowing. "Do you think I wanted to marry your father, Nadia? I didn't, but it helped my family and I was an obedient daughter. It's what good daughters do."

"Marrying Roland wouldn't help anything, Momma. When will you get that?"

"But lying beneath a stranger like a whore will?"

Nadia drew back. Hurt, and speechless, she stared at her mother, wondering where such hateful words could come from. Her vision blurred as her blood heated. "Elliot isn't a stranger. I ... love him."

The words crossed the short distance and seemed to silence even the birds in the valley. Everything stilled as reality settled into her bones. She loved him. It was dangerous and exciting and terrifying all at once.

"I love him, Momma," she repeated, her tone now protective and certain. The feelings she held for him were so intense she refused to let her mother's expectations tarnish them with ugliness.

Her mother rolled her eyes. "Two weeks ago you lived with a different man. What sort of woman does that?"

"This is different. I *never* loved Ian."

"And yet you shared his bed. All of these lovers, and not a single proposal. You think you're too good for Roland, but he's the only one willing to marry you after all of these years. He is secure and familiar. It could be much worse."

"How could anything be worse than binding my life to someone I don't love? Do you hear how insane that sounds? I don't want to be married, and I'm *never* going to marry Roland."

"At least he would make an honest woman of you. Men don't want to settle down with women who have a past. You need to do what's right *now*, while you're still young and beautiful enough for a good man to overlook your mistakes. "

Her mistakes, that was all her mother ever saw. Pressure built in her chest as bile rose in her throat. When would this argument end?

She didn't want Elliot to marry her. She just wanted him to accept her. Maybe he'd come to love her too and when he learned about her past mistakes he'd love her enough to not care that she was beneath him. She wanted to be good enough for him, smart enough for him, and kind like him.

"Elliot's different."

"But are you, Nadia? Are you any different from any other warm body he could lay with?"

A cold fist cinched around her heart. She wanted to be different to him—special to him—but her mother was right. Elliot could have any woman he wanted and he probably would grow tired of her over time.

"You don't understand what we have. He looks at me and…" Her throat constricted as her personal doubts and worries had her questioning her own words. Her voice warbled as she forced them out anyway. "He sees me as someone special."

"And I wonder how special you'd be if you kept your clothes on for him."

Her spine stiffened as her breath hitched, the urge to slap her mother's face stole over her, but she remained ramrod still. "We're leaving. I just came to find you to say goodbye."

Her mother blew out a huff of air and waved her away. "Go. Run to your American life and don't come back. We will be fine without you." Her mother turned and marched into the house, leaving Nadia shaking on the lawn.

"You know this is a mistake."

Startled, Nadia twisted to find Roland standing by the fence. He'd been listening to all the hurtful, humiliating things her mother had said.

Her blurred vision narrowed on him. "This has nothing to do with you."

"That man is using you, Nadia. He will lose interest and leave you destitute. Then what? Do you expect me to keep waiting?"

Elliot wasn't keeping her alive. He was merely cosigning a loan for her, yet everyone else acted as if she were signing her soul to the devil. Perhaps it was a survival tactic from years of dealing with this bully of a man that flipped her insecurities into bolstered outrage.

Shoving aside her doubts, she glared at him and let her hurt find a target. "For the love of God, Roland, *move on*. I never asked you to wait—" He flung open the gate and grabbed her by both arms, shaking her.

"*Liar*," he hissed.

A sharp, startled cry escaped as he took her off guard and shook her again.

"You told me you'd be back." He jerked her harder, rattling her teeth. She lost her footing as his grip tightened with every scornful word. "I could have had several women in your absence, but I— foolishly—remained loyal to you. You think I'm going to help now? That house could burn to the ground and I wouldn't waste a drop of piss trying to put the fire out."

Startled by the vehemence in his eyes, her arms swung forward and she shoved him off of her. *"Don't touch me!"*

She staggered back the second he let go. Elliot was right. He was a bully and she'd let him get away with far too much for far too long. *"You* will *never* have a right to lay a hand on me. *Never!"*

He laughed coldly. "What are you going to do to stop me, Nadia?" he sneered, towering over her. "Have your little man come after me? He can't protect you from a fly." His arm snaked behind her, grabbing a fistful of her ass and she inadvertently jumped closer to him.

His thick arms banded around her, pulling her feet off the ground as his steamy breath panted across the side of her face. "He just wants to fuck you, Nadia. He'll never love you. That's all you're worth to anyone, just a lousy, hard fuck toy. At least I would have put up with you for longer than a few screws."

"Get off me!" Tears burned her eyes as she shoved at his arm.

He groaned and chuckled, his body hardening behind her the more she struggled. "Does his little dick satisfy you? I bet you don't cry that it's too big with him. Not like you cried with me."

"Shut up!" She refused to go back to that time, but he was taking her there, filling her mind with those horrid memories. "I hate you!"

"Mmm, keep fighting the inevitable." He chuckled, his fingers curling in the material of her loose skirt. "You've said those words to me before, just before you came all over my fat cock. Maybe I'll remind you of what a real man feels like—"

She screamed in frustration, going ballistic in his arms and scratching until his grip loosened. "Let! Go!"

"Motherfucker!" The masculine roar came from across the yard and her body was knocked to the ground.

She rolled away from Roland, her hands and knees pushing up on the dry grass as Elliot's voice registered. His body blanketing Roland's as his hands choked the larger man just as Roland's meaty fist drove into the side of his head, knocking his glasses clean off his face.

"Elliot!" She scrambled to her feet as Roland's larger body rolled atop Elliot's, his arm jerking back and his fist slamming down with a gruesome crack.

"Roland, no!"

She threw herself on the larger man only to be tossed off as his fist connected with Elliot's face, again and again. She cried and screamed for help, but no one came. Elliot blocked his face, but the punches kept coming.

"Get off of him!" she screamed, grabbing ahold of Roland's hair with both fists.

All of her self-defense training came back to her as she gathered his shirt and twisted it around his throat, cutting off his airway. It only slowed him enough to take his attention off Elliot.

Beefy hands scratched at her arms as she held

tight and he toppled to his side. Rolling, she scrambled to her feet. He wasn't far behind. Coughing, he lifted to his forearm and started to rise to his knees.

"No!" She kicked him in the balls with all her might and he fell back to the ground with the thud of a downed oak.

"Fucking bitch!" He curled into a ball and groaned, cupping himself.

She skittered away, rushing to Elliot's side where he lay on the crabgrass, his face swollen and bloody, as he breathed rapidly.

Her hands trembled as they cupped his blood smeared face. "Elliot, look at me."

His breath panted and his eyes opened to slits, one full of red. "Did ... he hurt you?"

Her vision blurred. This foolish, bloody man was worried if *she* was hurt. "What were you thinking?"

He shut his eyes and groaned in pain. "Wasn't. Just acted."

Her smile was pained as she sucked in a stuttering breath. "My foolish hero."

His swollen eyes only opened slightly, his lip split and bloody. She broke into tears.

"Shh." His hand trembled as he cupped her cheek. "Don't cry. Not worth it."

Sniffling, she wiped her eyes and fought back more tears. "Look at you..." His face was so swollen and smeared with blood, she wasn't sure how he was conscious.

He winced and smiled at her. "I've had worse. Let's go home now, Nadia. I wanna go home," he slurred.

She nodded quickly, her gaze shooting back to Roland who still held himself and grumbled in pain. Her shoulders quaked as she looked back at Elliot and choked on a sob. "Why did you do that?"

He shut his eyes, resting on the grass, his breathing labored. He tried to smile but only winced. "I'll always defend you."

She lowered her face to his, nestling her nose to his cheek. This was not the way she wanted it to go. She wasn't worth this much trouble and now... Her heart seemed to swell until it painfully occupied her chest. Her voice shook as she leaned close and nestled his cheek with her nose. "You're hurt because of me. I'm not worth defending, Elliot."

He shook his head, his eyes reflecting his pain. "You're worth that and so much more, Nadia."

17

"I grew up watching 'Superman.' As a child, when I first learned to dive into a swimming pool, I wasn't diving, I was flying, like Superman. I used to dream of rescuing a girl I had a crush on from a playground bully."

~Tom Hiddleston

The flight home was long. Nadia couldn't fall asleep, but Elliot had no problem drifting off. He looked awful, his bludgeoned face with two black eyes, a gash on his cheek, and a split lip. That was her fault.

Gazing at the tarmac, she waited for the captain's instructions. Home. They were finally home.

Elliot shifted, drawing her attention. Brushing a hand over his nose, he winced and opened his eyes. "Did we land?"

"About a minute ago." God, he looked terrible. "I think we should take you to a hospital before we go to your house. You might need stitches after all."

He'd refused to delay their plans and see a doctor in Hungary, but now they were home and that lip still wasn't healing.

"I'll be fine."

"Your lip—"

"I'll be fine, Nadia. It's not my first split lip." He unbuckled his seatbelt before the light came on. "Did you sleep?"

He always seemed more concerned with her, so she lied. "A little."

The lights came on and passengers busied themselves with collecting their personal belongings. The next hour was passed exiting the plane and airport and finding a cab. Elliot was silent most of the way.

When they entered the house, he rummaged through drawers until he found an old pair of glasses. "These will have to do."

She hung back as he washed the lenses and checked his phone. He'd complained several times about how inconvenient it was to not be able to see.

"Tomorrow you can go to one of the one-hour places and get new glasses. I'll buy them for you since this was my fault."

He glanced over his shoulder, his darkened eyes narrowing. "I can buy my own glasses. The bank emailed us back."

"I know you can, but I—"

"You're not paying for my glasses, Nadia. That's the end of it." His tone left no room for argument and she let it go until he squinted through his out-dated lenses at his email.

She frowned. "Leave it for tomorrow, Elliot. It's the middle of the night."

Not sparing her a glance, he punched something into his phone. "It's morning there."

"Elliot..." Her gratitude for all his help remained, but this was silly. He was hurt and they literally just walked through the door after a very long flight. He was neglecting his needs. "Why don't you come upstairs and I'll fix a bath for us. Let me wash your face and—"

"I'm not so injured I can't wash my own face."

Her spine buckled and her mouth snapped shut. He was taking her concern all wrong. "I just want to take care of you the way you've taken care of me."

"That's fine, but first I need to handle the situation with the bank in order to get the mortgage transferred to you."

Her brow tightened. He was hyper-focused on this house situation but there was no rush. Placing her hand on his sleeve, she waited for him to look at her. "You've done so much to help me and my family, Elliot. More than I'd ever be comfortable asking of someone. I truly appreciate all your help, but right now I really need you to let me help you. That's what partnership means, we help each other."

"I don't need help. I need to finish what I've started. Men like Roland don't lose quietly and I want to see this through before there are any more complications. He might have me outmatched in a physical altercation, but this is how *I* win. He can throw the last punch like the Neanderthal he is, but I always get the last word."

She frowned as he brought the phone to his ear, pulling away from her touch. He stood and walked out of the room, leaving her staring after him. His kind gesture now felt more like a personal vendetta. She wondered how much it actually had to do with her. He seemed more focused on evening the score between him and Roland when all she wanted to do was leave Roland and the memory of him back in Hungary to stay.

Carrying her luggage upstairs, she continued to scowl. What started out as a selfless gesture to help her family had turned into a pissing match between two men. She was rather tired of games.

She went to her room, supposing this was where he expected her to sleep while he wasted the next hour or so in his office. She watched the door, waiting for him to come to her, but he never did.

The following morning, confused and unsure of how she fit into his life at home, she dressed and decided to avoid all confrontations. Elliot's bedroom door was closed. She crept through his house trying to guess where he hid his umbrellas. His home had so many doors, she'd forgotten which ones were private rooms and which were closets.

Turning the knob to a door on the second floor she peeked into the shadows, seeing the space was somewhat narrow and full of shelves. Maybe an umbrella would be in there. She felt for the light switch and stilled as the room illuminated with track lighting. It was much larger than she assumed.

Her gaze traveled along the custom shelving, noting all the various packages and strange items. Toys. It was a room full of unopened toys. Were these things his company made? Were they presents for little children? Maybe a donation he did during the holidays? Regardless, there were no umbrellas on the neatly organized shelves and she suspected this was one of those doors she wasn't meant to open. Shutting out the light, she closed the door and continued her search.

The day was anything but sunny. Calling a cab, she took it directly into the city and was the first patron at the bank that morning. She smiled politely as the bank clerk waited for his computer to turn on, making small talk, and offering her coffee.

"No, thank you."

The computer screen lit and he grinned in relief. "So, you want a credit card. That shouldn't be an issue."

Elliot said her credit score was low because she hadn't established any. She wanted to remedy that as soon as possible. This seemed the place to start. "I've never had a credit card before. I hope I'm approved."

The man, again, smiled. "I'm sure we can work something out. Where are you from?"

"Hungary."

"Beautiful country."

She perked up. "Have you been there?"

"Uh, no, but I've seen pictures. Beautiful people, too." He winked.

From then on she only answered the pertinent questions regarding her account. By the time she left she had a little plastic card with her name on it and a five hundred dollar credit limit.

Elliot texted her, asking where she was, but she only told him she had to be in the studio early. The last few days had been monumental and eye-opening, emotionally awakening parts of her soul she feared no man would ever find. But in the last twenty-four hours, he'd reduced their beautiful association to a sort of business deal. She didn't want a financial adviser. She just wanted him.

It seemed the issues with the house were forming a barricade between them, siphoning all the intimacy away from their newborn relationship and stealing something from her she never had with anyone else. She'd been with plenty of men, but she'd never fallen in love, never had a man tell her he loved her. She thought they were close, but now he seemed miles away. Where had her sweet man gone? This business side of Elliot was not the same person.

Maybe she was being overly sensitive. She appreciated how much he was laying on the line to help her family. Though it didn't seem like much to him, her family didn't have opportunities like the one he offered—at least not without rope-thick strings attached.

Maybe she was reading into things and tired from jet lag and being what they called a drama queen. She hated dating dilemmas and promised herself Elliot would be different. With him, she wanted honesty. No games.

Trying to do the mature thing, she told herself

she was being dramatic and called him, sure that after she heard his voice she'd feel better and things would go back to the way they were.

"Nadia?"

"I miss you."

"Oh, good. I'm glad you called."

She smiled, but then frowned as he went on.

"I need your social security number."

Had he even heard what she said? "What for?"

"I have someone on the other line. I'm ready when you are."

She rattled off the numbers. "Elliot, I was thinking—"

"I have to go, Nadia. I'll call you later."

She frowned at her phone as the call ended. Baffled by his behavior, she growled and threw the phone into her bag. "And he thinks I'm bullheaded?"

At the studio, she paid a few bills. She needed to make more money if she ever wanted her independence back and looking over her enrollment lists for the fall, she'd be just making her rent and utilities, hardly anything left to save.

She drove to *Reflections*, Steve's new gym. As expected, he was already there.

"Nadia," he greeted, pressing a kiss to her cheek. "Sorry. I just finished up a training session. I'm sweaty."

"It's okay." Once they made it to his office in the back of his gym she sat in the chair across from his desk.

"How have you been?"

"I'm okay." She folded her hands so she wouldn't

fidget. "I wanted to see if you'd be interested in teaching some self-defense classes at the studio."

His expression was friendly but regretful. "I wish I could, but my roster's packed. Did you check with the guys at my old gym? I might be able to reach out and find someone there for you."

She trusted Steve and didn't want to work with someone she didn't know. "I don't know."

He eased back, his eyes appraising her. "Are you looking to make some extra money? I could put out a signup sheet for jazzercise."

The pay for a class like that was promising, being that Steve's gym was one of the nicest around and catered to an upper-class clientele. But that meant leaving her studio at night and losing a higher profit margin by sharing the cut with the gym.

"Do you think there would be takers if we did the class during the day?" Being that most of her students were school age, her days were pretty open.

"Nah. You might get two or three students, but not enough to make it worth your while."

She slouched. It was obvious how great Steve's business had been doing since meeting Asher. Asher paid Steve an incredible sum of money—Nadia could only imagine how much—for Steve's help with some things. His gym lacked nothing and everyone that worked there seemed happy.

Envy cut through her and she hated not being able to feel happy for her friend without feeling sorry for herself. "You guys are doing so well."

"Memberships are up thirty percent this quarter. Pretty amazing, since summer just ended."

Yes, it was amazing. Autumn, however, was her affluent time of year, with students registering and buying new leotards and tights from her inventory. But she was still struggling to make ends meet, her enrollment down twenty-five percent from the year before.

"How are things at the studio?" he asked.

She sighed. "We have less and less each year. I don't know what I'm doing wrong."

"Maybe it's not you. The neighborhood isn't what it used to be. You know what they say, *location, location, location.*"

When she'd started her business, the area was thriving with little kids and families. Now, it had issues with gang violence and houses foreclosing. "I can't raise my prices. That's all my clients can afford."

"So maybe look for a new studio and keep the prices the same. That might get you an increase of clients at least."

"I can't do that right now. I'm saving for an apartment." Her lease at the studio was month to month, but a new place would require a deposit. "I have to find a place to live before I do anything about the studio."

He frowned. "Where are you staying?"

She hesitated, a strip of her pride bracing to tear away each time she admitted she could no longer support herself. "With a friend."

"Do I know her?"

"Yes, but it's a him."

His brows quirked. "Who?"

She shifted in her seat. "It's Elliot Garnet."

"You're living with Elliot? Since when?"

"It's new. We're ... dating."

Steve's jaw dropped. "You're dating Elliot Garnet? Asher's friend? I wasn't even sure he liked women."

She laughed. "He does."

"That's great, Nadia. I think you'd be good for him. And he seems like a..." His eyes tilted upward as if trying to think of the right term. "Straightforward guy."

Sure, Elliot was direct, but that was only the tip of the iceberg, a tip she was coming to realize others often mistook as the whole of him. "He can be very sweet."

Steve eased back in his chair and laughed. "You and Elliot ... shacking up. I never saw that coming."

"The living situation's temporary. He's just helping me out."

"But you two *are* involved?" He laughed and shook his head. "Dating?"

"Yes. Why is that so hard to believe?"

He shrugged. "I guess it's not. But I get why you wouldn't want to live with someone you just started dating. Sort of blurs the lines."

"Exactly."

"Well, maybe I can help you out. Asher helped me, and I'm in a position to pay it forward." He reached into his desk drawer and pulled out a pamphlet. "I've been toying around with the idea of buying up the space next door. It'd make a great dance studio."

She frowned. "I can't afford—"

"No, no." He waved a finger. "I'm not suggesting

you bid on it. I was thinking *partner*. We've known each other for years. I think you're great at what you do. I'd love to bring your talent in full time. A chunk of my members are women and our daycare is thriving. There's your clientele. You could determine the prices, control the schedule, and I'd get a cut of the profits in lieu of rent. It'll draw in new clients for both of us and probably keep you a hell of a lot more busy than you are downtown."

She sat back, understanding the appeal but thinking it was a lot of work when Steve already seemed busy enough. "You would honestly do that?"

He shrugged. "Why not? I mean, if the price is right and we can work the numbers. I've been thinking about opening up an area for kids to exercise, but I couldn't run it myself. I'd be outsourcing the position anyway. This could be exactly what we both need. Mom could drop little Sally off at tap while she gets an hour in on the elliptical. It could be a win for everyone."

"I don't know if my clients would drive this far."

"I know you love your students, Nadia, but you have to make a living. You'd have a full roster here. I guarantee it."

"How soon could this happen?"

He checked his schedule and reviewed the pamphlet. "We could probably make settlement a month or two after I put in an offer. I'd have to hire a subcontractor to do the construction. You could help with the layout. I'd say we could have you in there by the new year if all goes well with the sale. That gives you time to let your clients know you're moving."

"You say it like I've already agreed."

He tilted his head and grinned. "Come on, Nadia. I know you better than most people. You're a smart woman and you work like a mule when you want something. This is a good offer."

Her belly knotted as her mind searched for reasons to turn him down. "Would you need anything from me upfront?"

"It would be my property. You'd manage the business end of the studio. I wouldn't get paid until you opened for business, so, no. Once the details are ironed out, you could take your deposit from the old studio and put it toward an apartment. My neighborhood's nice."

She rolled her eyes. Steve lived in a gated community with modern rental houses. "You know I can't afford that neighborhood."

"You might be able to afford it soon. What do you say? Do we have a deal?" He held out his hand.

Biting her lip, she hesitated. It really was an incredible offer and as much as she'd miss the students she'd lose, she'd meet many more here. She stretched her hand sluggishly across the desk. "Thank you, Steve. I never expected this when I came here."

"I'm glad to help out a friend. I'll contact the realtor today and let you know if I make any progress."

While they were friends, this was a business venture. It was very different from taking money from someone she was intimately involved with. It was a big, scary change, but a good business decision for her company. And as she replayed the plan in her head, the more committed her heart became to the idea. It filled her with a sense of capability.

When she returned to her studio her mind was clearer than it had been in months. She purged many of her dated files and sorted through the paperwork she needed to keep. It was amazing how little she actually had to take with her to make this move in a few months.

She balanced her clients' accounts and contacted those who hadn't paid deposits yet. Tomorrow was her first class for the new school year, so she printed out notices about the studio's upcoming move and hung them around the building.

It was the same pre-season routine she did every fall, but with a big announcement for the future. Once she had all the paperwork for her students printed and updated, she set up a table for parents. Though she loved working with brides and grooms and teaching the occasional adult class, it was the children that really made her job a labor of love.

Feeling a bit anxious about the next day, she put on some music and did a run through of her favorite yoga positions to loosen up. Just as she was finishing up her routine, the bell on the front door jingled.

Elliot appeared, wearing a crisp suit and looking more like his usual self than he had in days, despite the bruises.

He rocked back on his heels and wedged his hands in his pockets. "Hi." He'd bought new glasses.

This man stirred so many intense emotions inside of her, his presence knocked her off balance. She'd been upset he'd been obsessing over the details of her grandmother's house, refusing to see a doctor about his injuries, but both were because of her. Maybe he wasn't the one being obsessive. Maybe she was obsessed with him and the slightest distraction made her jealous.

Crossing the room, she pressed her body to his and greeted him with a kiss. He pulled back too soon and she frowned. Putting distance between them, he cleared his throat and adjusted his glasses.

Trying to match his calm, she sipped her water. "I like your new glasses." The sharp, vintage frames gave him a Madison Avenue appeal. "They're sexy on you."

"I visited the optometrist at lunch today. If one more person asked what happened to my face I was going to strangle someone." He glanced at the wall where one of the notices hung. "What's this?" He stepped closer and frowned. "You're moving?"

"I actually had an interesting day. I met with Steve—"

"Steve the trainer?" He turned and faced her.

"Yes. I wanted to talk to him about possibly teaching some classes here this fall, but he's so busy he can't do it. He, um, made me an offer though."

His face blanked. "What sort of offer?"

"He wants to buy the building next to his and make it a studio. We'd be partners and I'd manage the business just like I do now, but he'd get a cut and we'd both profit from the shared clients."

"Did you have a lawyer draw up an agreement?"

She laughed. "No. Today was the first time we

talked about it. Besides, Steve's my friend. I trust him."

He pressed his lips together. She was already becoming familiar with his expressions and could tell he had something to say but didn't want to say it.

"What's the matter, Elliot?"

"That's a big decision. This is your studio, your business, and you're just going to sign over half of it to some guy? How long have you been thinking about doing this?"

"I wasn't thinking about it until the offer fell into my lap. But the truth is, I'm not doing well on my own. The studio would still be mine, but I'd have a partner to help with expenses."

"What if Steve's gym goes under? Where would that leave you?"

"Steve's doing great over there. He's doing me a favor, Elliot. If things don't improve, this could be my last season."

"A smart businessman wouldn't make a deal like that unless he had something to gain as well. Don't give him too much leverage. Partnerships are fifty-fifty."

She frowned. "I wouldn't have accepted the offer if I thought he was taking advantage of me."

"I'm not trying to offend you, Nadia. I know you're smart, but I also know you love the company you created. I'm just suggesting you think things over for a few days before you announce it to the world. Business deals fall through all the time and I don't want to see you get hurt."

He was acting like her financial advisor again. "I

appreciate your advice, but I have thought about it and this is what I want to do. It's a relief to know I have options. Honestly, I've been incredibly stressed trying to manage everything on my own."

His mouth flattened and he glanced away. "He isn't your only option. There are investors everywhere. Sometimes silent partners are better."

"Well, no one else has made an offer like the one I got today."

"What about me? I'd invest in a new studio for you."

She rolled her eyes. No more mixing business with pleasure. While he had a fascinating business sense, it embarrassed her every time she required his help. She didn't want him to see her struggle. She wanted to show him that she could be a successful woman, the sort that rose to his standard. She wanted to prove she could run her own life, like most American women.

"Thank you, but you've done enough."

"You said you were glad for my help. Now, you seem to be bothered by it."

She gathered her belongings and dropped them into her bag. "I appreciate everything you've done, Elliot, but it's enough. I need to do some things for myself."

He followed her toward the bathroom. "With Steve's help?"

She dumped her water bottle in the sink. "Is this about what's best for my business or something that makes my boyfriend uneasy? Steve's my friend, my colleague. That's it. You don't have to feel threatened by him."

"I don't feel threatened."

She glanced over her shoulder and arched a brow. "Are you sure?"

"Yes. I feel ... territorial. You're my girlfriend."

She smirked, appreciating his honesty. Shutting out the bathroom light, she faced him.

"And that's exactly what I want to be to you. I don't like being a charity case. I want to be your lover, your friend, not an inconvenience you support, or someone you have to constantly rescue."

"You're not an inconvenience." His chest lifted as he stared at her, his pupils dilating. "And I like rescuing you."

She stepped closer to him and cupped his jaw. "You've taken me into your home, flown me across the world, helped my family with getting approved for a loan, and brawled with Roland for me. I think your work in the rescue department is done." She kissed his bruised cheek. "I need my independence where I can get it, Elliot."

He caught her hand and kissed her wrist, his observant gaze stealing her breath as he once again showed her the affection she'd come to desire from him, the affection she'd been missing over the last two days. Maybe now they could move forward and put the pain of the last few days behind them.

His voice lowered to a soft whisper, his words teasing over her skin and putting her into some sort of trance. "I know you're an independent woman. I admire that about you. But I'll never stop trying to help you. That's who I am."

And she'd be lying if she claimed his heroism didn't touch something deep inside of her. "You are relentless, mister." She sighed, pulling her hand away. When he looked at her like that, she became a puddle of need, and in regard to her studio, she'd already made up her mind. "Let me do this on my own. Please. I know you can probably do it faster and easier, but I need to know I can, and you'll see I can take care of myself."

His mouth twisted. "You don't have to prove anything to me. I know who you are."

"Then you know why it's important for me to do this without you."

"Will you let my lawyer write up an agreement for you, just as a precaution?"

She groaned and turned away. "You are a pain in my *csikk.*"

"Does that mean ass?"

"Pretty much," She picked up her bag. "Let's go eat. I've had a very long day and I'm starving."

He didn't move.

She paused, trying to decipher the look in his eyes. "What?"

"I … want to kiss you."

She pivoted toward him and smiled. He could be so powerful and so vulnerable at the same time. It was the perfect storm and she couldn't help being drawn into those wild eyes. "*There* is the side of you I adore." She slowly approached him and looped her arms around his neck. "When you look at me like that—hungry and direct—I want to grant your every wish, like you're my master and I'm a slave to your desires. My mouth is yours, mister. Do as you please." His lips brushed hers as he caught her hips, dipping her back and not pulling away until she was dizzy.

She blinked up at him, debating if she wanted to go to dinner or his bed. "Will you sleep in my room tonight?"

"No." Her heart jerked, but then he grinned and said, "You'll sleep in mine."

Satisfied, she nipped at his lips and giggled when he growled, kissing her deeply again.

18

"My precious..."
~Gollum

THEY WENT to a little Chinese restaurant in the city. On the drive back home, Elliot was quiet, but she was coming to realize his silence wasn't a bad thing. It was simply part of the man he was, only speaking when he had something important to say, and that made his words all the more valuable. She, on the other hand, got squirmy when things got too quiet.

"I hate the rain," she said, hoping to stimulate some conversation.

"At least it isn't a storm."

"I'd rather a storm. At least then there's some passion. This endless drizzle makes me edgy."

He pulled into his driveway. "You don't seem edgy."

"Well, I am."

He glanced at her and removed the key from the ignition. "Maybe you need to catch up on sleep. It's been a long week."

"I'm not tired." If anything she had too much energy and needed an outlet—preferably sex. She shivered as the drizzle dampened her clothes.

He walked her to the door and flipped on some lights. "I spoke to the bank several times today. The paperwork should be ready in a day or two."

Dropping her bag by the front door, she shook out her hair and waited for him to look at her.

He removed his suit jacket and hung his laptop case on the hook in the hall. "You'll need to sign everything with a notary present, but we have a woman who does that at my office."

Toeing off her shoes, she placed them by the door. Elliot sorted through the mail on the foyer table, still not looking at her, so she removed her shirt. Nothing.

"Once that's done, we'll forward everything back to the bank in Budapest and your grandmother will have to sign off on everything."

"Elliot."

He turned and stilled, his gaze fastening to her bra. "I ... thought you should know."

He didn't move closer to her or put down the mail. Patiently, she sighed. "You talk too much about business. Don't you ever just want to have fun?"

"Business can be fun."

"Oh, yes, with all the acquisitions and mergers and money talk. Enough with the house. You said you'd handle it and I trust you to do just that. When the papers get here, I'll sign. Until then, could we please be a normal couple? I feel like we haven't had a normal conversation since we slept together."

His brow creased as he put the mail on the table, his posture defensive. "What does that mean?"

How could she explain her feelings to him without offending him? While she loved his intellect, he sometimes used it as a shield and it seemed he'd been doing that with her for days. She didn't want him to hide from her, she wanted his playful side. She didn't want to discuss business any more than she wanted to discuss the weather.

"It means forget about that stuff for now. We're home. Let's say goodbye to the stresses of the day and talk about something else."

He frowned. "I assumed hearing that things were working out would *relieve* your stress, not add to it."

Although she appreciated his help, it was overshadowing every minute of their time together since he woke her up that morning with the idea that he could financially save her family. She didn't want to be a problem he had to fix. She just wanted to be herself with him—no solution needed.

"Elliot, I want to be with you, but you have a habit of making every conversation a game of finding the solution. I know you enjoy problem-solving, but I don't want to be a problem you must solve. I want to be the woman you want to love."

"I..." He glanced away then quickly said, "Helping those I care for is the only way I know how to communicate my feelings."

"There are other ways couples communicate. There's body language." Let him try to talk finances that way. She was pretty sure it was impossible.

His expression turned wounded. "I want to be with you. I just…" He shook his head. "I'm not sure how normal couples act in private, but I'm pretty certain I can't maul you the second we walk through the door. We're not animals."

"But we are." Relieved he wasn't losing interest, she relaxed and tried a more delicate approach. "Well, we can talk about our day, make plans for tomorrow or the weekend, dream about places we want to visit together. But we need to talk about more than business. This is not business." She hooked her thumbs and pushed down her pants, standing before him in only her panties and bra. "This is very, very personal."

His gaze drifted to the floor. "I'm not good at small talk. I've never been good at it."

"Just say the first thing that comes to mind. What are you thinking right now?"

He glanced at her and looked away, mouth tight as if holding back his words.

"It's okay to tell me what you're thinking, Elliot. I want to know. You don't have to do me favors to make me want to listen. You already have my full attention."

He shifted but kept his distance. Never in her life had she met a man so closed off to simple conversation.

He cleared his throat. "I want to kiss you … all the time."

Well, there was something. She smiled. "Then why don't you?"

"Because..." His mouth flattened as he wedged his hands in his pockets. "If I kissed you every time it crossed my mind you'd get sick of me and I'd become nothing more than a pest."

She scoffed at such an absurd statement. "Your kisses are not pestering me. I happen to like when you're affectionate. Why hold yourself back?"

He glanced away. "I don't want to ruin what we have."

"You won't. Women like affection. At least I do."

He shifted his foot, his gaze diverted to the floor. Maybe she was putting too much pressure on him. She wanted to know him better, so she could read his signals easier.

"Then let's just talk," she suggested, trying to put him at ease. "Tell me something about yourself that I don't know."

"There isn't much to know. I eat, sleep, and work."

She waved a finger. "Not true. I know you have secrets. Tell me one and I'll tell you one of mine."

His brow creased, as he appeared to silently wager a mental debate. It shouldn't be that difficult for him to talk to her. If they couldn't find one topic in common they had a big problem. She tried to think about something she wanted to know about him.

She thought of that morning when she'd been searching for an umbrella, the room with floor to ceiling shelves seemed an interesting topic. It looked like a storeroom, brimming with little boys' toys, but not a single one was out of its package. Finding all those unopened toys said something about this man, but she wasn't sure what.

"Why do you have so many toys in that room upstairs?"

His head snapped up, his gaze connecting with hers for a split second then pulling away. "They're not toys. They're collector's items."

"But they are toys. They were made for children to play with, no?"

"They were. When were you in that room?"

"I was looking for a coat closet. I needed an umbrella this morning. Are you donating them somewhere?"

"No. They're mine." His jaw twitched. "Some of them are from my childhood."

"Oh." What would a man want with so many toys? "Why do you keep them?"

"I like them."

"Do you play with them?"

"No." His posture tensed and she sensed he didn't want to discuss this either. Another closed off part of him. Meanwhile, several of her vulnerabilities had been exposed over the past week.

"I'm not judging that you have them, I just wonder why they're not opened. Didn't you play with your toys as a child?"

"They're more valuable in their packages."

Her head tilted as she looked at him, his gaze skating away from hers. What child had so much discipline they could accumulate so many unopened toys? Little boys were meant to get dirty and break things, but Elliot was so meticulous, he preferred to keep his fun things packaged on a shelf. Had he been that way even as a child?

His restraint was as curious as it was baffling. "Didn't you ever want to open them? Play with them as they were intended?"

"Sure, but then they'd be worthless."

"But the experience might be priceless."

Expression tight, he glanced at her. "When you appreciate how rare something is, you understand it should be kept safe. If I played with them every time the desire crossed my mind they'd be ruined by now."

She was noticing a pattern. He didn't want to kiss her because he feared he'd pester her and scare her away. Did he see that he was treating her like another prized toy, too afraid to play with her because he might somehow damage their relationship?

The unopened toys were plastic, so it was foolish to feel sorry for them. But she was real. She also didn't come in a perfect package. She had flaws and emotions—and feelings.

"I once had a doll with a broken hand," she said softly. "Our dog chewed the fingers off and her hair was patched with bald spots from all the times I brushed it. Her skin was dirty and her one eye never stayed open, but I loved that dolly like she was my baby. To imagine never playing with her for fear that she might get messy... So many happy moments would have been lost."

His breathing became noticeably strained as if

her story made him uncomfortable. "I've collected them for decades. To me, they're not toys. They're worth a lot of money."

She frowned. Didn't he have enough money? "Do you plan to sell them?"

"No, but if I ever have kids I'd pass the collection on to them."

"And what if your child wants to open one and play with it?"

"That's not what they're for. I'd teach him or her how to treat them."

"Well, you have an answer for everything." She turned, sad for him and sad for the kids he might someday have. And sad that every time she tried to penetrate his walls he seemed to construct another one right before her eyes.

"Nadia, what's wrong?"

"Nothing. I just... I wonder why you hesitate, always measuring consequences before doing anything, but I guess that's just who you are. If there isn't a feasible outcome written in black and white, you hold back."

"What are you talking about?"

"You're so guarded, Elliot. Contracts. Attorneys. Shelves full of unopened toys. Where do all these trust issues come from?"

"Are you talking about your deal with Steve? It's poor practice not to protect a business agreement with a signed—"

She growled and covered her face. "Did you make a contract with Asher when you started your company?"

"Eventually, yes. It isn't an uncommon practice. I know you've worked with Steve before, but this is your livelihood. You'd be tying yourself to the success of someone else's company. Things could go wrong."

"I know that. But today I was excited. This is a new adventure for me, but when I told you, all you could do is worry. I know it might not work out perfectly, Elliot, but I'm okay with getting a little dirty in the process. You have to break some eggs to make a cake. Sometimes risks are fun."

"And sometimes being proactive is safest."

He wasn't making the connection. This was more than business. This was the way he approached *everything*—including her. He needed to let go.

She walked up to him and kissed him hard. His hands caught her waist as she drove her tongue into his mouth, pulling his jacket down his shoulders and reaching for his belt.

His fingers closed around hers and he broke the kiss. "What are you doing?"

"Let's be messy. Show me your reckless side."

He stepped back. "I don't understand what's happening. We were talking about your studio and now you're taking off my clothes."

Her gaze dropped to his belt. He wasn't aroused. As she looked back at his face she realized he was irritated and embarrassment spiked in a way she wasn't used to with other men.

"I'm sorry. I... I don't know what I was trying to do." She was begging for him to let her in.

"Are we in an argument?"

Feeling rejected and confused by his restraint, she put more space between them. "No."

"Then what is this, Nadia? I don't understand why you're picking a fight."

"I'm not picking a fight." The truth was, she was scared. Elliot was smarter than her and she enjoyed his intellect, but sometimes she felt two steps behind, with no hand reaching to help her catch up. And here she was making a fool of herself, throwing herself at him in her underwear when he only wanted to talk.

Maybe he had a point. Perhaps she was too reckless. If she behaved as cautiously as Elliot, she wouldn't have half the problems she had with men, money, and life in general.

She'd based so much of her future on the short conversation with Steve today only to have Elliot spot every possible pitfall in a matter of seconds. She was burying her head in the sand about her family's financial situation at home, while he was making phone calls across the world to solve her problems. She had nowhere to live and a boyfriend whose house was so immaculate even his playthings were put away on shelves.

What if it was only a matter of time before he realized she was too damaged to fit neatly in his orderly life? Maybe he'd grow tired of identifying all the ways her life was a mess... her family, her finances, her history. While she loved being with him, it was starting to feel like a privilege she might not deserve. And his recent preoccupation with her ongoing dilemmas seemed to be building additional space between them when she just wanted him to hold her and play with her, be intimate and close to her. Maybe her mother was right...

"I'm sorry. I... I think I'm just tired." Glancing down at her exposed body, she flushed. She stepped back and wondered if she'd always question if she was good enough, would always come to the uncomfortable conclusion that she wasn't.

Brow tight, he frowned at her but said nothing. She felt exposed and embarrassed the longer he studied her like a problem he couldn't solve.

She was humiliating herself. "I think I'll go to bed now. Forget what I said. You take care of things. More people should be as cautious as you."

She turned, scooped up her discarded clothes, and took the stairs, only wanting to escape her unstable life and the blinding perfection beaming from his. He took the steps behind her and once she reached the landing, he caught her hand.

"Are you mad about my collection?"

She worried that was the only way he knew how to enjoy life, by conserving the things he loved so nothing bad ever happened. He was always saying how beautiful she was, but what if that was all he liked about her? She didn't want to sit on a shelf. But the closer they became the less intimacy they shared.

She wanted him to play with her, muss her clothes and show his spontaneous side. But what if he didn't have a spontaneous side?

Elliot didn't appear to make mistakes. He was too meticulous and, sooner or later, he'd learn parts of her weren't so pretty. Some parts were beyond repair.

"I'm not angry. We're just different."

"But..." His eyes flashed with worry. "What are you saying, that we're *too* different?"

"No. I don't know. I've never met anyone like you, Elliot. It's intimidating."

"What is?"

"*You.*"

He took a step back and laughed without humor. "Do you have any idea how ridiculous that sounds coming from you?"

"I'm not being ridiculous. Look at your home, your life." She waved a hand, encompassing all the immaculate beauty that surrounded him. "I don't know where I fit in."

"I see." His hands returned to his pockets.

She didn't want to insult him. "I just wish you would open up with me so I can understand you better. I want to understand *you*, Elliot."

He looked at the floor. "I spent a lot of my life not knowing where I fit in. You asked about my collections... They're more than toys to me. You can't just go to the store and acquire those items. Some took years of searching. It's something that kept me busy when I had nothing better to do."

"But you have so many."

His gaze shifted to hers. "I had a lot of free time on my hands."

"Didn't you do things with friends? Go to parties or hang out?"

His cheek twitched as his eyes shielded. "No, Nadia. I collected toys. I never went to parties and I didn't date. The highlight of my social calendar has been Comic Con for the last decade. I'm not going to stand here and be judged for something that doesn't harm anyone and I find enjoyable."

She drew back. There was a difference between judging someone and trying to understand them. "Now *you* are angry."

Accusation flashed in his eyes. "What do you want from me? This is who I am. It's who I've always been. I don't judge you for the things you like."

"I'm not judging you!"

"Yes, you are. You don't understand the hobby so you see it as a juvenile pastime."

"Elliot, that's not how I see it. It's clearly important to you. The only reason I brought it up was because seeing all those unopened items scared me."

"Why should they scare you?"

She looked at him, wishing for a moment he could see that she had insecurities too. "I worry that's the only way you know how to treat things that are important to you."

"There's nothing wrong with taking care of my possessions."

"You're right. But I don't like feeling like one. If you put me on a shelf, I won't stay there. I'm your *girlfriend*. I want you to play with me. Show me I'm wanted and you have more to give me than business advice. Otherwise, I feel meaningless."

The color washed from his features as he blinked at her. "I... I don't see you as my possession."

"Then what *do* you see me as?" She took his hand and pressed it to her chest where her heart pounded. She knew she was putting it all out there but felt if she didn't do it now, the distance between them would only grow until they could no longer reach each other.

"I'm as human as you are, Elliot. I like to feel you next to me. My skin hungers for contact and I want to be touched. When I kiss you and you push me away, I don't know how to interpret that."

His brow pinched as he blinked at her. "I didn't realize... Damn it, Nadia, if you think I don't want you, you're crazy. I can barely breathe for wanting you. But I'm trying to be a gentleman. I'm not going to just ravish you like some caveman every time we're together."

"Why not? If that's what you want, then do it. Maybe I want you to."

His Adam's apple shifted as he swallowed, drawing her attention to his perfectly knotted tie. "I don't like craving things outside of my control. When people rely on others too much they end up disappointed, because a sense of entitlement takes over, but eventually ... people change their minds."

"I see."

"You have to understand that this isn't normal for me. You're the first woman to ever look at me like I'm worth anything—*me*, not my home or my assets. I've never gotten anything I wanted in this world without analyzing every possible outcome. And no matter which way I look at it, the probability of a woman like you falling for a man like me doesn't add up. The minute I lose my head, stop playing it safe, something will shift. I want you too much to get distracted and mess this up."

"Mess this up? Elliot, the only way we can ruin this is if we ignore our chemistry. Come at me with everything you've got. I want you to."

He didn't say anything, his eyes telling her how little he believed her. What could have happened to this man to make him so distrusting of others?

"You don't believe me."

He glanced away. "Women like you don't—"

"Women like me—what does that even mean? I am me and there is no other." She grabbed his jaw and turned his face so he looked her in the eye. "I am telling you that I love you, Elliot. I do not say those words easily. And my feelings are not because of your financial stability or anything else you want to blame. It's you I care about, you who attracts me, not your money or house or the way you look. You could have asked me out a year ago, Elliot, and I would have accepted, because I find you incredibly attractive, but I would have quickly learned how different you are from other men. There is no hiding how special you are. Why do you believe you are somehow less than the rest of the men out there when you're so much more? Why can't you see what I see?"

His expression was unreadable. "Trust me, Nadia, I see exactly who I am."

Her heart pinched as she realized how much she overestimated his confidence. Perhaps she'd even overestimated his affection for her, but his reserve did nothing to diminish her feelings for him. Everything she'd said had been true. Stepping close to him, she wrapped her arms around his waist and rested her head on his strong shoulder.

"I love you, Elliot. Because you are sweet and gentle and honest to a fault when you actually tell me what's going on in your head. You don't have to hide yourself from me or be some sort of savior in order for me to love you. I want to know all of you, the real you. I'm sorry if my curiosity came off as judgmental. I would never judge you because you have yet to judge me and there's plenty to criticize."

His arms slowly closed around her and squeezed. "I'm sorry for getting defensive. I don't want to lose you. I'll figure out how to do this, but it's going to take some time."

"I'm not going anywhere."

He let out a deep breath. "You have to be patient with me. I'm not someone who hurries things and I hate feeling like I'm being rushed, especially when it's something important to me."

"Learning curve."

He chuckled. "Right. A learning curve."

The walls that protected him were thick and reinforced by time. "I can be patient so long as you remember you are not a pest and passion shouldn't be controlled." She stroked his tie. "You have to let it out or it will eat you up inside. Don't hide your desires from me. I want the whole you."

His breathing labored as his face pinched and he seemed to struggle to get his words out. "I've thought about you every day since I first met you, Nadia. The amount of passion I'm holding in is frightening."

"Since the night you brought me here?"

"No. Since the day Asher brought me to your studio."

"But you barely looked at me. You never said anything."

His gaze drifted to the wall. "I figured you were taken."

She pulled his chin back to hers and brushed his lips with her mouth. "I would have gone out with you." To think, all this time she could have been with him instead of Ian and the two before him.

He swallowed. "I dreamed of returning to your studio and telling you how I felt. I've had countless fantasies. But never in a million years did I think that you'd actually be with me."

Her heart jerked at his admission, a piece of the wall shifting. Lifting her lashes, she smiled into his eyes. "Did you touch yourself when you had fantasies about me?"

His jaw twitched as color stole across his cheeks.

"I'll take that as a yes." She smiled. "You're a living, breathing, red-blooded man, Elliot. Stop pretending you're above carnality. Give in. Take what you want. You don't have to fantasize anymore. Be yourself. That's the man I want in my bed."

He glanced at her over the rims of his glasses. "You're sure."

"Positive."

"Now?"

She shrugged. "If that was our first argument, maybe we should make up."

His hand caught the back of her neck, tipping her head to the side as his mouth sealed over hers. He gripped her hip, backing her to the wall as his tongue pierced her lips.

Rising to her toes, she dropped her clothing and met his passion with her own. "Yes, take what you want," she rasped as his mouth worked down her throat, his hands stripping her bra to her waist.

He kissed her deeply, his hand gripping her breast as his other hand cupped her sex through her panties. She moaned, grateful to finally see his control slide.

"I want *you*," he growled into her mouth. "So much I can hardly think straight."

She cupped him, stroking his engorged flesh through his pants. "Take me."

His hand wedged into the front of her panties, delving into her sex and she gasped.

"You wear too many clothes." She jerked at his tie, loosening the knot as his fingers grazed her clit.

She ripped open his shirt and buttons went pinging across the floor. "Sorry."

He growled, his lips and teeth scraping down her shoulder as his finger surged deep and her body pressed into the wall.

"More."

He fingered her harder, his mouth dropping to her breast as he sucked her nipple between his lips. He switched to her other breast as his fingers worked her into a frenzy of pleasure.

Her focus somehow dropped to his belt, unfastening the leather and pulling it free with a hiss and a snap. She caught his scorching flesh in her palm, curling her fingers around his thickness and stroked hard.

"I want to be inside of you," he hissed, removing his fingers and staggering back.

Pressed against the wall, her breath caught as she stared at him, shirt gaping, chest heaving, eyes wild as his thick cock pushed hard against the elastic of his briefs. She licked her dry lips.

"Condom."

Reaching for his wallet, he quickly withdrew a condom and tossed his wallet to the floor. He sheathed himself and crowded her against the wall. "Is this okay?"

"Don't ask. Just do."

He glanced down, left, right, and back to her. "Turn around."

She twisted so she faced the wall, her body desperate to feel him inside of her. Angling her body, she quivered as he stepped close, lining up his cock with her sex.

His hands caught her hips, hitching her posture in a way that gave him easier access and he plunged into her. His fullness stretched her and she contracted around his length. Her palms slid up the wall, her nails digging into the expensive wallpaper as he thrust again.

"God, you're amazing," he growled, thrusting harder.

"Don't stop!" He was so deep, so possessive. This was the side of him she wanted, so unrefined, disheveled, and raw.

His hands released her hips and gripped her breasts, pulling tightly as he rammed into her, driving her up on her toes. He pinched her nipples, lowering his other hand to her pussy and teasing her clit. She keened breathily as pleasure knifed through her, her knees trembling.

A wave of ecstasy stole through her and she was coming. He fucked her harder, confessing a litany of naughty demands.

"I want to fuck you every hour of the day. I want your scent all over me. Mine all over you. You're like an addiction I need to feed and I'm tired of fighting it."

Her mind short-circuited as one orgasm folded into another. She wanted all of those things, too.

"I want to be everything you need. I want to know all your desires and make them realities. I want to make you happier than any other man ever has."

She surged forward as he pumped his hips hard, his flesh smacking deliciously with hers. He caught her at the waist, thrusting deep and groaned, his body shaking with a shiver behind her, his release escaping with a guttural moan laced with the relief of finally letting go.

They panted in the silent hallway, a sense of lib-eration blanketing her. He took a staggering step back and her body quivered as his support eased. She glanced over her shoulder and he looked away.

"Sorry. I don't know—"

She twisted and caught his face between her hands. "You do not apologize for that, Elliot. *That* was passion, and I'm glad to see you have so much." She kissed him hard and felt his tension ease as his arms gently wrapped around her.

Pulling back, she whispered, "I love you. I loved *that*. Don't you dare hide that side of yourself from me, do you understand?"

He nodded tightly. His clothes were a mess. His shirt was ripped, his tie was undone, and his part obliterated. "I didn't know women ... liked... You're sure I wasn't too rough with you?"

She smiled and arched a brow. "It shouldn't matter what women like, only what *your* woman likes. I like when you take control and I like when you lose it. Don't be ashamed of your desires. I want to know all of them."

His head lifted and something heady flashed in his eyes. It was as if her words unleashed a part of him he'd kept tethered for far too long, the metaphorical leash fraying with each praising word she spoke. Maybe if she encouraged him enough, that tie he kept fastened around his control would snap.

"Don't be afraid to tell me what you want, Elliot. It might surprise you the things I'd do to see you happy."

His hand caught her neck, his thumb brushing possessively over her jaw. "I want you to sleep in my bed."

Rising to her toes, she kissed him. "You're very sexy when you're direct. But I already told you I wasn't letting you go tonight. Take me to bed, Mister Caveman."

19

―――――

"IF I HAD to choose a superhero to be, I would pick
Superman. He's everything that I'm not."

~Stephen Hawking

Elliot awoke just as the sky faded from
sapphire to vibrant shades of gold, Nadia's
warm body curled into his side. Last night, the things
she said struck a nerve. At first, he thought she was
making fun of him, but then he understood her
point. He'd made a habit of collecting treasures but
never allowed himself the pleasure of actually
touching all he'd accumulated over the years.

It was scary, giving up the manageable control
he'd ensured after years of having none, but he
wanted to prove to her that he could satisfy all her

needs better than any other man. Urgency thrummed in his veins to demonstrate his virility every second she was within reach.

Part of him wanted to go into the spare room and rip open his Masters of the Universe Eternia Set, the Holy Grail of He-Man collectibles. But another part, the part that understood how infinite loneliness could be, shuddered at the thought.

Too many negative experiences from his past warned how dangerous it was to trust in others. Something always drove them away in the end. But maybe Nadia truly was different. Baby steps.

She seemed to truly want to know him and she promised not to judge the secrets he shared. He didn't know a life without judgment, nor had he ever met a person above judging others. Even he could be over critical of others at times.

Glancing at the stunning woman beside him, a wealth of thick, black hair fanning across his arm, he was filled with a surreal sense of possibility. Last night had been immeasurably liberating. So much pent-up desire burst from him and she hardly flinched when he showed her how desperately he wanted to possess her. The things he'd said, secrets he never dreamed of uttering, she greeted each confession with what seemed like genuine acceptance.

Though he'd entertained countless fantasies about her, each one the epitome of perfection, he much preferred the reality. Past her beautiful exterior, she was messy, stubborn, and exceedingly difficult at times. If those were her flaws, he was more than happy to accept them. That was the real her, not some fantasy he'd concocted in his mind.

He laughed to himself. *She's real. This is really happening.* He wondered if he'd ever come to terms with the surreal happiness filling him.

She made him step outside of his comfort zone. When Roland grabbed her, he saw red and the next thing he knew the son of a bitch was pummeling him. Yet, for some reason, those bruises felt different from all the others he'd earned over the years. He didn't care that his face was still sore and his lip still hurt. He was damn proud of those pains because he hadn't run away. He'd run to her defense and that was exactly the man he wanted to be, always there when she needed him. A hero.

She was worth every scrape and bruise. She was his girlfriend and no man would touch her so long as he breathed. That's how true heroes behaved. They weren't fearless, but they had the courage to act in the face of fear. Roland had terrified him, but Elliot hadn't balked.

Mine. The word rolled through his mind like a rumble of thunder. His body thickened as he again admired her naked form curled into his side. When was she going to wake up? Would he get to be with her again before work?

Take control...

Easing the blankets off of her body, he watched as her nipple pebbled against the cool air. He shifted, rolling her onto her back, still asleep. He glanced at the nightstand, mentally counting the condoms he had left in the drawer. He needed to buy more.

That's a new item for the shopping list. He chuckled silently.

Her arms rested on the pillows, her body stretched before him. He pulled back the sheet where it lay over her hips and his mouth went dry. Would she be upset if he touched her?

He ghosted a finger up her thigh and she sighed, her legs slightly shifting. "Nadia, are you awake?"

Nothing.

He traced a finger over her flat belly, circling the jade piercing, and she hummed in her sleep, her nipples pebbling tighter. Gently moving her legs, he kneeled between them and leaned over her, licking at the tip of her breast. When she didn't respond he licked the other one. His lips closed over the tip and he sucked gently, his body slowly rocking over hers.

She inhaled on a moan and arched into him. He raised his head, feeling like a kid caught with his fist in the cookie jar. "Did I wake you?"

"Yes, but it's a nice way to be woken up."

He nuzzled her throat, kissing her soft skin, his erection dragging heavily against her thigh. "I want you."

"I'm yours."

There had never more magical words. He slid lower, spreading kisses over her ribs and stomach until he was exactly where he wanted to be. Gently parting her folds, he teased her and she moaned softly. The scent of her arousal crawled into him and he tasted her heaven.

She mumbled something in Hungarian he interpreted as praise as her limbs stretched to give him easier access. Feeding his fingers inside of her, he took exactly what he wanted.

"There," she gasped as he thrust deeper.

He glanced up at her in question. "This?"

"Right where you just touched. Do it again."

Retracing his steps, he pressed his fingers deep. "Here?"

She moaned, her back arching into the pillows. "Yes. Right there."

He focused on that area, penetrating slowly. She sucked in an audible breath, her cries finding a quick rhythm and suddenly she was trembling beneath him, calling out his name.

Every time was more beautiful than the last. He reached for the condom and her legs opened in invitation. Lining his body up with hers, he entered her slowly and they both groaned in pleasure.

She held his stare as he rocked into her, her eyes replete and her cheeks flushed. Her beauty was staggering at times, especially when they shared such an intimate connection.

"You're so beautiful," he told her, stealing a kiss. She never showed much response when he complimented her beauty, but he couldn't hold back the words. Everything about her emanated sexiness. Even a blind man would find her stunning.

Her legs curled around his hips, her fingers digging into his shoulders and sides. At times, he'd simply hold himself deep inside of her, luxuriating in the comfort she brought him. Nothing had ever felt so precious, so right.

"I could stay like this forever."

She moaned, her lashes fanning low. "Me too. It's lovely, isn't it?"

There simply weren't words for how *lovely* it was, not because it felt good, but because it was her—Nadia. Though he had no basis for comparison, he was certain she made these moments so much more intensely satisfying than any other woman could.

He rested with her as long as he could, but time was not their friend. Hating the idea of pulling away, he sighed. "I'm going to be late for work."

"You should call out sick. Stay home and make love to me all day."

He laughed. He'd already missed more work since meeting her than he had in the last decade. "I wish I could, but we have a meeting today and I have to be there."

"Will you pick me up from the studio again tonight?"

"I'd love to. What time does your last class end?"

"Seven."

That should work. He could work a few hours late and... "Shit, I forgot I made plans for tonight." His promise to have dinner with Asher had completely slipped his mind, but he couldn't ask for another rain check. "You could come with me."

"Where?"

"Asher's. He invited me over for dinner. I haven't seen Anakin in a while and I promised I'd come by after our trip."

She rolled to her side, resting her head on her palm. "Is Anakin Asher's little boy?"

"Yeah. He's named after—"

"Anakin Skywalker." She tapped a finger to his nose. "I pay attention."

He chuckled. "Yes, you do. Will you go with me?"

"Will they mind?"

"Of course not. You know Lettie. I'll let her know to set out two places for dinner."

"Okay."

He checked his watch. "Damn. I really have to go." Forcing himself out of bed, he turned and looked at her one last time. That was a mistake. "You don't make it easy."

She stretched her naked body over the sheets and pouted. "I don't want you to go yet."

"I don't want to go. But I have to get some things organized before my meeting."

"Fine." She rolled to her belly, giving him a spectacular view of her ass. "I'll entertain myself."

"You could watch a movie. The remote's in the drawer."

She rolled to her back again and cupped her breast. "I'm not in the mood for a movie." Her fingers slid across her skin, twisting over her nipple as she tipped her head back and shut her eyes.

He couldn't move. "What are you doing?"

She slid her other hand down her belly and between her legs. "Enticing you to stay."

He swallowed thickly, his body stiffening to a hunk of granite. His eyes widened as her hand slid lower. He couldn't miss his meeting, but how much did he really have to prepare? It seemed more important to see if she'd actually finger—

She was in. Dear God, she was masturbating

right on his bed. Was this an ordinary thing women did? She seemed pretty skillful. His lips parted, shallow breaths making his lungs work double time.

"Does it feel good?" he heard himself ask.

"Mm-hmm." She parted her knees, giving him a clear view of what she was doing and he forgot how to breathe.

He couldn't look away. Couldn't blink. "Touch your breasts again." And apparently, he couldn't control his inner monologue from escaping.

Her other hand drifted to her chest as she did as he instructed. Amazing.

"Do you like watching me, Elliot?"

"Yes," he rasped, debating if he should join her.

"I like watching too." She peeked at him from under her lashes. "Show me how you touched yourself all the times you fantasized about me."

He looked away. He should have never told her that.

She turned her cheek to the blankets, smiling at him. "Please. If you show me, I'll finish you with my mouth."

He was suddenly stroking himself. She was like a high sorceress, casting spells on him and making him do things he'd be mortified for the rest of the world to see. "Keep touching yourself."

Her body writhed as she pumped her fingers slowly between her legs. "Like this?"

She was messing with him. How was she so good at this? "Yes. And your breasts."

His dick throbbed in his grip as she arched and moaned. "Do you want me to come, Elliot?"

Dear God. "Yes."

Her fingers rolled over her clit as she plucked at her nipple, writhing and moaning. Her breath came quickly, filling the silent room as he stroked harder. Her body trembled, toes pointing, as she let out a long, breathy moan and shivered.

Lifting her hand, she gazed up at him, the proof of her release coating her fingers. "I've made a mess of myself."

He had to pinch back his release because it was easily the hottest fucking thing he ever watched. "Fuck..."

She giggled. "Your turn?"

He nodded, unsure if he could handle more.

She slithered off the bed, sauntering to where he stood and dropping to her knees. "Is this where you want me?"

"Yes." His throat was so tight no sound came out.

She cupped him and he sucked in a breath. "Tell me what to do, Elliot. I like when you're direct."

His words were scorched, rasping through his dry throat as he trembled on the verge of exploding. "Your mouth..."

Her lashes lowered and she curled her fingers around him, tracing her lips over his sensitive tip. "Like this?"

That was nice, but he wanted the real thing. "More."

She licked up his shaft and he breathed heavily through his teeth. Slowly, her lips parted and he considered the situation, wondering if this was what other women did or something uniquely Nadia.

As her breath teased his flesh he found himself creeping closer to release. "You're messing with me."

Her head cocked to the side, her eyes hypnotizing. "No. I'm giving you control. You're in charge. You have to say the words."

His inhalation was jagged. Say the words? Which ones? There were so many to choose from. "Put it in your mouth—all the way."

Amazingly, she complied. His body shivered as a rush of adrenaline followed the command. He jerked as heat engulfed him, giving him little chance to find his balance as she gripped his hips and sucked him to the back of her throat.

"*Fuck.*"

He cupped the back of her head, panting as her lips pressed all the way to his pelvis. Pulling back, his skin flashed wetly with her saliva and she went down again. When she held him tight, greedily, there was no chance of lasting.

A few strokes and his body pulsed. His spine tingled as he rose to his toes and choked out her name. "Nadia."

She didn't stop and everything felt too incredible. His release came like an avalanche, too forceful to slow.

"Nadia wait."

It was too late. His legs locked as his release jetted out of him.

"Shit."

She continued to suck and moan, her fist working out every drop of come to the point he wondered if she tasted his soul. She slowed and hummed, stroking him lightly as she gradually pulled back. Blinking up at him, she smiled slyly.

"All work and no play? I think not, Mr. Garnet."

Jesus, she was going to kill him.

20

"Nerd. **One whose unbridled passion for something defines who they are as a person, without fear of other people's judgment.**"

~Zachary Levi

*E*lliot strolled into work an hour late and whistling. The guys looked up from the round table as he settled into an empty seat.

"Sorry I'm late." *Not really.*

Asher and Jet frowned at him as Hunter asked, "Were you mugged?"

"No."

Jet frowned. "Where's your jacket and tie?"

He glanced at his chest and shrugged. "I didn't feel like wearing a tie today. And it's warm outside."

"What's going on?" Hunter asked, glancing at Asher who looked back to Elliot and raised a brow.

While he'd told the rest of the guys he'd banged up his face in a minor fender bender, Asher knew the truth. Mostly because he knew he'd gone away with Nadia and wouldn't let it rest until he told him where the black eyes had come from. Who knew the guys would be more concerned over the where-abouts of his formal accessories than they were his battered face.

"Maybe you hit your head harder than you thought when you got in an accident," Jet suggested.

Well, this was awkward. "Nothing's going on. It just didn't feel like a formal day. Sometimes casual is good."

"Call someone, Ash," Hunter mumbled. "He's lost his mind."

"I haven't lost my mind." Elliot rolled his chair closer to the table. "Catch me up. What did I miss?"

"Why were you late?" Jet asked, ignoring his request.

"I had company."

"Is your mom visiting?"

Elliot scowled at the jab. "No."

"Then who did you have over?"

This was exactly the sort of tedious dialogue he'd hoped to avoid. It shouldn't be a big deal. People were late all the time. His justification shouldn't matter.

"If you must know, I was with my girlfriend."

"Whoa!" Jet threw his arms up and slid back

from the table, his head shaking dramatically. *"What?"*

Elliot's mouth twitched, Jet's reaction a bit extreme. Was it so hard to believe a woman might like him?

"I don't think it's unfathomable I'm dating someone. And don't make jokes about my maid. It's not her. And *no*, you can't meet her."

"Why? What's wrong with her?" Hunter immediately asked.

"Nothing's wrong with her, you tit. I just don't want everyone involved in my personal life."

Jet laughed. "Do we know her? Who is she? Or ... is it a he?"

"It's a woman." The guys just stared at him and he turned to Asher. "Tell them it's a woman, Ash."

Asher held his hands up. "I'm out of it."

"Wait," Hunter looked at Asher then back to Elliot. "Ash knows who she is? How?"

Asher shrugged. "He told me."

"Forget it. I shouldn't have said anything. Just assume I had a flat and that's why I'm late. Let's get to work." He didn't want to discuss his personal life anymore.

"How long has Asher known?"

Asher shrugged. "Before he went to Budapest."

Hunter's eyes widened. "Did she go with you?"

Elliot groaned. "Yes, she went with me. Now, can we please get to work? Our meeting's in an hour."

Jet passed him a folder. Asher quickly summarized everything Elliot had missed, but Hunter wasn't as easily sidetracked.

"Wait a minute. You wanted to go to Budapest but had nothing planned. You were scrambling to schedule last minute meetings. That means you were going there for a reason. Are you involved in some mail order bride scam?"

"Screw you, and no. Drop it."

"Maybe she's from there," Jet said, back on the investigation trail. "Are you perusing Hungarian dating sites?"

"Oh, shit." Hunter's lips parted as he leaned back in his seat. "No. Way."

"What?" Jet asked, looking from Hunter to Asher to Elliot. "What did I miss?"

Hunter laughed and clapped his hands, rolling his chair back from the table and laughing. "It's the dancer!"

Elliot's face heated. "Did we get the metadata back from yesterday's run?"

"Asher's dancer?" Jet asked, expression one of disbelief. "I thought she was Guatemalan."

"She's not *my* dancer," Asher amended. Then he snickered. "She's Elliot's."

"Wait," Jet interrupted, shaking his head. "You're hooking up with the hot Guatemalan dance instructor?"

"She's not Guatemalan, you moron! She's Hungarian. Did you ever take geography? They're on two different continents."

"My lack of geographical knowledge is what's shocking you here? We *are* talking about the same woman, right?"

"This is exactly why I didn't want you to know."

Asher stood and patted Jet's shoulder. "Yes, it's the same woman. Her name's Nadia and she's Hungarian. Get yourself a globe. And Elliot, I don't know why you're being so secretive about this. I have to make a call before the meeting."

Hunter and Jet gaped at him as Asher left the room.

"What?"

Hunter scoffed and closed the folder in front of him, following Asher out of the office.

Elliot looked at Jet. "What's his problem?"

"You could have told us." He closed his folder as well. "Did you honestly think we'd make fun of you for dating her? Hell, who cares who she is, we'd only be happy for you, Elliot."

"That wasn't why I didn't want to tell you."

"Then why? You told Ash. Clearly, you kept this news from us for a reason."

Elliot ground his teeth and inwardly groaned. "Since the beginning of our friendship, I've ... disapproved of how ridiculous you guys got around women. I didn't want to get my balls broken."

Being that he was basically obsessed with Nadia and could hardly think of anything else, he was currently a wide-open target. But he didn't want his relationship viewed with the same callous indifference he'd shown Jet so many times in the past when he had a new flavor of the week. Nadia was a serious person in his life. She was off limits.

"Elliot, we're your friends. If we break your balls, it's out of love, man."

"That's what I mean. I don't want to hear it. I'm already nervous enough. She's ... incredible."

Jet grinned, a bit of awe in his eyes. "I'm happy for you."

Feeling like he might have overreacted, he figured he'd come clean. "There's more." Eventually, they'd all find out anyway. "She's living with me—*temporarily*. She was in a bind and I helped her out."

The sincerity of Jet's smile faded. "Were you hooking up with her before or after she moved in?"

"After, but it's not like that." At first, he thought her attention might have been some form of gratitude, but now he was certain she honestly cared about him. She said she loved him... "She means a lot to me."

Admitting how deeply he loved her felt dangerous, like inviting a permanent vulnerability into his life he wasn't sure he could handle. But the truth was becoming impossible to ignore. He loved her the first day he laid eyes on her, loved her *still* the night he rescued her from that asshole at the restaurant. And if it were possible, he loved her a little more with each passing moment. His affection for her behaved like a formulaic equation that infinitely increased and the sheer unwieldiness of his ever-growing emotions overwhelmed him.

"Well ... she's just the first girl. I'm sure there will be many more. Enjoy it."

Elliot's guard went up. "Why do you say it like that?"

Jet stood, his gaze skittering to the door. "I'm just saying have fun. Get laid. It's all good."

Elliot frowned as Jet left the office. What the hell was that? It was as if Jet knew something about Nadia Elliot somehow missed.

Jet knew lots of things about lots of women, but this seemed personal. He stood and went after him. "Jet, wait. Did you and Nadia go out or something?"

His friend laughed and shook his head. "No."

"Then why are you acting weird?"

"You guys act weird all the time. Suddenly it's a cause for concern?"

But they *were* weird. Jet was supposed to be the normal one. "Do you know something about her I don't?"

"No."

Well, then why the hell did he say that? It not only insulted him, it insulted Nadia. "I'm not just *getting laid*, Jet. I'm in love with her." The truth flung out, his anger and fear postponing his regret for sharing such an intimate secret.

Jet's eyes closed as if this were unfortunate news. "Just ... be careful, Elliot. I don't want you to get hurt."

"Nadia wouldn't hurt me." Not on purpose.

His friend looked at him, all humor replaced with assumed wisdom. "Are you sure?"

No one could ever be one hundred percent sure about such things, but he trusted her and she said no games. "She loves me."

"Look, it's not my place to tell you how to live your life, but this all seems a little fast. How long has she been staying at your place?"

"Two weeks." A slight exaggeration, but if estimations worked in math why not apply them in calculations of love?

Jet leveled him with a stare, his concern clear. "Women can be con artists, Elliot. I'm not saying she's that sort of woman but look at all you're doing for her. I know you. You're a good guy, but you don't usually put yourself in vulnerable positions. Vulnerability's your kryptonite." He frowned. "And I saw your car this morning. How is it the car looks fine and your face looks like that? Did someone beat you up?"

Deja vu from adolescence came rushing back. Whenever they had a run in with a bully, Jet insisted on squaring things up and rushing to their defense. But he wasn't a kid anymore. "No one beat me up. I got in a fight."

"Did Nadia have something to do with it?"

"Yes, but it's not like she started it. I did. Me."

"Just ... be careful."

Elliot absolutely hated vulnerable situations, but with Nadia it was different. Others wouldn't understand. "She's not that kind of woman."

Jet sighed. "I hope you're right."

21

———————

"My love for you is a puzzle, for which I have no answers."

~Padmé

"Don't forget your water bottles," Nadia called as her junior jazz class bagged up their shoes.

She mopped her brow with a cloth and caught her breath. It felt good to be back in the swing of a new season, even if teenage girls were a handful. One by one, the students said goodnight as their parents arrived to pick them up. When the last student was gone, she hit the shuffle button on her playlist.

Touch and Go's sensual beats of *Straight to Number One* echoed through the sound system. The erotic thrum of drums and lyrics drew her mind to visions of Elliot.

Her body heated at the mere thought of his shoulders, the way the muscles bunched under her fingers and the way the sweet tang of his skin tasted on her lips. She loved how his strong hands held her so possessively, making her weak in the knees every time he touched her.

Though she'd had many lovers, she couldn't recall a man ever possessing her on the level Elliot did, physically, emotionally... Dare she say spiritually? It was as if he was fully present in every caress, every kiss.

His affection was evident in every glance, so hungry, embarking on fully trusting. Each show of his trust took her deeper into this strange obsession with him, made her yearn for more. He was such an intense man, and she wanted to push his intensity to the brink, feel just how passionate he could be once he fully let go.

Her love was there, but their trust was only starting to build. Past experiences told her to move slowly this time, guard her heart no matter how much her instincts told her he was different. She wanted to give in and give him everything, but on the other hand, she wanted to be smart and not spoil what might be the most incredible relationship she ever had.

He wasn't like other men and that meant being hurt by him would carry twice, if not more, the usual impact of heartache. She didn't want him to break her heart, and if he didn't, he'd be one step ahead of all the rest. There was something so unique about him, she couldn't help the teasing thoughts of forever, but there was still a lot to learn about the man currently occupying her heart.

She could be a handful, yet he tempered her jagged edges. Perhaps it was the intense way he cared for her. Despite his reserved shyness, she believed Elliot loved her. He brought her emotions to a new level, one that intimidated her and shined a glaring light on all her shortcomings. More than anything, she didn't want to disappoint him.

"What's that face?"

Startled, she pivoted toward the doorway. And there he was, the man of her dreams. "I didn't hear the bell."

"Exactly why you need better security."

Her heart jerked with newfound anticipation of what the night might bring. "The new place will have something better, I'm sure."

He glanced at the bench. A paper granola bar wrapper and a water bottle lay forgotten on the floor. "How was your first day back in session?"

"It was good." She found it hard to meet his gaze, as her body seemed to pull into his orbit. She didn't want to come on too strong. She'd promised to be patient with him. "I just need to change my shoes and then we can go."

"Take your time."

She shut off the stereo and switched into her sneakers. Her gaze skittered to the wall of mirrors, observing him. He stood with his hands in his pockets, appearing at total ease, something he hadn't seemed to be able to achieve in her presence a week ago.

"Did you have a good day?" she asked, lacing up her sneakers.

He glanced at his watch. "It was typical, for the most part."

"How was your meeting?"

A dimple flashed in his cheek as the corner of his mouth hooked into a grin. "Not quite worth leaving you, but so are the pains of life."

Her knees trembled as she stood. "I'm ready."

He cocked his head, scrutinizing her. "Are you okay? You seem shaky."

"I'm fine." God, she wanted him.

Accepting her answer, he walked her to the door and waited as she locked up. Her body pulsed with arousal, her blood thickening enough to overcrowd her mind and block any ordinary thoughts. Not since she was a young girl had a boy made her so jittery and excited. One look and she was mush.

This couldn't be normal to want a man this desperately, this consistently. Usually, she had to shoulder off her dates, but with Elliot, she was constantly anticipating the slightest graze of his fingers, the thinnest glance from his gray eyes. Love and lust, at first sight, the only way to explain her need—and her affection.

As he slid behind the steering wheel of his car, he gave her a skeptical look. "You sure you're okay?"

"Yes. I just have a lot on my mind."

She pushed away her impulse to straddle him right there in the parking lot. Was he still battling the urge to touch and kiss her? She wanted him to make the first move, but it was difficult to wait him out. His self-control was daunting, to say the least.

Once he backed out of the parking space he took her hand. His fingers curled around hers as he drove and that eased some of the sexual tension. One touch, an almost platonic one at that, and some hungry part of her was momentarily satisfied. He was that potent.

Once she had her insatiable hormones under control, she scrutinized the road, not seeing any familiar landmarks. "Are we going somewhere?"

"Asher's. Remember?"

She'd completely forgotten. Glancing at her sweaty clothing, she grimaced. "I should have changed."

"You look fine. They know we're coming from work."

Easy to say when his job required a suit. She sniffed her shirt. "I smell like sweat."

"I like the way your sweat smells."

She crinkled her nose. "Maybe you like it, but your friends might feel differently."

"They're your friends, too."

No, they weren't. They were her clients. She really didn't know them very well.

"Look," he said, turning down a road she'd never visited. "If you're that uncomfortable, we can swing home and you can change. I'll call them and let them know we'll be late."

She debated, but as much as showering would

relieve her, she didn't want to hold everyone up. "No, I don't want to make us late."

"It's fine." He turned the car around, heading in the opposite direction.

"Elliot, don't. I'll be fine. I'll freshen up in the bathroom when we get there."

"It's not a big deal, Nadia."

But it was. She didn't want to give the impression she was high maintenance, something Ian accused her of being, and he wasn't the first. "Just go to their house."

"It'll take five min—"

"Elliot, I said just go."

"Why are you getting upset?"

"Because you aren't listening to me. Just drive to their house and I'll freshen up when I get there."

He clamped his mouth shut and turned the car back around, once again driving toward his friends' house. They didn't speak the rest of the drive to Asher's. When they got out of the car, he stopped her by the passenger door.

"Hey." His fingers brushed her jaw and she trembled as she met his gaze. "I didn't mean to make you upset. What you're wearing is fine. I just wanted you to be comfortable."

Her reaction was embarrassing. "I overreacted. I just want to make a good impression for you."

"You make a great impression and they already like you. Relax." His lips softly brushed over hers, casual, not at all explicit yet the sexual tension thrumming in her veins twisted into a giant knot of desire and need. He pulled away and she dizzily followed him to the front door.

This wasn't normal. There had to be something wrong with her.

Lettie opened the door with a smile as soon as they reached the large porch. "Hey, guys. Come in."

Nadia tried for outward calm, but the home was some sort of medieval castle. They lived here?

Asher greeted them in the main den, which was a gigantic room with two mammoth fireplaces. The ambiance and architecture made Nadia's clothing that much more slovenly.

"Anakin, Uncle Elliot's here."

The furniture appeared so homey, despite the formality of the room. As they passed a large leather couch, her gaze fell upon a darling quilt and a pudgy-faced boy surrounded by toys.

"Your son's adorable," she told Asher, who smiled proudly.

"He gets his good looks from his momma. Ani, don't eat that." Asher took the remote control from the boy, replacing it with a plastic cube decorated with springs twisting from each side. "Can I get you guys something to drink?"

She glanced at Elliot who was staring at the little boy as if trying to solve a complicated math equation. "I'll have water," she said, waiting for Elliot to answer.

Realizing they were watching him, Elliot shook off the distraction and said, "Nothing for me."

Asher disappeared into what she assumed was

the kitchen. "This place is enormous," she whispered.

Elliot raised an unimpressed brow. "Asher takes every endeavor seriously. This was part of his *Win Over Lettie* plot."

He said it as if there were something underhanded in the way his friend met his wife. Did Elliot not like Lettie? She always seemed nice whenever they came into the studio, sort of easygoing and quirky.

Asher returned with her water and they stood in awkward silence, watching the baby play.

"How old is he, Asher?"

"Ten months. He just started standing, so we're in the middle of baby proofing everything. Pardon the locks in the bathroom. Lettie's nuts with that stuff." Asher glanced at Elliot and back to her. "Do you guys want to sit?"

She lowered herself to the couch and waited for Elliot to join her, but he just stood there.

Asher excused himself. "I'm going to go see if Lettie needs a hand. Elliot, are you okay with him for a minute?"

"Sure."

Asher left and they were, again, alone with the baby. "Elliot, you're making Asher uncomfortable."

He glanced at her, expression confused. "No, I'm not. Asher knows me."

"Well, you're making me uncomfortable. Why don't you sit down?"

He sat, but his new position did nothing to improve the mood of the room. She wasn't familiar with this strange vibe she was getting from him.

Scooting to the floor, she rattled a ball, rolling it toward Anakin. "He's so cute."

Elliot looked at her but didn't smile. His eyes observed her from behind his lenses, and she had no idea what he saw or what he might be thinking. "What is that look, Elliot?"

He glanced back to the little boy. "Do you want children?"

Her belly did a delicate flip. "I think so. I'd like to have my career in order first, have some money saved up."

His brow folded. "Maybe the dad will have money."

"Dads don't always stick around."

"What's that supposed to mean?"

She shrugged, adjusting Anakin's sock. "It's just the truth. I'd rather know I can support my children if I have any."

Lettie came into the room and scooped up the baby. "Dinner's ready. I'm just going to change Sir Stinky Pants before we eat. You guys can head into the dining room."

As Lettie carried Anakin up a sprawling staircase Nadia stood from the carpet. When they crossed the room, Elliot whispered, "My dad never left."

This wasn't the time to discuss something as personal as wanting children. But like her father, his had passed on. "Abandonment comes in all shapes and sizes, Elliot. Let's not discuss this now."

Their footsteps echoed and he whispered, "My father was incredibly loyal to all of us."

"Well, mine wasn't. He never cared what I wanted and the only times he spoke to me was when I'd somehow disappointed him. I don't want to discuss this here."

Her steps faltered, her brain catching up with her blinking eyes as they stepped through the vast doorway. The dining room was an average ballroom.

What is this place?

This home was absurd. Glancing at Elliot, she murmured, "Is this some sort of museum?"

Asher grinned, rising from the head of a grand table. "Why do you think it was so important for me to learn how to dance? Welcome to our ballroom."

She smiled at Asher's pleasantness, hiding the level of which she'd misjudged his wealth. She'd known he had money and was a successful businessman, especially when she heard what he'd done for Steve, but this was beyond affluent living. This was obscene.

She sat beside Elliot at the ornate table and settled her fidgeting hands in her lap. "It smells delicious."

Asher grinned. "Lettie's an incredible chef."

His wife returned and situated the baby in the highchair, which was as ordinary as every other highchair she'd ever seen, conflicting with the rich surroundings. Her mouth twitched as she mentally tried to meld the luxury of the home with the couple's ordinariness.

"Let's eat," Lettie reached for the breadbasket. "I

hope casual's fine with you, Nadia. With school starting, I've been trying to balance work and marriage and the little monkey all in one, so my game's a little off."

"Casual's perfect." It was her preference.

Though the serving dishes were ornate, they were filled with simple comforts like roast pork, mashed potatoes, and corn. Once she saw how laidback Asher and Lettie were, laughing when Anakin flung his potatoes on the floor and gesturing easily as they ate their meal, she let go of her insecurities and accepted a glass of wine.

Lettie was great, very easygoing and quick to laugh. "Don't you love salads from a bag? I swear my culinary creativity would be dead if not for shortcuts."

The more Lettie spoke, the more Nadia's tension eased. By the end of the meal, she felt a strange pull to get to know Asher's wife, finding her genuine congeniality refreshing and sincere.

"Let's go relax in the den, Nadia. I cooked, so Asher does the dishes."

She followed Lettie to the room with the couch and sat as she returned Anakin to his blanket of toys.

"He's such a pleasant boy," Nadia observed with a pang of envy.

Lettie smiled. "He's my little angel." She curled her feet underneath her knees on the couch and sipped her wine. "So, you and Elliot, that's unexpected."

Nadia cocked her head, a teasing pinch tightening her stomach. "Why do you say unexpected?"

Lettie shrugged. "He's not the easiest to get along with and he *never* dates. Not to mention you're like … supermodel gorgeous."

She shrank a little in her skin. "I don't know about that. I'd give anything for hair the color of yours." Lettie's hair had all the vibrant shades of fire. It was so alive compared to Nadia's drab, Morticia black locks.

The other woman blanched and laughed. "No, you wouldn't. But seriously, how did you two start seeing each other?"

Nadia explained the night she and Ian broke up and how Elliot sort of rescued her. "He just showed up at exactly the right time. We had some drinks and he did magic tricks for me."

"Elliot did magic tricks?"

"Yeah. He's really good at them."

"Huh. I never knew he could do magic."

Worried she might have betrayed his privacy, she whispered, "Maybe he doesn't like other people knowing."

Lettie didn't seem too concerned. "So, you two are serious?"

It was odd, measuring her relationship under another person's inspection, but Nadia never had a lot of girlfriends and maybe this was what they did.

"I like the way he talks to me. Most men don't show interest in my thoughts and opinions, and they tend to act put out when I share them. Elliot isn't like that. I've never liked a man the way I like him. He's so sweet and patient." She flushed at how deeply she'd fallen, sure she was under some sort of puppy love spell only magicians could cast. "And he's very sensual."

Lettie blinked. "*Elliot*?"

Nadia giggled at the baffled expression on her face. "Yes, *Elliot*. He's…" Her face heated another degree. "He's domineering and incredibly passionate when he wants to be."

Lettie glanced toward the kitchen door where the men still remained and back to Nadia. "*Our* Elliot?"

Why was this so difficult for her to imagine? "Is he different around you?"

She took a long sip of wine. "Well, out of all Asher's friends, he took the longest to warm up to me. He's very…"

"Precise?"

"I was going to say opinionated, but we'll go with your word."

Nadia frowned. "I don't find him opinionated at all. If anything, he's overly cautious about other people's feelings. It takes a bit of coercion to get him to let down his guard, but when he does, there's so much hidden inside of him." Keeping her voice low, she quietly confessed, "Sometimes I worry I'm not enough for him."

"Wow. Cheers to finding a side of him the rest of us missed." They clinked their glasses. "That's a really special feeling, sort of how Asher makes me feel. I used to be so intimidated by him. He was so closed off to the rest of the world. I think that's why he and Elliot are so close. They have common inhibitions and hide a lot of vulnerability inside."

It was a relief to meet another woman involved

with a man similar to hers. "Yes, Elliot feels things deeply. That's another attractive trait."

Lettie smiled, twin darts of pink forming on her fair cheeks, likely from the wine. "I think, regardless of what others see, you two make perfect sense. You'll be good for him."

Elliot was complicated, but in some ways transparently simple and kindhearted. How could anyone see something different in him? Or was she speaking of them as a couple?

"Do you mean what people think of us dating?"

She waved a hand. "It's nothing. Asher was just telling me that Jet was worried Elliot might get hurt." She leaned close and whispered, "He's never really been in a relationship before."

Feeling protective of Elliot's past, she sipped her wine. She didn't want his friends thinking she had any ulterior motives where Elliot was concerned. She only wanted to be close to him.

The baby crawled off the blanket and Lettie was distracted. When Nadia finished her wine, she excused herself to find the boys.

Cutting through the ballroom, she pushed the door to the kitchen open a crack and paused—

"But what if Nadia gets mad?" Elliot asked.

She drew back, unsure what they could possibly be discussing.

"Then apologize. I can only vouch for my own experience. I never thought Lettie would be into the things she's into and, as much as you made fun of the whole Mr. Stone thing, it helped in that department.

There was no personal consequence—at least for a little while. I could be ... myself."

"But you weren't being yourself."

"You're wrong, Elliot. Pretending to be someone else let me be more myself than anything else ever has. It took away any sense of blame or shame. Don't get me wrong, finding a balance between reality and fantasy wasn't easy—I swore I'd lost her—but we made it work and look at us now. Never in a million years did I imagine she'd accept me so completely. She'd been *blind* to my flaws just long enough for me to find the courage to show her my true self."

"But you two still argue."

"Of course," Asher laughed. "What couple doesn't? But that's over insignificant stuff. The truth is, once we stopped basing personal experiences on other people's standards the instinct to compare ourselves to others sort of disappeared. We're happy and that's all that matters to us. We liberated each other, accepted who we are on the inside."

Nadia peeked through the crack of the ornate wooden door, but Asher's body blocked Elliot's expression from her view. He patted Elliot's shoulder. "Let her see the real you, not the idea you want to portray, but who you actually are. Love can only be genuine. If it's not, then it's not really love."

Love? Her heart fluttered at what she might be hearing. But then she frowned. Why was he telling Asher this when he should be sharing his feelings with her?

Elliot sighed. "She's like a drug. It doesn't seem

healthy for one person to alter another's perception so intensely. She makes me feel stronger. I've *never* felt strong. And she likes…" He paused. "Never mind."

Her head tipped as she waited to see if he'd voice his concerns. Thankfully, Asher prompted him to keep talking.

"What? I'm not going to judge you."

Keeping his voice low, Elliot whispered, "She likes when I'm … aggressive."

A smile twitched on her lips as his words affirmed he, too, was struggling to manage the intensity of their chemistry.

His friend laughed. "Yeah. Lettie likes that, too."

Nadia's face heated as the conversation turned personal.

"So what's the problem? Does being aggressive make *you* uncomfortable?"

"No, it's the opposite. I like it *too* much. It's a rush and I feel powerful, but I'm afraid I'll accidentally cross a line. It doesn't seem right to treat a woman that way. Maybe it isn't. I don't know. This isn't what I expected."

"So make a safe word."

"A what?"

Asher shook his head. "I have some books you should read. There's no reason to reinvent the wheel, Elliot. Sex is supposed to be passionate. You're not the first guy to worry about losing his head."

"I just don't want to disrespect her. I can't screw this up."

"Have a little faith in yourself. Doing something

to a stranger can be a felony, but doing certain things to a lover who's begging for it—literally begging—can garner a whole new level of returns."

"We'll see. I think she's mad at me right now. She was really quiet on the way here and nervous about coming in her work clothes."

Asher laughed. "That's ridiculous. Let her know we're the last people to judge others for something as meaningless as clothing. We know she works."

Feeling terrible for assuming Elliot's friends could be shallow when they were honestly two of the most accepting people she'd come across in a long while, she stepped back from the door, letting it silently close.

She'd let her personal doubts run amuck in her head tonight. She had to stop doubting herself. All of these worries were groundless and creating unnecessary stress.

As soon as she got Elliot alone again, she'd explain that sometimes her past experiences mutated into insecurities, but assure him she was ready to trust what they had and stop comparing it to past failures. That was only fair, being that she'd asked him to do pretty much the same in regard to his past.

When she returned to the den Lettie smiled. "Did you get lost?"

"No, I was looking for the boys, but they were talking so I didn't disturb them." She settled on the couch. "Scarlet, can I ask you a personal question?"

"Sure. I'm not sure I'll be able to answer, but go for it."

Nadia thought of Asher's enthusiastic words, trusting he knew his wife better than anyone. "Do you think there's something broken in a woman that likes..." She went with the word Elliot used. "Aggressive men?"

Lettie snorted. "No. I hate having to make the first move or ask for things. I'd much prefer for Asher to be the aggressor."

"But what about ... physical aggression—in bed?"

Lettie frowned and then nodded. "Ah, you're talking about hair pulling and all the fun stuff."

Hearing her label it as fun untied the knot in her neck. "Yes." She leaned close and whispered, "Do you like that stuff?"

"Mmm-hmm." She giggled. Scooting closer, she cupped a hand along the side of her wine-stained lips. "Sometimes Asher will even tie me up." She sighed. "We haven't done a lot of that since becoming parents, but I *love* when he goes all Mr. Stone on my ass."

Nadia frowned. "Mr. Stone?"

Lettie waved a hand. "It's sort of an inside joke. But that's what I call it. He's so sexy when he gets all bossy and domineering. It's such a turn on. He gets in my head and I love it." She giggled, her eyes shifting as if a fantasy played through her mind. "I should leave a blindfold on his pillow tonight, let him know I'm overdue for some play."

Blindfolds? Tying up? Nadia didn't know if she could go that far, but she was intrigued. "When he ties you up, do you ever panic?"

"Hold that thought. My little prince is falling asleep and I have to get him to his crib or he'll wake up when we move him and never go back down."

Nadia waited, as she carried the baby upstairs, her mind rolling over several strange scenarios. Knowing Lettie had this whole other side really helped.

Because Elliot had limited experience, Nadia had been terrified she'd come on too strong and he'd think her trashy. But if Lettie did those things and there was nothing remotely wrong with her—she was a teacher for crying out loud—then Nadia was definitely overthinking things. Maybe there wasn't anything wrong with her. Maybe it was the men of her past that had been wrong.

Lettie returned, carrying a baby monitor. "Okay, I'm back. Where were we?" She rubbed her hands together. "God, it feels good to have another girl-friend I can talk to about this."

Nadia smiled, feeling the same way. "I asked if you ever panicked when he tied you up."

"Sometimes, but it's a good panic, the sort that heightens awareness and intensifies everything. We have a word in case I'm ever really freaking out. I've never needed it though. God, I really miss that. I'm glad you came over tonight. You make me remember how it was in the beginning."

"I'm glad we came, too."

Lettie's gaze drifted as her mind went somewhere else. In a dreamy voice, she whispered, "There's something so potent about feeling your man's weight pressed over you. It's dominating, but so telling. I love when Asher holds me tight and takes exactly what he wants."

Nadia nearly panted with the thought of Elliot doing the same. "I can't believe I was nervous coming here. Now, I realize how silly that was. I think you and I have a lot in common, Lettie."

Her friend smiled. "We should get together again, maybe have a girl's night."

"I'd love that! I don't have a lot of female friends."

As if they sensed their exclusion, the men entered the room. Elliot looked at her, his eyes guarded, and she smiled.

She'd been unfair to him tonight, again working out her own issues, and overlooking the fact he might have his own concerns to navigate. The fact that this was truly a relationship, not just casual fucking, made her so much more aware of what she could actually lose when it came to Elliot.

Rising, she went over to him. She was done limiting her impulses. He should know how addictive she found him. "Hi."

He studied her, his eyes guarded. "Is everything okay?"

She stepped closer, nuzzling his chest with her nose. "I'm sorry I was in a mood earlier. I had a lot on my mind."

"You can talk to me, Nadia."

"I know. But I think I needed a girl's perspective. I'm glad we came here."

He ran his finger under the strap of her tank top. "Even in these clothes."

She smiled, embarrassed for the way she acted. "Yes, even in these clothes. Your friends are nice people, not the sort to judge."

He pulled her closer and lowered his gaze. "Good." His lips traced over her pulse and she shivered. "Did you want to stay longer?"

She wanted him and now that he was teasing her with little kisses and touches, her body was growing more impatient than ever. "Let's go home, mister."

His gaze heated, firing up her blood and she rested her hands on his chest, hopefully implying everything she wanted to do to him. His fingers glided along the strap of her shirt, grazing the side of her breast.

"I want you," he whispered, dark promise in his eyes.

Sweet, sweet relief. She should have never doubted their chemistry. While they both struggled to communicate, the physical attraction they shared remained unhindered. Perhaps that was where their focus should stay for the time being.

Although Elliot seemed to be communicating his needs with naked clarity as he looked at her, his eyes direct and his intentions screaming in the silence. Maybe he needed a guy's perspective. She now felt his aggressiveness without having him lay a hand on her. It was palpable, thick and hot like the air of a small Baptist church full of sinners on a Louisiana summer day. Her skin itched to strip away every stitch of clothing. They needed to get out of there immediately.

Her breath trembled as she held his stare, the

gusset of her panties flooding with arousal. "I'm yours. Let's get out of here."

He glanced over her shoulder and she turned, surprised to see the other couple snuggling on the couch, Asher's fingers combing through his wife's hair as Lettie rested her head on his shoulders and whispered in her husband's ear.

Elliot, ever direct, announced, "I'll see you in the morning, Ash. Thanks for dinner, Scarlet."

The two turned, a look of uncertainty on their faces. Lettie's cheeks wore a deep flush as she smirked, understanding where their conversation had led.

"Let me know when you want to do that girl's night, Nadia."

A warm sensation unraveled in her chest as she recognized the beginning of a friendship. "I will. Thank you for a beautiful evening."

Elliot took her hand, the slightest contact drawing her nipples to needle-sharp points of need, as he walked her to the car. As he slid into the driver's seat his posture seemed stiff—aroused.

Once they were on the main road, she tried to distract her carnal thoughts by admiring the play of lights passing over the contours of his body. His posture appeared tight as a bow, so taut even the air around them seemed incapable of movement. "You're being very quiet."

"Did you want to talk?" he asked, gripping the wheel. The speedometer climbed as the car sped up, hugging the curves of the dark road and propelling them closer to home.

Her gaze lowered to his lap, her hand drifting over the console and brushing the bulge in his pants. The car swerved and slowed, his attention jerking to her. "What are you doing?"

"We have a few minutes. I thought we could pass the time." The wait was killing her.

He stared intently at the dark road. "I'm driving."

"I bet you could multitask."

He glanced at her again, the streetlights reflecting in the lenses of his glasses. His attention returned to the road and his jaw twitched. "We should probably wait until we get home."

Thwarted, she withdrew her touch and faced the windshield. Five minutes ago he was a lit fuse, firing towards an explosion. Now, the closer they came to his home, the more his mask of control slid over his features and that sparking fuse seemed more like a dimly lit candle. She wanted to playfully taunt him and keep him on edge. If he was a simmering ember she'd blow on him until he was burning hot.

She pulled her shirt to show off the curve of her breasts and reminded, "You don't have to be reserved with me, Elliot."

"It's not a matter of reservation. It's a matter of highway safety."

She smothered a laugh. "Oh." Such a law abider.

His fingers flexed on the wheel. "I know I don't have to be reserved with you."

"Good." If they were really going to do this, she wanted it to be authentic.

"It's not that I don't want your hands on me," he

continued. "I just want to give you my full focus. You deserve more than half of my attention."

And just like that, he turned his rebuff into a compliment, one that not only reaffirmed her self-worth but made her feel incredibly important to him. "You always know what to say."

"Not true. Half my thoughts are tossed aside as unnecessary."

"Well, the ones you choose make me feel good."

He glanced at her, his attention divided. "Never doubt that I want you. That's probably my most constant thought."

Her body burned for his touch and she tried to determine how far they were from home. "Will you prove it?"

The car picked up speed. "Prove it how?"

"Show me how much you want me."

The car switched into the passing lane. "When we get home."

Her mouth pursed with a tight smile, anticipation fueling her arousal. He could probably handle a little road play and not crash the car. "If you wanted something now—"

"Nadia."

He used that powerful tone she'd only heard a few times from him, the one that seemed to cripple her commonsense and turn her into a needy Elliot fiend. She shifted her shoulder so she was facing him.

"What's going to happen when we get home, Elliot?"

His attention shifted to her again. "What do you want to happen?"

"I want you to decide." Yes, that was what she wanted. She wanted him unrefined and demanding, telling her exactly what he needed.

"Then I'll decide."

Delicious wanting coiled tight in her belly. "I love when you take the lead, Elliot. It really excites me."

His Adam's apple made a slow bob under the stubble covering his throat. "Is that so?"

"Mm-hmm. My body's already pulsing. It wants you—deep and hard."

The motor growled as he drove a little faster. His chest lifted as his breath turned labored. "I can take the lead."

The heavy sense of desire grew in her belly. This was certainly a satisfying way to pass the time as he abided by all highway safety laws.

"I'd give you anything you asked for. Anything at all."

His jaw twitched. "No more talking."

She glanced at his lap, the shadow of his erection pressing hard against his suit pants, and she snickered. When he pulled into the driveway, he hit the brakes hard enough to rock her body. The engine silenced and he stared out the windshield.

The car cooled, but her body was on fire, their flagrant lust thickening the shared air of the car.

"Are we going inside?" she whispered.

His door popped open and her brows lifted as he rounded the car. Her door clicked and he was suddenly unlatching her seatbelt and hauling her out of the seat. Adrenaline shot through her veins as he pinned her to the cool exterior. His mouth crashed over hers, penetrating her senses and calling her body to full alert.

She leaned into him and he pulled back, eyeing her for an uncertain moment. "Is that really what you want, me to take control?"

A shaky nod and he spun her to face the car, her hips colliding with the curve of the hood and his hands groping her ass. His fingers slipped under the elastic band of her pants, teasing warm flesh and she hummed. He pressed his hips against hers, showing how hard he was.

Her arms stretched over the heated hood as the cooling engine pinged and he panted behind her. She waited, silently begging for more. His fingers stroked down her ponytail, giving a tug at the end. She moaned, arching back for him.

His hold released on her hair and her pants were shoved down her backside, exposing the top half of her ass. His fingers dug into her soft flesh, squeezing tightly.

"I can be gentle," he murmured, his strong hands massaging with a firm grip that belied his words.

Between shallow breaths, she whispered, "I don't want you to be gentle."

His fingers again dug into her flesh as his other hand massaged the front of her sex. His warm mouth closed over her ass cheek, kissing and seducing her. "I'm very wet, Elliot. You keep teasing me."

He paused, his exhaled breath cooling the wet

kiss mark he'd left on her skin. "I want you," he whispered and she smiled.

"I want you too, but if you don't stop teasing me I'm going to do the job myself." Her pants went up with a snap as her body was jerked away from the car and he hauled her toward the house, his fingers tight around her wrist. The alarm beeped as he punched in the code and pulled her through the doorway. She practically skipped over the threshold, giddy with eagerness.

Once in the foyer, he shoved her back against the wall and delivered another mind scrambling kiss, which left her breathless. Melting under his attention, she sighed and eased her weight into the wall.

"Eyes on me."

She sucked in a breath as he pinched her nipple through the cotton of her shirt, her gaze flashing to his face. Her body trembled with unrefined desire.

His hand slid down her front, toyed with the elastic band of her pants. "I'm in charge?"

She barely nodded, but it was enough. Permission granted, his fingers slipped into the front of her panties and she gasped at the first brush of his finger to her clit, her knees going weak. His finger teased her slit, sliding over her wet folds and delving inside of her sex with shallow dips. Her head rolled back as she drew in a deep breath.

"I said look at me."

She flushed, his distracting touch making it hard to focus on any rules. "Sorry."

"Do you want me to stop?"

She shook her head. "No." She gasped as his finger slipped fully inside of her.

"Then keep looking at me." He glided his finger in and out of her, and she was glad the wall supported her weight.

"I want to see your body," he commanded.

Her heart raced as the intensity of his gaze drilled into her. She lifted her tank top to the top of her chest and a masculine grunt escaped his throat. Her sports bra left her covered and she wished she'd chosen a nicer one that morning.

Elliot's thumb grazed her clit. "More. Pull your bra down."

Yes. She loved this demanding side of him, loved his directness and loved giving in to him. She breathed fast, her hard nipples pressing against the constricting bra. With jagged motions, she shifted her arms through the straps and lowered it to her ribs.

His head dropped and he licked over one turgid nipple as she gasped, her blood pumping like lava as her fingers combed through his hair.

"Elliot..."

His finger sank deeper, penetrating faster. His head jerked back, their breath mingling in the combined heat of their bodies. He yanked her leggings down, exposing her ass against the wall as his hands coasted over her hips and his mouth pleasured her breasts.

He nudged her thighs apart, but her pants limited her. "Take them off." His hot command sent his warm breath over her damp nipples.

She shimmied out of the constricting pants, kicking her shoes and socks aside. Elliot took a step back. She leaned against the wall, only a sports bra twisted around her ribs.

He eyed her from tits to toes then met her gaze. "Your nipples are wet."

She glanced at her chest noting the tightly ruched tips of her breasts, damp from his mouth. "Yes, they are."

"So are your thighs."

Arousal gathered with each word, her body begging for him to touch her again.

He glanced at his fingers and her face heated. He crowded her against the wall, his fingers stroking her folds and her body melted into him. "Look at you. I come close and you whimper. I tease you and you moan. I touch you and you're wet."

"Elliot please." She'd never been so aroused. Her mind teetered on the precipice of something dark and carnal, one little push and she'd tip over the razor-sharp edge.

"Please what, Nadia?" A damp trail teased up her stomach as he dragged his fingers toward her mouth.

"I need you."

Holding her stare, he dragged his fingers up her throat, over the curve of her jaw, and to her lips. The scent of her arousal filled her lungs. "Taste."

Her lips parted and his finger slid over her tongue, rich with the tang of sex. Her mouth closed around his knuckle, sucking gently. He pushed a little deeper and she moaned. His nostrils flared and he growled, pulling his fingers in and out in clear simulation.

When he withdrew his fingers their gazes held for a moment, implication dilating his eyes. She needed him and couldn't wait another second. Licking her lips, she whispered, "Do you want me on my knees, Elliot?"

He nodded and she slid down the wall, her lashes lifting to watch his expression as she un-latched his belt. Sliding his zipper apart, she leaned her head against the wall, letting him take the lead.

"Show me what you want," she rasped. "I'm yours."

His hand trembled slightly as he reached into his pants, his fingers curling around his thick length. Uncertainty flashed in his eyes as their gazes crossed, but it was quickly masked.

"I... want you to open your mouth."

Her lips obediently parted, but he hesitated, something holding him back. Trying to coax him, she reminded, "You told me you'd prove how much you want me. Prove it, mister."

Angling his body closer to hers, he brushed her lips with the velvet smooth tip of his cock, arousal painting the soft skin. Her tongue snaked out and he hissed in a breath.

"You're teasing me again, Elliot. Show me. Hold nothing back."

His fingers caught her jaw and he wedged his cock to the back of her throat, surprising and pleasing her at the same time. She closed her lips over him, sucking deeply as he grunted and thrust hard.

Showing him total trust, she folded her arms over her head and he grabbed her wrists, pinning them against the wall, his gliding hips pressing her head to the wall as he filled her mouth.

Her need to please him doubled as he took total control. She widened her mouth to take more of him and he thrust deeper, his fingers curling tighter around her hands. Moans vibrated her throat as he moved faster and harder, her body fully pinned against the wall. She looked up at him, coiling her tongue around his length and his jaw locked, his grip on her unbreakable.

He lunged into her mouth, penetrating the back of her throat. Her eyes reflexively watered as her lips worked over him, her shoulders tensing with each advance. *This* was the Elliot she suspected hid behind his polished exterior, the one she wanted to set free.

He grunted, flexing his hips with repetitive snaps as he plunged and practically cursed out her name. It was intense, but the force drove her higher. She reveled in his total claim and luxuriated in the sense of his unyielding need. Her lips tingled, and suddenly his motions turned jagged. She leaned into him, her arms trapped in his restrictive hold as he shifted, but she refused to let him go.

He released her hands and she grabbed his hips, holding him to her, but he was stronger. His cock ripped from her mouth and hot come splashed over her lips and cheek, mingling with the dampness from her eyes as he stumbled back.

He'd lost control, the proof lingering on her swollen lips. It was sexier than she'd imagined and she could hardly believe he'd trusted her with such an uncensored view of the beast he kept tethered inside, the animal she desperately wanted to untie.

Her fingers brushed along her cheek, catching traces of his desire and sliding into her mouth as she shut her eyes. *Elliot.*

On shaky legs, she stood and stepped up to him. "Your turn to taste."

Her lips brushed his and she slid her tongue over his, the salty essence of arousal mingling in their kiss. He jerked back, his brow tense. Uncertainty chilled her like a bucket of ice as she glanced up at him and saw the flash of doubt and shame in his gray eyes.

"Elliot?"

"I..."

His stark gaze showed fear and she sensed him emotionally retreating. "What's wrong?"

Without answering, he gathered her clothes and righted his pants. He glanced at her and quickly looked away, his face flushing behind his glasses. "I didn't mean to be so rough. That was too much."

What was he talking about? "I loved seeing you like that."

He shoved her clothes into her arms and took a quick step back as if he was afraid to touch her. Her shoulders hunched, trepidation pressing into her with relentless force. "I don't understand—"

"You're crying," he snapped, his body turning so she could only see his back.

Her fingers feathered under her eyes. Her lashes were wet, but that was just a reflex, not an emotional reaction. She hadn't shed emotional tears, though, now she felt like she could.

"I'm fine, El—"

"It's *not* fine." He paced, putting more distance between them.

She flinched at the lash in his voice. "Why are you angry? I gave myself to you and you took—"

"You should get cleaned up." He continued to move about, righting his clothes and avoiding eye contact. Shrewd eyes glared over his shoulder and she shrunk a little more, wishing her clothes were back on her body.

Her chin shook, not understanding any of this. "Elliot, there's nothing wrong with what we just did—"

"I don't want to discuss it." He closed his belt and turned to walk away.

Her mouth snapped shut. He'd rather leave it looming, festering between them? "You won't even look at me." Her accusing words barreled out with a lash of pain and humiliation. Shame, or something extremely close to it, registered in her stomach. She didn't know what to make of his behavior.

"Nadia, please."

Please, what? What was this? Where was this anger coming from all of a sudden? What changed? She wanted him to hold her, not shun her. Unwinding like a fraying thread, she tried to pull him back. "Why don't we take a shower together? Cool off?"

He paused and she held her breath. Maybe he just had a small moment of freaking out, but now she might be getting through to him. "I'll meet you up there. Start without me."

Thank goodness. Her body shook with relief, but at the same time every instinct told her leaving him was the absolute wrong thing to do. "Elliot?"

"I said I'll meet you up there."

Lowering her gaze, she nodded and walked up the stairs. "I'll be waiting for you."

22

~Sherlock Holmes

*E*lliot twitched under his clothes, unsure of what just happened. She'd asked him to take the lead, which he had, but then things got out of hand, and he was suddenly pinning her to the wall and fucking her mouth without restraint. He needed a minute.

He watched her take the stairs, noting the slight blotches on her backside from his grip. He waited until he heard her bedroom door close then marched up the steps, not thinking about where he was going.

He'd acted like some sort of animal. She'd *cried.*

Because of *him*. And he was too lost in his own pleasure to notice.

And then she lied, as if tears were somehow acceptable in what should be a tender act. He should have never let Asher convince him sex should have a darker side. This was how people got hurt. If anything, his friend's track record should have warned him away from any such advice.

While such behavior might be acceptable for the majority of men, it was not okay with him. He needed the security of his control. The moment he let that slip, his perfectly orchestrated world would unravel. Everything would fall apart—he and Nadia would fall apart. He didn't like leaving loose ends untied and he couldn't bear this sense of mentally checking out to feed some greedy emotion. He was better than that.

Or was he just the same as everyone else? Panic gripped him as he pin wheeled for balance. What was happening to him? He was meticulous, exacting, and never sloppy with his actions. The man he became when around Nadia was someone he didn't recognize, someone he wasn't sure he could tolerate.

He passed his bedroom and several other doors until he barged into the room where he kept his collectibles, the room Nadia visited when he'd specifically told her it was private. This was what he did when he felt like he had no control. He hid.

There seemed to be razor thin balance between his past and future, one safe and secure, the other dark and reckless. He didn't want to be in either at the moment.

He shut his eyes and the image of her looking up at him, lips swollen, face wet with tears and come painted on her skin. Jesus. What was wrong with him?

Seething, he stared at all the neatly displayed items and cursed. "*Fuck!*"

His hand flung out, clearing the closest shelf, as priceless items clattered to the floor. Not caring what they were, he kicked a box across the room, knocking several others off the shelf. He was supposed to be a fucking man yet had no fucking clue what was normal when it came to women. But it certainly wasn't this.

He'd promised himself he'd respect her. And yet he'd lost control. What good was he if he couldn't even keep his word to himself?

His hand flung out, tossing more objects across the room. Resentment boiled inside of him as every crutch he'd leaned on now seemed debilitating. Useless shit adding to his ignorance. Curtains to hide behind while the rest of his peers were miles ahead. He hated feeling uninformed, but he didn't have a fucking clue what he was doing.

"Stupid. Childish. Nonsense!"

He grabbed hold of a box, clutching it in both hands and stared at the collector's item. It was the 1978 special edition, Luke Skywalker figurine, one of only twenty in existence.

He knew everything when it came to valuing action figures, child playthings, but he knew nothing about women. The filthy way he'd treated her tonight was wrong. Despite his lack of experience, he was certain any man that made a woman cry during intimacy was doing something evil.

His thumbs pressed into the plastic, denting the protective packaging and his heart thundered. A woozy sensation washed over him, but he didn't ease his grip.

Knowing the consequences and not caring, he squeezed harder. Anxiety spiked as he imposed his own penance. Damaging something else he couldn't replace seemed an irrational but fitting punishment.

He gasped as the packaging buckled, the aged glue breaking its seal from the paper backing.

"Shit," he hissed, the haze of his rage dissipating fast enough to leave him disoriented and sick to his stomach.

What was wrong with him? More careless damage done from reckless behavior. Was his brain on fucking vacation today? How was he going to fix this? How was he going to make things right with Nadia? What if she left? He couldn't breathe.

Glancing around, he looked for any sort of glue, but his eyes widened at the disaster he'd made. The second he registered the result of his destructive behavior his lungs went into an almost asthmatic spasm. Fuck. Everything was a disaster. Because of *him*.

Panting, he placed the collectible on the shelf and quickly gathered the others, his hands trembling as he inspected each package and returned them to their rightful places. What was happening? This wasn't him. He wasn't reckless. He took care of the things he loved, cherished them, and *never* gave in to passing urges that came with high stakes.

A cool sweat coated his skin. A few minutes of fervent anger and he'd cost himself twenty-five thousand dollars. Ten minutes of taking what he wanted from Nadia and he might have ruined the best thing to ever come into his life.

How could he face her? He couldn't bear the sight of himself and didn't want her to see him so shaken and disturbed by the uncharacteristic urges inside of him. He couldn't bare facing her only to see her walk away. Her rejection would destroy him and experience promised she'd eventually leave once she got back on her feet—yet he kept helping her get there financially and otherwise. Was that love or some sort of masochistic self-sabotage?

There was no playbook, and the man he became around her was unrecognizable to him. Fist fights, spontaneity, sexual impulses... Life never used to be this complicated. Despite all his hard-earned patience and perfected reserve, he didn't trust himself not to disrespect her again. And he couldn't bear the thought of her tears. What if she was crying now?

His head was a mess. What if he already ruined it? Oh God, what if she hated him? She'd said it was fine, but... It wasn't fine.

He went to his bedroom and locked the door. He couldn't deal with this side of himself and she shouldn't have to either. The feelings she stirred were too intense. It was too much, too fast, too reckless, and he needed to find a sense of stability again.

The memory of her looking up at him flashed in

his mind again and his palm pressed into the door. He couldn't stop picturing it. What kind of man slaked his own pleasure while holding a woman down?

Shame choked him as the urge to turn back time and temper his desires twisted in his gut. Nothing would undo what he'd done. Nothing could unshed her tears. He wanted to throw up.

23

"NERDS GET CAUGHT *up in minutiae, because there is a tremendous and fulfilling sense of control in understanding every single detail of a thing more than any other living creature.*"

~Chris Hardwick

Nadia shut off the shower and frowned. She was turning into a prune waiting for Elliot to join her. Wringing out her hair with the towel, she slipped into a cotton T-shirt and went to see what was taking him so long. With every step her trepidation returned, tying her insides in knots and leaving her distrustful of his promise to find her.

The foyer lights were still on, but the rest of the house was dark. "Elliot?"

She mentally replayed his words, holding onto

her relief that they were okay, but now she felt like a fool for trusting him. He said he'd meet her in the shower. He said he'd be right behind her, but he was nowhere to be found.

Had he gone to bed? Seeing his bedroom door closed, she reached for the knob and frowned when it didn't give. Jiggling it again, she scowled. Since living there, he'd never locked his door.

"Elliot? Are you in there? The door's locked."

He didn't answer, but when she looked at the floor she saw the shadow of his feet under the crack.

"Elliot, why is the door locked?" A whisper of movement from the other side caught her ear, but he didn't answer.

Her hand released the knob and she stepped back, a sinking sensation filling her stomach. During her long shower, she'd talked herself down from another self-deprecating ledge. She sensed him putting up walls downstairs but decided she was being over analytical. She promised to be patient and let him move at his own pace with these things.

But this... This was more than an emotional barricade. This was a solid, locked door. "Elliot, what's going on?"

Silence.

The unwelcome ache in the pit of her stomach moved to her chest, tightening with every passing second he didn't answer. She knocked again.

"Elliot, open the door. I know you're in there."

The shadows on the carpet moved and she knocked harder.

"I don't like games. What's going on?" She jiggled

the knob again, her hand stilling when the light on the inside of the room went out. He had to realize she knew he was in there. She gave herself to him and he was now hiding from her? Why? Her uncertainty nipped, pricking at insecurities she tried so hard not to awaken.

Unsure what caused this, she slapped her palms on the door, a sting reverberating from her trembling fingers down to her pride.

"Elliot, I know you're in there. Open the door, right now."

Her chin quivered when he still didn't respond. He was shutting her out, hiding worse than she ever imagined he could. Why couldn't they just discuss whatever was bothering him? *Be a man*, she wanted to yell, but that wouldn't help.

She shoved down her panic and softened her voice. "Please, open the door."

Nothing. Her throat contracted with an urge to truly cry, a very different and painful reflex compared to the one that caused her tears earlier.

"You're scaring me," she whispered, believing he was close enough to hear the fear in her voice.

Her breathing turned ragged as she stumbled back, her throat tightened around a painful lump.

"I don't understand what happened." Erotic images flashed through her mind, the heady memories distorting into disgraceful acts of a desperate woman as she tried to picture what they'd done from a different perspective. To her, it had been beautiful, but what if to him...

No. She wasn't doing this to herself. She loved

and trusted him. There should be no dishonor to how they interacted intimately and in private.

But there was the shame, dark and oily, slithering through her, hissing terrible truths that she would never be like other women. She was asking for too much. Sex was always fine, but anything more... Why was there always a catch? And why did Elliot's distance hurt so much more than anything else? His silence was terrifying.

People didn't lock doors on the women they loved. They crossed Milky Ways on magpies and built bridges to be together. Clearly she'd misinterpreted his feelings, assumed he'd loved her when he'd been very careful not to use those words. But she still felt his desire to connect, and this inexplicable derailment every time they seemed to get a little closer. Only this time was worse than any time before.

"Why are you shutting me out?" Her plea was too soft to penetrate the wood door, but it announced every truth she didn't want to see.

There was emotional rejection and then there was physical. This was a combination of both. Humiliated, she silently admitted someone who loved her would never do this. Whoever was on the other side of that door suddenly seemed cruel and not the person who stole her heart. A cool tear slid down her face and she batted it away.

Her palms slapped into the door again. "Answer me!"

When he didn't, she stumbled back. Denial and worry twisted into regretful acceptance.

She had believed he cared for her, trusted him not to judge her. Her feet made a graceless trek to her room and she slammed the door, hopefully shutting out all the insecurities on the other side. But those dirty thoughts slithered through the cracks and stole her breath as true panic crept in.

Digging her phone out of her purse, she called his cell, her desperation a boundless hope this wasn't happening. Not with him. He was different. She *loved* him.

When voicemail picked up, Elliot's indifferent voice suggesting she leave a message, she gripped her phone so tight the case whined. Her head hung in defeat. He wasn't different at all. He was abandoning her like all the rest, only this time it was deeper.

They all lost interest. They all eventually treated her like baggage. Even Roland had come to the conclusion she was no longer the marrying type. She thought she was finished using her body that way, and that hadn't been what she'd been thinking with Elliot. With him it had meaning. Yet, here she was, being shoved away, not worth a word of explanation for where she went wrong.

In those silent moments of revelation, each shard of self-doubt sliced open old wounds until she could barely bear the weight of her skin. People assumed beauty came with confidence, but deep down she was a fragile disaster hiding inside a porcelain shell. Her demons battered her thin veneer until the last shred of dignity seemed to scream inside of her, scream nothing but ugly things.

She couldn't bear it anymore. Her life was an endless cycle of choosing men who only hurt her. He was supposed to be different. She trusted him. She loved him. But clearly, he didn't love her. She batted away more tears.

There would be no staying here after this. She had her pride.

Gathering her belongings, she stuffed them into her bag and shoved her legs into a pair of dirty pants. Once she had everything, she marched down the hall, forbidding herself when she wanted to knock on that damn door again.

She ordered a cab with the app on her phone and walked to the foyer. Only then did she recall the cameras everywhere. She stilled, her eyes glazing as she blinked back tears and stared into the little lens on the ceiling, certain he was watching her.

Stiffening, she raised her chin. "I thought you were a man, but you're just a coward."

She walked out the door and to the edge of the drive, refusing to look back as her heart slowly crumbled. This was the last time. No more. She could not beat herself down on behalf of another man's shortcomings ever again. She had all the battle scars she could manage and her heart simply couldn't take the ache anymore.

Her hair was damp and she was shivering by the time the car arrived. Holding her bag on her lap, she buckled her seatbelt and gave the address to her studio.

She thought of Lettie, certain she wasn't the one to confide in about whatever just happened. After all, Lettie's husband was Elliot's best friend. She might have answers, but Nadia was sure calling her at this hour would only make things worse. She had no one to talk to.

Desperate and confused, she leaned her head into the car window as the world went by in silence. Her gaze caught on the driver's wedding band. People had counterparts everywhere, but she seemed destined to be alone.

Her aunts were gone. Her mother despised her—called her a whore. Her father had left this world feeling much the same way. Ian was just one of many men who decided they were better off without her. She thought Elliot was different. She thought he...

A crushing pain clamped around her heart. She was stupid. A hopeless romantic who expected a fairytale when the world was actually a cold and unwelcoming place.

When she reached her studio she paid the driver and went inside. Her back hit the wall as she dropped to the floor, still holding her phone and crying in the dark. She couldn't do this anymore. She couldn't keep resting her hopes on love when she needed to actually start using her head.

Her eyes followed the shadows and a shiver crested her shoulders. No bed. No blankets. This was her best option? She should go to a hotel, but that would destroy her budget for the week and she needed to feed herself.

Wiping her eyes, she thumbed through her contacts, the light from her phone dancing like a firefly in the dark. She couldn't stand the thought of sleeping on the floor so she checked the time and texted the only friend she could think of, though he was more of an acquaintance.

Are you at the gym?

Her phone pinged back a moment later.

I'll be there tomorrow at six. What's up?

Humiliation kept her fingers unsteady.

Never mind.

Her phone suddenly rang, Steve's name lighting the screen. She debated not answering, but she couldn't let him worry. "Hey."

"Do you need something from the gym?"

Her emotions slipped and she struggled to keep her voice level. "No, I just wanted to see if you were there. I was going to stop by."

He was silent for a beat. "It's eleven at night."

"I know. I don't know what I was thinking. Go back to bed, or whatever you were doing. I'll be fine."

"Nadia, stop. What's going on? Where are you?"

She bit her lip, the view of the dark studio wavering behind an unshed wall of tears. "At my studio."

"Is everything all right?"

A tear slipped past her lashes and fell onto her bag. "I don't know. I left Elliot's and I'm not sure what's happening."

"I'll meet you at the studio in twenty minutes. Don't go anywhere."

"Steve, you don't have to—"

"Knock it off, Nadia. You're my friend. I'm not going to let you sleep there. I'll see you in a few minutes."

"Okay," she rasped, ending the call.

Several minutes later the bell rang and she heard his heavy footfalls racing up the stairs. She stood but had a hard time meeting his eyes. She hadn't even put on a bra and her hair was still damp.

His gaze made a quick assessment of her shambled appearance. "Get your things. I'll take you to my place."

He followed her down the steps and took the keys from her unsteady hands, locking up. Rounding the front of the car, she climbed into the SUV and he shut the door behind her. When he returned to his seat his grip was tight on the wheel.

"Thank you for doing this. I didn't have anywhere to go."

His jaw ticked, but he said nothing.

"I'm not even sure what happened. We got home and… It's embarrassing."

He laughed without humor. "Trust me, Nadia, whatever you have to say won't shock me. I've seen a lot since getting involved with Asher."

She frowned, more uncertainty moving in where good assumptions lived. "I thought you two were friends."

"More like business acquaintances. He offered me a job. I did it. And then I collected a debt and cut ties. I'll go to things here and there—for Lettie—but some shit isn't easy to forget. If Elliot's anything like Asher…" He paused for a moment. "Sometimes victims become the worst bullies of all. Those guys all went through some shit, but I don't think they ever got over it. They have no comprehension of how powerful they actually are now. None of that past shit matters anymore, but it's molded them into the men they are, and I'd hate to say it, but they're fucked up. It takes some devotion to get involved with anyone who needs that much work, which is why I cut ties."

"I wish I had known you felt that way."

"Why do you say it like that?" His knuckles bleached as his grip tightened.

"I just do."

They made the rest of the drive in silence. He parked the car outside of a small but pristine home in a suburban district and faced her, his shoulders tense.

"Do you need to go to a hospital or anything like that? I need to know now before we go inside."

She drew back. "What? No. God, Steve, Elliot would never hurt me like that." He could break her heart, but he would never get physically rough with her.

Steve didn't appear convinced, but he nodded anyway.

His home was nice—lived in—and she could see he wasn't expecting company as he gathered scattered dishes the moment they walked in. "Do you want something to drink?"

She stared at the couch, wondering if that was where she'd sleep. Her feet refused to move. Here she was again, begging another man to give her a place to stay. What happened to her life? When had this become her norm? There had to be something wrong with her.

"Nadia?"

"No, thank you. I'm fine," she murmured, anything but fine.

"Will you be okay here?"

"This is just for tonight," she reassured him. "I really appreciate you helping me."

"Don't mention it."

She nodded, only wanting him to go so she could fall apart in private.

Likely sensing her desire for privacy, he sighed. "Bathroom's down the hall. Kitchen's there. My room's at the top of the stairs if you need anything, and I mean anything."

"Thank you," she murmured again.

"Hey," he gripped her shoulder and she looked

up at him, her composure fraying. "If you want to talk, I can listen."

So tempting, so redundant. "Thanks, but I need to think right now. Maybe we'll talk tomorrow."

"Okay." He released her and stepped back. "Try to get some sleep."

She nodded and went to the couch as he took the steps. Her body folded as she rested on her side and she pulled the throw blanket over her shoulders. Confusion escaped in silent tears.

This needed to be the last time she let something like this happen. From now on, she could only depend on herself.

As much as she judged her family for letting Roland bail them out time and again, she'd developed the same tendencies, leaning on men for security and never learning how to depend on herself. It seemed ironic Elliot had been the one to say depending on others was dangerous. He was right. She should have never depended on him—or trusted him with her heart.

24

———————

It was probably the most heartbreaking decision Nadia ever made, but it was her only choice if she wanted to salvage what was left of her pride and find some independence again. Her landlord slid the check across the desk and her stomach bottomed out as she reached for it.

"Thank you. I left the metal desk and moved the old bench to the curb. Someone will probably take it before the trash men do."

"I wish you luck, Nadia."

"Thank you, for the luck and for all the times

you've been patient when I needed a few extra days to make my rent."

Her landlord grinned, his veneers flashing an unnatural white against his deep hickory skin. "I know what it's like to start a business in a foreign place. Not always easy."

That was the truth. She felt empty-handed as she left her landlord's office. It was as if she literally put down her dreams to make room for a more practical future.

She'd contacted all of her clients that morning, trying hard to disguise her tears as each parent asked why she was closing so suddenly. She couldn't offer a professional explanation, so she simply promised a reimbursement and an invitation to join her at the new studio that should be opening in a few months.

She took a cab to Reflections Gym and found Steve with a woman working her thighs. Hanging back, she observed his mannerisms and how hard he pushed the client. He had sizable knowledge about what machines worked which part of the body, and a presence that backed up his credibility.

When he was finished, he noticed her and smiled. "Nadia. When did you get here?"

"About twenty minutes ago. You're good at what you do."

"Thanks. Come back to my office. I'll split my lunch with you."

She followed him to the back and accepted half his turkey wrap as they settled around the desk. "How'd you make out today? Any word from Elliot?"

She was trying not to think about Elliot because

every time he entered her mind she felt sick—more so because he still hadn't called.

"No." She finished the last bite of her wrap and brushed the crumbs off her fingers. "I closed my studio today."

He stilled, his eyes growing wide. "What?"

She shrugged, holding back the urge to scream and cry at the awful doubts scraping her insides raw. "It would have happened eventually anyway. My roster was too light and it was costing me too much. So I'm going to find work somewhere else for the time being until we open the studio here."

"Nadia..." His brow pinched. "They haven't accepted my offer yet."

"But ... they will. You said you put in a bid."

"Yes, a bid." Worry flashed in his eyes, sending the claws of doubt deeper into her stomach. "I wish you had told me your plans."

"I'm sure you'll get it. Has anyone else put a bid in for the property?" Swallowing, she ignored the pinch of panic. "It doesn't matter. Something will work out."

It made her situation a lot more precarious, but knowing this information didn't change the tough choice she had to make today. Numbers didn't lie and she could either afford shelter or her studio. Having both was no longer an option. Right now, her best solution was to find a good paying job, make some fast money, and get herself a new place to live.

"I won't know anything for a few more days."

"Well ... hopefully, they accept your offer. If that

doesn't pan out, then my clients will just have to move on. I'll move on, too."

"You can teach here a few nights a week. The other girls have kickboxing and Zumba covered, but maybe you could manage a jazzercise class."

"Thanks." It wasn't her first choice, but she was done being picky. "Let me know what nights and I'll be here."

"I will, but it won't bring in more than a hundred bucks a week. I'm sorry I can't offer more."

"I have other options. I think I could flip burgers if it got me out of this rut, so anything remotely related to my field is a blessing."

"Do you still need a place to stay?"

"I found an apartment in my budget and I'm going to look at it today. But I can't afford to be picky. I got my deposit back on the studio, so that helps."

"Well, if you need anything..."

She stood, the temptation of simple, temporary solutions something she needed to overcome. "I just wanted to come by and thank you for last night. I'm heading over to Maple Crest Village now to meet the landlord."

His gaze held too much concern and she hated taking responsibility for putting worry there. Before he could voice another offer, she said, "Call me about the dance classes when you figure out a schedule."

"I will. And you call me if you need anything."

"Thanks, Steve."

As she walked across the parkway to the apartments, she ignored the uncomfortable weightlessness she felt. Her life was once nailed down, both feet on the ground, and now she felt utterly untethered—untied—insignificant enough to blow away under the slightest breeze.

The Maple Crest apartments weren't glamorous, but they were affordable. She signed a lease for a second story efficiency and wrote a check before the money was in her account to clear it. By the time she made it to the bank, it was dark.

It seemed like the longest day of her life, and it wasn't anywhere close to finished. The silver lining was she was finally making productive decisions in her life. They weren't the best, but they were productive.

She stopped at a discount store and purchased some necessities along with a few boxed meals. When she got back to the apartment, she switched out a few light bulbs and showered.

As she wiped the steam away from the mirror, she couldn't manage a smile. This was her reality and it was just fine. It would afford shelter over her head and food in her belly, and soon enough she'd be back on her feet, able to invest in her dreams once more.

Unzipping her makeup case, she pulled out her pallet of colors and went heavy, false lashes and smoky shadow. Next was her hair. She used all the volumizing products she owned and blew it out to twice the normal size.

Rummaging through her bag, she found her nicest lace bra and matching panties. What she put on top didn't really matter, but she went with her red dress—the one she'd worn the first night she had drinks with Elliot.

Her motions slowed as she dragged the material through her fingers, her mind turning back to that evening. Things had gone so terrible and then he'd shown up, rescuing her and amusing her with his delightful magic tricks.

Her lashes flickered, the weight reminding her that her makeup was done and she couldn't afford to get emotional right now. Sniffing, she lifted her chin and finished getting ready.

The cab showed up as she slid into her five-inch heels, her legs trembling with uncertainty as she locked the door. Directing the driver was a distraction, but as the taxi neared her destination her nerves returned with a vengeance. What if this was just another mistake?

You can do this. You can do anything for a little while. Do this now and you'll be able to afford your pride later.

Her pep talk was enough to keep the contents of her stomach down, but nothing stopped her palms from sweating. She checked her phone again, disappointed but not surprised Elliot hadn't called.

Her biggest problem was waiting for men to save her. She had no hope for little boys. Using the corner of her nail, she switched the ringer to silence and put the phone back in her bag.

When the cab parked, her breath shook and her fingers trembled as she passed the driver the fare. Maybe she should ask him to wait? Her appointment might tell her to leave the minute he saw her.

No. She was being stupid. She could do this and

she had her phone to call for a ride home once it was over. She thanked the driver and stepped out of the cab.

Though she never set foot in this establishment before, she'd passed it several times. Its reputation spoke for itself.

A broad-shouldered man stood beside the interior doors. Bass pumped loud enough to rattle the walls and everything was dim. The doorman arched a brow the moment he noticed her.

"Do you know where I can find Joey C?" she asked.

His gaze drifted to her shoes and back to her breasts. "Are you Nadia?"

"Yes."

He pushed open the doors and pointed. "Past the stage, down the hall, last door on the right. I'm Big Z."

"Thank you, Big Z." The stench of booze and lust left a cool sweat on her skin as she took her first step into the next chapter of her life.

25

———

"Love is poison. A sweet poison, yes, but it will kill you all the same."

~Cersei Lannister
Game of Thrones

*E*lliot sat on the bed in the empty guest room, Nadia's scent lingering in the air and stabbing into him like a rusted blade. His phone rested in his hands as he deliberated over too many uncertainties to manage.

He'd messed up. And like everything he did in life, he'd messed up so flawlessly, there was no erasing what happened. He couldn't take away the last twenty-four hours. She was gone and an abyss separated them, so wide and overwhelming no sane person would dare to cross it.

His thumb brushed the screen of his phone, drawing up her contact information. He should call. Find out where she was, where she'd stayed, if she was safe. It was the right thing to do. It was everything he wanted to do, but fear held him back.

You're a fucking coward.

The words rattled like a broken record in his head, the old tune played out since childhood. When he was younger, he'd dreamed of normal, imagined a simple home with a modest life, but that wasn't where he ended up. His career had given him other options, and one by one old hopes fell away as new, unexpected opportunities arose. Why could he fearlessly move forward where business ventures were concerned, but anything having to do with the heart utterly paralyzed him?

He was so fucking lonely, a feeling he hadn't admitted in a long time. But since Nadia disappeared—no, since he practically chased her away—he felt it like an ax in the center of his chest.

The mistake was inviting her into his life too soon. He wasn't ready. He hadn't prepared. Navigating without a compass or a clue had cost him in ways he might never fully calculate. He'd lost her.

He overshot and missed the target completely. Over the years he'd pieced together a self-effacing amalgam of what he might achieve in a partner. She'd be shy, well-educated, but not pretentious. Her hair would be ordinary and her body average. Maybe her teeth were a little crooked and her clothes a little frumpy, but she'd still be a little outside of his league, despite those flaws.

They'd read at night until the bedside lamps turned off, and perhaps discuss children down the line. She might not love him with the fiery passion authors wrote stories about, but she'd like him on some personal level and respect the life he could provide.

None of that was Nadia.

Nadia was wild passion and sultry hedonism. She was his darkest fantasies in living flesh. She was kind and funny and agreeable to anything. How did some people manage such emotional flexibility? He envied her resilience and adaptability, the ease at which she greeted each oncoming day. She was everything he didn't deserve, and nothing he should ever dream of having in real life.

The other night when she'd played with Anakin, a strange sensation came over him. Seeing that softer side he hadn't anticipated threw new worry into his life. Where was this leading and would he be able to give her everything she deserved? All the things she might someday request of him? The daunting un-knowns were mounting to terrifying heights.

He loved her and wanted nothing but to please her, yet he'd done the exact opposite and succinctly destroyed all they'd had in one stupid evening. He was beyond angry with himself. One, for mistreating her, but also for hiding like a goddamn coward. And she'd called him out on it.

Jesus, he fucked up.

She was the most enchanting woman he'd ever met and the greatest of her beauty hid on the inside. She said she loved him, wanted all of him, desired him completely. Leave it to him to destroy something so irreplaceable. He seemed on a crash course of self-destruction where doubt was the driver and regret his only companion.

God, what had he done? She deserved better than him, and that was the most honest truth he knew at the moment.

His stomach knotted, tension twisting up his back until he could barely stand the indecisiveness smothering him. His thumb tapped her number and the phone dialed, ringing three times then dumping into voicemail.

He couldn't blame her for not answering, but he couldn't leave her thinking she'd done anything wrong longer than he already had. It took him nearly twenty-four hours to find the balls to call, but he had to fix this. This was his doing, his inexperience and fear corroding something beautiful and his actions and self-doubt hurting someone he loved.

The voicemail beeped, prompting him to leave a message. "Nadia... It's Elliot. I..."

I'm sorry. Please come back. Please give me another chance to try harder. I never meant to hurt you.

"I ... found some of your clothes you left behind. If you want them, call me back."

He waited a few seconds, willing himself to say more. But deep down he feared if he asked her to come back for him, she wouldn't and hearing that level of rejection might destroy him in irreparable ways.

"I hope you're okay," he muttered and ended the call.

Staring at the blank screen, a sort of numbness took hold. "And I'm sorry. I..." He couldn't bring himself to confess his love to her voicemail. "I hope you can give me another chance."

His body fell back on the bed as he shut his eyes, lifting off his glasses and scrubbing his palms over his face. "You're such a pussy," he groaned, hating himself to the point that he felt a physical ache in his chest. "You can't even leave her an honest voicemail, you useless fuck."

His fingers loosened and the phone fell to the comforter. Maybe his inability to fix them was for the best. How much longer would she honestly be satisfied with a man like him? She deserved so much better. He didn't have a clue what he was doing and, as much as he wanted to be the strong hero in her life, that shoe would never fit.

Reaching for his phone, he scrolled through his apps, searching for a distraction. Nothing held his interest and soon he was staring at her number again, unsure how he'd gone from staring to hearing the phone ring.

"This is Nadia. Leave me a message and I'll call you back." As her voicemail picked up again, his frustration doubled.

"It's me again." He grit his teeth. "I'm sorry. I shouldn't have acted like that last night. I just ... this is a lot for me and I hate having to keep explaining that. I ... never meant to hurt you."

His eyes closed. What the hell was he doing? He should have rehearsed this, made a list of points to address instead of just rambling like an unstable lunatic. But like a derailed train, he couldn't stop or get back on track.

"I'm sure you don't want to talk to me. I just wanted you to know I'm sorry. For everything."

He hung up before the words *I love you* fell out. Saying such things would only make the situation worse. He needed to fix this, then he'd tell her how much she meant to him.

Forcing himself off the bed, he shut the door and went to the kitchen. Halfway through making dinner, he was speaking to her voicemail again.

"Did you ever hear about butterflies, the kind people say they feel in their stomach? I never understood that. Those sort of comparisons always confused me. When I was little, I'd feel snakes in my stomach when I was afraid, which happened to be a lot, but never butterflies. Then… then I met you."

His thumb pressed into the prongs of his fork, leaving little divots in the pad of his finger as he rambled and stared at his dinner, wondering why he couldn't just leave her be. All these messages were probably making things worse.

"But you didn't give me butterflies, Nadia. You set off fireworks inside of me. Simply looking at you put me under siege. Cannon fire, that's what it feels like. Certainly not delicate butterflies."

His gaze drifted across the table as he questioned the little he knew about love and all the assumptions that seemed shortsighted to what he felt. "I never felt anything like that for anyone else. Sometimes you scare the hell out of me."

His shoulders drooped as he stared at his plate, appetite gone. "I don't know if I give you snakes, butterflies, fireworks, or something else. I wish I knew, because ... maybe then I'd know if this was normal. If I'm normal."

His mouth pursed as his voice lowered with each word. "I'm rambling again. Just delete these messages. Sorry to keep bothering you. I'll leave you alone now."

With a sigh, he scraped his plate into a glass container and wedged it on a shelf in the fridge. He was kidding himself if he thought he could swallow one bite. He had no appetite and his stomach was knotted too tight to get a single bite down.

He went to the den to find a book. Nothing appealed, so he settled on an old favorite, hoping he could pass the hours until he fell asleep. After staring at the same paragraph for a solid ten minutes he tossed the book aside and grabbed his phone. Furious curiosity plagued him when she still didn't answer.

"Okay, I get it. You don't want to talk to me. I'm a complete asshole. Last night, I acted like... I got scared. I lost control and..." He sighed, his eyes closing in shame. "My control's all I have. I can depend on it and without it..." Memories of screaming in absolute panic raced through his mind and he shuttered. It didn't matter that those memories were decades old. The sense of no control they stirred was still fresh and excruciating. But he wasn't only concerned with protecting himself.

"Nadia, my control… It's what's kept me sane most of my life. But when I touch you… The thought of hurting you terrifies me. And I know it's only a matter of time before I permanently mess this up."

Maybe it was already fucked. His gut twisted painfully, those knots tightening until even his breath wheezed out of his lungs. Everything he wanted also happened to be everything he feared.

"I … I know we've only been together a short time, but I don't remember how to start my day without you. I forget how to think without your presence lacing each thought. It was childish to lock the door and I'm sorry. I wish I could take it back. I'm failing at this and it's gutting me. I hate to fail, but this is worse than every other failure because I'm failing *you*."

And when things didn't go his way he made a habit of minimizing their importance, convincing himself he didn't want what he couldn't have. But he couldn't minimize Nadia. He couldn't even pass a minute without thinking about her.

"I hate that I've screwed this up. I hate that I hurt you. I hate that I don't know where the hell you are right now or what you're doing or who you're with. If you're okay."

"Can we just talk? Please?" He waited as if a response might come. Eventually, the automated voice asked if he was happy with his message and he hung up.

His head dropped to the back of the couch as he blinked at the ceiling. "I hate that I'm impossible to love when I'm so madly in love with you," he whispered to himself, wondering how long this unbearable pain and doubt would last.

As he closed up the house and made his way to bed, the urge to speak to her didn't fade. If anything, it intensified. He'd purposely left his phone in the den, but climbed out of bed to retrieve it sometime around eleven, worried she might actually call back. She hadn't, so he called her again.

"Are you doing this to punish me? I shut you out so now you're doing the same? I know that's what I deserve, but it's not what we need, not if we both want to fix this."

His head cocked as the answer slapped him in the face. "But you probably don't want to fix this."

He hung up and took his phone back to his room, swearing that was the last time he'd contact her and knowing his vow was a lie.

As he lay in the dark his patience disintegrated. He couldn't take it anymore. He needed to speak to her.

"Look, you want a man who's in control? Fine. Answer your phone. We aren't throwing this away without talking it over first. Pick up the phone, Nadia. I fucked up. I'll own that, but I'm not a quitter when something is important, and *this* is important. *We* are important. I don't want to go back to the way things were before. I ... need you."

But no matter how persuasive his words, he was speaking to a machine. She might not even listen to his pleas. He didn't know where she was or how to find her, and these stupid messages were all he could do to reach out to her aside from driving to her studio at this time of night and praying she'd be there.

She wouldn't be there...

He was out of bed and getting dressed two seconds later. He needed to get her to listen. He needed to make this right.

26

---

*"Failure means a stripping away **of the inessential.**"*

~J. K. Rowling

*N*adia stood in the small office, her eyes threatening to water as a haze of cigarette smoke hung beneath the ceiling. She kept her motions loose as she shook the man's hand, his fingers holding onto hers long enough to cross the line between polite and unnerving.

"Well, look at you." Joey C kept his grasp on her fingers and directed her in a slow twirl. "Beautiful. Mexican?"

Nadia refused the urge to roll her eyes and forced a smile. "Hungarian."

He nodded. "Good. Exotic."

She pulled her fingers out of his hold and

reached into her bag. "I brought my resume. I've been teaching dance for many years."

He took the slip of paper and placed it on his desk with barely a glance. His gaze weighed on her front, inspecting every curve and dip. "Good. Have you ever performed?"

"Not outside of recitals, but I've taught every sort of dance there is."

His gaze dropped to her five-inch pumps. "Any scars or notable birthmarks?"

The breath in her lungs expanded. "I have a few birthmarks, but nothing out of the ordinary."

He rested his hips on the desk, folding his arms over his chest. "Okay. I'll have to take a look."

"O—of course."

She turned, her gaze lowering to the outdated loveseat squeezed between a filing cabinet and mini fridge against the wall. She stepped closer to the seat and remained facing the wall as her fingers trembled to untie the belt of her dress.

Cool air bathed her front as she opened her attire. The weight of her hair hung like an insignificant shield down her back as she slid the dress off her arms.

"Nice."

She folded the garment and placed it on the arm of the loveseat then slowly turned. Her gaze clung to the floor.

"Are you nervous?"

Her head shook as her mind screamed. If she gave her feelings too much thought, she might make herself sick. "No."

"You have a great figure."

Her voice shrank with every breath. "Thank you."

"Let's see your tits."

Her throat tightened as her fingers fumbled the clasp.

"Need a hand?"

"I have it." Thankfully, she managed to still her fingers enough to unhook the bra. Lace pulled away from her breasts and her chest burned under his attentive inspection.

"Beautiful." He stepped closer, making a slow circle around her back and returning to the space in front of her. "Arms up."

She raised her arms, her nipples puckering in the cool air and lifting. Though he didn't touch her, there seemed to be a notable weight to his gaze as it crawled over her.

"Now, the panties, please."

The snap of a match preceded the scent of sulfur as she bent to lower her bottoms. When her body unfolded her face was hit with a cloud of exhaled smoke. She tried not to react.

Joey C eased back against the desk, staring intently between her legs. "You'll have to take care of that hair. The girls have a waxing station in the back. One of the others will do it for you. Have a seat."

She glanced at the loveseat, noting stains she'd missed a minute ago. She lowered herself to the edge of the cushion and folded her hands on her knees in an attempt at privacy.

"I'll need to see everything, Nadia. You don't have

to be nervous. I've seen it all—before. Pussy's pussy. It no longer shocks me."

She blinked, finding it impossible to move. "I thought it was just topless dancing."

"No, we do it all here. The girls that walk the bar usually wear a skirt so when they take orders the men get a nice peek down Broadway."

Hopefully, she wouldn't be working the bar. She unfolded her hands and rested them on the cushion beside her hips. Turning her face away, she willed her knees to part, but couldn't move.

"Don't be nervous, gorgeous. You have a boyfriend?"

The pounding of her heart stilled with a bludgeoning smack. A cool sweat beaded around her hairline and on the crest of her lip. "No. No boyfriend."

"How about we grab dinner after this?"

This. What was this? Was this what her independence should feel like? Her heart ached as she tried to hide her tension. "I don't know what I'm doing."

"The girls will give you an orientation. Just show me what you got and I can introduce—"

"This was a mistake." Her hand fluttered to her dress and she fumbled to unfold the material and slip it over her head.

"We're not finished."

"I'm done." She stood on unsteady legs. "Thank you for your time." She had to get out of that smoky office before she vomited on the stained carpet.

Pushing through the door, her ears were assaulted by male voices and music. The scent of stale alcohol and cigarette smoke choked her as her emotions spun wildly in her stomach. She raced to the exit on her tall heels, thrusting open the doors and gasping for fresh air.

"You okay, lady?"

Her gaze jerked to a strange man reaching for her and she backed away. "I'm fine."

"You sure? Why don't you let me buy you a drink?"

Shaking her head, she walked deeper into the parking lot, unsure where to go. A cab waited in the distance and her unbalanced legs wobbled over the broken pavement, heading in that direction.

Where would she go? How would she afford her apartment if she didn't have a job or a studio? A hundred dollars a week at Steve's wasn't enough to live on. She'd made so many mistakes. Finding balance again seemed a hopeless wish.

The cab window lowered as she approached. "Can you give me a ride?"

"Hop in."

She slid onto the worn leather and shut the door, her mind a carousel of failures, her confidence an untethered thread. She was done. It was time to admit defeat.

"Where to?"

Faces of her past mistakes flooded her memory, but there was one man who hadn't been a mistake. He'd been the only man to treat her kindly and care about her. He'd also been the only one to break her heart.

She gave the cabbie Elliot's address and stared

out the window as he drove. Was this what the end felt like? She needed to see him one last time, to thank him for all he'd done and say goodbye. She couldn't leave him worried about her and she now had a financial obligation to honor back in Hungary. She'd pull her deposit and use it to buy a plane ticket. One way.

They'd know she didn't have what it takes once she returned home for good. And while they hissed their *I told you so's,* she'd find a job and remember where she fit in this world. She'd tried. No one could take that away from her. She'd tried with all of her heart to live the American dream and run her own business, but her heart could no longer take the failures and rejection. At least at home, she knew who she was supposed to be.

Her eyes closed as she thought about her mother and Roland. Thank God for Elliot's help with the loan. So long as her family made the payments on time Roland would no longer be necessary in their lives. But he'd weasel his way back in eventually— that's what weasels did.

The car pulled up to the gate outside of Elliot's. "Do you need to be buzzed in?"

She knew the code but wasn't sure she was welcome to use it anymore. She also didn't want to give it to a stranger. "You can let me out here."

Once she spoke to Elliot she'd take it from there and get a ride to wherever she needed to go. She paid the cab driver and watched as he drove away. Approaching the lockbox, she entered the code and the gate opened.

The night was cool and her arms were exposed. She'd left the club in such a rush she'd forgotten her bra. Chafing her arms she took the long driveway to the front of the house. When she reached the door, she pressed the buzzer and waited.

When no one answered, she pressed the buzzer again and stared at the security camera wondering if he watched her. "I just want to talk, Elliot. Please let me in."

Her shoulders sagged as disappointment knifed through her. She couldn't leave things like this with him.

"I'm coming in." She punched in the code and the door unlocked, but the house was dark and silent. "Elliot?"

She searched each room, calling his name and flipping on lights. His car wasn't in the garage. Returning to the foyer, she dropped onto the bottom step and removed her shoes. Where could he have gone at this time of night?

She pulled out her phone and sucked in a breath, only then seeing the multiple missed calls and voicemails from Elliot since she'd set it on silent. Her heart rattled as she drew the phone to her ear.

27

___

"BEING *a geek is all about being honest about what you enjoy and not being afraid to demonstrate that affection.*"

~Simon Pegg

Elliot stared at the FOR RENT sign on the door of her studio, a new lock fastened to the freshly painted door. What had she done?

He'd given up leaving her voicemails and searched for her, only to find every trace of her gone. Sitting on the curb was the bench her students sat on to tie up their shoes. A sickening feeling latched on as the world suddenly seemed enormous. She could go anywhere and never answer a single call from him again.

He got in his car and gripped the wheel. Where

could she be? Pulling up his contacts he dialed Asher through the blue tooth and started to drive toward home.

"Do you realize what time it is?"

"I need Steve's number." Maybe the guy pulled through with the studio deal and she'd moved her business there.

"Elliot, what's going on?"

"I need his number, Asher. I don't have time to explain."

"Where are you? You sound upset."

"I'm losing my fucking mind! Are you going to give me his number or not?"

"Okay. Okay. I just sent you his contact." His cell pinged with the text. "Did something happen?"

"She's gone. Nadia's gone. I fucking ruined it."

Lettie's voice murmured in the background, and Asher whispered something as the phone muffled. Elliot gripped the wheel, his molars locked as he sped toward Steve's gym.

"Elliot, I'm sure you didn't ruin anything. Tell me what happened. Is this why you called out today?"

His eyes prickled as he stared at the dark road. "It's me. I can't do this. I don't know how to do this, Asher. I don't know how you let yourself be this vulnerable for Scarlet."

"Okay, calm down. Are you driving?"

"Yes."

"Maybe you should pull over."

"I need to find her."

"You will, but you need to calm down. Take a breath. Do you think she's with Steve?"

The old him would have gone into a full-fledged delusion by now, picturing her with another man, but his mind couldn't go there. No matter how much damage he'd done, he knew her well enough to know she wouldn't do that.

"No. I don't know. They're supposed to be going into business together. He's the only person she might have contacted. He's the only person I can think to ask."

"I'm texting him now. Where are you heading?"

"I don't know. I'm just driving. She could be anywhere. She gave up her studio, Ash. It's like she's giving up on everything." If she'd give up on her dreams he didn't stand a chance.

"Elliot, you need to calm down. Wait, Steve just texted me back. He saw her today, but he says he doesn't want to be involved in whatever's going on. Says Nadia's his friend and his loyalty is to her."

Elliot's hand slammed down on the wheel. *"Fuck! Fucking mother fucker!* What's his address?"

"Whoa. Slow down. You are not going to barge into his place demanding answers, Elliot. Think for a second."

"I am thinking."

"Really? Because Steve's a bodybuilder three times your size."

He ground his teeth. "What am I supposed to do? She could be anywhere. What if she's leaving the country? What if I never get to fix this or tell her I'm sorry I'm such a dysfunctional prick? What if I never get to hold her again or kiss her or hear her laughter..."

His voice ceased as emotion choked him. His foot eased off the pedal as his vision blurred. "I love her, Asher." His breath escaped in a shaky exhalation. "And it's ripping me to shreds."

"Elliot, whatever happened, you can fix it."

"What if I can't?"

"I believe you can. You're Elliot Garnet. You can fix anything."

"Not this. Not relationships. I'm good with numbers and guarantees. I've never been good with people."

"That's not true. Do you remember when we were kids and I was getting picked on for my stutter? You were the only person willing to be my friend. You were patient and never made me feel stupid when I tried to get something out. You made me feel safe and eventually, I stopped stuttering around you."

"And then you stopped stuttering around everyone else."

"Yeah. But you made me believe I could overcome my nerves. You made me believe I could do anything if I found the right approach. We just need to find the right approach."

His breathing slowed. "Everything was so hard. It got easier the second we got out of school, you know? Fewer people watching over our shoulders, less pressure to be like everyone else. Being with Nadia puts incredible pressure on me to measure up and be better than every other man. What was I thinking?"

"Maybe she doesn't want you to be like every other man. Maybe she wants you to be Elliot."

"No one wants that."

"Enough!" Asher snapped. "I get what it is to be your worst critic, but I'm sick of you ripping my friend apart. You give yourself no credit, Elliot. If I needed something, you'd be the first guy I ask, because I know you're dependable. And yeah, you're opinionated and anal, but so what. You're fucking brilliant and honest and always putting other people's feelings before your own. It's why people exhaust you so much. You're not an introvert because you're a social outcast, you're an introvert because you want to fix everything. You only know how to be the hero and you hate letting people down. Look at how you've stepped up for your mom after your dad died. Look at all you've done for Nadia. My God, when Lettie was pregnant and complained of back pains, you set up weekly prenatal massages. I'm her fucking husband and I didn't even think to do that. When will you realize how much other people appreciate you?"

"Scarlet hates me."

"My wife loves you, you idiot. But you're not the easiest person to small talk with. She was thrilled you and Nadia came for dinner the other night."

"Small talk's a waste of time."

Asher groaned. "You're such a dick. Can you just take a compliment for once?"

His speed slowed as he turned into his neighborhood. Since calling Asher his panic had subsided into a low grade freak out. "Thank you."

"You're welcome. Now, how about you go home, get some sleep if you can, and tomorrow morning I'll meet you at your place and we'll find her."

Knowing he had a friend like Asher on his side helped. While Elliot might be addicted to fixing things, Asher was one who couldn't accept defeat. Together they made an unstoppable team. "Okay. Thanks. I ... needed..."

"I know. We all need to hear it from time to time."

He drew in a shaky breath. "I'll see you tomorrow."

"Goodnight, Elliot."

The call disconnected as he pulled up to the gate and punched in the code. His body was overwrought from a sleepless night and a day of whiplash emotions and worry. He'd fix this. Tomorrow he'd find her and he'd insist she listen to him. He could be the man she deserved. He just needed to convince her to give him a second chance.

Walking up to the front door, he keyed open the lock and flipped on the foyer light and stilled. His heart jerked hard in his chest and the wind knocked out of him.

"Nadia."

She looked up at him, her eyes smoky and her cheeks streaked with rivulets of makeup. Her chin trembled as her hands gripped her phone. "I got your messages."

28

"Did Superman really want to save the world, or did he just feel like he had to?"

~Gerard Way

His hair was a mess and he was in wrinkled jeans and a plain white T-shirt. His jaw wore a shadow of stubble and his lips parted when he spotted her.

Her entire body trembled as she held his stare. His brow creased and he briefly glanced away and shut the door. When he looked back to her, he said, "You're dressed up."

She should have known her clothing wouldn't escape his observant nature. It was her turn to look away.

"Elliot, I messed up." Her eyes flooded with more

tears and she smudged them away, her hands wearing more mascara than her eyes. "I didn't know what to do and—"

"Hey, hey, hey..." He was suddenly in front of her, on his knees, lifting her face and looking into her eyes. "Don't cry. We can fix this."

She wasn't even sure how they were broken. "What did I do?"

His eyes closed behind the lenses of his glasses and he swallowed. "You didn't do anything, Nadia. I did this. And I swear, if you give me another chance, I'll fix it."

He wanted another chance. His messages had said as much, which was why she waited for him, but she needed to hear the words from his mouth, see the promise in his eyes. Now that she had, her relief released a jolt of adrenaline and she started to tremble.

"Why did you shut me out, Elliot? I begged for you to let me in and you left me there—alone like a fool."

"No, Nadia." He pulled her into his arms, pressing his face to her neck and holding her tight. "I'm the fool. I'm an idiot, paralyzed by imperfection and terrified of damaging the irreplaceable."

She choked on a gasp. "No one is perfect. Especially me!"

"Not your imperfections, baby. Mine. I'm not good enough for you, but I want to be." He drew back and looked into her eyes. "The biggest obstacle in my life has always been me. I set such high standards that when the time comes to try something new, if I'm not sure I can succeed, I balk and back down. I pass so many opportunities up because I'm afraid I'll screw up and let someone down. I only feel confident when I'm in complete control and see a clear cut path to success."

"No one expects you to be perfect all the time, Elliot."

"I know. But I wanted to be perfect for you."

Her throat tightened as she swallowed back the lump that had been choking her all day. "Maybe you're perfect for me just the way you are. I know you're stubborn and you think stars are nothing but rocks when I want them to be wishes, but you're still incredibly sweet and caring. You're gentle and kind. And there's so much that makes you different from everyone else. I just want to be a part of that. I want to know all of you, and I want you to know all of me. I never want us to hurt each other."

"I never want to hurt you either, but I did hurt you and knowing that I did the one thing I hoped to avoid..." His jaw ticked. "It's turning me inside out."

He had hurt her and there was no pretending these last twenty-four hours hadn't happened. She needed to understand his reasoning if they were going to get past this. "Why did you shut me out?"

He leaned his back against the wall and she scooted beside him. His knees drew up and he draped his arms over his legs. He looked straight ahead, unconsciously picking at a fingernail.

"When my dad got sick I paid the best doctors in the country to examine him. He had the best treatments available and every time my mother cried I promised he'd be okay. I gave her my word I'd get him through it. But I couldn't. I offered more money and was willing to try anything. But in the end, my dad said it was enough and refused any more help. He told me to be there for my mom ... because he was ready to die."

"Oh, Elliot." She rested her head on his shoulder and looped her arms around his. "Some things can't be fixed. It's not your fault. You did everything you could."

"I know. I'm not an irrational man and science is the one thing that makes sense to me—science and numbers. But ... my heart..." His brow creased and his gaze swung away. When he looked back to her, stark grief showed in his eyes. "I didn't want to lose him. I wasn't ready to give up fighting for him, but I couldn't force him to stay in the battle."

Hearing the strain in his voice, she shifted to her knees and caught his face in her hands. Tears shimmered in his eyes and he blinked them away.

"I'm so sorry you lost him. I wish I could have been there for you during that time. I'm sure your father appreciated everything you did for him to the very end." Her lips brushed his. "You honored his last wish, Elliot. Do you know how noble that is?"

He nodded, his lashes now hiding his eyes. "But it still felt like failure, only worse, because it was heartache. It's hard for me to cope with loss. That's why I preferred to be alone. I always hoped I'd find someone. But after losing my dad..." His hand rubbed over his chest as if an old ache still pained him there. "It hurt so much. I felt like part of myself died with him, and yet, I knew my mom hurt even more. I couldn't imagine the pain of losing someone you woke up next to every day for over thirty years. I never wanted to love anything that much. Never wanted to be that vulnerable."

Her heart cinched as his words sliced through all her tender hopes and emotions. She understood his fear but also didn't know where that left her or their relationship. She loosened her hold. "I see." As she pulled away he caught her hand.

"I don't want to be alone anymore, Nadia."

"You don't?" Her heart fell into an erratic rhythm, unsure where this was leading. She needed to be more to him than mere company.

"No. I can't lose you because I love you, and the thought of living without you for even a day is more than I can bear."

She sucked in a long breath. "You love me?"

He nodded. "Falling in love wasn't something I planned or calculated. That night I ran into you was purely accidental. I had no intention of intruding on your situation, but when I saw you were upset..."

"You wanted to save me."

His brow pinched. "I just wanted to make it better for you. I didn't like the way that man spoke to you."

"Elliot, you did make it better. You are always making situations better. But that's not why I love you."

"Why then?"

She wasn't sure, only that she did. "I suppose I love the curiosity in your eyes, the way you analyze everything. I love the way you know every word in the English language. I love that you can do magic and that you're always so patient with me when I try something new. I love that you hate jeans but will wear them for me."

"They're not so bad once they're broken in."

She glanced at his disheveled appearance. "You look very hot right now, all wrinkled and messy."

His smile was strained. "I should have told you how I felt. The truth is I've felt this way for a long time, but I didn't want to scare you."

"You could never scare me, not when it comes to this. Knowing you share my love and that I'm not crazy and alone in feeling this way... It's a relief. I almost did something drastic, but changed my mind because I want to be the woman you love, Elliot. I want that more than anything else."

"You're the only woman I've ever felt this way about." He touched the strap of her dress, his brow creasing. "Where were you tonight?"

"Everywhere I shouldn't have been. My life is a mess and I'm afraid if I tell you how messy, you'll run away screaming."

"I can handle it."

"Are you sure?"

He was finally opening up and she didn't want to spoil it.

He nodded. "Realizing everything I had to lose made me stronger. I can handle it, Nadia. For us, I can handle anything."

Her lips formed a thin line and her brow pinched as she met his stare. "I can't seem to straighten my life out. I had to get rid of my studio and now I don't know if the deal is going to go through with Steve on the new property. You were right. We should have made a contract before I made any changes, but I didn't listen. I just assumed everything would work out and now things are worse off than before." She forced out a harsh breath. "You're afraid of failure and I feel failure is the only thing I do right."

"That's not true. Why won't you let me help you, Nadia? I want to see you succeed. That's all I'm trying to do in terms of your business—just help."

"Because I'm prideful and stubborn, but now I think I'm ready to wave my little white flag and admit defeat."

"You're not defeated. You just need a little guidance. You have the bones of a practical business. You just need to beef up your practices a little. When more experienced people offer guidance, it's good sense to at least hear them out."

"Says the man who refuses to accept failure."

"I'm working on that and you can work on this. We both need to learn to depend on others a little bit more than we do."

"But I don't want our relationship to change into a business one."

"Nadia, you're the first girl I brought into my home. The first woman I've let into my life. The first person I've ever opened up to this much. Trust me when I say I want to do more than business with you. Besides, this is *your* business. I just want to help you achieve everything you've dreamed of doing with the company. Let me help you."

"You're very charming when you want to be."

"It's a gift reserved solely for you." He kissed her lips, "It would help me a lot if we could start looking at things in the long term."

"How long?"

He laced his fingers with hers. "Forever works for me. I love you. Now that I've admitted it, I see no sense in playing down my emotions. I don't ever want to lose you."

"I love you, too." And losing him wasn't an option. Nothing made sense without him. "I think you're a drug to me."

"I feel the same about you. It's..."

"Intense," she supplied.

"*Very*." He let out a breath. "But I'd rather have that intensity than nothing at all. The other night I freaked out. I have no basis of comparison, and I was embarrassed by my actions. I saw tears in your eyes and... I never want to hurt you. I lost control of the situation and—"

"Sometimes losing control in the heat of passion is a good thing, Elliot. I told you I was fine. You make me lose control all the time. I hunger for it."

"You do?"

"Yes! It's freeing and exhilarating." It wasn't like they were the first couple to do something a little rough. "I think next time we watch a movie, I'll pick it."

"A foreign film?"

"Sure, we can find one with foreign actors if you like. I want to broaden your horizons. I think you will thank me."

"Okay." His expression quickly returned to a more serious one. "Do you forgive me?"

All humor faded with her smile. "Don't ever shut me out like that again. I love you, Elliot. And while I like to play rough, my heart is breakable. I'm trusting you with it."

He swallowed and nodded his understanding. "You can trust me with it."

She believed she could. If anything, Elliot knew how to take care of the things he valued. Her hand slid into his, their fingers lacing once more. "Then I forgive you."

He kissed her, soft at first and then hungry. Relief flooded her when he pulled away and her chest felt as if a weight had been lifted.

"Will you take me to bed, now?"

He stood and helped her off the floor. "My pleasure."

Together, they walked up the stairs, leaving the past behind and stepping into their future. There were no guarantees, and it was scary tying her heart to someone else's, but for them, it was right. For them, it was beautifully messy, intensely addicting love. And they wanted all of it.

EPILOGUE

"The future is worth it. All the pain. All the tears. The future is worth the fight."

~Martian Manhunter

"Don't forget your costumes for the spring show," Nadia called as the rambunctious junior ballerinas fled the studio to greet their waiting parents. They were going to make adorable dandelions.

She gathered up the recital props and cued up the music for her next class—a private lesson for a new client. Her roster was full since moving into the new studio, and why wouldn't it be? Elliot had designed a state of the art facility, one that no other dance academy in the area could compete with. He also provided her unlimited advertisement on Geek-Peek, which created an invaluable buzz way before their grand opening. And of course—because he was Elliot—everything was secured by a top of the line security system. He truly was a magician, because with him anything was possible.

In the months it took to get the studio off the ground, she and Elliot truly got to know each other and fell more in love with every passing day. He no longer pulled away when the intimacy tightened around them. Instead, he pulled closer, knowing that the intensity was a shared gift they should relish rather than fear. She'd thought this sort of happiness only existed in romance novels, but it turned out to be very, very possible in real life.

And while her outcome had been an unpredictable one, Elliot showed her that a good partnership didn't involve one person leading the other. Her independence remained. She was stronger than ever, and her success had flourished since falling in love with a man who emotionally supported and encouraged her.

Switching her pointe shoes for a pair of heels, she awaited her new client. They'd probably run through the basics, maybe touch on a tango or foxtrot if he wasn't too inexperienced. Then she'd go home to her man.

As she twisted her hair into a bun, a breaker blew and the entire studio went dark. "Oh, no." Pinning her hair in place, she headed to the hall to check the breaker box, but before she made it across the dance floor violins began to play and she frowned.

The stereo glowed as Etta James crooned the slow intro to *At Last*. "Hello?"

She jumped as twinkle lights suddenly illuminated the rafters like stars. Turning, she searched the shadows. "Who's there?"

Elliot stepped through the doorway, holding a single long stem rose. She smiled, unsure what he was doing there. "I thought a breaker blew. What are you doing here?"

"I have an appointment."

"You...?" She laughed. "You're my new client?"

He nodded. "I was hoping you could teach me how to dance." He crossed the floor and handed her the rose.

"You hate dancing."

He shook his head. "Not anymore. Not since I found the perfect dance partner."

Pressing her nose into the bloom, she smiled. "And where will you be dancing?"

"My wedding."

She stilled, unsure if she heard him right. "Your...?"

"Wedding. I'm asking her to marry me tonight."

Trapped in some sort of trance, she blinked at him. "I can't feel my feet."

He laughed and took her hand, dropping to a knee. "I won't let you fall."

Her heart raced as she stared at him, kneeling before her. "Oh my goodness."

"Wait, there's more." He looked to the door where something buzzed. A small robot with tank-like wheel treads and big eyes rolled onto the floor.

"That's your robot." She recognized it from his collections. But she'd never seen it out of the box.

"His name's Wall-e. He's a hopeless romantic."

She laughed as the little robot rattled its way across the floor. A little velvet box was affixed to its head with a red bow.

Elliot untied the ribbon and opened the box, revealing a stunning diamond ring. "I want to dance with you for the rest of my life, Nadia, you and nobody else. I want to be your partner, your lover, your best friend, and the man who makes all your dreams come true. I've loved you since the moment I met you and I plan on loving you for the rest of my life. Do you think you could put up with me that long?"

Her vision blurred and when she blinked twin tears fell. "You've already made my dreams come true, you silly man."

"Is that a yes?"

She nodded, her fingers covering her mouth as she lost control of her emotions. "Yes."

He stood and pulled her hands away from her face and kissed her. When they broke apart, she was wearing the ring. "You've made me very happy," he whispered, kissing her again. "I love you."

"I love you, too." She burst into happy tears, blindsided and still in shock. "I didn't know any of this was happening today."

He laughed. "That's how it's supposed to be."

She looked down at the little robot. "You took it out of the box."

"It was worth it."

She admired her ring, leaning into his chest. "I'm stunned."

His fingers closed around her hand, the one holding the rose. He pulled the other to his shoulder. "I was promised a dance."

She laughed. "Now, I'm sure I'm dreaming. What have you done with my boyfriend?"

"I traded him in for a better model. This one's called a fiancé. Now, dance with me. I paid a lot for this lesson and in a few minutes we're going to be interrupted."

She let him lead her in a slow turn. "Who's interrupting us?"

"Just those who knew this was happening. The guys, Lettie, my mother."

"They all knew?"

"I've been obsessing over it for weeks. They're all going to be relieved you said yes."

"Was there ever any doubt?"

He met her gaze and smiled. "Do you know how out of my league you are, Nadia? The fact that you even look at me is amazing."

She tsked. "Do you know something, mister? I feel the exact same way about you." She wiggled her fingers, flashing her ring in the twinkle lights. "And now I get to look at you forever. I'm never letting you go, Elliot."

"Promise?"

She nodded. "Promise." They sealed it with a kiss.

THE END

Want more billionaire romance from Lydia Michaels?
Read *One Billion Secrets* next!

ALSO BY LYDIA MICHAELS

BOOKS BY SERIES
Many first in series books are FREE
Grab them here!

Free Books Here!

MCCULLOUGH MOUNTAIN
Almost Priest *

Beautiful Distraction

Irish Rogue

British Professor

Broken Man

Controlled Chaos

Hard Fix

Intentional Risk

JASPER FALLS

Wake My Heart *

The Best Man

Love Me Nots

Pining For You

My Funny Valentine

Side Squeeze

CALAMITY RAYNE

Calamity Rayne Gets a Life *

Calamity Rayne Back Again

Calamity Rayne Gets Hitched

BONUS: Calamity Rayne Veiled & Railed

Calamity Rayne Over the Moon

Calamity Rayne Knocked Up

THE SURRENDER TRILOGY

Falling In

BreakingOut

Coming Home

Ruthless Billionaires

One Billion Secrets *

Two Billion Enemies

MASTERMIND

Blind

Untied

NEW CASTLE

First Comes Love *

If I Fall

Shattered Vows

ADDICTED TO YOU

Crush *

Bang

Throb

THE ORDER OF VAMPIRES

Original Sin *

Dark Exodus

Prodigal Son

Immortal Bastard

Primal Kill

Blood Moon

STAND ALONES

La Vie en Rose

Simple Man

Sugar

Breaking Perfect

Hurt

Protege

ABOUT THE AUTHOR

To receive Lydia's Newsletter and 7 FREE Books, click HERE !

Lydia Michaels is the bestselling and award-winning author of more than forty novels. She writes heart-clenching, unpredictable romance with dark elements and high heat. Her work is character-driven and bursting with broken heroes and badass females. With a sweet spot for overbearing, territorial types, her deeply emotional books are spicy, emotionally satisfying, and guaranteed to leave readers with many book hangovers.

Lydia is the consecutive winner of the *2018 & 2019 Author of the Year Award* from *Happenings Media* and the recipient of the *2014 Best Author Award* from the Courier Times. She has been featured by *USA Today*, *Romantic Times Magazine*, the *Women in Publishing Summit*, and more.

Michaels started her author career in 2007, becoming a recognized presence and advocate within the publishing industry. She is the CEO of LMC Consulting, a certified author coach specializing in character and plot development, and the founder of the *East Coast Author Convention*, the *Behind the Keys Author Retreat*, and www.LydiaMichaelsBooks.com.

She is happily married to her childhood sweetheart. Her favorite things include cooking Italian cuisine, hosting extravagant dinner parties, sipping espresso martinis, listening to her husband play piano, and escaping to her coastal home on the Jersey Shore. She's an LGBTQ ally, a BLM supporter, a firm believer that the patriarchy must end (women's rights are human rights), and an advocate for pediatric cancer research.

LYDIA

Follow Lydia Michaels on social media!
Facebook | Instagram | TikTok

THANK YOU FOR YOUR REVIEW!

Reviews help authors so much! If you left a review for this book, I greatly appreciate it!

Thank you,

Lydia

Click here to leave your review!

www.ingramcontent.com/pod-product-compliance
Lightning Source LLC
Chambersburg PA
CBHW060945190726
48286CB00005B/1433